Dyst

By

Mark Tufo

DEVILDOG PRESS
SWANVILLE, MAINE

DevilDog Press

Cover Art by Dane@ebooklaunch

Dedications:

To my wife thank you for helping me through this one!

To my incredible beta readers: Kimberly Sansone and Amanda Walker for helping make this book a better version of its self.

To the men and women of the armed forces, all you do and all you sacrifice will be something I am always grateful for.

PROLOGUE

Where does one start when there are so many beginnings? Do we venture back to Winter and Tallow's discovery of the library? It's as good a place as any; but should we travel further back? To Mike Talbot's abduction from Red Rocks? Perhaps the chase and subsequent murder of Drababan's family...but events were already in motion, long before any of those things happened. If one is really looking for a beginning, my best guess is the day the Progerians stepped out of their primordial stew. Seems that was the catalyst for all that followed.

But that was another world; another Universe. For this story, maybe it is best to start with Earth's involvement, our homeworld's entry into a war that has spanned thousands of years and involved countless planets. We could lay blame for the destruction of the world as we knew it on Heinrich Hertz, but it hardly seems fair; he was the first to send and receive radio waves now the radio waves were out there. Picking them up merely opened a channel. Like answering a ringing telephone, it allowed a Progerian Scout ship to discover us and lead them back here like an ill-thrown breadcrumb trail. From that moment, we entered the fray, became victims in a war they'd fought elsewhere for millennia, and it all but guaranteed our end. With some outside help and an incredible degree of luck, humanity held on and finally persevered, in a fashion, and for a while, at least. Then an unfortunate series of events that came to be known as The Happening took place—an era so violent that humanity felt the only way to survive was to vacate. And so we fled from our only known home.

Most left in ships designed to last for generations in space, but many could not escape. Others chose not to. This is the story of those people, the ones who fought on, even as everything around them collapsed. From the heights of our greatest technological advances, to something not much removed from the Stone Age, humans endured.

And this is the story of Winter and Cedar; distant progeny of one of Earth's greatest heroes, Michael Talbot, and, somehow, one of her most treacherous villains, Beth Ginson. When faced with a choice between giving their lives to create babies for the Dystance war machine or fighting for the freedom of Humanity, they chose to fight. An unlikely ally, Brody, a disillusioned Broker whose primary job was to keep the populace and any troublemakers in line, trained Winter, Cedar, and their friend, Tallow in the hope they would find some answers as to why they fought and died.

Once in the War, they first fought against the Comanchokees and then befriended them. It seemed their situation had improved further when they allied with the powerful Klondike clan, until their leader, Haden, double-crossed them in a move to join himself to the despot, Mennot, the Hillian commander. Serrot, Haden's second in command and others loyal to him, helped Winter and Tallow escape into a vast and unknown world. But escape wasn't enough. Winter wanted to free the Comanchokees, a people that had suffered greatly from Haden's betrayal. She went back through the deadly borderline, the Pickets, only to encounter a Bruton death squad. After defeating their leader, she advanced into that role and befriended Lendor, the squad's second in command.

She led the Comanchokees on a terrifying retreat from Haden's thundering cavalry. Once through the pickets, she was able to use the full might of her army to capture Haden, subsequently killing him in a duel. Thinking the battle was over, they let the remaining Klondikes go, realizing too late that Mennot and the Hillians had followed and regrouped. Most of the battle took place near the downed pickets, and all might have been lost if not for the arrival of the strange flying ships that appeared to repair the pickets, taking no notice of the people below.

Winter and Cedar, along with others from their group, decided to discover what and from where the machines were. They could not have begun to imagine the events that would unfold from that point forward, engulfing their entire world. If they had, perhaps they may have decided to pass back under the mountain and into the War. The Dystance way was not an easy life, but it was a known entity. Sometimes living with the devil you know is a better choice; sometimes we don't realize that until it's too late.

As they searched for a place to call home and for answers to the strange ships, they learned about two species they had no idea existed: Rhodeeshians and Stryvers, bitter enemies who had fought against each other in the wars. Frost, the Rhodeeshian leader, discovered that there was a link between herself, Winter, and Cedar. As they ventured forward together, they discovered the old hangar where the Picket repair equipment was housed, along with a shuttlecraft. Cedar became instantly enamored with the idea of flying. She read and practiced relentlessly until she was ready to return to camp, a trained pilot. When she arrived, she found that a great battle had happened and pushed the group away to the mountains.

She raced to get there, as Winter and the rest fought desperately for their very survival. Her flight, in the meantime, caught the attention of the Intergalactic War Ship *Iron Sides,* who was given orders to investigate. The commander of the ship took it upon himself to lend aid. But with one hand he gave, and the other he took. The Rhodeeshians, Frost and Ferryn, he held captive onboard his ship, while Winter and the rest were scheduled to be brought back to the planet's surface…until the ship was attacked. They found themselves once again prisoners within a war, only this time, the scale was much grander.

CHAPTER ONE

IRON SIDES

"You have got to be kidding me!" I yelled angrily as the door closed behind me.

"I know, right?" Cedar said from across the room. I turned to look at my sister just as she leaned over a small, brown, hinged box and opened it. "Look at all these bottles! You think we can drink what's inside them?"

"I was referring to us being locked up, Cedar." I was exasperated.

"I realize that, Winter, but there's nothing we can do about it at this very moment. I'm just being practical." She twisted the lid off a green-tinged bottle. It dropped from her hand when we all heard the escaping hiss of air; it sounded much like a snake getting ready to strike. Pale, foamy liquid spilled across the floor. "Smells like citrus," Cedar said, taking a step closer. She reached down and picked up the half-spilled remains. She placed the top under her nose and sniffed. "Smells good. Wish me luck!" she said. Before I could protest, she tipped the bottle up and drank a fair amount of what was left.

Her eyes went wide and one hand flew to her mouth. "Are you alright?" Serrot asked with concern.

She looked at each of us, her eyes seemingly getting larger with each contact made. "I suggest all of you should stay away from this." She took another large guzzle, finishing off the rest.

"This one of those baccoon things, or is she being serious?" Tallow asked. He was referring to the feast we'd had on a wild boar we'd killed in an underground hallway; Lendor had pulled off a particularly tasty portion and Cedar went nuts over it.

"What do you think?" I asked, jutting out my chin to Cedar's backside as she greedily began to hoard up the like-colored bottles.

"Don't you dare!" she said to Tallow when he went over to investigate. She sat down on the spacious bed and twisted the top off another. "Ahh." Her face colored in embarrassment when she involuntary let go a small burp. "The bubbles…they tickle my nose!"

"Sure they do," Tallow said as he grabbed a reddish bottle. He sneezed when he opened it up, his nose too close. When he sniffed, the carbonated liquid went straight up his nostrils.

"Serves you right," she told him. She attempted, unsuccessfully, to stifle another burp, this one much bigger than the last.

"This is all quite fascinating." Serrot seemed angry. "But we have serious problems here."

"More than we might think," Cedar said.

"More than Frost and Ferryn being taken? More than us going who knows where? More than the fact that we are leaving all of those people behind?" I asked.

"More." Cedar stood. "Belnot said something that has me thinking."

"Him? He's just a broker in another uniform," Tallow said hotly.

"Maybe," Cedar said; she was thinking.

"Cedar," I prodded. While she was thinking, my heart was racing. I'd felt something I could not explain; had she maybe stumbled across an answer? I needed to know, though a whispered voice told me I didn't want to.

"He was talking about the weapon designed to kill the invading Stryvers. Said it targeted their DNA, or actually, any alien DNA."

"What's that got to do with us?" Serrot asked. "I don't even know what DNA is or how it pertains to us."

"I only know what I've read about it in my books; it usually revolves around what a criminal leaves behind at a crime scene…but my understanding is it's an integral part of what makes us, *us*."

"Huh?" Tallow's head was cocked to the side in confusion.

"It is a substance inside of us, a *hereditary* material, a genetic make-up. If we had the know-how and the equipment, Winter and I would discover not only that we share our looks, but our very cells would show that we are related."

"Cedar, I don't know what you're telling us." Tallow was lost, and I admit, I was on the same path he was; maybe not as far gone, but unsure where all this had her leading us.

"These cells would all be unique in their own way, much like we are, but they would also share a commonality, just like we do."

Because we're all human," I said, jumping from Tallow's track to something closer to Cedar's.

"You're saying the people on this ship aren't human?" This from Serrot.

"What is going on here? How can they not be human? They sure do look it." Tallow replied.

"Cedar, your beauty is only rivaled by your smarts," Serrot said as Cedar blushed.

"Something I can understand, please?" Tallow asked.

"Yes; Cedar could you Tallow it down?" I asked.

"Funny, Winter, but I bet if I asked you a pointed question right now, you'd be as clueless as me," Tallow said.

Cedar was still rolling along. "The weapon targets alien DNA. If we were all the same, it would not target any of us at all."

"I saw the way they looked at us; it was much like how Haden and Mennot looked upon their enemies and even some of their underlings. As if those people were beneath them—hardly even of the same species. Is it possible these people see us the same way?" Serrot finished.

"So much so that they would believe we are not even the same creature?" I asked.

"What if Belnot was lying or just didn't know?" Tallow asked.

"That presents a whole other set of problems. Do we dare to test out this extremely dangerous and deadly weapon? And who among us do we designate as the test subject?" Cedar asked though she was continuously looking at Tallow.

"You're a funny one. If I'd known you were going to get so mad, I wouldn't have stolen one of your fizzy drinks. I should have left it where it was."

"Now you know," she told him.

"Trapped by the truth or by a lie, still means we're trapped," Serrot said. "Seems to me our entire lives up to this point we've been trapped by lies, too afraid or too unwillingly to ever question them. I don't want to live whatever time I have left like that ever again." He strode to the door. He placed his hands upon it and pushed, then tried to pull, though there was nothing he could grasp. "What kind of door is this?" he yelled.

Cedar seemed amused as she came up next to him; she pressed a button on the wall next to her. The door slid noiselessly open.

"What do you want?" the guard outside asked. He had been leaning against the far wall in the hall but stood when he saw them staring at him.

"We'd like to go home," Cedar said, sweet as syrup.

"Me too, come to think of it. Haven't seen my girlfriend in two months," the guard said.

"Great, let's get a ship."

"I don't think you understand how this works. Even if you are half the pilot they say you are, they'd never give you a ship. And if you're thinking about stealing one, don't bother."

"They're saying I'm a good pilot?" Cedar blushed.

"Not really the point," I told her.

"Right," she answered. We were now both in the doorway.

"You should go inside."

"And if we don't?" Tallow asked.

"Last time I checked this thing," he held up his rifle, "it shoots deadly plasma bursts. Not something you want to experience."

"Why are we being held prisoner?" I asked. "We've done nothing wrong."

"Don't know, don't care. They tell me to guard this room and make sure no one leaves or enters, that's what I do. It's pretty simple once you cut out all the rest of it. Now go." He motioned with his hand. "You just being at the doorway could get me in trouble and now I have to call someone and figure out why it's not locked."

Cedar pretended like she hadn't heard one word he'd said and took another step out.

"Do you have air sandwiched inside that pretty little head of yours?" the guard asked. He was getting tense; it was easy enough to see his arms tightening as he gripped his rifle.

"You think I'm pretty?" She tilted her head and made some obnoxious braying sound that was more like a horse than my warrior sister.

"Yeah. In a savages-gone-wild type of way, I'd say you're extremely pretty. Unfortunately for you, it doesn't look like you got much in the smarts department."

"What about my sister?" Cedar turned to me and winked.

The guard was gazing over Cedar to get a better look at me. "I'm more of a redhead type of guy, but…" That was all he got to say as Cedar moved lightning quick. She kicked him square in the crotch and wrenched his weapon free as he bent over in extreme agony.

"*What did you do that for!?*" He was still hunched over, wincing as he spoke, drool falling from his mouth.

Cedar motioned for Lendor and Tallow to pull him into the room then checked both sides of the hallway before entering the room herself.

"You think you could have maybe told one of us what you

were planning on doing?" Lendor asked her.

"Didn't know I was going to do it until I did," she replied. "How do you think this thing works?" she asked, looking at the plethora of buttons on the stock of the weapon.

"What do we do with him?" Serrot asked.

"Tie him up somehow; I'm sure we've got bunches of questions we can ask him, and if he doesn't answer, I'll just point this thing at him while I press buttons and turn dials until something happens," Cedar said matter of factly.

The guard swallowed noisily. Serrot held the man in place while Tallow ripped up strips of the bedding to use as makeshift bindings.

"You're all idiots."

"What's your name?" I asked.

"Why? So you'll know who is accusing you at your trial?" he asked.

"Try the gun out, Cedar," I said.

"Wait…wait." He was gathering himself, still in a great deal of pain, his face red from it.

"Manuel. Listen—if you let me go now we don't even have to tell anyone what happened."

"You'd do that?" I asked.

"You're not thinking of letting him go, are you?" Tallow asked.

"It's an option. I'm sure he'd be in some pretty big trouble if it was found out we took him prisoner. Not sure I would have gone about it this way, but it appears our hand has been forced."

"You're welcome!" Cedar said from across the room. She was sitting on the bed, looking over the gun.

"Seriously, what do you think is going to happen? You think you can take me hostage, force me into the hangar, take a ship and somehow get away? Well, I've got some news for you. That kind of stuff doesn't happen."

"I beg to differ," Cedar said. "What?" she asked when we all looked at her. "I read about it in a book once."

“Fiction or non-fiction?” Tallow asked.

“Does it matter?”

“Yeah, yeah it does,” he replied.

“Stop touching those buttons! You don’t even know what you’re doing! You’re like a monkey with a bongo!” Manuel yelled over to Cedar. She got up angrily.

“This button marked ‘joules’…if I turn this up to 10 megawatts, I’m thinking that would be enough power to burn that head of yours clean off. Now, this button here changes the rate of fire from semi-automatic to fully automatic. When I depress this button, it tells me how much of a charge I have remaining, which pertains to how many rounds I have at my disposal, and since this is fully charged, I’m going to say I have quite a few. What say you?” she asked. Manuel was silent and seething. “This back here? When I click the knob, it opens up where a traditional magazine would go to expose two metallic leads. Now I can’t say for sure because I’ve never seen one, but I would imagine this is how you charge it up when it begins to run low. How am I doing? Any better than a monkey? And this, this button right here,” she made sure to shove the side of the rifle into his face, “this button has an F for Fire…or for what you are right now (but I can’t say in mixed company), and this S stands for Safe, which you most definitely are not. We on the same page?”

Manuel said nothing.

“She asked you a question. I suggest you answer it,” Lendor said.

“I’m betting this little pully tab makes the gun fire,” Cedar said. She had the rifle pointed around where she had kicked him; Manuel took that threat seriously.

“Same page,” he said reluctantly, but there was relief when she moved the muzzle.

“Who are you people?” I asked.

“We’re the people that saved your asses from the Stryvers on top of that mountain. Or have you already forgotten?”

“He does have a point,” Cedar said.

"Seriously?" I asked her. "You're the one that took him."

"Someone should have maybe talked some sense into me; I can't be trusted."

"They took Frost and Ferryn; that makes them the bad guys," Tallow said.

"It's a war. How many unsavory things do you think are happening all around us? When you all were stuck up on that mountain and were about to become spider food, what wouldn't you have done to save yourselves? Now I'm not talking about any one of you personally, but the entire group?" Manuel asked.

"He's making sense," Cedar said.

"Cedar!" I nearly stomped my foot. She'd set all of this in motion and now looked to us to stop the ball from rolling.

"What about us? We're stuck here too." Even to my ears, Tallow's argument sounded weak.

"You heard the ship-wide warning of an imminent arrival, right? Don't normally get one of those if the ship is a friendly. There's a good chance we'll be under attack soon. You think Commander Breeson would risk this entire ship to make sure you four got home? There aren't any four people on here that he would do that for. But don't do anything stupid; I can't guarantee it, but I think if the opportunity presents itself sometime in the future, he'll get you back, even if he has to defy an order or two to do it, that's just the kind of guy he is."

"Wow, I'm sort of feeling bad we hurt him now," Cedar said.

"We?" I asked.

"No need to split hairs," she replied. "So what about the sensors in the hallways, the ones that have the lasers?" She turned her attention back toward Manuel.

"What about them?"

"Belnot said if he turned them on, they would kill us, but not you. How are we so different?"

He was tight-lipped. He answered with: "I don't know." But the stiffness in his voice and how uncomfortable he looked led me to believe he did know. "My replacement is due in ten minutes, so this can go one of two ways. Winter was right; this will look really bad for me if they find out I was overpowered and taken hostage. Might lose a stripe and some pay. It'll be a lot worse for you, though. They'll have you all in the brig, which is far worse than this room—this is an officer's quarters, by the way. Better than I stay in. Right now, you're guests. If you get bumped to being prisoners, the odds Breeson is going to want to bring you home goes down. I'm not exaggerating when I tell you that there is not much you can do with me to further your cause. If they think you're gaining any sort of advantage, they'll take us all down and I'll just be a casualty of war."

We stepped away from Manuel and the four of us had a small huddle, attempting to figure out our next steps.

"He's full of crap. I say we at least use him to force a meeting with Breeson," Tallow said.

"That won't work," Serrot said to him. "If they are indeed preparing for war, he's not going to waste any time on us."

"I think the guard is right. The best thing we can do is to let him go," Cedar said.

I wanted to slap my palm against my forehead. "Okay, I'm for letting him go too."

"What are the chances he's lying and the moment he gets free he doesn't harm us or at the minimum tell his superiors what happened?" Lendor asked.

"I know!" Cedar said excitedly. She went back to Manuel and searched his pockets.

"What are you doing?"

"How does this work?" she asked, holding up a small rectangular device that could have fit in the palm of my hand and was no thicker than one of my fingers.

"That's mine!" Manuel surged in his chair.

"I realize that; I got it from your pocket. Or have you already forgotten, silly?" Cedar asked.

"Give it back!"

"I'll smash it under my boot if you keep yelling. Listen, we have about five minutes before we're all in trouble. How about you tell me how to work this thing before my incredibly idiotic fingers do some irreparable damage to it."

"It's not just some *thing!* It's a Pear Pie 21B, the state of the art comm device for all star travelers."

"Pear pie? Sounds delicious," Tallow said.

"Better hurry, Manuel. I'm thinking that something like this must cost a small fortune and from what I've read, military people aren't paid a whole lot. Didn't stop Isabella from marrying Troy though. Now, Isabella, she didn't care about the money or the security Conrad could have offered with all his millions."

"Huh?" Manuel tilted his head, attempting to follow Cedar's tangent.

"Go with it, much easier," Tallow informed him.

"Okay! On the bottom, there are four small tabs. Press the second one twice and the first one three times."

Cedar did as he said, the device expanded to nearly three times the size it had been and a display came up, much like on the shuttle. She had to swing her hand out and catch it in mid-air when she dropped it as the device began to speak to her.

"Your facial features are not recognized. This Pear Pie will only open when its owner is recognized."

"It needs to see me," Manuel said. Cedar turned it around. "Unlock."

There was a small chime. "Unlocked, Manuel. How can I be of assistance?"

"Well?" he asked Cedar.

"Have it take a picture of you tied up."

"Is she serious?" he asked me.

I shrugged.

"Fine. Dierdre, take…."

"Wait, wait!" Cedar said as she handed me the device. She quickly ran her fingers through her hair and got behind Manuel, smiling widely.

"What is going on here?" Serrot asked.

The only two that seemed to know weren't saying anything.

"Smile, Manuel," Cedar whispered in his ear. He gave a weak one before telling the device to take a picture. There was a snapping sound and that was it.

"How'd it turn out?" Cedar asked, coming from around Manuel and grabbing the thing from my hand. "Manuel, what kind of smile is that? You look like you just ate frogs." Cedar frowned. "I, on the other hand, look ravishing!" She held it up so we could all see.

"What is this sorcery?" Serrot asked. "Did it make small copies of you both? Are they trapped inside now?"

"You've never seen a camera before?" Manuel asked.

"Up until recently we'd never seen a light bulb," I told him honestly.

"Make it print," Cedar said, holding the Pear Pie up.

"I can't." Manuel's head sagged a bit.

"Print?" Tallow asked.

"Like in the books," I told him.

"It'll make a copy of this and then we have proof we had Manuel as our prisoner so he won't turn us in after we let him go."

"Oh," I said. "That's pretty smart."

"Looks like I got all the brains of the family and you the brawn," Cedar said playfully. "Now make a copy," she demanded.

"That's the 21A, okay? I couldn't afford it. It's incredible; prints out pictures on these translucent discs. You can stretch them out to cover a whole wall if you want and not lose any resolution. Someday…maybe when I make sergeant or I leave the service and take a job at my cousin's ship repair shop. He said he'd get me a job there."

"No picture? I guess we'll just hold on to this."

"You can't!"

"I thought I told you enough with the yelling."

"Sorry." Manuel did seem very contrite. "It's the only way I can stay in touch with my girlfriend back home. It's the only thing that makes all of this bearable."

"How far away is your girlfriend?" Tallow asked.

"Right now? I don't even know…millions, billions of miles, I guess."

"And this thing lets you talk to her?" Tallow was pointing.

"Listen Cedar, you let me go and take that with me, I swear to you I won't say anything."

"We can't believe him," Serrot warned, but I was looking at his eyes. They were focused on the Pear Pie, picturing the girl on the other end.

"Let him go. I, for one, trust him and I don't want to go to the brig, whatever that is. Just sounds foul," I said.

Tallow immediately began undoing the binds. "What are we going to say about all the ripped-up sheets?" he asked, holding them in his hands.

"I'll get you replacements on my next shift." Manuel had stood and was rubbing his wrists. "Can I have that?"

Cedar handed him the Pear Pie.

"Probably going to need the rifle as well."

"Fine." Cedar reluctantly let it go. "You turn us in and when I escape the brig, you'll be the first person I hunt down and kick in the crotch."

Manuel hunched over a bit and protectively covered himself. "Duly noted." He fixed his uniform, gave us all a once over before heading out the door.

"We shouldn't have let him go," Serrot said sourly.

"And do what with him?" I asked. "Our choices were fairly limited and I'm not much for killing if we don't need to."

"Did you see the way he avoided my question?" Cedar asked. "What's that all about?"

"Do you think he'd answer now that we're not holding him captive?" Tallow asked, heading for the door.

We were just in time to see Manuel's relief come and change out with him.

"Get your scurvy asses back in that room. I almost feel like I could catch something nasty from just looking at you," the replacement said, his rifle pointed at us menacingly. Manuel looked back as if to say sorry.

"I don't understand the hostility," I said once Cedar shut the door. "They definitely think less of us."

"Part of it might be that, by comparison, our world is so less advanced than theirs. Kind of what we thought about the Comanchokees. We inherently assumed we were better than them just because of how they chose to live. This disparity is many times greater than that," Cedar said.

"I get that part of it, even maybe understand it, but it's more like not only do they believe how they live is better, but they themselves feel superior. There's something weird going on here and I don't like it," I said.

"I don't like it either, but I'd be able to think on it more clearly if I could find a bush to use." Tallow was nearly dancing from foot to foot.

"Should I tell him?" Cedar asked.

"No clue what you're talking about, sis, but if you have any ideas feel free to share, because…now that he brought it up…"

Cedar looked at me funny. "You don't know either?"

"Don't know what, either?"

"Come here." She grabbed my hand and pulled me to a small room in one corner and pointed to a strange, oblong device sticking out of the wall. Couldn't have been more than a foot deep, and when she turned on the light, I could see water at the bottom.

"That a well for drinking?" Tallow asked as we all crowded in.

"It's a toilet."

"A what?" I asked.

"You do your business on it."

"How?" Tallow asked getting close and sniffing at the feature.

"Well, it's not like I can show you," Cedar said,

embarrassed.

"No way," I said. "You have no idea what to do right now either."

"Whatever. It's not like they have pictures in the books I read, but this is a bathroom. This is where people do what they need to do."

"Oh, I get it." Serrot had moved over to a small basin about hip high. "This is where…" He made a motion as if to pull out his privates.

"Oh!" Tallow said in surprise. "Perfect. Okay, everyone out. Wait, what do those handles do?" He twisted one then stepped back as water jetted out. "Clean up. Perfect."

"Wait, that's a *sink*, I think." Cedar messed with the handles; copious amounts of water came pouring out.

"That's not helping," Tallow replied, crossing his legs.

We all left the bathroom and Tallow to his own devices. I looked up as the color in the room changed from a natural sunlight tone to a glaring red; this was immediately followed by a loud, three-round blast of sound.

"I do not think any of this signifies something good." Lendor went to the door and pressed the button.

"You open that again and I'm going to shoot you," the guard said harshly as Lendor made sure to shut it quickly.

"It would seem he is nervous," Lendor said, not overly concerned he'd just had the muzzle of an extremely dangerous weapon pointed at his abdomen.

"The 'imminent arrival' has arrived," Cedar said.

I reached out and grabbed my sister as we were violently rocked to the side. The entire ship thrummed, sounding much like the rumble of a sleeping hog. This was followed by an extremely uncomfortable sensation. I felt like someone massive and powerful had wrapped one hand around the entirety of my head, wrapped my feet with the other, and then attempted to pull me apart. I could barely focus on the others to see if they were experiencing the same thing that I was. Then as quickly as it started, I snapped back into my normal self.

The door to the bathroom opened up, a haggard looking Tallow walked out. "I'm never doing that again."

"This ship was attacked and they ran." Lendor had his hand upon the wall.

"You know this how?" Serrot asked.

"No more explosions and the feeling of being pulled apart; similar to the sensation one gets when they are running down the face of a mountain at an excessive and uncontrolled pace," he replied. "That, and there are no more explosions," he repeated, still suffering some after-effects.

"The lights are still red," Serrot challenged.

"How quick are you to let your guard down after being attacked?" Lendor countered.

"So we're traveling further away from our home?" I asked.

"It would appear that way," Lendor said.

After a while, the lights turned back to their normal color. We took turns sleeping, though if these people wanted to do us harm, there was very little we could do to prevent it. It is nearly impossible to tell how much time has elapsed when you are in an enclosed room, much like a cave. It sometimes felt like a week, but knowing plenty about shift changes, it hadn't been more than twenty-four hours when Manuel returned.

He came in apprehensively; two others were with him, one pushing a large cart. It had more food on it than I'd ever seen at one time. I was convinced this must be for all the personnel upon the ship and they were going to give us our allowance. When the one with Manuel turned quickly and left the room, I thought he'd made a mistake.

"You coming?" the man with Manuel asked; he was the guard that had threatened Lendor.

"Yeah, be right there."

"Don't linger—you don't know what kind of things you can catch from these animals," he sneered. "I don't like that they know how to speak, like they're making a mockery of us."

"It's alright, Blainer, I've got this."

"Okay, your funeral. Death by feral animal, that would be

a horrible way to go. Better than by Stryver, I guess. Back in four. These cannibals kill and eat you, that's on you—I'm going to tell the Old Man I warned you."

Manuel nodded at Blainer; he waited for the other to leave before speaking. "How you all doing?"

"This is all ours?" Cedar asked around a mouthful of food she was double fisting into her face. "What is this? It's delicious."

"The blueberry muffin or the croissant?" Manuel asked.

"Yes," she sighed contentedly.

"Can you tell us what is going on?" I asked.

"Eat first. I'm sure you're hungry. As you've heard, I've got four hours."

The food was incredible. There was fresh fruit, vegetables, pastries and meats of a variety we'd not even known existed. We ate to a level none of us were accustomed to.

"Now, before I fall asleep," I prodded.

"As I'm sure you're aware, we were attacked."

"By whom?" Lendor asked.

Manuel hesitated.

"You must have wanted to talk to us; you said you would," Cedar said, cutting to the chase.

"In terms of the order of this ship, I rank near the bottom, so it's not that I don't want to say something, it's that I don't know anything. Rumor has it we were attacked by Gengruns." He shuddered at that word, but it meant nothing to us and he must have picked up on that. "Think Stryver, only worse."

"That would be an unfortunate enemy," Lendor said.

"Thing is, they're not supposed to exist anymore. Supposedly wiped out over a hundred years ago. We learned all about them in school, how they had nearly brought the known galaxy to its knees. They allied with no one, destroyed everything they encountered, seemingly for the joy of destruction. For that, they were dubbed the angels of death, but that didn't make any sense. Death only takes its due; the Gengruns took everything."

"How were they stopped?" I asked.

Manuel shook his head. "Our lessons got fuzzy there. I never saw anything that was definitive—mostly speculation."

"Then how were they speculated to have been defeated?" Cedar asked. She was somehow stuffing another muffin into her mouth, this one chocolate chip. "I juff knew chclate was going to be this good." She started pulling out the deep brown, cone-shaped pieces and slowly rolling them on her tongue.

"Depending on the source, it was a virus."

"You don't believe that though," I said.

"No. More likely it was some terrible weapon we created but no one talks about it."

"I wonder if this is the 'Happening' we keep hearing of," Lendor said.

"Where are we going now?" Serrot wanted to know.

"You can't say anything." Manuel looked around as if we were being observed.

"Who do you think we're going to tell? Blainer? That guy is an ass," Tallow said.

"We're going back to the where the high council is, our home world."

Had another hundred or so questions for him when the door slid open and Commander Breeson, along with five others, filed into the room.

"Private Jimenez. Imagine my surprise when I saw that you were not at your duty station," the Commander said.

"This one here was choking, sir, I came to her aid." Manuel pointed to Cedar, who on queue began to cough.

"Sorry, I can't stop eating these." Crumbs fell to the floor. "Got it lodged in the back of my throat, can still feel it there. Want to take a look?" She stuck out her tongue and opened her mouth wide.

"As long as you are all right, that is all that matters. Private."

"Yes, sir." Manuel made a motion with his hand, bringing it up to his forehead before quickly departing.

"I hope you enjoyed your breakfast," the Commander said pleasantly enough but the words did not have the ring of kindness behind them, as if he spoke per custom and not that he cared in any way.

"It was wonderful. Is there any chance we can discuss going home now?" I asked.

"As much as I would like to say we can get you there, this ship was damaged in that attack and we have to return to our home for urgent repairs."

"Who attacked us?" Tallow asked.

"We are unsure," Breeson replied, though he looked away for a moment before answering.

"Can you tell us why your people are hostile to us?" Serrot asked.

"I have no idea. If you tell me who, I will talk to them personally. You are our valued guests and as such, should be treated kindly."

"Do you always keep your guests guarded and locked in a room?" I asked.

Breeson looked at me sternly. "This is a military vessel, not a cruise ship. It has been a pleasure to talk with you all but I need to check on the rest of my ship." He let his thin smile fall from his lips as he turned and left. "You go in there again and you'll find yourself in an extended stay in the brig, you understand me private?"

"Sir, yes, sir." Manuel stood rigidly as Breeson and the other five walked out of the room and disappeared around the corner.

"Does anyone think anything he said was the truth?" I asked.

"We're prisoners. Well-fed prisoners, but we're stuck here," Cedar said.

Hours once again passed. The old food cart was removed and a new one replaced it. I was not the only one still full from the previous meal. Perhaps had we known that they would be coming with a frequency we would not have eaten until it felt as if our bellies would burst. But where we are from, when food is presented, you eat until you no longer can. A next meal is never guaranteed.

"Something's going on." Lendor was standing, yet he was looking to his feet. "Do you feel that?"

I got up off the bed, trying to feel what he felt. I shook my head in negation.

"Nothing," Tallow said.

"There it is." Cedar was smiling. "We're slowing down. That's it! Right!" She was happy she'd felt it, not that we had potentially reached our destination.

"Imminent Arrival," came through the walls.

"Another attack?" Tallow asked.

"It does not seem likely that they would slow down for it," Lendor replied.

"Maybe the machine is broken," Tallow said. Hard to argue with that considering we had barely any idea how any of it worked. For all we knew, it could have been magic from any number of Cedar's books. We occasionally picked at the food, only because it seemed like such a waste not to, but other than that we didn't do much. We could ask each other all the questions we wanted, but without any corresponding answers, it seemed a frustrating and worthless venture. I enjoyed my quiet times, peaceful times of reflection as much as the next person, but this wasn't that. We were all ready for action—even if we had no idea what was coming. Luckily, all we needed to do was wait some more; that was something we were getting good at.

CHAPTER TWO

INTERCEPTION

"Is what I heard correct?"

"It is, High Councilman Lodilin," Trekoton, his aide, replied. "Our source within the people's high command says that Commander Breeson has five inhabitants of Earth and something else, though we were not able to decipher that part of the transmission."

"Is my imperial ship ready?" Lodilin stood.

"Of course."

"Let's go then."

"May I ask where, sir?"

"To intercept the Iron Sides. It is imperative we get to those humans before Breeson can get them home."

"Intercept?"

"Diplomatically, of course. We have not yet been to war with our new allies."

"This is a dangerous game you play, High Councilman."

"These are dangerous times, Trekoton."

"We are receiving a request to board by High Councilman Lodilin," Major Dillinger, the communications officer said, speaking to his commanding officer.

"You have got to be kidding me," Breeson said as he sat upon his chair in the bridge. "Put him on the screen." Breeson gave a slight nod of his head when Lodilin's image came on the massive viewing screen. "High Councilman. It is good to see you. How may I be of assistance?"

"You must have received my message; otherwise, we would not be speaking now. You may be of assistance by slowing your ship from its buckle," Lodilin stated.

"High Councilman, we have sustained damage from an attack. It is of the utmost importance that we seek repairs at our home base."

"Nonsense. I have some of the finest technicians aboard this very ship. We will board and be of assistance."

"High Councilman, I am under orders to return to base as quickly as possible."

"Commander Breeson, if I were to order you to stop, which request would be of higher priority?" Lodilin asked.

Breeson clenched his teeth but smiled nonetheless as he gave another small nod. "Of course, High Councilman. We are slowing now. I look forward to meeting with you soon." He nodded to his comms officer and the screen went blank. "Major, you have the bridge." Breeson walked out and to his quarters.

"Commander Breeson, may I ask the reason for this communique? There are proper channels to be used." Front Admiral Lowrie was impeccably dressed in a red military jacket. Medals which he had earned in dozens of campaigns adorned his chest.

"I am sorry to bother you, Front Admiral. High Councilman Lodilin has requested an opportunity to board."

"Damn him. He must know. The coincidence is too great. Commander, you get him off that ship as quickly as possible.

Is that clear?"

"It is, sir." The small screen went blank. "And just how am I going to do that? What's that old saying? Stuck between a…" He gripped the sides of his desk as the ship came to a stop much quicker than he'd been expecting. The lights in his quarters turned a dull red as a general alarm was sounded.

He ran to the bridge. "What's going on? Something fail in the buckle drive?"

"Don't know, sir," Major Gralter told him. She was busy looking at her displays, attempting to ascertain exactly what had happened.

"Have we pulled out of the buckle?" the commander asked.

"No, sir. The buckle was stopped," Gralter said.

"The buckle was stopped? That's impossible."

"Up until thirty seconds ago, sir, I would have said the same thing."

"Where's Lodilin?" Breeson asked, wondering if the wily Genogerian was up to something.

"Still an hour out, according to our scans," Captain Tilton replied.

"Are there any ships in the area?" Breeson asked.

"None that we can detect," Tilton said.

"That sounds like a qualifier. What's going on, Captain? Put it on the screen."

The captain did so. From his seat, he circled an area in the upper left quadrant. "Here, sir. We cannot detect *anything*, almost as though the continuity of space does not exist there."

"A black hole?"

"Not quite—a black hole can be measured. This is just a hole. A void."

"Theories?"

"Nothing yet, sir. I've never seen anything like it in my life."

"Major Gralter, can we get back into a buckle?" Breeson asked.

"Sir, all systems are green, but we cannot, for some reason, ignite an opening."

"Propulsion?"

"Online."

"Let's move. Major Dillinger, get on the line with High Councilman Lodilin. Tell him we are about to be under attack and he should leave the area as quickly as possible.

Ogunquit

"I usually have a difficult time deciphering the vast facial array the humans can display, but sir, I think I can safely say that Commander Breeson was most angry."

"It is easy enough, Trekoton, when you know what to look for. Now we wait. I would imagine he's sending off an encoded message to his superiors letting them know about my request."

"Do you believe he will heed your order?"

"He has no choice in the matter. If he does not, he risks weakening everything we have been working on for centuries."

Lodilin was on the bridge. He was watching the long-range sensors as the *Iron Sides* came out of its buckle. "That was much quicker than I expected. I truly thought they would delay." He had also feared that the humans would bring in more ships as a display of power—a heavy-handed reminder that he was sticking his snout in places it did not belong.

"Imperial Ship *Ogunquit*, this is Major Dillinger from the *Iron Sides*. We are under threat of attack. Commander Breeson has requested that you vacate the area as quickly as possible so as not to come in harm's way."

"That would be one way to discourage us from coming onboard," Lodilin said to Trekoton as an aside.

"It very well could be a ruse, High Councilman, but it would have been difficult to do what they did in regards to the buckle; they would need to employ a technology we are as of yet unaware of, and with our connections within their system, it is highly unlikely that we would not know about it."

"You are correct in that matter. Someday, I hope that we become confident enough that all this clandestine subterfuge is no longer needed between us. Bring up the communication screen."

"Major Dillinger, what kind of ally would I be if I fled in your hour of need?" Lodilin asked.

"High Councilman." Breeson came on to screen. "With all due respect, this is a war vessel equipped to handle myriad hostile situations. Right now, we have no idea what we are dealing with and I cannot also be concerned with your ship being involved in something I cannot control."

"Commander, the *Ogunquit* is more than capable of defending herself. I daresay perhaps even better than the *Iron Sides* herself. We will stay close for now, especially since it would appear that your buckle drive is unavailable to you, rendering you especially vulnerable."

"As you wish," Breeson said before abruptly cutting comm.

"I do not believe he likes your decision." Trekoton wore a ghost of a smile.

"You are getting better at this. Have our techs discovered the source of the *Iron Sides'* problem?"

"No sir, but I have just received word of an anomaly."

CHAPTER THREE

BUCKLING

I fell into Lendor, who himself fell onto the bed.

"What just happened?" I asked as I helped Cedar up. She had bumped her head against the food cart as she looked for more of the bubbly sweet water.

The lights in the room shifted to red, though there was no sounding of an alarm.

Lendor was shifting on his feet, testing the deck plates. "We've stopped."

"How can you tell? There're no windows," Tallow asked.

"It is a sense; also, there is a minute vibration in the floor as we are moving, an engine in motion, like in the trucks and the shuttle. It is no longer there."

"Maybe we're wherever we're going." Serrot looked to the door.

"More likely they stopped for the 'arrival' they are expecting. Friends, maybe?" I said.

"Very well could be, if not for that." Lendor pointed to the red lights. "One would not think it would be worthy of shipwide alarm as you awaited guests."

"Well there's that," I said.

"We're guests. Look how we're treated." Cedar was rubbing her head.

"What does any of it mean to us? We can't do anything, and I, for one, am going insane waiting," Tallow said.

"Yeah. We should do something. Tallow doesn't need to be pushed far to get the end of his rope," Cedar said.

"Funny one," Tallow mock-laughed. "Probably has more to do with the company I keep."

"He is right, though," I said, "the first part, anyway. I am going a little stir crazy as well and worried over leaving everyone we know. They could still be in danger. And it always circles back to the fact we are helpless." I was grousing. Our spirits seemed to have dampened with the lighting. Nothing happened for a seeming eternity, with nothing more to do than digest food, I fell asleep. Possibly a few hours later, I was awakened by a soft tapping coming from the door. No one else in the room had heard it, they slept on where they lay.

"Manuel?" I said as I hit the button that opened the door. "Is it wise for you to be speaking with me?"

"Probably not, but I've never been one to adhere to all the rules." He stood there for long moments, just looking at me, to the point where I became increasingly uncomfortable.

"Is there something you wanted to say?"

"You are quite beautiful, you and your sister both. Are all women from Earth like you two?"

"If you've spoken your piece, I'm going back to sleep."

"No, no—I'm sorry. I only meant…it was merely a compliment. I am happily in a relationship."

"Again, Manuel, I have not slept well in days and my body is still sore from the battle we were involved in." I was turning around.

"We're under attack," he blurted out.

"What?" I turned back toward him. "Stryvers?" I could think of no worse enemy to be confronted with.

"We don't know."

"You don't know who is attacking you? I don't understand."

"It's more of an electronic attack right now. My friend Halsey works in engineering—he says we were ripped out of a buckle and cannot get back into it."

"Until recently, the most advanced thing I had ever seen was a rifle. I don't understand most of what you just said."

"Okay, just the basics…not like I understand it either. Space is huge, like, *enormous*. Numbers that hardly make any sense. So buckling was created. It's a way to travel across vast amounts of distance without taking centuries to do so. Here, I'll give you a quick demonstration." He pulled his communication device from his back pocket. "Say you wanted to go from the top of my Pear Pie device down to the bottom." He traced a straight line from one to the other. "You would think that would be the quickest way to achieve this, right?"

I nodded, wholly unsure where any of this was going and still greatly missing my bed.

"But what if I did this…" he bent the device. "you see now how much closer the top is to the bottom?"

"I do. Your ships do this with space? They somehow fold it over?"

"Yeah, it's called buckling. Supposedly it has been around for ages, but it was us that improved upon it, found a way to increase the number of folds so that the points are that much closer."

"So something interrupted this…buckle?" I asked.

"Not interrupted, took us out of it completely. Halsey says it's something that absolutely cannot happen. Not even theoretically."

Tallow must have heard us. He'd come up beside me; he had been there longer than I thought because he seemed to have heard most of the conversation. "Are you sure it was an attack? I mean, shouldn't things be blowing up, if that was the case? Or shouldn't you be firing on somebody? Something like that?"

"Did your machine just break?" I asked.

"Halsey says it has to be from the attack. The buckle drive itself is checking out perfectly."

"Then start it up again and get moving," I said.

"It won't do it." Manuel looked plenty nervous. I suppose I should have been too, but I just didn't know enough to be scared. As far as I could tell, there had been a malfunction and that as soon as these technologically-driven people fixed it, we could get moving again. The sooner that happened, the sooner I could get back home. That was all that concerned me. I was rapidly realizing that the world, no, the universe was entirely too massive a place. I just wanted to be in my small piece of it and do what I could there.

"Why are you telling us all of this, or any of it, for that matter?" I asked.

"I just thought if it is an attack and something should happen to any of us, that you would want to know why."

"Thank you, Manuel," I told him. "You've given us lots to think on." I closed the door.

"Well, well, well. Looks like someone has a crush." Cedar was smiling.

"Before you think you're all funny and everything, he said we were both beautiful, so my guess is he has a crush on you as well."

"He said that?" Cedar blushed.

"I'll kill him." Serrot was up and heading for the door, but Lendor intercepted him.

"You think Manuel would wear a kilt?" Cedar asked me.

"How can we possibly have the same mother," I told her.

I was about to ask Tallow why he wasn't defending my honor when the ship was hit, and hit hard. Unlike the hard stop when I fell into Lendor, this put all of us on our butts. Lendor even had some blood on his forehead from where he'd hit the corner of a desk.

"You alright?" I asked as I helped him up. I had to shout over the blaring of an alarm.

"That's not helping!" he yelled, pointing to where the sound was coming from. It only rang out for another ten seconds before quitting, then a notice came over the speakers.

"All crew members. Battle Stations. This is not a drill, repeat, this is not a drill."

"Manuel?" I went to the door to seek out some answers. He was out cold.

"Must have hit the wall. Lucky for him. I would have hit harder," Tallow said as he reached over and grabbed the weapon.

"What are you doing?" I asked him. "He'll get in trouble if they find him like this, unarmed."

"We're under attack, Win, by who knows what. I'm not taking any chances that we get caught without a way to defend ourselves."

"You're right, but help me drag him in. We can at least try and keep him safe if we need to."

"Is this because he called you beautiful?" Tallow asked as we moved the soldier.

"It certainly didn't hurt," I smiled.

"I'll put him back."

"I'm mostly kidding," I told him. "We can use an ally on the inside."

"We could hear men and women running back and forth, sometimes yelling orders at each other or just hurrying to get where they were going, but none of them ever bothered to check on us. Then came sounds we were wholly unfamiliar with: loud twangs that reverberated throughout the entire ship.

"I bet that's weaponry," Cedar said. "Sounds similar to what the shuttle was shooting, only much more powerful."

"I don't like this," Tallow said. "It was one thing when we battled the Stryvers on that mountain; sure, we figured they were wild animals bent on killing us, but they weren't hyper-intelligent beings flying space ships and shooting crazy guns at us—at least those ones weren't."

He was right; it made it much worse to think that a being like that was capable of this level of warfare. How would we have felt if the wild dogs we all feared were driving trucks and shooting rifles out the windows at us?

CHAPTER FOUR

ATTACK

"Incoming!" Captain Tilton warned.

"Evasive maneuvers." Before the commander's order could be completed, they'd been struck on the side. "What was that?" Breeson asked as he sat upright in his chair.

"Don't know sir; it would appear our deflectors and shields have held integrity as there are no signs of damage, according to my instrumentation."

"Where was it heading?"

"C Deck level seventeen," Tilton said after a moment as he scanned the ship.

"Officers' quarters," the commander said. "Did the *Ogunquit* fire upon us?"

"No sir, the shot came from the void."

"Magnify the area. Has the vessel shown itself?"

"Still nothing."

"Anyone else think it's suspicious that Lodilin shows up just in time to witness us getting punched?" No one spoke, unsure if the question was rhetorical, and to say something like that against a High Council member was a sure way to derail one's career. "Scan the ship again." Breeson was seething; something was happening that he was completely unaware and not in control of—two things that he had actively made sure to avoid in his twenty-two years of service.

"Nothing, sir. All shows as well," Tilton said.

"Something is wrong here. Major Dillinger, have all decks report in."

"Aye aye, sir."

"Colonel Runger, can you get me a firing vector on that void?"

"Commander, it's the damndest thing; the computers are acting like there's nothing there. I can't even get a lock because that small piece of space won't even show up on my system."

"So not only has this unseen enemy shrouded themselves and their ship, they are somehow concealing a piece of space. Is this even possible?"

"Commander," Runger spoke up. "Five minutes ago, I would have told you unequivocally that this wasn't possible, but it is hard to deny the proof we are staring down."

"Gralter—any change in the status of our buckle?" Breeson asked. They were faced with an enemy they could neither see nor fire upon; the best thing he could do now was to report his findings to his superiors and hope that they had a solution for this new threat.

"None, sir."

"Anyone have any theories as to why they have only fired the one shot?" Breeson asked.

It was Gralter. "Sir, it's possible that the power needed to warp the space around them makes the charging of their main guns a long process."

"Possible," Breeson said, though he didn't have much faith in it. Any beings with the ability to do what was being done would have already figured that problem out. "Have the fighters on standby."

"Sir?" Colonel Runger asked.

"I think they could fire upon us whenever they wished. That they have not done so leads me to believe that they are planning on attacking soon, and we will need the fighters out there as an added layer of defense."

There were tense moments where nothing happened; the expectation of battle was usually far worse than the battle itself.

"Sir, all levels have reported back with zero casualties, some minor injuries, and no damage to the ship except for

Deck C level 17." Major Dillinger looked to his Commander.

"What are they saying?" Breeson queried.

"That's the thing, sir; I can't get them to respond at all."

"Colonel Runger, get a Tactical Response Team down there and check it out. Probably comms took a hit, but I'm not liking the number of coincidences happening today."

"Captain Collins, this is Colonel Runger. Send TReaT units four and five to Deck C level 17."

"Threat level, sir?" the captain asked.

"Yellow. Can't get a response from that area and the Commander wants it checked out."

"Sending them out now, sir. We'll have some word to you in five."

CHAPTER FIVE

RESCUE

"Winter, I am going to check on what is happening," Lendor said.

"Be careful, and no further than that doorway," I told him. Something was definitely not right. "Don't go thinking heroics either, Lendor. If something is going on, those hallway sensors will be on."

"I had forgot about those." Lendor shivered thinking about the invisible blades that would cut him to pieces. He pushed the button to open the door, cautiously poked his head out and looked to the left. Satisfied there was nothing in that direction, he turned to the right. He quickly pulled himself in and slammed his palm against the door button. "Back room now!" he yelled, his eyes wide and his voice tremulous.

"What's going on?" Cedar asked.

"No time, go!" He was pushing everyone to the back.

"Lendor?" I asked once we were in the far corner.

"*Monster*," was all he could manage to get out, his eyes riveted to the door.

"I guess that answers that question. I had hoped to never see a Stryver again," Serrot said.

Tallow had the rifle trained on the door. His eye to the sight. I felt completely exposed with no weapon to wield. Cedar had grabbed a heavy looking object off a shelf and had her arm cocked back, a look of grim determination upon her face. The closest thing to me was a pillow, and I would not be caught dead using that to defend myself.

"What's happening?" Manuel said he was on the far side of the room, closest to the door. He was sitting up with a hand to his head.

It was a dead heat as Cedar and I raced out to get him. He looked genuinely scared that we were going to do something to him. Cedar strapped her hand across his mouth to keep him from shouting out. Neither of us waited for him to get his legs under himself as we dragged him back to where we were.

"We're under attack," Lendor explained quickly. "Monsters in the hallway."

"Can I have my rifle back?"

"Not a chance," Tallow said. "You can't even stand."

"If it's my men that come through there…"

"It's not," Lendor told him.

"Cedar! Winter!" was yelled through the door. "We are coming in, do not fire upon us."

"Looks like we repelled whoever it was," Manuel said. "You'd better give me the rifle, so there're no misunderstandings."

"Not yet," Tallow said as the door slid open.

A man walked in, dressed all in camouflage. He had strange facial hair: a moustache and a small beard that surrounded only his mouth. He looked fit and ready for just about anything, but he was overshadowed immediately by the monster coming in behind him.

"Son, put the rifle down." The man had his hands outstretched. "I know this might be hard to believe, but we're friends."

"Michael, convince them quickly. We are running out of time. This ship has sent tactical response teams to our location." The monster appeared to be listening to a device attached to his head.

"Who are you?" I asked, standing up.

"Get down!" Lendor begged as he himself stood. Seven more camouflaged men and women poured through the door, all of them armed. There was now a standoff between Tallow and them.

"Son," the Michael man said again. "Listen, you pull that trigger and some people are bound to get hurt and if anything happens to my great, great, great...." The man looked up at the monster. "How many greats did you say it was again?"

"Michael, it does not matter. Make your point."

"Dee, can you not see I am attempting to develop a repartee or is it rapport, with my kin?"

"Kin?" Cedar asked, she was standing now as well. "Tallow, put down the rifle. Your safety is on anyway." His face turned red as he placed the gun on the bed and put his hands over his head.

"Put your hands down. This isn't a surrender; it's a rescue," the Michael man said.

"Michael? As in Michael Talbot?" Cedar asked, coming around the corner.

"You know? We weren't sure if you would, been debating that for a good long while. Seems I owe this big galoot behind me now. And if you think Dee's pretentious now, you should see him when he has a fresh victory under his belt."

"I have yet to understand why you keep betting with me, Michael. I have not lost."

"Someday buddy, you'll stumble, and when that happens, I plan on pouncing. And yes, Cedar, I am Michael Talbot."

"I don't know how." She had tears in her eyes. "And I care even less about why. But I cannot tell you how happy, how overwhelmed, really, that I am." She ran at him as he did his best to move his rifle out of the way. She wrapped her arms around him tight and sobbed into his chest.

"Oh, my sweet, sweet girl, you have no idea what we've gone through to get here, but every last bit of it was worth it. I cannot believe how much like my wife you look. And you too, Winter, like you two jumped right out of a photograph."

I was more guarded than my sister, but the pull of him was magnetic; I found myself drawn. The feelings my sister felt for him…what emanated from him in waves…could not be fabricated. He had somehow and for some reason traveled across time to this very moment, for us. And he was family. I found myself smooshed up against Cedar as we sought solace in his arms.

"Michael…" Dee urged.

"Alright, alright, I get it, but how many times can I say I hugged the greatest of great-grandchildren? And don't be scared of Dee here. He is a Genogerian, and he is the fiercest warrior you will ever come across. Also, the most loyal of friends."

"General Talbot, we have thirty seconds," one of the soldiers with him announced.

"We need to go," Michael told us.

There was a quick scuffle as Manuel grabbed the rifle from Tallow's outstretched hand as they both went for it. He'd seen Manuel dive for it but was slow to react. "You can't take them." Manuel was wobbling as he stood, the barrel of the rifle swaying as he did.

Every invader in that room had their rifle pointed at the uniformed boy.

"Who's Shaky here?" Mike asked, referring to Manuel as he gently moved us to the sides and away from where the guard was pointing. He took a step front and center to dominate Manuel's line of sight, should he start to fire.

"That's Manuel; he's our guard," I told him.

"Manuel, you don't want to die here today."

"Do you?" He looked scared, the bravado ringing false, the whites of his eyes clearly on display.

"Honestly, no, not really, but I'm not afraid of it. I've done a lot in my life I can be proud of. I have a wife and children that love me dearly. I have friends I cherish; I have done all that I can to make sure that all of them are safe and live the best lives that they can. What more can a person ask for? And what of you, Manuel? After you pull that trigger and kill me, you follow a moment behind. For what? What will you have accomplished? No matter how far astray your people have come, you have roots in humanity and from what I know, myself, Dee here." He threw a thumb over his shoulder at the much larger being. "And those with me…we are heroes of your history. How's that going to look for your legacy? Got to imagine the weight of you being called a traitor for all eternity is going to be a huge burden for your family."

Manuel looked confused, scared, and indecisive. All could have lethal repercussions. I looked up to Michael; he had a tense look on his face. There was just the slightest movement from the fingers on his right hand.

"Wait!" I stepped out in front. The distraction was enough to keep Manuel from getting shot—or anyone, really—as Tallow leveled him with a punch to the side of his head.

"OW!" He danced around and shook his hand. Manuel fell away to the bed, out cold.

"Good job," Serrot said as he grabbed the rifle. "Maybe next time don't punch someone in the skull."

"I'll remember that," Tallow hissed. Mike's men surrounded us all and within seconds, we were on the move down the hallway.

"You know about the breech inhibitors?" I asked, although we were already twenty feet in the kill zone.

"I should. I was in the meeting when Mad Jack brought up the theory of them."

"Is it true, then?"

Michael looked angrier than when Manuel was getting ready to shoot him. He was about to answer that until we came under fire.

"Have you two ever shot guns?" he asked as we ducked down a side hallway. "Dee! The bag!" he called out as we stayed pinned to a wall. A green bag that looked to be made from the same material that he was wearing was tossed over; he had to move quickly to keep it from smashing into his head.

"You did that on purpose, you giant piece of luggage."

"Next time I tell you to move, it would perhaps behoove

you to do just that. Now we find ourselves in a firefight we may very well have avoided."

"He gets angry with me when we get shot at," Michael said as he rooted around in the bag.

"Don't you?" Cedar asked.

"If he got mad every time someone shot at him, he would know no other emotion," the huge Genogerian replied.

Michael looked up as if he were thinking on Dee's words. "Some truth to that, unfortunately." He pulled out two small rifles—carbines, he called them. They looked very much like our previous rifles, though they shot a blue ray instead of a traditional bullet. "You've shot?" he asked, his head nodding in the hopes that we agreed with him.

"Yes," we both answered.

"Good. No…not good. I'm sure you've had to shoot out of self-defense, just good that you know how. Okay, safety is here." He pointed to a small green button. When he depressed it, it illuminated a bright red. He pressed it again and it turned green. "You know, now that I'm looking at this, the color scheme seems wrong. Green usually signifies go and red means stop, but this time green means stop and…"

"Michael!" Dee admonished.

"Right. Red is for fire, danger. This is your charge." He was now showing us a series of seven green lights, all of which were lit. "Trigger, barrel, all the rest is the same." He handed them over.

"Now what?" Cedar asked. "There has got to be hundreds of them onboard this ship."

"More like thousands. Don't plan on fighting them. My goal is to get you off this ship and to a Genogerian ship parked nearby."

"And what of you?" I asked.

"I've got to get back to where I'm from. I'm already breaking every known law of physics and I'm sure a few other sciences. I'd tell you what they were, but I never really paid much attention. Usually too busy getting familiar with sweet leaf."

"Sweet leaf? Marijuana?" Cedar asked.

"Dammit. You weren't supposed to know that." He stood as did we. "Reynolds, we ready?"

"Almost sir."

Streaks of red were blistering down the hallway, coming from the men on the ship.

"Can't you just tell them who you are?" Cedar asked. "Wouldn't they stop firing then?"

"Oh, I think at that point they might just deliberately blow up this entire section of the ship. In public, this would be considered some horrible accident…now, if my name was somehow associated with it, they would pretend how distraught they were, but inwardly, they would be thrilled because of what me and my cohorts represent."

I had no idea what he meant and would have loved to hear some clarification, but we were in an active firefight and were preparing to move. And as much as the man in front of me seemed to be a joker, he was all seriousness now as we got down to the business of escaping.

Michael swore as one of his men was shot and lay bleeding in front of us. He turned the corner and savagely burned through dozens of rounds. Dee motioned for us to get moving, as the covering fire was being leveled.

"Fire in the hole!" Michael yelled.

"Run!" Dee shouted. Neither my sister nor I needed to have worried as our feet left the ground. Wind was whistling past my ears as we moved at a pace I would never have been able to produce on my own. "Cover your ears!" Didn't hear the last part of that sentence; figured out what it was he was getting at when there was an impossibly bright light followed by the single loudest noise I had ever heard. I could not be certain because of the jostling I was taking on my forced ride, but the walls of the ship appeared to be vibrating from the assault.

"There's a wall!" Cedar was yelling as the Genogerian was

running headlong into one. We were about to be completely flattened between the immovable wall and the unstoppable force. I was trying to twist away, but I was more heavily secured than I had been when I was captured by Haden and tied up. "Slow down!" she shouted.

Just as we were at the point of no return and he could neither stop nor turn, and I was preparing myself for the bone-crushing collision, the wall began to shimmer and then it turned translucent. I was now looking into the dark interior of another vessel. We were jarred as Dee stumbled; there was a drop-off to this new ship we found ourselves in and the hallway we just left. He was still moving, but slowed as we got to the end of the vessel. He quickly placed us down and went back to the front where he began to grab the trailing men and women out of the air so that they would not have the same unexpected, harsh fall. We could see into the ship we had been on; Michael was firing while also dragging the wounded man.

"Down!" Dee shouted to him as he grabbed a large-barreled weapon and poked it through the opening. A green ray of energy nearly as large around as the Genogerian's head whooshed out of the barrel and narrowly missed Michael. The column expanded until it touched the walls of the hallway where it stopped and solidified.

"Good idea!" Michael yelled as he shouldered his weapon. He grabbed the arm of the injured man and pulled him up and over his shoulder.

"Temporary force field," Dee turned to tell us.

"Are you alright?" Tallow asked, wrapping me up in his arms.

"I'm fine."

"Who are these people, Win, and should we be trusting them?"

"Your lives could not be in better hands," the one called Dee said.

But how does one trust the words of those that have potentially captured you? The only thing I could think of was:

why would they bother making us feel at ease if they meant us harm? It was a weak argument, but it was all I had.

"Well that was close," Michael said as he handed the wounded man to two meddies who immediately brought him over to a table that had medical equipment all around it.

"Close? Michael, your shirt is smoking," Dee said to him.

"Like I said: close. Dee, help me get our guests buckled in."

"Are you shot?" The woman I had seen in the pictures was standing there. I felt as if I had hit my head and was staring at a little older version of my sister.

"I don't think so." Michael was tapping around his body. "One minute, Tracy, then get us over to Lodilin's ship…Crazy, right?" Michael said as he saw his wife staring at Cedar then me.

"How is that possible?" Tracy asked her husband.

"Beats me, but if we had any doubts about this mission being worthwhile, I think we can lay that worry to rest now."

Tracy came over and introduced herself as she helped to buckle us in. Dee was manhandling Serrot, Tallow, and Lendor into their seats.

"I cannot tell you how incredible it is to meet you both. I'm sure you have a thousand questions, and I wish we could go through them all," Tracy said.

"About ready, woman? Running out of time here!" Michael shouted as the small ship we were on was rocked violently.

"Funny how you tell others that we are running out of time but seldom heed your own advice," Dee murmured.

"Physician, heal thyself," Michael replied, though I did not know what that meant. Dee found it humorous.

Tracy left us quickly, her voice coming through the ship's interior. "For those of you new to this experience, you are going to want to take the small bag to your right and place it over your mouth." There were groans from the other soldiers as they did just that. All of us except Lendor followed suit, until Michael scowled at him.

I don't even know how to describe the sensation. We moved so fast it felt as if we were in two places and every point in between at the same time. My brain could not even conceive of what I'd just been through, and neither could my stomach; it evacuated everything within its possession as if I'd had my fill of tainted water. I was embarrassed until I realized that everyone aboard that small ship, even Michael himself, was now stowing the used bag.

"That's one thing Mad Jack never warned us about. That first flight was umm…unique." Michael was smiling at me.

"We have twenty-seven minutes!" Tracy yelled as she came back into the crew area. "Twenty-seven minutes Mike, not one second more."

"How do you recover so quickly?" he asked as he stood with a groan.

"Because I'm not a baby," she responded.

Dee chuffed. "That is funny because it is true. I have seen you with the slightest of fevers; you appear as if you are in need of emergency medical procedures."

"Give me crap all you want, Dee. You still look a little tinged behind the gills, though."

Their words were light-hearted, but they were also hard at work as they helped set up devices that linked our ship to this Lodilin's, and whatever magic they used to make the metal disappear was employed again. Michael stood front and center as the cold gray metal shimmered, then began to lighten until finally, it was translucent. A few seconds later, the hull was as clear as if it had never existed. We were looking at a short hallway and ten or more heavily armored Genogerian soldiers.

"Thought this was supposed to be clear," Michael whispered to Tracy out of the side of his mouth.

"Reynolds! Shut the gate!" Tracy ordered.

"Belay that. No time for another insertion point," Mike said.

"You're going to regret it if you get yourself killed," Tracy said angrily.

Mike turned his head slightly; he had a confused expression on his features. "Yeah, I would think so."

"You know what I mean."

"As far as I know, the living can't haunt the dead."

"I'll find a way," Tracy said matter-of-factly.

"No doubt," Mike said to her as he took a step forward. "I'm Michael Talbot." He raised his arms above his head. "I need to speak with High Councilman Lodilin."

"You are a murderous pirate intent on kidnapping the High Councilman for profit," one of the Genogerian soldiers shouted back.

"Pirate? I'm not a pirate. I mean, I guess back in my day I downloaded a song or two, but that hardly qualifies."

"Come forward so that we may apprehend you and execute you for high crimes," the same guard shouted.

"There's a problem with that command; there's no real incentive for me to follow through."

"Twenty-six minutes, Mike," Tracy told him.

"Perhaps all the humans look the same…." Dee stepped up and next to Michael.

"Hey! That's specie-ism." Mike seemed genuinely hurt.

More than one of the Genogerian guards went to one knee and bowed their heads.

"This is a trick of some sort!" the same guard yelled.

"Perhaps you should let High Councilman Lodilin make that determination, as we are related by blood."

"Are you hearing this?" the guard asked.

"Drababan…is that truly you? How can this be possible?" A voice came through the ship's sound system.

"High Councilman." Dee bowed his head slightly at the words. "There are matters of physics here I could not even begin to explain. Just know that our time is extremely short, and we are here for the same reasons you are."

"How could you possibly know?"

Drababan motioned with his hand to Cedar and me. I didn't know what else to do except go to him. Everything we were doing had a heavy dream-like quality. It was so surreal; it seemed impossible it could happen, and I doubted my waking state.

"Dee, I'm not a fan of having them exposed like that," Mike said quietly, though I heard him.

"These are the humans from Earth: Cedar and Winter Talbot."

There was a long pause, Michael looked as if he was going to vibrate right out of his skin.

"Why are Genogerians always so deliberate," he hissed.

"I am sorry that my entire race has not adopted the practice of 'hold my beer and watch this.'"

Mike turned to the much larger being, a smile beamed across his face. "That is comedic gold, my leathery pal."

"Twenty-five minutes." Tracy was looking to a small machine on her wrist and to us and then the hallway beyond with quick furtive movements.

"What happens to us?" I asked.

"Well, the hope is that Lodilin takes you in and gets you far away from here so that one of the destinies that you have laid out before you can become reality."

"And if he doesn't? Can't we go with you?"

He turned and we looked at each other; I could see the worry and pain that flooded through him. "Honestly, kiddo, not much would make me happier if that were the case. It's just not possible. Like Dee said, we are traveling in uncharted territory. Right now, we're like bumblebees. Shouldn't be able to fly, but here we are anyway. All I know with any degree of certainty is we can't stay here, and you can't come with us. This gambit has been an 'all or nothing' exercise right from the beginning."

"How dare you!" I shouted. "How dare you put all of my friends and family, *our family,*" I hit his chest, "in jeopardy?" Michael registered surprise at my outburst, but it quickly moved to internal pain. Yet I felt the need to spur on. "We were making our own way. We escaped the Pickets—a hell you relegated us to for generations. How long did we need to pay for the sins of our fathers? Or mothers, in our case."

"It's not like that. There's so much you don't know."

"Educate me then. We're listening. If you all are so powerful, why didn't you come and rescue us when we were children or maybe get my mother out of that prison when she was a child!?"

"Winter, we had one chance at this. The sheer number of cataclysmic events we have witnessed as we searched for a linchpin point, someplace where we could change the plotted course of events, to really make a difference."

"Saving our mother would have made a difference!" I screamed. I was shaking with rage. Cedar came over, either as support…or for comfort.

"Little girl!" Drababan boomed. "This is greater than any one person, greater than any group of people. All of us here have risked our lives for just the smallest of chances to change a great many wrongs and make it right. We have watched billions upon billions die, we have witnessed the worst displays of life's disregard for itself that it is very possible none of us will ever find peace again, all in the name of this war. We have spent uncountable sleepless nights dissecting timelines and predicting probabilities of success. We have done our part more times over than I wish to count, and now we are passing that responsibility on to you."

"And what if we don't want it?"

"Then we will bring you back to the *Iron Sides* and you can suffer that fate," he said.

"What's so bad with that?" Tallow asked. "We get to eat all the food we could ever want."

Tracy spoke up. "None of you will be alive seven days from now and your deaths were less than pleasant."

"They were nightmares," Mike said. His eyes took on a heavy sadness. "I can't—I *won't* allow that to happen. If you don't want to get on the Genogerian ship, or if they will not let you, we will stay with you until our end in the hopes that you five can make it somewhere, anywhere, and live out your lives unaffected by what happens in the galaxies."

"Why should we believe you? We don't even know you," Serrot stated. "You show up out of nowhere and take us away from the *Iron Sides,* where we were at least safe, and now you want to drop us off onto a ship with monsters like this one?"

Drababan growled.

Mike dismissed Serrot offhand and looked directly at me and my sister. "Winter, Cedar, in the depths of your heart you know what I am saying is true. How did you feel aboard that ship?" He motioned with his head.

"I felt…." Cedar was thinking about it. "Uneasy, I guess, is the best word I can come up with."

"I'll agree with her statement," I said. "There were some people that were decent to us, and yeah, lots of food, but for the most part they were rude and dismissive, condescending, even. And then there was the fact that they would not allow us to leave our room. They said they plan on taking us back home someday, but I do not believe them. And their commander…he took the Rhodeeshians and…"

"Wait, what?" Michael asked.

"Frost and Ferryn," Cedar replied, "they took them."

"Are you telling me that there are two Rhodeeshians on that ship?" Mike paced away from us, took his hat off and ran his hand through his hair.

"Mike, that wasn't in any of the paths we looked at," Tracy said softly.

"How much time?"

"Twenty minutes."

"This isn't happening." I watched as Michael stepped onto the other ship, the guards in the hallway did not like that and looked on the verge of sending him home in a variety of independent parts. "Lodilin, your men recognize Drababan. I'm sure your scans have confirmed this. That and the earthlings, you know the importance of them. There is no time to be any more thorough; we have two urgent matters to attend to before we have to go."

"I'm listening." Lodilin had come forth through the forest of his guards, though they looked none too pleased about it.

"There are two Rhodeeshians aboard the *Iron Sides.* They have been taken captive; we need to get them and bring them back here with your blessing."

"Impossible. Trekoton, scan *Iron Sides* for…"

"He tells the truth. Two of the animals are on the ship, Deck A level twelve. It is their medical facility."

"Guards, bring the humans onboard. Michael, do you wish help in obtaining the Rhodeeshians?"

"No, High Councilman. The best thing that can happen for you is to use plausible deniability, that you have no idea how any of this happened. By the time they figure out the time-trap we placed on their buckle drive, you can be long gone. Tell the council we sabotaged your ship as well and took off with everyone. I know that look, High Councilman, and I hoped we would have a little more time together to go over things, but the Rhodeeshians change everything. They need to be freed."

"Good luck." He shook my hand and Dee's as well.

"Cedar, Winter." Mike grabbed us tight. "I know you only by the paths I have watched, but that does not stop the love that fills my heart for you both. I don't know if we've made your lives better. Difficult is a word I would use, full of hardship, war, pain and loss, but it is life. We have given you opportunity, potential, and that is what I am thankful for. I truly wish that we could be with you the entire time, it is just not possible. Just know that you do have family and they love you more than you could ever imagine." He hugged each of us and kissed our foreheads, a move that Tracy mimicked, though she was much more tender where Mike seemed to pull us in tight with a quiet desperation.

I know I was crying; I believe Cedar was as well, though I could not see her through my haze of tears.

"Quiet, little ones," Dee said tenderly. "You have Talbot

blood running through you. I expect nothing less than greatness from the both of you. Do you understand me?" He got down on a knee and hunched over so that he could see into our eyes. "There is nothing the universe will throw at you that the two of you cannot overcome. Now nod your heads that you have heard me."

Once I did, he pulled me in close. For such a large and rough looking being, it was an incredibly tender gesture. "Go, make us proud." He stood and turned away from us. I don't know if Genogerians cry, but that appeared to be what he was doing.

"And Tallow, Serrot, you do anything to harm either of my girls, I will chase you through the cosmos and into hell itself to personally deliver a justice that will make you wish the Stryvers had taken you back on that mountain top. We clear?" Mike asked.

Tallow nodded. Serrot gulped and told him, "Yes."

"You keep an eye on these two," he said to Lendor as he gripped his hand and shook it.

"Which two?" he asked.

"Both sets."

"I will do that, Michael," Lendor replied.

"Let's go. We have two Rhodies to round up. How much time, Tracy?"

"Not enough," she said as they retreated to their ship.

"What other way would there be?" Dee asked and then they were gone.

CHAPTER SIX

FROST & FERRYN

"Dee, I don't like the fact that we somehow missed two Rhodeeshians were on that ship," Mike said.

"It is easy enough to understand when you realize that this is a variable we had thus far not encountered," Dee replied.

"Can't say I like that idea; if that's the case, just how many other variables have we missed?"

"Likely, an infinite number of them."

"Yeah, that's rather terrifying, don't you think?"

"You might view it as such. It's just as likely this one could be extremely beneficial, perhaps there are others."

"Dee, I hate to be construed as a pessimist...maybe let's say, pragmatist. But if there are good possibilities, what are the odds there will be bad?"

Drababan could only stop to think on the question as Tracy cut in over the intercom. "Five seconds to takeoff. You know the drill."

All the crew members grabbed fresh bags.

"You think we'll ever get to the point where we won't need these?" Mike tossed his used bag into a receptacle. "I swear to God, Mad Jack designed this flight so this would happen; probably gets a chuckle every time he thinks of us heaving our guts out."

"Perhaps next time we are invited to his fiancée's house for dinner you won't tell her you would rather pull up and eat poisonous mushrooms from the backyard than the ham she spent all day preparing."

"It was *ham*, Dee. How could she not know I don't like ham? I'm pretty much a national treasure; she should know everything about me."

"If she knew everything, she would have never invited you."

"True." Michael had to acquiesce; he stood as the breach team put the hull disconfigurer into place. "As always, Dee, if this goes sideways, just know I could never have a truer friend."

"Likewise," the Genogerian replied as he checked his armor then the charge on his weapon.

The disconfigurer rearranged the atoms in the hull to the point they were far enough apart that matter could move through; now all the occupants could see down the entire length of the corridor they were about to step onto.

"It's dark," Tracy needlessly told them. "General, I think we should abort."

"Because of a burnt-out bulb or two?" Mike attempted to make light of the situation, but he knew better. "Are the DNA sequencers off?"

"Should be, sir," Crewman Reynolds replied.

Mike was about to step off the ship and into the hallway before he turned back toward the crewman. "Should be? That doesn't exude confidence."

"Sir, all of my equipment is working. It says the signal was sent, but I am not getting confirmation to that effect. Sir, this did happen in training though, occasionally the send back signal would get lost or not be strong enough to reach the receiver."

"We should have brought that Tallow kid along; he would have been a great test dummy."

"Mike!" Tracy admonished him.

"What? I'm just saying, you saw the way he looked at my…"

"Eighteen minutes. You going to keep jabbering or get this done so we can go home."

"Here goes nothing," Mike said as he stepped out into the inky blackness

"Should have led with your head if that was the case," Dee said as he strode past, illuminating a bright light mounted on the front of his rifle.

"How far?" Mike asked as the small squad moved quickly down the corridor.

"This should be it," Dee said as he hit the entry button and nothing happened.

"Corporal Bircher, you're up," the General said.

The munitions expert attached a piece of wadding no bigger than a skipping stone. When that was sufficiently adhered to the door, he stuck in a small, metallic rod roughly the size of a toothpick.

He took a half step backward and said, "Fire in the hole!" with enough volume that his team could hear. The explosion, if it could be called that, was no louder than if a large paperclip had fallen to the floor. The door whirred then opened, as whatever had been keeping it locked had been released. Mike had his hand on the corporal's shoulder, about to tell him "good job," when Bircher was blown back with three large, burning, gaping wounds. Two to the chest and one had seared the right side of his face into a charbroiled mask of curled and blackened skin. Dee pulled Mike back as more rounds were shot through the opening.

"Spinner!" Mike said, holding his hand out but never taking his eyes off the doorway. When he had the small device in his hand, he held it up to his face, pressed two buttons, one to arm the device—the other to calibrate the weapon to know when to do what it was named for. He underhand lobbed the spinner. As it left his hand, the flat device opened up enough to allow three rotors to unfold. They increased speed enough to enable the spinner to hover in the air. It flew to the door then hooked a hard ninety-degree angle and flew in.

From inside the room, the five soldiers watched the unknown device come in. Before any of them could fire upon it, thin whips of fire lashed out and sliced through the necks of the two closest guards. Their heads fell to the floor, neatly cauterized by the very flame that had done them in. Blasts of fire spewed forth from the three remaining rifles as the men attempted to neutralize the new threat. Mike flipped a cover on the wrist device he was wearing. On the small screen, he could see the room as the spinner recorded it. He moved his finger, taking remote control of the weapon, bringing it closer to two of the men that were scrambling to get behind a table. Mike double tapped the screen and the needle thin flames once again burst forth, neatly removing the scalp of the closest man. His skull glistened wetly as his eyes crossed and he dropped to the floor.

Mike made the spinner dive to get the other man, who had gone to the deck. The beam cut a swath across his back, neatly severing his spinal column. He hollered out in pain and fear, instantly paralyzed. Just as he was turning it to pick up the fifth and final soldier, his screen went blank.

"Son of a bitch," Mike said as he looked back up. "He shot it."

"More soldiers are coming, Michael. We either do this now or we have to leave. We are running out of time."

"Not sure how we can be running out of time when we are manipulating it for our own use," Mike remarked.

"You know exactly what I meant."

"You in there. Surrender and we'll let you live!" Mike yelled.

Rifle blasts exited the door and were absorbed by the far wall in the hallway.

"I do not believe he is going to give himself up," Dee said.

"No time for negotiations." Mike poked his head in the door to see where the man was then ducked back just as a blast slammed into the doorframe, narrowly missing his ear. "Far back on the left," he relayed the information. "Parker, go through straight to the side. There's a large workbench; you won't be exposed more than half a second. Don't worry—he doesn't have the greatest reaction time, or aim, for that matter. Otherwise, he would have taken my head off."

"What do I do when I get there, sir?"

"Nothing. You're my distraction," Mike told him.

"He doesn't look overly pleased with your idea; perhaps I should go," Dee stated.

"Not a chance. The guy could be asleep and blind and still hit your oversized hide. You're up." Mike clapped Parker on the soldier.

As he dove in, there were two shots. Mike was happy to note neither of them had hit his man. Mike fired three rounds as he framed himself neatly in the doorway. The first two were all it took. The surprised guard was shot twice in the chest and once in the neck; his rifle dropped noisily to the ground.

"Parker, you good?" Mike asked as he moved into the room, checking for any other surprises.

Dee had also come in and bent over to help the soldier up.

"I think so, sir," Parker replied.

"He has not sustained any injuries," Dee said as he roughly turned the man in a circle, looking for any wounds.

"Where the hell are the Rhodeeshians?" Mike asked. As he looked around, his gaze settled on a row of cages, all of them empty, though two of them had their doors open.

"I think I found one of them." Dee was looking down.

"Grab it and let's go," Mike said.

"It would appear to be the other way around. Her fangs are pressing tightly against my calf. I fear if I move, she will bite."

"Um, sir?" Parker gulped. "I think I found the other one's friend."

"Calf as well?" Mike's view was obstructed by the bench.

"Thigh, sir." Parker was looking down, beads of sweat falling from his brow.

"I'm coming around. Frost, is it? Ferryn? We're friends, you and me. I was recently with Tabor; you remember her? Is she still part of your legacy?" Mike asked as he approached the two animals. The larger male hissed, snarled, and showed more of its teeth.

"Pressing harder sir!" Parker gritted.

Frost's ears perked at the name "Tabor." Mike knew where to direct his talk.

"You're Frost, right? All white, seems a fitting name. You know what I'm talking about, girl. Tabor is a legend among the Rhodeeshians. I fought, well, to you it's fought *for* me, I still fight alongside her. My name is Michael Talbot. Does that name mean anything to you?"

Frost did not let go, but her gaze was kept watchfully on Michael.

"You cannot be Michael Talbot," the voice broadcast directly into his head. "Your species does not possess that type of longevity."

"If you know Tabor and you know me, you also know we did…something with time. Something that Mad Jack was able to recreate in a more stable environment without all the side effects. I'm not of this time; I'm just here to help."

Frost wasn't budging.

"Frost, normally I realize that trust is something slow-forged, but time is something we have very little of. More of this ship's personnel are coming, and they will overwhelm this position, killing us and recapturing you."

"I will not allow us to be recaptured!" She was angry. "Those beings are vile!"

"Frost, I need you and Ferryn to trust me, to let me get you back to Winter and Cedar."

"The sisters are well?" She softened.

"They are for now, but if we don't get you back to them so you can escape, they may not remain so."

"General! Footsteps!" was called in from the hallway.

"Look around, Frost. Even if you have doubts about who I am, you cannot doubt we are not on their side."

Frost let loose a high-pitched chirp. Ferryn immediately let go of Parker's leg just as Frost let go of Drababan's.

"Thank you," he told her.

She took many long sniffs of him before going over to Michael. He bent over so she could better smell him, she backed up and looked at him when she was done.

"It is true!"

"You ready to go?" he asked her.

"Anywhere is preferable to here."

"They're here, sir!"

"Get inside now!" he yelled.

The black hallway became a blazing shadowplay of lights as dozens, then hundreds of rounds blew through the darkness.

"This is Master Sergeant Belnot; there is no escape. Give yourselves up and you will be tried and then executed."

"Lots of potential executing going on," Mike said to no one. "Will the trial be fair?" He was stalling.

"If the trial ends in our execution, I do not think it will be fair," Dee whispered.

"Shhh…I just want to see what he says."

"All of our trials follow the law and are just."

"How many end in execution?"

"Mike, you realize I can hear you, right?" Tracy asked, listening in on the conversation from the microphone and speaker built into his uniform.

"Of course I can. I'm just stalling so that more of them will pack in."

"I'm not understanding how you think that is going to help."

"You're not going to like it, but we're gonna need a shockwave."

"You're too close."

"No choice. We've got half the ship's combat force bearing down on us, not going to be able to fight our way through. I can hear you hemming and hawing, woman. Coming to attempt to rescue us isn't going to work—we don't have the forces available. Trust me on this; we'll be alright."

"Your spouse is correct. We are too close," Dee said. Mike

hurriedly attempted to cover up the pickup.

"What was that?" Tracy asked. "Did he say you were too close?"

"He said he has to pick his nose."

"Are you coming out?" Belnot asked.

"We're going over the benefits of a peaceful surrender. Parker wants to know if he could expect a decent final meal or will it be standard military food."

"Come out now and I will personally make sure to spit on everything you eat."

"I'm really starting to like this guy," Mike said sarcastically. "He starts with one persona and rides it all the way to the end."

"Bring the flayer," Belnot said loud enough to make sure that those in the lab heard.

"Woman, I love you more than the earth and the moon, but you know what else I'm really, really fond of? My skin and the Master Sergeant out there wants to remove it from me. If I knew that was going to happen, I wouldn't have bothered to go through my daily moisturizing routine."

Parker looked to Dee. The Genogerian shrugged. "It is high time you knew, Corporal, the general has, for a long time, been clinically insane."

The corporal didn't know whether to think Drababan was joking or if his General was indeed crazy; both things were confusing to him.

"If I wasn't clear, I'm saying they have a flayer, hon. You know their version is about the size of a toaster and is remotely operated. I could be a very red version of myself soon."

"Give me a minute, Mike. You can't just expect me to do this with you in range."

"Might not have a minute, and yes, I fully expect you to do this."

"You ordering me?" she asked.

"Well, since you are a colonel and I'm a general, I most certainly could, but you're not so good at obeying orders, especially when they come from me. So no, I'm not ordering you, I'm asking you as your husband to hit this area with a shockwave now, before it's too late. Dee? How far are we from our ship?" Mike finished.

"No more than a hundred feet."

"Tracy, pitch the shot two degrees."

"You've got fifteen seconds," she replied. Mike could tell she was worried.

"Really wishing we still had that door in place. Let's go, everyone, as far into this room as possible and get low to the ground. I want you all to pretend you're part of the flooring. No looking up at all, for any reason. Could very well be the last thing you do."

"Sir, the flayer is at the door," Parker said.

"What the hell did I say about looking up? Belnot!" he yelled. "We surrender! We surrender. Don't shoot…we're coming out!"

"Too late. If this goes to trial I'll only have to use up some of my free time to testify, and I hate that."

Mike figured it was going to be a neck-and-neck photo finish to see who pushed the trigger of their respective weapon first. Ultimately, he didn't think it mattered all that much. Death by shockwave or death by flayer—both were going to be exceedingly horrible.

"Looks like Tracy won," he said to a confused audience.

"What the hell is that?" Belnot asked in time to the heavy vibrations of metal scraping against metal. A truck with worn-out leaf springs, carrying a cargo of unwrapped, fine china and traveling over an unpaved, washed out roadway would have made a similar noise, but not with the same volume and vehemence as whatever was racing toward them like a runaway freight train.

"Don't even try to cover your head! Too high!" Mike yelled. There were screams from the hallway as men and women were shaken apart.

A live demonstration had been performed of the weapon's capabilities the previous year. It was the only time he'd had any compassion whatsoever for the Stryvers; at least, for this one in particular. The animal had been placed in a tungsten shipping container usually reserved for radioactive material. The walls were over a foot thick, and seemingly, nothing could break in or out. He'd not wanted to be there; all the mucketymucks were out in the desert for the test. Mike had never been one for a dog and pony show, and honestly, he'd seen enough Stryvers blown up to last a lifetime. But this was the business of being a general in the United Earth Marine Corps; that, and the fact that MadJack had begged him. Mike kept looking over longingly to his shuttle, knowing it could whisk him back home, some two thousand miles away, in less than the time he could eat the lunch that he'd left aboard.

"Ladies and gentlemen, we stand on the edge of a new dawning. A new day is upon us. We know that the Stryvers favor the tactic of burrowing deep into the core of whatever planet they have infested." MadJack spoke; there was a lilt in his voice. *He's excited for this*, Mike thought. "Never again will we have to send soldiers down into their lairs or release megatons of explosives in a vain attempt to flush them out. I present to you the Shockwave!" A tall, green tarp emblazoned with the logo of the UEMC was pulled free from a device that was close to the size of a blue whale. Mike didn't think it looked all that impressive, truth be told; it resembled a giant red school bus, though this thing had components sticking out from it on all sides.

"I know it looks enormous, but we are already working on a model that is half the size and nearly double the power of this prototype. Soon we will have the capability to mount this device on shuttles," Jack said proudly. His audience did not react, as thus far, there was nothing worth getting excited about, and a slight disappointment fell across MJ's features.

Mike was concerned by the size of the machine; if anything went wrong, he knew the spectators were entirely too close, and it wasn't like MJ hadn't had a test show go awry before. Just the previous year in Germany, he had launched the Spinner and quickly lost control; it had cut through two shuttles and the Germany Chancellor's ski chalet.

"Okay, let's get this started," MJ said, not quite so inspired when he realized he hadn't roused the kind of enthusiasm he'd predicted. There was the short bark of a siren as the machine started up and then...nothing. Thirty seconds passed. Those in the stands with me began to get uncomfortable in their embarrassment for the scientist, who was even now smiling madly as if he'd just created sliced cheese, the thought of which brought Mike back to his lunch. A minute later and now there was loud talking amongst the guests. Mike had even stood to go down and see what the matter was, or perhaps to thank everyone for their time as he dismissed the event.

Someone came off from the side and whispered in MJ's ear. "Sorry!" he said loudly as he leaned down into his microphone. "The prototype has a significantly longer warm-up period; this was done to ensure safety. I can assure you, though, that in real-life scenarios the warm-up will be under thirty seconds."

Mike was thinking that thirty seconds when the bullets were flying would be the end of a lifetime for many. The crowd was getting restless as the three-minute mark passed on by and still nothing happened; the desert sun was beating down upon them mercilessly.

"Ah, we're ready," MJ said, though how he knew was a mystery as nothing had changed; no lights went from red to green, there was no increase in noise, nor an explosion of any kind. "You'll want to keep an eye on the monitor." MJ pointed to the large screen behind him that should have been displaying the Stryver inside the large box off to the side.

"The screen is blank!" one of the men in the stands shouted, then under his breath he added, "Dumbass."

"Colonel Trasker, could you bring whoever shouted that to me?" Mike asked, "And his commanding officer."

"Of course, sir." In less than a minute, a very red-faced Captain Garrett was standing ramrod straight in front of the senior-most officer in the entire world, along with his Commanding Officer, Colonel Killian.

"Captain Garrett? Hmm, who exactly are you? Can't say I remember you from any of the many battles I have been in. Your name rings zero bells in terms of any significant contribution to the war effort, and I can see by your ribbonless chest you haven't even been in long enough to earn a merit badge."

"Graduated Annapolis last year sir, top of my class. Still in my MOS school," the captain said proudly.

"Top of your class, good for you. Got to say I'm a little disappointed in Annapolis. I thought they were in the business of putting out some of the finest military personnel the world had ever seen. But that doesn't seem to be the case, does it?"

"Sir?" the captain asked.

"Let's see. I've got this smart-ass captain that hasn't so much as seen a battlefield making derogatory comments to a man who singlehandedly found a way to turn the tide of a war we were losing rather badly."

"There was no disrespect meant, sir."

The general put his hand up. "I've got nothing else to say to you; you've already wasted more of my time than I'm comfortable with. Dismissed."

"Sir." The captain appeared as if he wanted to plead his case.

"Which part of dismissed has gone over your head? Colonel Killian, you and I have seen our fair share of battles. Have you perhaps worn yourself so thin that you would allow such insubordination in your ranks?"

"No sir, Captain Garrett is an anomaly."

"An anomaly that you plan on taking care of?"

"You have no idea, sir," the colonel replied.

"Captain, you were dismissed. If you can't follow this most basic of commands, I suggest you go back to the street corner you were hanging out on before you joined my Marines Corps!" Mike shouted. The captain double-timed it back to his seat.

"My apologies, sir," the Colonel said. "He actually is a good soldier; sometimes, he just likes to try too hard to get a laugh from those around him."

"Don't go crazy on him, George; I just wanted to put a little fear into him."

"Yes, sir," the Colonel replied.

"Good to see you. How are the wife and kids? And that Great Dane you had to have, what's her name, Sadie? I hear that they're still cleaning drool out of the shuttle you transported her in. I had to throw that uniform away, by the way." Mike was smiling.

"All doing good, sir. I'll tell the wife you were asking about her."

Mike shook his hand. "Alright. I think MJ is finally ready; don't be a stranger." The colonel got to the position of attention and saluted. Mike returned it and the colonel went back to his seat just as the show really got underway.

Colonel Trasker was smiling. "That captain is in for a rough ride."

Mike was about to respond but he thought he noticed something flicker across the screen; it looked like a picture that would have been on a damaged old VHS tape. The edge of the tungsten box wavered; he at first rejected it, believing it to be something attributed to the video feed. But the wave moved across the screen and toward the Stryver, who knew something was happening and had pushed up against the far side of the box, its arms out in a defensive gesture. Mike noticed more and more people's heads were turning from the monitor to the actual box. He turned quickly, not wanting to miss anything, and his gaze stuck there. The box had somehow become invisible—or worse yet, disappeared, which meant that a pissed off and scared Stryver would soon be running amok...but if the box had melted away, the Stryver made no indication it had seen it.

A piercing squeal ripped the audience's attention from the disappearing box and to the Stryver; the strange wave had come into contact with its forearms and they shimmered and vibrated at a pace that, for a moment, looked as if they were in a paint mixer. Unlike the box, the animal's arms did not disappear but began to expand—as if they were being shaken apart. Black arms gave way to red muscle. Mike thought it looked like a textbook illustration, an exploded view image of the Stryver. The Stryver threw its head back as the wave came into contact with its body. The beast was attempting to climb the wall, but there was no escape from this grisly end. When it was over, the box itself was a twisted, mangled wreck; the body of the Stryver had been reduced to pieces no larger than a dime.

MJ looked back to the audience once the test was complete. The expressions on the faces that looked back at him ranged from disbelief to disgust with a smattering of awe. The weapon was a game changer; one that could finally change the already altered course of man, and one that might, hopefully, put them back on top for good.

"Any questions?" MJ asked.

It was Drababan who stood. "What are the repercussions to the earth once you start sending this signal into it?"

"We are currently working on devices that will be able to discern between organic and inorganic material. There will be some residual damage to the surrounding terrain, but not to the same magnitude as what you are seeing here."

"MJ." Mike stood.

"Yes, General?"

"And what about damage to other organic material?"

"I'm sorry, sir, everything not considered the enemy will be collateral damage."

"Hmm," Mike replied. "The weapon is incredible, MJ, and I applaud you and your entire team, but I would also like a cursory study on the projections for damage to the ecosystem."

"Of course, sir. We've already got something drafted up. I can have it on your desk in half an hour. And we can't take all the credit; we are building off some plans we found for a shelved project called the Pulsinator…Sam something. Apparently, he was trying to patent a bug-killing machine."

"Seems it finally came to fruition," Mike said.

"Mike!" Tracy yelled frantically through the microphone.

"We're fine," Mike replied, looking at the twisted and skewed room.

"Not for long. There is a hull breach, about three feet long at the moment, but it's expanding quickly."

"My ass he figured out the physics of 'just hitting organic compounds.' Up, everyone, up." He quickly explained that there was a hole in the side of the ship but it became unnecessary as they heard the whistle of oxygen and saw nearby objects being pulled out into the vacuum of space.

"Tracy, going to need a new extraction point," Mike yelled over the rush of air and the blaring klaxon.

"Undocking now…wait one." He could hear the strain in his wife's voice as she sought another way out for them. "Same hallway, one deck lower, but hurry before the hull split catches up."

"How much time?" Mike motioned for those with him to follow.

"Three minutes."

"Anything else?" Mike asked.

"At least it doesn't bring you past every gun on that ship."

He got the message. "We're headed to the deck below this one, same hallway. Let's move!" It was not lost on anyone that the red mist flowing past them was what remained of the men attempting to kill them.

"Anyone have a clue where the stairwell is?" Mike asked. "Parker?" The corporal had studied the layout of the ship for the mission.

"No stairwells in this area, sir."

"That would explain the reason it took them so long to respond," Drababan replied.

"Elevator?" They were still running.

"Pneumatic tubes, sir," Parker said breathlessly.

"Like old school banks?"

"Something like that, sir."

"Get us there."

Parker looked over his shoulder at his commanding officer as if to say: "What do you think I'm trying to do?"

The sound of the venting air was much less loud the further they moved. It gave them an opportunity to hear their labored breathing as they ran hard, but also the many footfalls of boots that were coming on an intercept course to stop them.

Frost, who had been running alongside Michael, pulled out into the lead. A soldier dressed in all white camouflage, the better to match the environment, turned the corner and was bringing his rifle up when Frost launched and struck him square in the chest, sending him sprawling backward. She immediately sank her fangs deep into the side of his neck, pumping him full of venom. His body went rigid before she could jump off of him.

"Sir, we need to cross over the juncture point, tube is right past it," Corporal Parker pointed.

"Of course it is, why wouldn't it be," Mike said. "Dee, going to need you to feedback a rifle."

"That will take too long," the Genogerian replied. The running had stopped as the soldiers began to get into position. Mike knew at any moment they would begin to flood out of the hallways they were in and rout their position.

"When I shoot, do your best to cover your eyes and hold your breath and go straight for the tubes," Michael said as he aimed upwards.

"I take back some of the less positive things I have said about you," Drababan said when he realized what his friend was attempting to do.

"At least you say them to my face," Michael replied as he fired into the ship's flame-retardant system. Instead of a controlled burst of the smothering material, it looked as if a bomb had exploded in a Christmas tree flocking factory. The air was thick with the particulates; Mike became disoriented. Thankfully, Drababan had grabbed his shoulder and guided him the way they needed to go. They stumbled their way through; Parker had pressed the wrong button, and they found themselves seven levels higher than they needed to be.

"Out," Mike coughed, expelling a heavy, white breath. He shook the material off himself and helped the two Rhodeeshians. The tube itself was packed with the spray and it was practically impossible to see through to the back. Two crew members spotted the usurpers but turned and ran.

"Other tube," Parker coughed as he pointed across the hallway and toward a clean transport.

"Mike, you have less than thirty seconds." Tracy sounded as if she'd been waging her own battle.

In ten they found themselves on the correct level and running down the hallway; if they encountered any further delay whatsoever, the chances were very good they would never leave the ship alive.

"Got the opening, sir!" Parker exclaimed, peering through his helmet's heads up display. "Crap," he added at the end.

"Can you elaborate?" Michael asked as they moved quickly. Very rarely in a combat situation did the word "crap" equate to anything even remotely good. "Crap, the reinforcements have arrived! Crap, the enemy has surrendered!" Never anything like that.

"The crack in the hull is almost on the opening. There was no need to explain; once the split hit the seal it would break it and Tracy would lose contact with the ship and they would have to once again find an egress. But not only was the clock within the ship ticking; time was running out on the much more dangerous one that dictated how much time they had in this realm. Even if they somehow eluded capture or death from the *Iron Sides'* personnel, they would not be quite so elusive with time itself.

"Frost, Ferryn, go!" Michael urged, knowing that the animals were much faster than the people they were running alongside. They did as he asked, knowing that to die now would make everything the humans had done for them in vain. "Dee!" Mike knew the Genogerian could also easily outpace him.

"No, Michael, I will not."

Mike knew there was no way he could force his friend. He just put his head down and redoubled his efforts. His lungs burned, partly from the exertion, but mostly from the irritant he had breathed in.

"Hurry!" Tracy yelled through his earpiece; he didn't respond, as that would take precious air away with the effort.

Mike was thankful when he looked up and saw Ferryn's tail cross the threshold. *So close*, he thought as he looked to the ceiling of the hallway. He could see the material buckling under the strain of metal being twisted from the stresses being placed against it. They were within twenty feet when Mike's hat was ripped from his head, and, for a micro-second, it plugged the hole that had opened up—at least until the hole widened.

They'd gone another five feet and they could feel

themselves attempting to defy the ship's gravity as the void beckoned them. Drababan had grabbed hold of Corporal Parker and heaved him through the opening.

Holding on to my dignity, Michael thought as he dove forward. Drababan and he landed on top of the stunned corporal as the small ship bucked wildly.

"Reynolds, they in?" Tracy yelled and begged at the same time.

"Got them, Colonel! GO!" he said as the ship fell away.

Drababan sat up; the entirety of his upper half was coated in the white, flame-killing material. Mike sat up as well, looked over to his friend and began to laugh in coughing bursts.

"I fail to see what is so funny," Dee stated.

"Sorry…you look like you've been dredged through batter and are all ready for a good frying."

"I cannot begin to count the number of times we nearly died or were gravely injured and yet here you find humor that I could be turned into some tasty carnival fare."

"We lost a good man on that ship, and later tonight I'm going to grieve, mourn, and then write his loved ones a letter about his sacrifice and what it meant for us. But right now, my friend, I want to smile. I want to revel that we are still alive and that even with some losses, we did ultimately succeed, and his death *did* mean something. And, oh yeah, I didn't say anything about you being tasty."

"I would be absolutely delicious! Look at these muscles!" Dee flexed. "And unlike you, I am not so inclined to ingesting food that is bad for me, like snack cakes. I am a delicacy."

"Oh, who are you kidding. You drink Moxie by the drum-full—look like an old moonshiner sucking on one of those jugs."

"You know the drill," Tracy said evenly as everyone fitted their bags on and strapped in.

"Prepare for docking with the *Ogunquit*," Tracy said.

Michael turned his attention to Frost and Ferryn. "I don't know what parts you two play in all of this; I would imagine it is more than I can imagine." Mike looked up and to the side. "Not sure if that makes sense, but the meaning is in there somewhere."

"We thank you for all you have done for us, and especially for our species. We have lived through a great many generations, as we were meant to, thanks to you. That debt will never be forgotten. I can feel your anxiety for your kin; we will do all that we can to ensure their safety as you did ours," Frost replied, bowing.

"Thank you. It means everything, knowing that you are by their side. Can you give them this? I was unsure if I would get any time with them and wrote this beforehand. Difficult to write a letter to someone you've never met."

"They are much like you," Frost replied.

"Not sure if that's a good thing." Mike smiled.

"Sir, the door is opening. The Colonel wanted me to warn you that we have very little time for any of your long goodbyes," Reynolds said.

Frost gently took the letter from Mike's outstretched hand into her mouth.

"Our prayers are with you," Dee said as he nodded solemnly to the departing Rhodeeshians.

"They're through," Reynolds announced into the intercom.

"Buckle in—this is going to be close," Tracy announced.

"Michael, I do not believe I have ever had a pleasant ride with your mate at the helm," Dee said.

"She can hear you. Are you trying to get us killed?"

CHAPTER SEVEN

THE OGUNQUIT

"Frost! Ferryn!" I exclaimed, running to meet them. "Are you alright?" I hugged them both. "What's all over you?"

"We are surprisingly well." Frost shook her body, much like a wet dog is apt to do, as she attempted to clear all the debris from her fur.

"Come," Yondario said. We'd learned he was a young Genogerian diplomat, responsible for the care and treatment of any guests onboard the ship. "We have rooms where you may get yourself cleaned, find food and rest."

"All of that sounds wonderful," Frost replied. "This is for you and your sister." Frost thrust out her snout for Winter to take the letter still firmly clutched in her mouth. I wasn't thrilled when Frost and Ferryn were escorted somewhere else, but Frost told me everything would be all right, and I had to believe her.

My hands shook as I took it; the desire to open it up and read it immediately was almost too great for me, but first I had to get back to my sister, who was at this very moment getting a wound on her leg dressed. I quickly traversed the hallways back to the medical bay.

"Hey, Winter," Cedar said as she sat on an oversized table. Serrot was hovering nervously nearby as two large Genogerians worked on the gash she had suffered.

"Does it hurt?" I asked. It was a nasty looking thing, five inches long and fairly deep.

"Nope. They gave me something and I can't think about much besides clouds and chocolate. You look sad; please tell me nothing bad happened to any of them." Cedar's bottom lip popped out in a pouting manner.

"No, nothing like that. Frost and Ferryn are even now getting cleaned up. It's just, we had family here, Cedar, and now they're gone. We'll never see them again…that makes me sad."

"Good thing you have me, sis," Cedar said, opening her arms wide. I found myself in the warm embrace of my sibling, much to the consternation of the Genogerian working on her.

"He left us a letter." I held it up as I stepped back from her.

"Your wound will be incredibly itchy for the next hour. Do not scratch the wound or I will be forced to bind your hands up," the Genogerian meddie told her. I don't think he was going for humor; he looked and sounded completely serious. "I will be back in fifteen minutes. Leave it alone."

"Leave what alone?" Cedar asked, a dopey smile upon her lips and glassy look in her eyes.

"Do you want me to wait to read this?" I asked her, though if anyone was itching to do something, it was me. Cedar looked like she could be attacked by a swarm of bees and wouldn't have cared.

"Is she going to be all right?" Serrot asked, stroking Cedar's forehead.

"I think it's like the Cahol chips; it'll wear off. I hope," I added under my breath. I didn't like the idea of my sister being perpetually loopy.

"Read the note, sis." Cedar seemed to have a moment of clarity.

"You sure?" I asked.

"The meddie wasn't kidding. If I could drag a cactus against my leg right now to satisfy this itch, I would. I need to think about something else."

My hands shook as I ripped the envelope open. I cleared my throat and read. "My dearest Cedar and Winter, my hope was that we would have at least a few hours to sit and talk. But as they say, even the best laid plans have a way of going awry. I have no way of knowing if we had five minutes or five seconds or if this letter you hold now is all you will ever know of us. You need to know right from the beginning that Tracy and I love you both as if you were our own children. I'm sure the doubts within you are huge—you doubt us, you doubt your purpose, you doubt that it is possible to have a worthwhile outcome; we have felt these doubts as well. There's so much Tracy and I want to tell you, but I've been warned by MJ that to do so could have dire consequences. Seems weird that people from the past have to be careful what they say to those from the future; it really seems like it should be the other way around.

"One of the hardest things we've had to do was to hide some of our technology from those that would come later. If not for Mad Jack, this wouldn't have been possible. And neither would have been your rescue, which I'm assuming went well because you're reading this. We know all about your past, another something you have doubts about. Just know that your mother and father loved you deeply. And don't worry that Beth is part of your lineage; it matters little. Events happened around her that broke her down; unfortunately, she could not build herself back up to her full potential. She was flawed—well, she was Human. She did possess a single-mindedness that was strong and unique in its own way."

"That's one way of explaining her file." Cedar stuck her tongue out and swirled her finger up around her temple as she rolled her eyes. "Crazy. It means she was crazy," she explained to me to quell the confused look I wore upon my face.

"Now, I'm sure you're asking why. Why did we have to hide things? I cannot go into detail—somewhat because it is important that you discover this on your own, but even more importantly, if I am captured or killed this letter might fall into enemy hands, and that would not do. Just know there was a reason for where we were and what we were doing. If you made it on to the ship we were trying to get you on, then these beings are your greatest allies; you can trust them implicitly. I know that especially for you, Winter, this will not come easily. Follow Cedar in this regard. We wish more than anything we could walk with you in what are going to be incredibly trying times, but you have each other, and it seems some decent friends you have made along the way. Good luck to all of you, and Godspeed. Tracy and I love you both dearly, always hold that thought deep within you."

I turned the note over hoping there was more but knowing there wasn't. He had said so much without saying anything at all, really. I felt a touch of sadness, but there was a fair degree of anger there as well. There was so much we needed to know that we knew nothing about…how could we possibly succeed?

"It'll be alright, sis," Cedar said in a sing-song voice.

"How can you know that?" I snapped back.

"Because the alternative is that it isn't and I don't accept that, silly. Now everyone needs to go. I'm tired."

"I'll stay with her," Serrot told me as he grabbed a chair.

"If I start to snore you need to ignore me," Cedar told him as she lay down, fluffed her pillow, closed her eyes and was immediately asleep.

"What are you doing?" Tallow asked. "I've seen that look in your eyes before, Win."

"I'm going to demand some answers," I told him, heading out the door.

"And if the scaly ones don't want to give any?" Lendor interceded.

"I guess we'll see." I was in such a rush to head out to somewhere and get answers from someone I wasn't paying any attention to where I was going. I slammed my head hard into the breastplate of a Genogerian.

"Come, I have more permanent quarters for you," he said.

"I'm sick of being relegated to quarters. I want to see your leader."

"You will, but not now."

"I demand it!" I thrust my hands down by my side. The Genogerian seemed put out by my petulant demeanor.

"I do not believe you understand the complexity and fragility of our immediate situation. High Councilman Lodilin is currently talking to the Commander of the Battle Class Ship *Iron Sides*. It seems strange that you have already forgotten the events that have so recently transpired, but since that seems to be the case, I will once again explain them to you. You were rescued from the *Iron Sides* by figures that are legendary among both our races. You were deposited here. They returned; the human ship suffered damage with the next rescue attempt and once again, a legendary race we thought long extinct is resurrected, and, once again, brought here. Humans and Genogerians share a long and rich history. In the beginning, we were mortal enemies, doing all in our power to destroy the other. Then we discovered who our true enemy was and aligned with humanity. This was one of the most prosperous times in either of our existences. For generations, we lived in peaceful harmony, but all things must pass. When war once again broke out upon the planet's surface, even with our combined forces, we were losing, The only way to save what remained was to take the fight from the planet and into space. This was the beginning of the Happening, an event so cataclysmic it caused humanity to diverge from its natural evolutionary path. We have been fighting in space for so long, Earth has been forgotten by most."

"But not by you." I knew that to be the truth.

"Not by us, but we have not been able to go back. We have stayed in the alliance with man; we feign ignorance to what they have done. Always we maintain the hope that we can go back to Earth and right this great wrong."

"We keep hearing about this 'Happening,' but no one is saying what it is exactly," Tallow said.

"And you will not hear it from me," he replied curtly. He seemed sorry that he'd even brought it up.

"What's your name?" I asked. I wasn't sure how familiar I

wanted to get with him—with any of them—but for a reason I could not put my finger on, I felt more comfortable around the crocodile giants than around those on the other ship, and that thought, in and of itself, was disconcerting.

"For your tongue, it would be easier if you called me Porter," he said.

"Porter, we really need to get back to Earth," I told him. "We have friends there that need our help; there are Stryvers there. The pickets still exist; our new settlement has been destroyed. We can't afford to be up here being shuttled back and forth from one ship to the other as *guests* of anyone." I made sure to lay a heavy emphasis on guests.

"If we were to bring you back to your home planet, it is very likely that the *Iron Sides* would come back for you."

"Why? What is it about them? Why are they so important?" Lendor asked. I gave him a sidelong glance. "I did not mean it like that," he said to me. I smiled.

"I do not have the authority to discuss such matters. Now come; my orders were to escort you to more suitable quarters." Porter turned away from us and was heading down the hallway. None of us followed. There was a loud chuffing sound as he blew air around the large jowls of his snout. He slowly turned. "You are not following me."

"Nope." I folded my arms across my chest. He was easily five or six times my size and I didn't have a weapon; maybe I should not have felt quite as confident in mine or any of my party's safety, but I had the distinct impression that they would do all in their power to keep us from harm, and whether it was acceptable or not, I was going to use what I hoped was that fact to our advantage.

"What gives?" Cedar shouldered past me. "You know I get *real* cranky when I get my sleep interrupted." She stood on her tiptoes and looked Serrot in the face, even made her eyes go wide as she stared at him for a long uncomfortable moment. The poor guy had been quiet throughout and was going to take the blame, most likely because he hadn't quelled the discussion.

"This is your sister's fault." He pointed.

"Winter, don't make me wear your favorite white cardigan sweater and spill mustard all down the front of it. Even with bleach, that's not coming out. You'd likely have to dye it black; it would never be the same."

"Cedar, I understand about as much of that sentence as I do everything else going on around us," I told her.

"Battle stations; prepare to buckle. Battle stations; prepare to buckle." This was announced throughout the ship. Unlike on the *Iron Sides*, the announcement was much more subdued; even the lighting, which had flashed an angry red on the other ship, only pulsed a brighter white, rapidly, three times before returning to its normal state.

"Come; this is no time to be obstinate," Porter said as he turned back to us.

"Who you calling obstinate?" Cedar yelled. She was dragging Serrot with her and following Porter, who had started to move.

"Whatever you choose to do, I am by your side," Lendor said to me.

I wasn't entirely sure what I wanted to do. I had made a stand and now was deciding if I should stick to it to the end. But to what end? If we were truly heading into battle, me standing in the middle of the walkway looking all irritable would accomplish little. We had to move to the side as Genogerians poured forth from whatever room or parts of the ship they had been in so that they could get to where they needed to be for whatever was to come.

"This is unprecedented." Porter looked nervous, at least as much as I could tell from his mannerisms and minimal facial expression. "Winter, the events that are happening now can directly be attributed to you and your sister's presence. It is imperative that you are moved to a safer portion of the ship, and I must get to my duty station quickly. Please," he said.

I relented, if only to get out of the path of the giants flowing around me. They had done their best to avoid us, but we'd been sideswiped half a dozen times already, wouldn't be long before we were trampled underfoot. We moved quickly; Porter was moving so fast it was difficult to keep up with his long strides. My legs were beginning to burn by the time we got to the appropriate door.

Porter made a hand signal and an opening appeared. "This is High Councilman Lodilin's private chambers. I have not had much contact with humans, but I know enough to realize you are an inquisitive species. It would be best for all involved if you did not touch anything while you are in here. He waited until we'd all filed in before he followed. The room was much like the one we had vacated, though it was laden with decorations; there were frames upon the walls that displayed pictures that moved in brief, ten-second clips.

"Are these movies?" Cedar wondered as she went closer, her hand reaching toward one of them.

"I just spoke the words. Have they not had enough time to sink into your brain matter and be translated into action?" Porter asked.

"Sorry," Cedar said sheepishly. "I've…we've never seen anything like this."

Some of the pictures were of what we presumed was a younger Lodilin in some sort of prestigious ceremony; there were a bunch of those. There were also ones of Lodilin getting into a fighter or smiling atop a mountain and waving to us. Each one seemed to tell a story, and it was difficult to pull one's gaze away from them.

Serrot had gone over to a high table where a stone roughly the size of his head glowed a bright golden color.

"I knew it was unwise to bring you here." Porter was watching Serrot, whose hand had been moving involuntarily toward the stone. "If you lay your hands upon the Fendrical plant from Kilfario, it will be the last tangible thought you will possess for the next twenty-four hours."

"What, that's a plant?" Serrot asked, though he pulled

back as if it was aflame.

"It is a powerful hallucinogenic that will transport your mind to realms that are beyond fantasy."

"That does not seem extremely bad." Lendor had moved closer.

"Ah, yes, but at a significant cost. If the being has not properly prepared themselves, it can be a quite um…an uncomfortable experience."

"Why?" I asked.

"To begin, there is an immediate and explosive release of one's entire bowel system."

"Bowel mean what I think it means?" Serrot asked Cedar.

Cedar nodded. Serrot backed up slowly, as if fearful that the vibrations from his footsteps might be enough to make the plant fall from its perch.

"Observe. Lodilin requests your presence here for this reason." Porter stepped over to the far side of the room and pressed something that I could not see. The gray wall turned opaque and then illuminated. We were looking on the bridge. Lodilin was seated in the commander's chair and was talking to Commander Breeson on a much larger screen in front of him. Breeson had flares of red crawling up his neck; even without the sound on it was clear he was angry. Porter touched something else and Breeson's voice came through.

"…Don't play the diplomatic immunity card with me, High Councilman. We were attacked. We've suffered casualties. My ship's hull has been breached and cracked by a means we are not even aware of."

"And that is why we are here, Commander, to assist you in any way possible," Lodilin said calmly.

"You can assist me, High Councilman, by giving back what was illegally taken."

"Taken? Are you suggesting that we somehow attacked you? Boarded your ship and stole something?"

"Lodilin, we have known each other a great many years. While we may not be considered friends, we have always been respectful of each other, so I am unsure as to why now you have deemed it necessary to insult my intelligence."

"I have not, nor will I ever doubt your intelligence, Commander."

"Do not talk to me in circles, Lodilin! The mere fact that you have met us out on a buckle is highly suspect. We were attacked by a technology that we cannot detect or track; what do you expect me to believe other than you had something to do with it?"

"First off, Commander Breeson," Lodilin stood, the timbre of his voice taking on more depth and breadth as he spoke and moved closer to the screen, "my title to you is High Councilman Lodilin, a status I worked for decades to achieve through numerous battles across the cosmos and was elected to by a panel from all the allied races. I did not get to my present station because my father was a famed figure during the Staffington Campaign."

Breeson's entire face turned a bright red as he swallowed back the vitriol that flew to the tip of his tongue.

"And if you did not notice, Commander, because you were too busy attempting to mistakenly lay blame upon the *Ogunquit*, we were also fired upon twice by the strange war machine."

"We do not detect any damage to your vessel whatsoever, *High Councilman*." Those last two words came out through clenched teeth.

"Perhaps we are better equipped to deal with the power surge that struck us. Perhaps you should think about that before you decide to do something rash. Something that would jeopardize all of the great things our two peoples have accomplished through the millennia."

"We are still in a state of battle, High Councilman. I will keep active scans and my weapons trained until such time I deem that this ship and my personnel are no longer in danger."

"Admirable, Commander, but our detection systems show that a significant portion of your weapons are pointed at us."

"It is our chance to repay the favor of your offer of help,

High Councilman. As you yourself have said, you were attacked twice as well, and if it were to happen a third time, we would relish the opportunity to shoot our mutual attacker down. My colonel here says your buckle drive is active; I do not think it wise you leave right now; there are many unresolved issues and we are all aware that traveling in a buckle is not quite as safe as we'd once thought."

"Is that a threat, Commander? You do realize that under article 72 of the Interspecies Treaty, all High Councilman Star Cruisers are equipped with the kill codes for every ship in all our respective fleets, do you not?"

"I never much liked that executive order. I'll tell you what, it sure is a blessing to have an Engineer as gifted as Major Gralter."

"That is not good," Porter said aloud to us.

"What's going on?" Tallow asked, not picking up on the subtleties of the conversation.

"As part of our peace process, we wanted to make sure that the leaders of all our species were never fired upon by any commanders or rogue units that did not agree with the treaty. All ships carrying high councilmen have in possession a signal that they are able to execute that will render any other ships inert. It would appear, however, that Commander Breeson has circumvented this safety procedure. It is likely we will be firing at each other soon."

"Can we take them?" Serrot asked.

"It would be much better for us to run. The *Iron Sides* is one of the newest ships in either fleet, the most heavily armored with the newest technology in weaponry. We would not last long if she turned everything against us."

"And we let ourselves be taken onto this ship, why?" Serrot asked.

"The alternative was a slow, painful death," Porter said in all seriousness.

"Yes. A majestic, fiery death would be more suitable," Lendor said, fascinated by what he was watching.

"I bet I could fly this ship to safety," Cedar said to me without an ounce of boasting. She was merely stating fact.

"Why so much fuss over us? No one even knew we existed a few days ago," I told her. I grabbed her hand and pulled her a few feet from the screen. "This doesn't feel right to me. How can the Genogerians be saving us from…people?"

"Because we were told that, Winter. You have to have a little faith, especially considering the source."

"You're alright with all of this?" I asked her.

"Alright with it? Are you crazy? I'm angrier than I've ever been! We keep getting pulled back and forth and none of it through our own decision. When….and *not if*, we get free and I get a flying machine to pilot again, I am going to make a lot of people pay."

"Okay good. I thought it was just me. Do you know who you plan on shooting first?"

"I'll figure it out when I get there." She gave my hand a slight squeeze. "I want to see what's going to happen." She was pointing to the screen.

"Any update?" I asked Lendor quietly.

"Breeson wants to send a boarding party this way to *help* with any repairs we may need. Lodilin respectfully declined, said the situation was well underhand."

"It's pretty tense," Tallow interjected.

"Would have never been able to figure that out if you hadn't told me." I smiled at him.

"Funny, Win. We're about thirty seconds from a space war and we don't have anything but our hands to fight with."

"Well, when you put it like that." My mood soured quickly with the truth in his words.

"Commander Breeson, we will be leaving now," Lodilin stated.

"Perhaps we should dispense with the banalities and civility, High Councilman. I am not letting you leave; at least not until we have thoroughly gone through your ship. I do not know if you attacked us, but you were complicit. We show no damage to your ship, yet we have suffered a loss of structural integrity and have also lost possession of some high-value assets."

"I am sorry, Commander, that your ineptitude behind the helm has caused damage to your ship for which you will undoubtedly be held accountable, but you will not use the *Ogunquit* as a means to acquit yourself of whatever happened aboard your vessel."

"You are going to power down your buckle drive and I am going to send four teams over. If you attempt to leave or my teams are not met with extreme courtesy, I will declare it an act of war and open fire."

"Have you lost your mind, Commander? Colonel Runger, I see you in the background. I am executing order 112, subsection 12. I want you to relieve Commander Breeson. He is unfit for command. You will be acting Commander until such time as the *Iron Sides* is brought back to her base and Commander Breeson is brought before a judiciary tribunal."

"That going to work?" Tallow asked Porter.

"Not very likely. High Councilman Lodilin is stalling."

"For what reason?" Before Tallow could even get his question out, there was a quick blink of the lights in the room we were in and then a warning issued so softly it sounded like what one might whisper into the arms of their lover in the middle of the night.

"Prepare for Jute Buckle in five minutes."

"This is not good." Porter looked alarmed.

"We're going to buckle?" Cedar asked. "Will we be able to do so before they fire?"

"High Councilman, it is you that needs to stand down. Commander Breeson has done nothing to warrant implementation of the Uniform Code of Military Justice relieving of duty. If anything, he has shown unbelievable restraint in the face of your acts of aggression. Had I been at the helm, I believe the time for talking would have been long over."

"Very well," Lodilin replied. "Send your shuttles; we have nothing to hide." He nodded and the screen to the *Iron Sides* went black. The leader turned to us, though I do not think he could see us.

"Portaliton, get our guests secured. I will come and see them as soon as I can."

"Of course, sir." Porter nodded. "Come, we must get strapped in. The Jute Buckle happens with such a speed that when not properly secured, there have been instances of living tissue melding with walls, ceilings or equipment. Sometimes it is merely a loss of skin or limb, but oftentimes the price tag is much higher."

"Yeah, strapped in sounds good," Tallow gulped.

"We've buckled before; what's different?" Cedar asked as we left the room and were moving quickly down the corridor.

We came to a door with markings on it that meant nothing to any of us except Porter.

"Jute Buckle warning, three minutes and counting."

"These special chairs were not designed with your size in mind, but we should be able to adjust the straps firmly enough," Porter replied.

"Should be?" I got into one, as did everyone else.

"We do not have much time. Pull the lap harness across," he explained.

It did little to ease our fears when we pulled the strap, which was over a foot wide and nearly an inch thick, across our laps.

"Into the buckle." He demonstrated. There were five audible clicks. "There is a button on the seat, down on your right-hand side; it will adjust the strap until it fits snug. There will be an uncomfortable pressure."

There was a soft whirring. There was so much extra material I did not think the slack would be drawn in. I was wrong and then some. Lendor, being the largest of us, was the first to feel the effects.

"This is a little snug," he said as the whirring on his seat got louder. "I do not like this. This must be a mistake."

I was looking over at him; he appeared to be getting shorter as the strap pulled him deep into the chair cushion. I thought he was being overly dramatic until my strap pulled taut.

"Whoa," Tallow exclaimed, then said no more. I gritted my teeth and waited for it to stop. Cedar had her eyes shut and was breathing in through her mouth and out through her nose.

"I can feel you looking at me; this will prevent panic," Cedar said through the corner of her mouth, not breaking her breathing rhythm.

The pain was tolerable; it was more the discomfort that was getting to me, but I thought I could make it for the two minutes plus without complaining too much. That changed when Porter reached behind my chair and pulled a webbing of the same material across my chest; he had to fold it over to keep it from covering my head. He buckled it in, hit another button and then moved on to Cedar.

"Wait…" I said weakly as I watched the straps begin to be pulled into their respective slots.

"All I can offer you is that time does indeed keep marching along, even though it will feel as if it has stuck and oftentimes even backed up."

I was close to panicking; Cedar's breaths came a little faster, but she still looked as if she could have been resting.

"Get this thing off me!" Lendor looked angry as he fought against the restraints. He could not do much, though, as his arms were pinned to his sides.

"This makes me wish Haden had struck truer with his sword," Tallow lamented.

"In through your mouth…hold the breath for a count of three…exhale through your nose for the same count…count to three again, repeat," Cedar offered.

The panic welling up in me was beginning to take over my higher reasoning. I wanted to thrash, much like Lendor; instead, I took my sister's advice. I was not immediately comforted, nor did I completely forget about my surroundings, but the technique eased the runaway panic; I was able to rein it in before it took off with me bouncing around wildly upon the saddle.

"I need to get out of this!" Lendor shouted. Where he got the wind in his lungs to do it, I have no idea.

"Lendor, do as Cedar said," I managed to get out, fearful that if he did not do as I asked that he would once again drag me into the frenzy he was feeling.

Serrot, who was abundantly quiet, was doing the best of us all; he had passed out.

"Happens sometimes," Porter said as he finally got into a seat and buckled in.

"Jute Buckle, two minutes."

"Two minutes? We'll be dead by then! Undo me! I would rather be part of the wall!" Lendor was like a wild animal in a cage.

Of all the lies I'd been told through my life, it was Porter's that seemed to carry the greatest weight. He assured us that time would indeed keep flowing along. That was a lie that lasted for nearly a decade.

"Jute Buckle, one minute-thirty seconds."

Even when the ship began to announce each passing second, I thought maybe Genogerians had a completely different type of time cycle, that a second for them equated to a week for us. All the breathing exercises in the world weren't going to work much longer and then I felt like I was being stretched, but not like a regular buckle. Those felt like something had grabbed your head and your feet and was slowly elongating you through a steady and firm pull. This was a violent tearing, as if hooks had been placed in my rib cage on each side and I was being cracked open, like one might split an orange. A normal buckle was mentally disorientating; this buckle was physically painful.

As quickly as it had started, it was over. The straps immediately loosened, and I hunched forward, pulling in large draughts of air and wincing at the pain my body registered.

Lendor was already out of his chair and nervously pacing the room.

"Never again." The whites of his eyes showed as he pointed at the chair.

Serrot had not stirred.

"You alright?" Tallow managed to swivel his head to me.

I nodded.

"Cedar?" I asked.

"We done?" She opened up one eye.

"Your sister is a few arrows short of a quiver," Tallow said as he stood then came over to help me stand up.

"I am glad to see that worked." Porter was standing. He gently placed a large finger against the side of Serrot's neck. "He is fine, though it is not recommended to travel that way; he is going to have a headache he will not soon forget."

Cedar had gone over to look at him.

"Now what?" I asked.

"We wait," Porter replied.

It wasn't long until High Councilman Lodilin strode in. "I wish I had more time to explain. At best, the Jute Buckle has provided us with thirty minutes. There is little I will be able to do to stop Commander Breeson from boarding this ship. It is imperative that none of you are aboard."

"What exactly do you propose to do with us?" I asked.

"Porter, as he desires to be called, is quite an accomplished pilot and was brought onboard for this possibility, which has led to an eventuality."

"High Councilman, you have said we do not have much time, yet you have told us nothing." Cedar seemed impatient, like she knew where this was headed and wanted to get to the good part quicker.

"The *Iron Sides* is not the only one presenting surprises today. I have an unregistered ship and an unregistered pilot aboard. He will take you away from here so that we may rendezvous at a later and safer time," Lodilin said quickly. We had already exited the room and were presumably heading to where the ship was. Porter carried a limp and groaning Serrot.

"And the Rhodeeshians?" I asked.

"They will most likely already be onboard, as they were much closer to the hangar."

"What are you going to tell the commander? Will you not be in trouble?" Lendor asked. "Especially after your escape maneuver?"

"I will tell him that I feared for the safety of my crew and I wanted us both to have time to calm ourselves and think the situation through. And if that doesn't work, there are four Genogerian destroyers en route; that should be enough to dissuade him from doing anything rash."

"Are we worth all this?" I needed to know.

"More than you know." Lodilin turned to Porter. "Be safe, my son." He leaned in and placed his head against the other in what appeared to be a gesture of affection. "I hope to see all of you soon." He had turned and was heading back the way he had come.

"We do not have much time." Porter led us into a large area where there were ships of all various sizes docked.

"Won't they be able to detect our departure?" Cedar asked, running her hand along the hulls of the ships we passed.

"The humans are not the only ones with new technology. They mistakenly believe that we only use what they give us; I can assure you that is not the case."

"We taking one of these shuttles?" Cedar's eyes were wet with excitement at the prospect of flying. Personally, I was sick of that particular mode of transportation; I would never again complain about walking.

"It is a shuttle in that it will allow living cargo, but that is the only similarity these ships have with that." Porter pointed ahead of us to one of the sleekest, most menacing vessels I had ever seen. Unlike every other ship in the hangar, this one was difficult to keep in sight; it looked more like a hole had been created where a ship had been.

"We call this *Deep Onyx*. It is a black so dark it absorbs

nearly all light that comes in contact with it," Porter explained.

"The protrusions, are they weapons?" Cedar was moving quicker than any of us to get to the vessel. I had the irrational fear that I would be pulled into the depths of the hole the ship created if I got too close. Lendor and Tallow, to some degree, seemed to share that same feeling.

"There are two phase cannons, two electron barrels, and a mini-railgun; there are not many ships that could suffer all her potential."

"Defensive capabilities?" Cedar asked astutely.

"You have knowledge of flight?" Porter studied her.

"You could say that," she replied.

"Stealth is her one and only asset, but it is most effective. Armament was sacrificed to make her as invisible as possible."

"Doesn't shooting the weapons give away your location?"

I was happy when Porter hit a switch and a hatch opened up and we were able to view a well-lit area inside; it broke up the illusion that we were traveling into a cave from which there was no exit. My happiness was compounded upon seeing Frost and Ferryn sitting on their hindquarters, patiently awaiting our arrival. Frost came over and rubbed up against me and Cedar.

"It is good to see you again. I am happy that we will continue our journey together."

"As am I," I told her, stroking the side of her face as she leaned into it.

"Stealth and maneuverability. Those are what she relies on. That is what we will rely on," Porter continued.

Within five minutes we were all onboard. Serrot was loosely strapped into a bed, Porter assured us it was only so he did not roll out, and that the ship did not have Jute Buckle capabilities.

"What are you doing?" Porter asked when Cedar unbuckled herself and followed him into the cockpit.

"I am going to watch everything you do and you're going to teach me how to fly this thing."

"That is wholly unnecessary." He snorted as if she had

questioned his ability to pilot.

"Can you be injured?" she asked. "Or killed?"

"I am mortal, if that is what you are asking."

"According to Lodilin, we are of the utmost importance, correct?" Cedar prodded.

"That is the reason for this escape, yes," he replied.

"What if something were to happen to you?"

"What is going to happen to me?"

"I don't know, Porter, there are a million and a half things that could go wrong. Don't our chances of a successful escape increase dramatically if there are two skilled pilots aboard this ship?"

He gave her a sidelong glance. "Strap your harness on; do not touch anything," he warned.

Cedar clapped her hands together. "I really do love when I get my way…how fun!" I could see her perfectly from where I sat; she was nearly dancing in her seat from excitement. She had to finally sit on her hands to keep them from touching any of the seemingly thousand buttons and switches in front, above, and beside her.

"*Deep Onyx*, you are cleared for lift off." This was Lodilin speaking directly. "Good luck and may our gods bless us all."

I wasn't sure what to expect as the ship rose; I could not help but grit my teeth and grip the edges of my seat. So far, little about space travel had been what I would consider *fun*. I wish I had my sister's attitude in regard to it.

"You can open your eyes now," Lendor said softly. We were out in the vastness of space. Instead of my unease dissipating, it had billowed like a heavy cloud. Looking out at all the stars through the front window was slightly overwhelming.

"What do we do now?" Cedar was bouncing on her chair.

"We wait. The *Iron Sides* is fast approaching." Porter moved a stick nestled close to his knees and we slowly spun so that the *Ogunquit* dominated our view. "We will start our first lesson in the meantime."

I watched as the young Cedar fell away and a much more mature and serious version replaced her. I had a feeling that those of us in the back ceased to exist for the time being as she did her best to soak in all the knowledge Porter was imparting.

Ferryn went over to sniff at Serrot. "He is beginning to awaken."

He groaned as he placed his hand on his head; there was a moment of confusion and panic as he tried to get up and was met with resistance.

"It's okay, it's okay," I spoke soothingly and quickly undid the belt. "How you feeling?" He took my hand to sit up.

"What hit me?"

Porter turned from his chair. "There is a small galley in the door behind you; he will need to drink plenty of water and eat something—it will help immeasurably. No, no! Do not touch that!" He lightly smacked Cedar's hand away from the console.

"What do you think they eat?" Tallow asked. "I'm starving." He was the first up.

I was quickly behind. Lendor stayed with Serrot to keep him from toppling over.

Tallow was opening up all the drawers and cabinets. "Protein bars? Everything is a protein bar." He pulled one out; it was the size of his forearm. He sniffed it and was about to take a bite.

"You realize it's in a wrapper, right?" I smiled at him as I grabbed a large bottle labeled "water."

"Duh, of course I did," he ripped the wrapper, again sniffed the bar and took a bite.

I got the water over to Serrot, who protested at first. Tallow came out with a stack of protein bars. "Not half bad," he said, putting them down on a small table in the side of the area.

"Protein bars?" Lendor and I had changed places and he was looking over the food. "Any idea what kind of protein?" he asked Tallow.

"What's that mean?" Tallow said around a mouthful of the tan bar.

"Protein comes in many different forms," Lendor said, slowly ripping his wrapper.

"Yeah, like a boar, right?" Tallow was powering through his food. "Don't look at me like that Win, spacefaring is hard business."

"I didn't say anything." I laughed. "And what exactly did you do that was so difficult?"

"Existing. Just existing seems to be a full-time job," he replied. It was hard for me to argue with that.

"A boar is one way; insects can also be a significant source as well."

"Are you saying I could be eating a cricket bar?" Tallow let his arm drop.

"Or whatever the Genogerians consider protein. Could be human meat."

"It is not human meat!" Porter shouted from the front. Much softer he added. "We stopped that practice once we became allies."

"Good to know." Tallow gulped. "I could have been eating human," he mouthed to me.

"I said it wasn't human!" Porter seemed offended. "Mostly." I saw the smile he gave Cedar.

"Tallow, I'm going to break that thing over your head if you interrupt my lesson again!" Cedar had got up and was berating him, her hands on her hips. "And give me one of those." She strode over to the table and snagged one. "How are you feeling?" She leaned down to look at Serrot, gave him a small kiss and left before he had the chance to respond.

"Most of the protein in the bars is plant based," Porter said as Cedar regained her seat.

"Whew," Tallow replied, then took another bite.

"He said *most,*" Lendor reminded him.

"I liked it better when you were the enemy and I could just kill you." Tallow put the bar down.

"As if," Lendor snorted.

"I don't feel so good." Tallow gripped his belly. For a moment I was concerned that maybe the food stores were old and he had gotten food poisoning, like Fletcher, when he'd foolishly eaten the ancient MRE.

"One more thing…do not eat too much. For your size, no more than a tenth of the bar. It is so protein-rich it will take a while for your digestive systems to process. Eat too much and it will feel like you have sunken stones inside you," Porter said.

"Too late." Tallow moved to lay down where Serrot previously had been. "You should get up; you're kind of crowding me." Tallow was getting into a fetal position, muscling Serrot out of the way.

"They are here," Porter said flatly. There was no need for an explanation of who *they* were. For as large as the *Ogunquit* was, the *Iron Sides* dwarfed her. Nearly one entire half of the front viewport was taken up, and I could not even imagine the distance we were from them.

"What exactly are you trying to pull, Lodilin?" Breeson asked.

"How is it possible that we are listening in on their communications?" Cedar asked.

"This is an espionage ship and for now, if you would remain quiet, I will answer your questions afterward."

"Your weapons were trained on us, Commander, and you told me that you have broken protocol by disabling safety features designed for this very occurrence. I feared for the safety of my crew. I thought that with a small respite, we may be able to have cooler heads prevail."

"My head will be much cooler when that which was taken from me is returned. If you even think of powering up your buckle drive, I will consider that an act of hostility and will be forced to fire upon you. I am sending the shuttles to search your ship; are you willing to comply?"

"I do not agree, Commander, and I will file a grievance upon my return. But if it keeps the peace, then do what you must," Lodilin replied.

"Was that so hard?" It sounded like Breeson was sneering. With some small changes to pitch, I could have imagined it was Haden's voice, with its arrogant superiority over all others I was hearing.

Porter had to point out the shuttles to us; they were so small in size compared to the behemoth they flew out of.

"Are those fighters escorting them?" Cedar asked, referring to the dozen other small ships surrounding the shuttles.

"It would appear so." Porter seemed extremely tense. "Commander Breeson is an intelligent individual; he will know that my father only acquiesced to this search because we have somehow escaped."

"Why bother with the search then?" I asked.

"It is a display of power. He is letting the High Councilman know his status before he strikes."

"Before he strikes?" Lendor asked.

"I fear that Commander Breeson will attack once he knows for sure we are not there."

"We need to do something," I entreated.

"All we can do is sit and remain quiet. To do anything else would be an affront to all that those on the *Ogunquit* have sacrificed." Porter let his head nod down, his eyes closed as he spoke what appeared to be a prayer, though it was in a language I did not understand.

"Porter, we're not worth it!" I said, interrupting him.

"Hey!" Cedar interjected.

"I didn't mean it like that, but I don't want to trade our lives for all of theirs."

"Okay, that I get," Cedar agreed.

Not much was said in our ship as we watched the shuttles dock with the *Ogunquit.* The fighters buzzed around her like incessant mosquitoes; I almost wished that Lodilin would swat them out of the sky, just on principle. It was long hours later that the shuttles left, the fighters quickly in tow. Serrot's head was starting to feel better, and Tallow had come up to the front with us; the groaning had subsided.

"Where are they, Lodilin?" Breeson said, the anger clearly evident in his tone.

"As I have told you before, Commander, there is no one on board that is not authorized to be here."

"Last chance."

"Their weapons are powered up," Porter hissed. He was looking at a small display off to his side, then nervously up to the screen.

"We have shared a long, proud history of peace between our races. You would…." That was the end of the transmission as an array of violent blues and blistering reds streaked across the expanse of space and collided with the hull of the *Ogunquit*. There was a fireball twice the size of the ship as it at first exploded out and then collapsed in on itself. When it was all over, there was hardly any debris at all to let anyone know that the High Councilman's ship had been there.

I was in a state of shock with what I had witnessed—the loss of so much life. I had barely known Lodilin and those with him, but *noble* felt like an apt word to describe them. That they had not given a second thought to sacrificing themselves for us was profound.

"Fire on them!" Serrot was so angry he was leaning over Cedar looking for the weapons controls.

Cedar's hands were hovering near to what I suspected where those very controls.

"Do not, little one." Porter's head was down. "I would do so in a moment if I thought that we could inflict enough damage to make it worthwhile."

"He can't do that!" Tallow couldn't comprehend what had happened. He wasn't the only one. "He'll have to pay for that, won't he?"

"Humans control the council. They will attempt to cover this up or diminish the importance, say it was an accident of epic proportions."

"They can't do that!" Tallow cried, so upset he was repeating himself.

"Injustices have been happening as long as there has been life," Porter replied.

"Something is going on." Cedar was looking at signals on one of her control panels.

"Look at all the shots; they are scatter-shooting," Serrot said.

Porter sat up, his remorse pushed away for the moment as we faced this new threat.

"It is called an active scan; it is modeled on an old system your navy developed in ages long past…it was called SONAR, and was based on sending out an acoustic signal—a ping. If the signal bounced off an object, they could tell how far away the ship was by the length of time it took the return echo to reach their sensors. In space, however, sound does not travel; that is why they are using high powered lasers."

"So, they aren't shooting?" he asked.

"Not in the traditional sense, but LARA, laser ranging, is only used in active war because the ship being targeted can have many of its sensor arrays damaged."

"Are we going to run?" Cedar looked primed to do her part.

"No, we are going dark. I am going to pull in and shield anything that may be harmed. We will sit here and hope we get lost in the vastness of space."

"Nothing? We're going to do nothing?" I asked.

"We are going to live, hopefully," Porter said as he flipped some switches.

"And if we get pinged?"

"It will be best if we do not."

I was frustrated that he said no more on the matter. It was intense and exhausting. The *Iron Sides* was taking her time doing a thorough grid search of all the space around them. Each time the laser array moved on to another location, we were happy it was not on us but worried that it was one step closer to where we were.

"Are they going to get tired of doing this?" Tallow asked

"It has been eight hours; what do you think?" Cedar was moving so much if I didn't know any better I would swear she'd sat on an ant hill.

"I think they're going to keep on going until they find us," Tallow said angrily.

"How long has it been?" A yawning Lendor had returned from taking a nap.

"How can you sleep during a time like this?" Cedar asked.

"Not sure what else I can do. Unless you get me on that ship, then I'll be happy to attack all that get in my way. Until then, I plan on eating and sleeping."

Cedar looked back at him, then over to Porter. "Those lasers, will they detect this ship?"

"In theory, no; the ship's hull will absorb 99.92 percent of the light."

"The other point zero eight percent?" she asked.

"Will reflect back to the *Iron Sides* but their sensitivity will only be calibrated to one percent margin of error," Porter responded.

"Meaning what?" I asked.

Cedar turned to me. "That their ship will hopefully disregard the signal as erroneous. What aren't you telling us, Porter?"

"It all depends greatly on the technician doing the scan. If he is inattentive, we will be overlooked, but if he is paying attention, he will notice that the lasers that hit us are not continuing to travel further out into space."

"So we light up as a dark spot," I said, understanding the implications.

"I've been watching how they are conducting their scans; we have about another four hours. There has to be some slip in vigilance," Serrot stated.

"They are being methodical and slow. They will have the ship's computer checking everything, and I would think they will have multiple people looking at the findings. Before you say anything," Porter was looking at me, "I said, *in theory* we will be safe."

"I don't get this. Isn't there a better chance of surviving if we start flying as fast as we can to get away from them?" Tallow asked.

"The propulsion system would be detected immediately."

"I learned about inertia while I was training for the shuttle flight. What about a micro-burst to get us moving?"

"To what end?" Porter asked.

"Get us closer to their ship, possibly even underneath it so that we are not in the path of the lasers."

"We are shielded to a degree, but if we power up the engines and fire them for even less than a millisecond, it will spike on their sensors," Porter replied.

Cedar was thinking hard, her eyebrows furrowed. Her eyes grew wide. "The airlock."

Porter's eyes closed for a moment. He appeared to be thinking on it; I was glad I wasn't the only one that had a confused look on my face.

"The thrust from the escaping air…" Cedar began.

"It could be enough to push us forward." Porter was tapping away at a small board with strange figures on it.

"How could escaping air be enough to move us very far?" Tallow asked.

"In space, once something is moving, it will not stop until there is an equal reactionary force…"

"Or we hit something." Lendor was pointing at the *Iron Sides*.

"That is a valid concern." Porter looked up from his device. "It is difficult to say exactly in which direction we will move, and the next problem does indeed become: how do we stop?"

"Next idea." Cedar was working through the problem. "They have already scanned the far side of the ship. Won't we be alright if we just travel on past them and into the cleared zone?"

"Ingenious!" Porter exclaimed. "They will have no reason to sweep the area again. Everyone back to their seats, please, and buckle in!"

We did as we were told. I was nervous, but Tallow looked terrified.

"Win, how long do we have to hold our breath? How long can we?"

"What do you mean?" I asked him.

"Those crazy two up front are going to let all the air out of the ship. I mean, what good does it do if we avoid the *Iron Sides* only to suffocate in our seats? I don't want to go out like that."

"What is Tallow complaining about now?" Cedar yelled from the cockpit.

"He's worried about not having enough air to breathe," Serrot said.

"Aren't you?" Tallow asked him, Serrot shrugged.

"I am now. Hadn't thought about it before you said something."

"You hadn't thought about suffocating? How could you not?" Tallow shot back.

"Both of you relax. There is an airlock where we came in; it is sealed from this main compartment. We are going to open the outer door for a split second—just enough to give us a shove. You'll hardly even feel it, I think, but there will be no loss of breathable air in here. I promise. I think."

"Win, I really hate when she adds, 'I think,' on to the end of stuff. She makes me fearful, and her confidence loses credibility in my eyes."

"If she says we'll be all right, I trust her."

"That doesn't work; you *have* to say you trust her, she's your sister." Tallow pulled his straps tight.

"I have decided that space sucks," Lendor said, completely out of character; he was generally so stoic. "I do not like fighting my enemy, no matter who they are, without being able to peer into their eyes."

"I don't know," Cedar replied. "There's something to be said for being as far away from Stryvers as possible."

"I would agree with that statement," Porter added. "Are you ready?" He was talking to Cedar. "When you open the door, count to three and close it. The calculations I have performed say that will be enough to get us into a moderate drift. Nothing that should be picked up by their sensors."

"Here goes everything." The lights in the ship turned from white to red; we could hear a loud whooshing behind us. The ship jumped a little. Whether we were moving, it was difficult to say. "Three." The sound stopped and the lights returned to normal. "It worked, Porter!" Cedar was excited. "Though we seem to be moving more toward them and not the cleared space."

I had undone my straps and gone to the cockpit. The *Iron Sides* did indeed seem to be getting larger. "Umm, guys, I'm not much into drama, I like to leave that department to Tallow, but shouldn't we be going under, or at least over, their ship? Because it really looks to me like we're heading right for it."

"Funny, Win." Tallow's eyes grew wide as he looked out at the same thing I was.

"I'll redo the calculations; the door was closed within the parameters." He paused. "It will work out, we should be going under her, missing by a mile or more." Porter was looking at his read out.

A mile sounded like a good distance when avoiding an enemy on the ground; out here, where everything was measured in terms of millions, I didn't feel quite as good about it.

"Can I see that?" Cedar had her hand out for Porter's tablet.

"You can read Genogerian?" he asked, reluctantly handing it over.

"What else was I going to do while they were looking for us?" she replied as naturally as if she had merely been combing her hair out. "The buttons, Porter. What good would it be if I didn't know what they meant? I'm not proficient yet; another couple of days and I'll have it down."

"What happens if we hit that thing?" Tallow asked.

"We are not going fast enough for any structural damage to either of us, but it will ring like a bell inside here and there. They will most assuredly know at that point something is out here."

"Space: the final f…" Lendor started.

"Lendor!" I said.

"What? You don't know what I was going to say."

"I think I know what happened." Cedar's fingers were a blur on the device she held. "The door opened from the bottom; enough air blew out to force us upward just enough. Your calculations were based on the door being completely open the whole time."

"This is a dreadful time to discover I made an error."

"Just enough for what?" I asked her.

"Just enough that the next few hours are going to be extremely tense." She looked up to the *Iron Sides*.

"How tense?" Frost had found her way through the tangle of legs and was in between Porter and Cedar.

Porter looked to her. "I thought the 'speaking in the mind' only a myth; I am happy to see that is one rumor that has been proved wrong. Welcome, Frost." She swished her tail at him. I think she was still waiting for an answer.

"Well, there's a margin of error of about ten feet. We either miss by eight feet or we don't." Cedar kept tapping, hoping for a different outcome.

"How is it possible to go from having a hard time finding enough blueberries to eat, to crashing into a spaceship, millions of miles away from earth? Is such a thing even possible? No offense, Win, but right now I'm kind of wishing you'd been able to get out of that mud hole on your own. Or better yet…never even stepped in it."

"Tallow, I don't want to state the obvious, but there's a

very good chance, you, me and Cedar would all be dead right now if you hadn't helped me."

He ran his hands through his hair and turned back to the crew area, attempting to reconcile what was happening as best he could. I could hear a protein bar wrapper being removed.

"I eat when I'm nervous!" he shouted up. "A good old-fashioned belly ache should keep my mind off things."

An hour crept by, then another. The laser grid was fast approaching us, as was the wide, white underbelly of the beast we were trying to avoid. Without any enhancement to the viewing screen, we could begin to see individual sensors, towers, and gun emplacements as they came into focus. It would not be long before we could see the ship's portholes and individual people walking past them or staring out.

"I have been updating our trajectory as we move forward. We are now more likely to hit than not. It has changed to a three-foot miss window with a five-foot margin of error." Porter looked up.

"Okay, we need to think of a solution. I can't just sit here and hope for the best. When I was learning how to fly the shuttle, I realize now that it was antiquated technology, but it talked about the sensors and the range that they employed. It talked about how far they could reach out, but it never discussed how close," Cedar said.

Porter was thinking. I could see the consternation on his features. "It's…" He stopped and thought some more. "It's possible. Risky, but possible."

"Could you flyboys explain it to someone that loves to find her feet on the ground?" I asked, looking from Cedar to Porter. Both were grinning with a smile that I would say bordered on lunacy.

"Your sister's intuition continues to astound me. It is likely that the *Iron Sides'* sensors are calibrated so that they only start picking up data from a set point away from their ship, otherwise, the vessel itself could cause interference."

"Okay?" I had an inkling of what they may be talking

about, but it is difficult to ascertain what crazy people are truly thinking.

"When we get close enough, we can start our engines and give us a small burst that will be enough to keep us from banging off their hull." Cedar was excited that she had offered a solution.

"That'll work?" I asked, hopefully.

"It is better than waiting for Providence to decide," Porter said cryptically.

"Nobody's going to see that?" Tallow asked.

"There is no way to tell for certain; all we can do is try." Porter was once again doing calculations on his tablet. "When I am done, Cedar, I would like you to look over my work and see if you notice anything. I have entered in the distance from which I feel it will be safe to power up, the amount of thrust it will take, and how long we have to once again shut down so that we do not show as a heat signature."

"So even after we stop the engine, they can see the heat?" I asked.

Porter nodded.

"I like the plan, I do," I began, "but it seems to me of all the scans and sensors they may have on that ship that anything that deals with heat would be pretty sensitive, especially that close."

"That is a valid point. It is very likely they will notice something; we can only hope that they believe it to be an anomaly of some sort or their own faulty equipment."

Porter and Cedar were going over the information they had at hand, constantly revising and practicing what they needed to do. I, for one, could not keep my eyes off the approaching ship and the sweeping lasers.

"Um, guys," I said, "we have another problem."

All eyes were on me when they should have been straight ahead.

"That can't be good," Lendor said as we watched hundreds of fighter ships pour out of the *Iron Sides*.

"Have they found us?" Cedar asked.

"Seems like an over-response," Porter said. "I believe we can expect company. My father said that he had called for assistance."

"There's about to be a war here? We're going to get squashed like an ant under horses' hooves," Tallow said.

"Any chance we could escape during the din and confusion?" Serrot asked.

"Screw leaving! I want the *Iron Sides* to pay for what they've done," Cedar replied.

We all held that sentiment to varying degrees. Cedar likely the most, but probably because she could actively do something. Besides Porter, the rest of us could only be observers.

The grid stopped as more fighters moved into position. The *Iron Sides* moved as well. We were now staring straight down the front of it, which meant the Genogerian ships were going to show right behind us. If it came to shots being fired, we were in the thick of it.

"This is crazy," Tallow said. "I can almost feel them looking at us, makes me itchy." He absently began to scratch his arms.

"How long until we reach them?" I pointed.

"An hour." Cedar looked concerned, caught in the crossfire between goliaths was never a good place to be. The fighters were moving out in front of the ship in what I could only describe as a disturbed hornets' nest of activity.

"Anyone change their mind about how much space sucks?" Lendor asked.

"If we start up and fire our engine now, Porter, one of those fighters is sure to see it. Gonna be hard to pass that off as an anomaly," Cedar said.

"This is getting exceedingly complicated," he replied.

"Just now you're thinking it's getting exceedingly complicated?" Tallow looked ready to jump out of his skin; I understood the sentiment.

"We have another problem," Porter said. We all looked at him. "It is unlikely that they can see this ship, but what they will be able to notice is that as we move, we will block out stars in the background. From this distance, we are too small in their field of vision to make a difference in the expanse, but the closer we become, the more light we will block."

"Win, what is he talking about?" Tallow asked.

"It is a dark night on Earth. There is a quarter moon that sheds very little light. Not even enough to see your hand in front of your face, unless, of course, you hold it up and block the moon from your sight," I said quietly. "Then the outline of your hand will be perfectly visible. This ship will be just like that."

Tallow held his hand up; he got it now and he looked none too pleased about it.

"We have a difficult decision to make and I would like for us to either agree on it or let the majority rule," Porter said. "We either make a stand when it becomes necessary or we run. I do not believe either choice offers us much of a chance. If we stand and fight against the fighters that will be upon us soon, we have less than a five percent survival rating."

"And if we run?" Lendor asked.

"If the confusion is great enough, it could go as high as twelve."

"I would rather die being hit from the front as I fire than shot in the back running away," Lendor said. "I vote we stay."

"As do I." Cedar put her hand in the air.

"Any harm to them is good," Ferryn spoke. It was such an unusual occurrence; it halted the discussion immediately.

"If my mate is for fighting, I am by his side," Frost replied.

"Wait, wait," I interceded before the deciding vote could be made. "I also want to make them pay for what they have done, more than anything. But we need to reason this out. The chances of making it through the day are slim and I would imagine that the chances we can inflict any serious harm are even more marginal."

Porter nodded in agreement.

"We need to live; running nearly triples that. We find another way to strike out when we have a better chance of hurting them. I vote run," I said.

"Well, I'm with Win. I've always been with Win, and not just because she'll kick my butt if I don't vote her way, but because she always makes sense," Tallow said, placing his arm around me.

"These are all valid arguments, and, as much as I would like to avenge my father, it may be better to plan a more forceful counterattack."

All eyes turned to Serrot; he was either going to deadlock it or send us into oblivion.

"Much like Tallow, I am afraid of what Cedar would do if I went against her." There were strained smiles. "There has never been a fight I have shied away from, but Cedar, Lendor, Frost, Ferryn…I don't think this is the time."

Cedar had undone her straps and was either heading over to him to punch his arm or hug him for his stance; this was when everything changed dramatically. We had been listening to the background chatter as the fighters got into position; it had all been routine—right up until it wasn't.

"This is Lieutenant Summers. I've got something here, directly in front of me. It's the weirdest thing. It's not showing on any of my scans, but there is something moving out there."

"Whatcha got?" Lieutenant Ned "Pounder" Summers asked his sister.

"I wish I could tell you," Lt Susan "Beachie" Summers replied.

"Lieutenant, this is Commander Breeson. Can you identify the object?"

"I cannot, sir. It's moving slow, drifting, but it's headed straight for me. Permission to leave formation."

"You have eight minutes before you're in no-man's land; I expect you to be back in tight formation with your squadron long before that."

"Aye, aye sir."

"You heard the commander," Squad Leader Captain Yamato said. "Sacks, you watch her six," he said to Lieutenant Phil "Sacks" Dentrof.

"Been doing that for a good long time now," Sacks replied. "Sorry, Pounder."

Susan laughed while her brother groaned.

"Uh-oh." Cedar had sat down and was getting ready for whatever came next. We all watched as the fighter sped toward us.

"What if she fires on us?" Cedar asked. "She saved us." She looked back to me.

"If she saved us just to kill or capture us, sis, then you know what to do," I replied coldly. She nodded, but I don't think she was quite as sure of herself as she had been a moment earlier.

"Can she see us? I mean, *us* specifically, not just this ship?" I asked.

"The port is as black as the rest of the ship. There is a way to change that, but for what purpose?"

"She's going to discover us soon enough; maybe we give her a reason not to see us," I said.

"But she will see us, Win." Tallow was clearly confused. Cedar got it, though.

"Sure, she was nice, and she did help to save us on that mountain, Winter, but what makes you think she would go against her kind to continue to help us?" Cedar asked.

"What other choice or chance do we have?" I asked.

"There is definitely something out here. I'm about two miles out. It's drifting toward the *Iron Sides*. Moving in for a closer look," Summers said.

"Five minutes, Lieutenant, then I want you back here," Captain Yamato ordered.

"Yes sir, Captain."

"I am projecting the interior of the cockpit to the portal; it will look very much like a standard viewing area," Porter said.

"I don't like this at all," Cedar said as we were staring

down the business end of a sky fighter.

The lieutenant was maneuvering so she could get in closer. Her eyes grew big as she took us in.

“Safe to say she can see us now,” Tallow said.

“Commander, this is Lieutenant Summers, I have…” That was the end of her transmission as a beam as thick as a tree trunk obliterated her ship; the shock wave sent us spiraling away. Tallow had grabbed Cedar’s seat and me to keep us from pummeling against the wall. Serrot and Lendor disappeared from view from the centrifugal force. Frost and Ferryn seemed fairly rooted to their spots.

Porter’s arms were jumping as he wrestled with the controls. Cedar was helping him while also manipulating things I had no idea the purpose of. We were coming back under control but above us, a battle was waging.

“Noooo!” came through our speakers; it sounded a lot like Beachie’s brother. His scream was cut short when I believe he joined her in the afterlife.

“Stryvers and…and something else,” Porter said. “Now would be a good time to make our retreat.”

“I’m going to see what’s going on out there. How do I get it up on the screen again?” Cedar asked.

Porter quickly pointed and then started the ship. I don’t know how fast we were going, but I think it was nearly to its maximum.

“We’re alright back here. Thanks for asking!” Serrot grunted.

“Help me up,” Lendor said.

“You’re on top of me,” Serrot replied.

I had my hand over my mouth as I watched what was happening. The *Iron Sides,* while seemingly our enemy, was now on the defensive as two Stryver ships and something I couldn’t even identify were firing on the *Iron Sides’* fighters and the mothership herself.

Barrages of blues, greens and yellows battered each other. Tiny explosions dotted the space where the fighters were.

Great pocks were forming where the traditional ships were sustaining damage.

It was impossible to say if the unknown vessel was taking any damage whatsoever. The ship was loosely shaped like something I had seen on one of the covers in one of the books in the library. The center was a pulsing yellow, though the outer fringes, which were continually expanding and contracting, were more of a blue color. From that fluctuating rim, what looked like impossibly enormous tendrils surrounded the entire structure, and at the end of each were white puffs that appeared suspiciously like dandelions gone to seed. Occasionally, one or more of these would detach and engulf a fighter or head straight to the *Iron Sides*. Wherever they made contact, the ship would glow a dull red.

"Do you know what that is?" I asked, hoping for and simultaneously dreading an answer. "It looks…familiar."

Tallow looked like he had swallowed his tongue. "*That looks familiar?!*"

"The *Iron Sides* is spinning up their buckle drive," Porter said.

"The fighters—they're not going to make it back." Cedar was confused.

"The good of the many at the expense of the few." Lendor had made it back up; he had a knot on the side of his head but looked a sight better than Serrot, who was bleeding from his nose.

"They're not even heading back," I said.

"They are trying to give as much cover as they can in the hopes that their ship can get away," Porter said.

"They're sacrificing themselves," Frost said.

"Just a little longer," Porter said. "The more they fight, the better our chances of escape."

It was difficult for me to distance myself that much from what was happening. Yes, they were both opposing forces to us, but we shared some destiny with the *Iron Sides*, didn't we? There was a bright flash and in an instant, the *Iron Sides* left;

her fighters, however, still waged a vicious war. Stryver fighters poured forth from the battle vessel closer to us; the one further away buckled immediately after the *Iron Sides* left. The pulsing ship began to quiet; its tendrils, no longer waving about and the seed pods, for lack of a better term, did not detach.

The *Iron Sides'* fighters were outnumbered and now had no back up; they were easy pickings, yet it was the Stryver fighters that seemed to be taking damage, occasionally flaring up from explosions. It took me a minute to realize that some of the *Iron Sides'* vessels were drifting aimlessly around, some lazily swirling or spinning slowly.

"What's happening?" I asked.

"The Stryvers are firing something that is incapacitating the human ships," Porter said.

"For what purpose?" Tallow asked.

"They will round them up, take them prisoner, question them to the point of death and then consume their vessel," Porter replied matter-of-factly.

"They're going to eat them?" Tallow looked how I felt.

"While that is extremely distasteful, I must remind you that your fate, while not quite as gruesome, involved a similar outcome. Do not spare them too much pity. We must now think upon our own survival. It is my hope that we can move past the range of their sensors. Cedar, please shut down the drive."

"Inertia, right?" Tallow looked to Cedar.

"You're getting it. You'll be a pilot soon enough," she said without looking back.

"I'd rather not." I was the only one that heard his answer.

"Biology," I said quickly when the thought popped into my head. "That is what that looks like."

All eyes were on me with varying degrees of question upon their countenances.

"I didn't look for long; I was in the education section of the library, I was trying to learn more about the world around us, rather than in us. It was a biology book. That thing looks like something that was on one of the pages. I mean, from the limited portion I read, they're supposed to be tiny, impossible to see without something called a microscope, but that looks a lot like a germ."

"A germ? Something that makes you sick if you're dirty?" Tallow asked.

We knew about basic hygiene because of what we'd been taught in the bio-buildings, though none of us had ever seen a picture of what could make us sick. Like everything else, we just took their word for it because that was the way it had always been. They told us and we believed.

"Apparently, Michael Talbot knew more than he let on," Frost said. She seemed slightly bemused. "It is well known that he had a fear of all things germ related, and with good reason."

"If he ever saw that, he sure did," Tallow said.

"Something detached from the germ-thing," Cedar said. "And it looks like it's heading in the same direction we are."

"Can we outrun it?" Serrot wanted to know.

"Passive scans show it moving at a slightly faster pace than we are," Porter replied. "It will take more than seventy-two hours to overcome us."

"They'll pull back long before that, right?" Tallow asked, but no one could answer that.

There was also the possibility that the much larger ship it had broken free from, or the Stryver ship itself, would come for us. It seemed strange that the tendril would have acted on its own, but what could we possibly know about an enemy so entirely foreign to us? For a long while we watched as the large ships began to fade from view, and then for an even longer time, we kept tabs on the piece that was still following us. When nothing happened and didn't appear like anything was going to happen any time soon, we went back about our normal routines. For most of us, that meant eating and resting. Cedar was pouring over the Genogerian manuals, which, luckily for her, had been translated to our language, although I really don't think that would have stopped her for very long.

We'd been traveling for hours. The intensity of the battle had begun to wear off. I hadn't thought to ask at first because just getting away was of paramount importance, but now it seemed like a question that needed asking.

"Porter, where are we going?" The way he looked at star maps gave me every indication he had a destination in mind and wasn't just flying around looking for a place to land.

"It is not by chance that we stopped the *Iron Sides* where we did or that we Jute buckled in the direction we had."

"Are we going back home?" Tallow asked. I knew that wasn't the case, but I can't lie and say my heart didn't race at the possibility that maybe that was the answer.

"It is more than likely, even if we possessed the food stores to make such a trip, that we would all die of old age long before we arrived at Earth," Porter replied. "There is a habitable planet less than two weeks from here; that is our destination."

The thought of spending the next two weeks confined in this small ship held absolutely no appeal, but that was far from the most troubling aspect.

"And then, Porter?" I asked.

"There is an abandoned Genogerian base there, or so we would lead others to believe. We can get help there."

"Can't you just call in help from here?" I asked.

"The machinery necessary to make those types of transmissions is enormous and requires a much larger vessel to house it. Our best chance is to arrive."

"And what of our uninvited guest?" Cedar asked about the germ tendril still following us. "If your base is to remain a secret, I don't think it's such a good idea to bring it there with us. They are still following, and we are no longer in sight or range of the other vessels. We've got to assume that they're going to keep on coming."

"I do not like attacking an enemy when we have no idea its capabilities. But you are right; we cannot bring it with us. First, we will change course and see if it alters as well. If so, we will move to intercept."

"About time." Cedar rubbed her hands together. "May I?" Cedar grabbed the controls, Porter nodded. "Oooh, so much smoother than the shuttle! I feel like I could fly this in a cave."

"No!" Serrot exclaimed. "Winter, you're her sister; can you tell her that's not such a good idea?"

"Let's just hope flying into a cave never becomes necessary," I told him.

"You and I both know this is foreshadowing." He walked back to the crew area with his head bowed. He was mumbling as well; I didn't pick up on it as I was so tense waiting to hear what the alien craft was doing.

"Nothing so far," Cedar said. There was excitement and a little disappointment in her voice, if I'm being honest. "Hold on," she said, tapping at a screen. "Porter?"

"I saw it as well, though it is an impossibility—at least according to all of the astrophysics laws I am aware of."

"What happened?"

"The ship disappeared then reappeared nearly ten thousand miles closer, and on our new course."

"Something like a Jute Buckle?" I was trying to understand what happened.

"Again, the machinery to do something like that is large; it would not fit inside something of that size, and besides, the movement was much too quick. It is unlike anything I know of."

"If they have the ability to do this and could seemingly do it at any time, then it seems safe to say that their primary mission is to follow us," I said, letting the tactical side of my mind think like my enemy. "How long can we stay out here?"

"If your boyfriend stops trying to explode his stomach, we have enough stores for two months," Porter replied.

Inwardly, I groaned at the thought of two months cooped up in here, eating the mystery protein bars. "Maybe we can outlast them."

"Perhaps. Or maybe it is nothing more than an unpiloted reconnaissance craft that could be out here indefinitely,"

Porter responded.

"I don't think that's the case," Cedar interjected. "I think the craft itself is alive."

"As hard as this is to fathom, I agree with you, Cedar, but that doesn't answer the question of how long it can stay out here with us," Lendor said. "And the longer it keeps tabs on us, the more chance it has of communicating with the big ships, and if they show up, Porter has already said we don't stand much of a chance against them. If we are voting again, I say we go straight after them. If we are victorious, we can get to this hidden base quicker. If we lose, well, at the very minimum we will no longer be stuck up here."

Lendor was very much of the same mind as I was regarding being trapped in this small ship, though I wasn't keen on not being in the ship because we weren't alive anymore.

"Cedar, make a course for the ship. I will man the guns," Porter said. "The rest of you are going to want to be restrained in your seats."

"Win, you sit there," Cedar said, referring to the first seat directly outside the cockpit. "If this goes poorly, I would like to be within hand-reaching distance. Serrot, you sit next to her. Wait, that's not fair; I'm sure Tallow would want to sit next to her just in case. Win, would you mind sitting on Tallow's lap? That really does fix two problems at the same time."

"Cedar, we are piloting a craft into a battle situation. Now might be the time to concentrate on that," Porter said.

"Serrot, how about you sitting on Tallow's lap then?" she said quietly.

"There will be no lap sitting!" Tallow demanded. "Just go and win this thing and then we won't have to worry about it!"

Cedar's eyebrows furrowed. "Okay! If that's the case, just let Serrot have your seat."

"Fly the ship, Cedar. I'm sitting right here," Tallow told her. She stuck her tongue out at him before turning back around.

"Yup, humanity's best chance right there," Tallow said

sarcastically.

I laughed when I saw Cedar stick her hand up over her chair and only one finger was raised. It was even funnier because Tallow didn't know what it meant.

"Turning now," Cedar said aloud, more for us. I got the feeling she was going to narrate so we weren't sitting back here in the dark; for that, I was extremely thankful. I noticed Frost and Ferryn were exceedingly quiet, though, on some level, I sensed they were speaking with each other.

"Burn the engines for five seconds and no longer," Porter told her.

"If anyone wants to know, that's because in five seconds we will be up to maximum speed and it makes no difference to keep the engine running, except to consume resources, which, because of the way this drive operates, are fairly unlimited, but not quite infinite. Just because you have an ocean full of fish doesn't mean you should indiscriminately kill one."

"Pretty soon I'm not even going to know what she's saying anymore," Serrot said with some pride and some measure of angst.

"They've stopped." I sat up straighter as Cedar said the words. I was watching on the screen. The tendril top pulsed slowly, yet did nothing. "Five minutes to contact." We were hurtling through space straight at it and still it did nothing. "Three minutes to contact." The words had no sooner come out of Cedar's mouth when the ship pulsed brighter, then just disappeared. Loud whooshes reverberated through the ship.

"Railgun deployed," Cedar told us. "Ship visible. Shots wide right."

The alien ship was no longer stationary; it had moved much closer with its mysterious propulsion system and was now coming forward and staying in view.

"Do you wish me to take command of the controls?" Porter asked.

"No, I'm better at piloting. You stay on the guns; I think we're going to need them." Cedar was concentrating.

Porter was studying her; if he hoped to see some falsehood in her face, he was going to be disappointed. Cedar was a spritely, fun-loving person, but she took flying seriously.

"If there is something you don't understand, you will let me know immediately," he told her.

"Uh-huh," she replied noncommittally.

We were now flying straight toward the craft as it was coming toward us. If what we had seen happen to the *Iron Sides* was any indication, a collision greatly favored them. Their ship was a weapon unto itself. This fact was not lost on either of those locked in combat with it.

"Evasive maneuvers in thirty seconds. Pull hard right; I will fire at that time," Porter told her. "Five, four, three…"

I held on as the pressure mounted from the ship pulling to the side. I felt like I was going to be deposited onto both Tallow and Serrot. There was the now familiar *whoosh* of the railgun firing and also the lasers or rays. It was a combination of all Porter had on hand, I figured.

"Hit." Cedar did not use any inflection of excitement and it was easy enough to see why. A few of the railgun projectiles punctured the walls of the craft and passed through, seemingly without any affect. "That can't be good," she said aloud.

"One would think not," he replied just as the ship once again blinked out of existence.

"Whoa!" Cedar shouted as she pressed us down hard; if not for the belt across my lap and chest, I would have become one with the roof. The alien vessel had materialized directly in front of us, and if not for Cedar's fast action, we would have flown straight into it and whatever it had in store for us.

"Safe to say they are no longer content with just following," Porter replied. "That is good news."

"Um, excuse me…" Tallow asked when we finally leveled off, "how is that possibly good?"

"It means that even though the railgun did not appear to cause harm, it has. It is my belief that otherwise they would have continued on with their original mission."

"Your belief?" Lendor asked.

"Nothing else to go on," Porter replied candidly. "It's following and gaining…" he warned Cedar, as if she didn't already know.

"If you have guns to the rear, now would be a good time to use them," she told him. I looked to the floor by her feet; I imagined there would be a growing puddle of sweat pouring off her brow. "As soon as you start firing and they once again do their voodoo disappearing act, I want you to fire high left and to the front. You got all that?"

"I think I can manage," he told her. "And if they don't fade out?"

"You'd better tell me about another way to make this ship go faster."

"There is none."

"Then this is going to work like a charm," she assured him.

"Firing. Hit! Now, Cedar, Now!"

We rolled with enough force that I felt light-headed and my vision began to tunnel.

"Everything again, Porter!" Cedar yelled, fighting against the same forces I was.

We were in what felt like a free-falling dive; if I could have released my grip, I would have wrapped my hands around my stomach to keep it from coming up through my mouth. As if that wasn't bad enough, we took a hit to the side that rattled the teeth in my head.

An alarm began to trill: "Alert; Collision…. Alert; Collision." Like we weren't already aware of it. It continued that way for another five minutes, the ship bouncing around like one of the Earth trucks on a rough road. I could not even focus on Frost across from me, as my eyes seemed to be swimming in my skull.

"She's listing to the side," Cedar said. I had no idea if she was talking about us or the enemy. Maybe both.

"Bring us around." Porter had a gash on the side of his head, wounded by a panel that had given way and crashed down. Small electrical bursts issued forth from the vacancy above him. I was pushed and pulled as Cedar fought with the ship.

"We've got flight control damage." Her hands were a blur as she moved them around trying to right the myriad wrongs we were dealing with.

"At least we can't crash land." Serrot seemed somehow pleased with that notion.

"I'd crash land a hundred times rather than be stuck out here." Lendor looked scared; that in itself was cause for concern. This was the same man that wanted to take on the entirety of the Klondikes with just one death squad.

"Who said anything about being stuck out here? That germ thingy is ripping this ship apart; we're going to be free floating in it soon if we don't do something," Cedar yelled back over the din.

"That bad?" Tallow asked me.

"No air and cold to the point we can shatter," I told him.

"So pretty bad then?" He was serious in that moment.

"Stabilizing!" Cedar shouted as Porter thankfully turned the alarm off. We were squarely facing the germ ship; it didn't appear to be doing anything and it looked like it had suffered damage as well.

Porter unleashed everything we had into the vessel. Parts of the enemy ship blew away further into the void. We watched the yellow, throbbing light become dimmer and then finally wink out. It was a victory of sorts, but we were still very much in trouble.

"We going to make it to this outpost?" I asked Cedar.

"Sis, I just don't know. Our flight system is a mess, and I think the hull has suffered a breach. Not horrible now, but as the cold works its way in it's going to damage more and more components, and well, once that happens…." She left it there.

Porter pressed a button and a hidden panel folded out; it contained a few dozen buttons and a much smaller flight stick.

"What's that?" Cedar asked him.

"Sky Drone. Usually used for reconnaissance, but right now I think it would be best used for ascertaining the damage we have suffered." A compartment opened up on the nose of the ship and what came out was similar in shape to what we were in, though on a much smaller scale. Porter changed the camera angle to that of the small ship. As it turned, we could see ourselves. Half of the ship looked as it ever had; the smooth black finish that made it look like a hole, but the other side had deep, metallic scratches through it like we had been attacked by a mountain lion.

"That is where our breach is going to be. I'm going to need to go outside," Porter said, rising up out of his seat.

"Outside where? Winter says it's pretty cold," Tallow told him.

"Cedar was right about the hole. I need to see if it is repairable."

"Can Genogerians hold their breaths for a really long time?" Tallow asked.

"He'll have a suit, goofball," Cedar said as she switched seats.

Porter looked back at her before nodding. "The coordinates are programmed into the ship, if something should happen."

"Hurry back," Cedar told him in response. "I'll keep an eye on you with the drone."

Porter went into the airlock, suited up, grabbed a tool kit he said was designed just for this problem. "Normally, the fear is micro-meteorites," he said over the speakers.

"Great, something else to worry about." Lendor threw his hands in the air. Once Porter went through the airlock and out into space, we all crowded into the cockpit to watch him. Cedar moved the drone so that he was always in our field of vision.

"How does he move around out there, Cedar?" I asked.

"His suit has small jets that will propel him." As she said this, we saw faint white puffs exit from his back and he floated forward.

Porter moved clumsily around. "I did not do well on spacewalk tests," he mumbled as way of explanation.

"Steady, Porter, you already used five percent of your tanks." Cedar sounded concerned.

"Five percent doesn't sound that bad," I said.

Cedar hit a switch. "In this situation, it's a lot; there's a very limited amount of fuel in those suits. He should have barely registered a hit. The same inertia principles apply to him as to this ship. A little gets you a very long way. He's nervous, bordering on scared…if his heart rate is any indication.

"And if he runs out of tanks?" Tallow wanted to know, as did we all.

"It's not the tanks," Cedar corrected. "It's what's inside them. But if he runs out of fuel, he might not be able to get back inside."

Porter hit the side of the ship with a jarring impact. We could hear his "oomphs" as he braced himself from injuring anything vital.

"Cedar, please move the drone closer to the damage on the wing. There is some sort of coating left behind by the attack."

I didn't like the fact at all that we could no longer see Porter as Cedar pulled the tiny ship in close.

"Does that look like it's glowing to anyone else?" Serrot was pointing to the screen.

"Yes, Porter—it did leave something behind, and at least from here, it looks active," Cedar told him.

"It is likely it is eating away at our hull," he said. "I do not know if this will work, but there is a hose in the airlock. I will need one of you to unwind it from its spool, and then reopen the hatch so that I may retrieve it without using too much of my power."

"Porter, how are you going to use a hose out there without flying off into space?" Cedar asked.

"I will have to counteract the effects of the force with my suit," he said.

Cedar was shaking her head in negation.

"You cannot think too much on this, Cedar." Porter said. "I see the hole we have now; it is reparable, but if those grooves are eaten through any further, I do not have the material available to fix it."

"Winter, can you get that hose ready? Let me know when you're back here."

"You think he can do it?" I asked her.

"He can do it, he just won't be able to get back in," Cedar replied.

"Just have him hold on to the hose; we'll reel him in."

"Don't think that will work, Tallow," Cedar said. "You'd have to be inside the airlock. Wait, Porter…are there extra suits?"

"Three, but why?" he asked. "I cannot change out here and we are running out of time."

"Not for you. We'll have the hose ready; when you're done with it, do not let go. We are going to reel you in with it," Cedar said.

"I'll do it," Tallow volunteered. "The suit, I mean."

"Figured you'd say that, but do not do anything heroic. You have no idea how the suit works, and odds are it's going to be much too big on you."

"Hose is ready," I called out as I came back. "Where you going?" I asked Tallow as he was coming toward me.

"Ceed says Porter is going to run out of suit juice or whatever the heck it uses. I'm going to pull the hose in with him on it, once he's done. Stop looking at me like that. I know that it's in the airlock. There's extra suits in there too."

"Don't do anything stupid," I told him.

"Why do people keep saying that to me? And if we're being honest, this whole thing is stupid, so there's that."

I kissed him.

"No time, lover boy." Cedar was looking back. "Get suited

up. Porter says the damage is getting worse."

I helped Tallow as best I could, tucking, pulling, and locking buttons until I was fairly certain he was ready to go.

"We're good!" I yelled up front.

"Big green button on the side of his helmet—press it!" Cedar ordered.

There was a loud hissing and a small alarm rang inside Tallow's suit.

"No pressurization." Cedar was moving quickly toward us. I did not like the idea that no one was flying this ship or the sky drone, either. "Gloves aren't on right. You going to be able to use your hands?" She was looking in his faceplate. He nodded.

"I'll be fine." I was scared; he sounded so far away, though I was standing right next to him. Cedar smacked the button again; his faceplate lit up.

"There a funny little symbol…looks like a fat buffalo…on your righthand side?" Cedar asked.

Tallow turned. "Nope."

Cedar's head bowed. "Inside the helmet."

"Oh yeah, there it is." He smiled.

"You're ready. I'm tethering you to the ship, okay?"

"Gotcha." He tried to do a thumbs up; didn't work out so good as the entire hand part flopped over.

Cedar found a thin metallic rope and latched it to a loop on the back of Tallow's suit.

"Why didn't Porter use that?" I asked.

"Not long enough, maybe, or he forgot. Alright, come on. We have to get out of here."

There was the cautionary light for the airlock being opened; we watched as the hose and Tallow were pulled to the exit. The hose continued where Tallow's flight was cut short. The hose looked much like a light pole for a moment; it was so straight and rigid. Within a few more seconds, it began to drift in the airless environment.

Once Cedar was certain everything had worked correctly and Tallow was fine, she raced back to the front.

"Hose is in place."

"On my way," Porter told her.

"He's moving too fast," Tallow said through his headset. Cedar didn't think he realized he was coming through the comm system. "*He missed.*"

"I have him on the drone. How you doing, Tallow?"

"Oh hey, I didn't know you could hear me. I don't think Porter knows what he's doing."

"I also can hear you," Porter replied.

"No offense, but you're zipping around like a bumblebee that drank turned nectar."

"Are you saying I'm inebriated?" Porter asked as he grunted. He was coming back the way he had gone.

"Less thrust, Porter. Ease up." Cedar was trying to calm him down.

"Gonna be close," Tallow said. "Ooh…" I could hear him wince. "He bounced the nozzle off his face and the hose has wrapped around his neck. Other than that, he's got it."

"Porter, are you alright?"

"I have a spider-web crack in my faceplate; it should not impede my mission." He was grunting as he wrestled with the trajectory of his suit.

"This is painful to watch," I said quietly to my sister, having joined her back in the cockpit. She had multiple camera angles up, including one in the airlock. It was somewhat comforting to be able to hear Tallow talk.

Cedar leaned over and switched off the comm. "I have a feeling all of his knowledge of that spacesuit he got from a book. It's terrifying that right now he's our best chance of getting out of this mess." She flipped the switch back on.

"Turning hose on in three…"

"Hold on Porter!" Cedar exclaimed.

"You didn't tell me this." She was looking at a row of switches. "I can remotely take control of your suit?" It came off as a question, but it wasn't.

"I originally thought it for the best if I was the master of my own fate."

"How's that working out for you?" Cedar asked him. "Alright, I am now controlling your suit. I'm going to get you closer to the damage. Make sure your spray is directed correctly; we're going to barely have enough fuel for you to do this. When I say stop, you have to do as I say, no questions asked. You hear me?"

"It would be difficult not to," he responded.

"Yeah, everybody hears Cedar for miles around," Tallow said, I guess forgetting she was listening to him as well.

"Alright Porter, I have you in position. On my count of three, you start spraying, and I'll do my best to move you along the damage. And remember, my worst is better than your best," she told him.

"Ouch," Serrot replied.

"One, two, three." Cedar began to control Porter's suit. He was moving forward quickly, not having turned the hose on. He was very much in danger of smashing against the hull. "Porter!"

Brown foam shot out and splashed across the wing an instant before he was to collide. He began to move erratically as Cedar struggled to find a balance to the forces being applied to him. I was worried that the foam would hit and go flying off into space, but it clung tightly wherever it struck. Porter was doing an admirable job of holding on to the pressurized fixture.

Cedar's head was shaking. "Move faster, Porter, burning through fuel."

"It does no good if I don't smother the damage." He was breathing heavily.

Cedar kept shaking her head as Porter moved methodically from section to section. He had just got to the final portion as a small buzzer sounded and a red button on Cedar's controls began to blink.

"You have two minutes," Cedar said through pursed lips.

"Push me closer," he panted.

Cedar did as he asked. My eyes kept shifting from my sister, who was concentrating and looked extremely worried, to Porter, who was moving far too slowly.

"Twenty seconds, Porter. You have got to stop before we run out. Tallow, be ready to reel him in."

"Ceed…not so sure how I'm going to do this. The hose feels like a tree trunk."

"Once he stops pumping it'll soften up."

"Ten…five…two! Stop now!" The small jets on Porter's suit flared and then sputtered and still he sprayed.

"Porter!" I yelled as he flew backward at an accelerated velocity. He was in danger of coming around and smashing against the hull on the other side at bone-breaking speed.

We could hear Tallow grunting as he tried to pull the apparatus in. Porter turned his head, knowing that if he held on to the hose, he might not survive the contact.

"I did it," he sighed as he let go of the hose.

"Nooo!" Cedar cried out as Porter flew off into space. She spent a moment desperately trying to squeeze more power out of his dead suit.

There was a thud in the airlock as Tallow, who had been straining against a weighted object, now found that he was pulling on air and had fallen into the wall. "Where is he?" he cried out.

"You fool!" Cedar spat as she pushed the suit controls away and grabbed the sky drone.

"I saved you; I can join my kin in celebration of my deeds," Porter said.

"You can join them at a later date." The drone took off toward him.

A Genogerian chant came over the speakers; it sounded like a final prayer.

"Not yet, Porter. I'm sending the drone. You grab a hold of it or I swear I will imbed it into your thick skull and fly you back here that way."

"I believe her," Lendor said.

I could only nod, as I did as well. "That going to work?" I asked, hopeful.

"I don't know. The drone doesn't have much power, or fuel, for that matter. But I've got to try something. Getting the drone to him and matching speed so he can grab it is going to be tricky. Then getting his momentum changed…I…I just don't know." Her forehead creased deeply, bringing her brows together as she concentrated on all the moving variables she was dealing with. I felt as useless as the cookbooks we found in the library. Sure, all the recipes looked delicious, we just didn't have any ingredients to make them with.

"Sorry Porter," Cedar whispered as she made the small flying machine accelerate.

He grunted heavily as the machine struck him somewhere in the chest/stomach region. He coughed and groaned at the same time, but his arms did wrap around it. He was still rapidly fading from our view as more red buttons lit up on the new display.

"Fuel again?" Serrot asked me, not wanting to interrupt Cedar, who looked like she could chew through bone.

"Come on, come on." Her hands were steady on the controls, though her whole body was tense. We could hear the struggled whirring of the drone as it fought against forces it wasn't designed for.

"Broken rib," Porter coughed out.

"Do not let go!" Cedar implored. "I've got this Porter, I've got you."

Later, when I reflected on this moment, I truly believed it was Cedar's sheer force of will that created the successful outcome. She was her own destiny and those around her had no choice but to comply.

"I think I've stopped moving!" Porter sounded as excited as someone could, speaking with a broken rib.

The light on Cedar's panel had gone from blinking red to a solid, ominous color. "One last push," she said.

"It's working, it's working!" Cedar and Porter said

together.

"Cedar, the drone is no longer functioning," Porter told her, "but I am headed back your way."

Relief flooded through the cockpit. If there had been room, I would have melted into a puddle on the floor, my legs were so weak. It was five minutes longer. Cedar was looking at the controls when another alarm sounded. Lendor was onto something; never got all those menacing sounds on the ground.

"No, no, no!" Cedar was frantically checking and rechecking.

"What's going on?" I asked, not sure if I could handle more stress, especially when I could do nothing about it.

"Tell them," Porter replied.

"You, you stop talking." She flipped off the comm. "He's going to run out of oxygen before he gets here and even if he doesn't, he's not on a trajectory to bring him back to the ship. At his closest, he's going to miss by about a hundred feet…might as well be a hundred miles." Her head fell against the console she was sitting at. It was the first time I had ever seen my sister's unflagging optimism not only wane, but completely falter.

"Yee-haw!" Tallow shouted.

Cedar's head came up fast, as did mine.

"Tallow, what are you doing?" Cedar asked before she realized he couldn't hear her.

"I see the big lizard! Going to go and get him!" Tallow sounded like he was having the time of his life.

Cedar flipped the switch. "Tallow, you have no idea what you're doing!"

"Don't be mad, Ceed! You're not the only one that can fly! If I'd known how much fun this was, I would have stayed with you at the shuttle!"

I ran to the airlock. I saw the retreating back of my boyfriend as he headed out into the abyss of space. "Get him back, Cedar!" I yelled, never taking my eyes off him.

"I can't manually take control of his suit without him

allowing it, and Winter, he's Porter's only chance," Cedar said.

"Tallow!" I shouted, slamming my fist up against the small window. Of course, I was concerned about Porter's wellbeing, but Tallow, he was the love of my life, the light that kept me going when all around was dark. I could not lose him; I could never lose him. I smacked the window two more times in frustration. I ran back to the cockpit to get a better idea of what was going on.

"Whoa!" Tallow was laughing; he had started to spin in place, the tether going with him. If he didn't correct it soon, he was going to end up hog tying himself and be no help to anyone.

"I'm going to 'whoa' up the side of his head."

"I heard that!" Tallow said.

"What's going on?" Porter asked.

"Porter, don't speak. You have about a minute of oxygen. At the speed you're traveling you'll be flying past Tallow in three; we'll have you back in the airlock in four. You can do it."

"Three minutes without breathing?" I asked in hushed tones. The incredulity of that hit me hard. Must have done the same to Tallow.

"Ceed, no way. No way can someone go that long without breathing. I'm going to undo my tether and I'm flipping control to you. Get me to him and get me back."

"Don't you dare take that rope off!" Even as I shouted, the cable lazily drifted away from him.

"I've got this, Winter," Cedar told me. If she was trying for comfort, it fell short. Nothing short of having him in my arms again was going to make me feel safe.

We could hear Porter taking small gasps of air. Didn't need to look at his vital signs to know what was happening. At a time when he needed to be calm and focused, he was likely the most panicked; not being able to breathe is a primal fear and my heart went out to him.

"Tallow, you're going to get some warning signals; it's only because of the acceleration, I'll slow you down in time."

"This seemed like a better idea when I was attached. Alright…get me there. Damn—he's huge! Am I going to be able to heft him up?"

Cedar smiled. "Of course! You've got superhuman strength right now, and plus, he weighs as much as a feather out there."

"Is that because he's out of air?" Tallow asked.

"If that's a joke, it's kind of funny," Cedar responded.

"Sure, yeah, that's what it was."

"Tallow, stay away from his rib cage—I don't know what kind of damage he's already suffered, and we don't want to make it worse."

"Hurry," I whispered.

"Ceed, he's coming up fast."

"Slowing now. Easy," she said more to herself. "Tallow, I'm going to start sending you back. Porter will be coming up on your right; his left arm is out. Grab it and I'll after-burn you back to the ship. Winter, there's one more suit. I've pulled the tether in with its motor. You need to suit up quickly, attach yourself, and grab them. I'm good; I don't know if I'm *that* good. Serrot, Lendor, help her."

I don't know when she'd had the opportunity, but the airlock was shut and pressurized by the time we got back there. I was getting turned, pulled and pushed in seemingly a dozen different ways as the suit was fitted on to me.

"Winter, you've got about thirty seconds! Lendor, slap the button on the side of her helmet; if it turns green, you and Serrot get out of there!"

"Green!" Lendor shouted excitedly as I heard the hiss of oxygen being injected into the suit. "Come on!" He was pulling on Serrot.

"The tether!" He was fumbling with the buckle.

"Winter, they're almost here!" Cedar yelled back. "Only have one chance!"

"I got it, I got it!" Serrot shouted as Lendor physically

dragged him from the room. I barely waited for the door to shut, nearly trapping his foot before I opened the airlock.

I didn't think at all as I propelled myself from the relative safety of the ship. I turned in time to see Tallow grab hold of Porter.

"Out of juice, Ceed," Tallow said, much calmer than I felt.

"Winter, they're coming your way. Not overly fast, but it might hurt some—just want you to be ready for it."

"I will not let go. I will not!"

"Put your hands down, Tallow, you'll push her away!" Cedar shouted.

"I'm sorry, Win." He was so close I could see him close his eyes as he braced for impact. My left hand slid around in the much too big housing it found itself in, making it completely useless as I tried to grab them through the sleeve of my stiff suit. I had three fingers of my right in position—made sense; three lives hung in the balance, one for each finger. Because if I missed, I was going to untether and chase them through the cosmos.

The impact was much more jarring than I had been expecting, even though I'd been warned. My faceplate immediately fogged up with the amount of air I had expelled. We spun. I closed my right hand; I could not tell if I had made a purchase or not. I hadn't. My fist was empty and I cried out in anguish. If not for the spin and the tether winding around us, I would have lost them all. It was that close. I wrapped my arms around Tallow in a bear hug.

"I got them! I got you!" I shouted into my headset. Fear and excitement warred within me.

"Reeling you in," Cedar said. "How's Porter?"

"Get us in quick," was all Tallow said.

The trip back seemed to take indeterminable minutes; my arms hurt from how much force I was exerting on them to make sure no one went anywhere. Once we were in the airlock, I heard Serrot shout that fact and the door to space shut behind us. We fell to the floor in a tangle of cable, arms, legs, and spacesuits.

"Help me get his helmet off!" Tallow was scrambling as Serrot, Lendor, and Cedar rushed in. Serrot and Lendor immediately went over to Porter while Cedar helped me get my helmet off. She gave me a quick hug before seeing what she could do.

"He's not breathing! What do we do?" Tallow was cradling the large Genogerian's head.

"I know about this thing called mouth-to-mouth resuscitation, though I've never tried it. It sounds like you just put your mouth over his and breathe into him." Serrot said.

"Serrot, his mouth is about ten times the size of yours," Cedar said as she looked upon Porter's snout.

"We have to try." He was pushing his way through to get to Porter.

Cedar wasn't sure how she felt about the man she loved getting that close to those huge teeth and the damage they could do, if only inadvertently.

Porter's eyes opened, rolled around for a moment as if they were adrift, one arm came up slowly. "Dormant," he said with a slur. "Dor…mant. I'm…okay." Though it didn't sound like he was okay. The words were drawn out and slow to come.

Within a few minutes, Tallow, myself, and Porter had been moved enough that we were sitting with our backs resting on the walls in the airlock. It had taken a considerable effort with Porter because he was sure he had at least one rib broken.

"I know we're all reveling in the fact that we somehow made it through this last mess, but, um," Cedar paused, "we still have damage to the ship that needs to be addressed."

"The suits need a recharging and I could use a short rest. Then I will get back out there."

"This time you'll use the tether." Cedar gently touched his shoulder before getting ready to head back up front.

"Thank you," Porter said. "I don't think anyone else would have had the skill or the mindset to do what you did."

"You're welcome, and I'm just that good," she with a wink.

"Yes, you are," he replied in seriousness.

I joined my sister up in the front once I got out of the suit and felt more like myself.

"Good work out there," she said, not looking up from the manual she was reading. Periodically, she would look over to her instruments.

"Couldn't let my sister have all the glory for the day. How's it looking?" I asked after she didn't respond to my jest.

"I think we stopped any more damage from happening, but we're still in a bad way. The propulsion system and the power converters are working great; could go on indefinitely, but without the ability to steer, we're basically bobbing around on the top of a lake. Our only hope, if we can't get moving, is that someone stumbles across us."

"What about calling for help?"

"Problem with that is we don't know who is going hear us and come and check it out."

"I liked it so much better when the hardest part of my day was figuring out how long I could hold a sword up."

"Yeah, that's another thing. I could go for a good old food cart right about now. Porter's protein bars taste like bark. No, I take that back. I'd rather eat a tree."

"Can I help with anything?" I asked.

"You can check in on Porter; right now, he's our only hope, and I don't think he's up for it. Wait." She looked over at me. "That sounded kind of mean. I'm just saying that he's wounded, and he's been through an ordeal none of us want to relive."

"I got what you meant. Plus, if I stop asking you questions, you can read more."

She smiled; I didn't need her to answer to know how right I was.

"How you doing?" I asked Porter when I went back.

He was on a cot, drinking generous portions of water. His ribs were bandaged up, thanks to Tallow and Serrot. He was staring off into a void of his own making.

After a moment, he reeled his thoughts in and looked my way. "I thought perhaps that I would face my death with better grace. My forefathers of old were among the greatest my species have ever known; you would think that some of that blood would still run through me."

"I don't think you're fully comprehending what you accomplished out there, Porter. You saved this ship. You saved all of us inside of this ship, and you were willing to do all that knowing it meant sacrificing yourself to do it."

"I know all of that, Winter, and I would do it that way every single time if need be, but I was scared. Terrified, in fact."

"First off, any more 'next times' and you will be securely cabled to this ship. And secondly, what makes you think that your forefathers, that Drababan, wasn't afraid? When authors write down the events that happened throughout history, they cannot possibly know the thoughts running through a person's mind. They can only record the deeds done. How do you believe your actions today would appear from that vantage point?"

I saw the beginning of a smile. "I think it would translate very well," he said. "I might even look good for a picture...if I didn't cringe every time I took a breath."

"Are you going to be up to doing this again?"

"It would not read well in the annals of history if I did not; I wouldn't want it to say 'He was too weak to finish the task.' When the suits are ready, please come and help me up. In the meantime, I think a bit of sleep would do wonders."

I laid my hand upon his.

"You have a good soul, Winter Talbot, and I take great pride in knowing that my family's name is once again linked to yours."

CHAPTER EIGHT

REPAIRS

We worked on a suit for Tallow, pulling it as tight as possible and using something called tape to make it fit better. It was still only going to be used in the event of an emergency, something we all wanted to avoid. Every one of us, including Frost and Ferryn, checked the attachment on the back of Porter's suit before any of us would let him go out again. He looked slightly embarrassed about the sheer amount of attention we were giving him. I don't know how I could tell that, as his species' facial features were much more subtle, different from ours, but I'm convinced that was the case. Unlike the previous jaunt out, where seemingly everything that could go wrong did, this one went exceedingly well, though there were more grunts from Porter as he worked, admirably, through his injury.

Once he and Cedar were convinced the damage had been abated, he told us in no uncertain terms he was going to sleep and if anyone woke him up without good reason, he would not be happy. We left him alone, especially since we were all exhausted as well. Now seemed as good a time as any for everyone to join him in slumber. Everyone, that is, except myself and Cedar, who appeared to never need sleep. Frost joined us, as well.

"I find it amusing that males of all species tend to do half the work and sleep twice as much," Frost said mirthfully.

We all shared a smile with her at the thought.

"How long you planning on keeping this up, sis? Even you

have to rest sometime."

"As long as it takes for me to get it," Cedar replied. There was a great length of silence as I looked out at the stars; I may have been drifting back and forth between wakefulness and slumber as I stared out at the hypnotic expanse.

Frost broke the silence. "Tracy Talbot, by all accounts, was one of the greatest Earth pilots." Frost was studying Cedar.

"Uh-huh," Cedar said, her nose buried in a manual.

"Although it has been told she crash landed one out of every three ships she flew."

"Uh-huh," she answered again, I sat up.

"She also is rumored to have had an interspecies relationship with Drababan, unbeknownst to her husband."

"Uh-huh.... Wait, what did you say?"

I had to laugh at the confused expression on her face.

"I said that perhaps you should also rest with the others."

"There's so much to learn, Frost, and I feel now, more than ever, our time is running out."

"You have an instinct that is unparalleled. I watched you work as your friends' lives were in danger."

"Instinct is one thing, knowing which controls activate what is something I need to know by rote. I lost precious seconds deciphering and debating. There might come a time where I don't have that luxury."

"I will stay with you then. It seems strange to me that a creature, any creature, would want to travel the stars."

"It does? Seems like the most natural thing to me." Cedar was looking off into the distance, as I had been.

"The world we walk on…there is water, there is food; air to breathe and room to play. A mate to have kits; what greater thing is there? Here is only cold, merciless, death…alone."

"To explore, Frost, to see what lies beyond the borders of what you know. To discover new worlds and the treasures they might possess. Curiosity. To see new things, learn new things."

"It was the Progerians that first left their homeworld; the only treasure they encountered were the Stryvers. That has not worked out well, for any involved. Curiosity is sometimes better left undisturbed."

"On that point, I might have to yield. It can't all be bad though, right?" Cedar was thoughtful.

"There may be some good; it brought our two species together and for that, I am thankful."

"You say 'our species,' but I know you're not including the people on the *Iron Sides*. Do you know what happened?" I asked. Would we finally get some answers to what was going on?

"Some, not all. For my kind were only there for the beginning of what is called *The Happening*. The man Mad Jack, who is considered a hero of the war, he did something that had never been done before. He used Stryver brain matter and injected it into himself."

"To what purpose?" Cedar was aghast. So was I, though I think she displayed it better. Her hands were up by her mouth and her eyes wide. Maybe I was just too tired for the spectacle.

"It is said that this procedure increased his brain power and allowed him access to all manner of knowledge previously unreachable."

"So, did he do something? Did he wreck the world?" Cedar asked.

"It was his actions, in part, that helped save the world or what remained. No, it was others that are credited with the destruction. There was no lack of villains and enemies desiring to achieve power through his work. Michael argued against it, he said that Mad Jack was a special case and that others ought not to tamper with something that was not truly understood."

"Why are people always so willing to do bad things?" Cedar asked.

"It didn't start that way. At first, it was believed if there was one that could help, why not two or ten? Just think how quickly they could bring an end to the conflict. And seemingly, this was working, in the beginning, anyway. Quickly though, as these people grew in power, they wished to expand their sphere of influence. To display their dominance, not only over the enemy, but all creatures, including Man."

"That's The Happening?" I asked.

"It is not specifically one event; it was a culmination. Many will argue that it started the moment Mad Jack, or Peter Pender, became tainted with the influence from the Stryver's; that from that moment on, events were predestined to travel down that particular road. Others will argue it was the moment President Talbot declared war on the Others."

"The Others? They're the ones on the *Iron Sides?* So they won the war?"

"Like most things, it is not that simple. Many wrongly blame Michael for the continuation and escalation of the war. So many races of beings were exhausted of fighting, even the Stryvers, we had all lost so much that it became not so much killing your enemy as just trying to survive. Humans were winning; they had the Genogerians on their side and had strong-armed the Progerians to their will. All that was left to deal with were the Stryvers. They were doing everything in their power to hide in the remotest parts of the universe, to either die in peace or lick their wounds and regroup before striking out again. Peace was what most wanted but were least likely to get. The Others were not content to sit back and allow those that had wronged Humanity to go unpunished. Michael was attempting to stop them; the only way was to strike them down before they could do any more harm. He pulled the battle away from Earth, where we were told it raged for decades, and we do not know much about what happened from that point forward. Just that the earth was mostly forgotten by everyone."

"I don't understand, then. How are the Others aligned now with the Genogerians and Progerians?" I asked.

"These may be questions for Porter when he is up for it," Frost said. "I am going to take my leave."

"Good sleeping," I told her. "How you doing, sis?"

"Confused, I guess. There's so much going on and we

know so little. A part of me wants to go home, to find a nice valley to live out our lives. Live the way we were supposed to, the way we fought for. You know?"

"I do," I told her honestly.

"That doesn't seem like it's going to be our lot in life."

"It doesn't."

"You've got to stop hogging the conversation. I can't even get a word in edgewise."

She smiled softly. "It's Michael. They somehow had the ability to comb through their future, and for a reason we don't know and right now can't fathom, they chose to get us off that ship. Why not get us out of the Pickets, or save us from the mountain top where we lost so many good people? Or ten thousand other scenarios before we were born or after our deaths? Stop the Others from even experimenting with the Stryver blood…wouldn't that have solved everything?"

"They had their reasons."

She seemed much less concerned with the whys of it than I did, and it was driving me crazy. "That's it? They had their reasons?"

"Winter, you know as much as I do. How can I possibly offer an explanation? If they took us from the Pickets, maybe we don't learn to fight like we did. To hone our skills. They save you from the mountaintop, then I don't learn how to fly a shuttle. There're a thousand what-ifs; unlike us, they had the fortune to be able to view events before they happened. We don't have that luxury."

"Don't start making sense now."

She placed her hands up in placation.

"Would have been nice if they gave us some pointers, though, right? A little clue as to what might happen," I lamented.

"Not me. I don't want to know."

"What?" I asked her incredulously. "If you had the ability to know what the future held, you wouldn't want to know?"

"You really think any of us would have left that library if

we knew we were going to encounter six-hundred-pound spiders?"

"What if you knew you were going to meet the love of your life?"

"Serrot?"

"Who else? Ooh!" My eyes grew wide. "You have a thing for Porter?"

"I meant flying, creep." She was smiling.

"Well, since we're the only two up here, maybe you should run me through some of this stuff."

"Really?" she asked excitedly. "No one else seems all that interested in it, but I really think it would help me learn it better if I had to teach it too."

"Then let's go ahead. I don't think you should be the one to have all the fun."

We spent the next six hours going over the controls, what they did or what they could do. It was exciting, but I was also happy when Porter came up and relieved Cedar so we could get some sleep.

CHAPTER NINE

ARRIVAL

According to Porter, we had been traveling for seven days, though it was impossible for me to tell this without a sun rising and setting each day. One moment was as indefinable as any other when it came to telling time, anyway. Cedar was a patient teacher as I attempted to catch up to speed. When Porter would come up, he would make us go over everything we had been learning just to make sure we were doing it right and as a way to reinforce that knowledge. He was reluctant to discuss the Others, even when pressed. All we really knew was they were uncertain allies because the *exterior* threat was larger than the *interior* threat and that preparations were being made for once that balance changed.

"That's a tough way to fight, having to always look over your shoulder at the man you are fighting next to," Lendor said one night when we were talking about it.

"Really, how different is it from inside the Pickets?" I added.

Lendor had to nod at that. "It just seems to me that when you get to this grand of a scale, things would be better, not worse."

"That is always the hope, hardly ever the case," Porter replied.

"Still don't know why we're so important to them," I said. Every time I even hinted along this line of questioning Porter would find something else to do or a way to divert the conversation. This time I held his gaze firm.

He sighed. "Humans are not constructed in the same way that they used to be."

"Constructed humans? Wait.... What's he talking about?" Tallow asked.

"Born you mean? Humans aren't born anymore?" Cedar asked.

"As they have tampered with their DNA, most have lost the ability to reproduce. New beings are engineered in labs. People are created by machines that three-dimensionally combine genetic material, then they have basic memories uploaded into their minds. We call them blanks; they have to spend two years learning how to interact before they are allowed to begin living an actual life."

"I don't know most of what you said but it sounds horrible," Tallow said.

"It is not pleasant; I have seen it. We were able to break into their surveillance systems. They would have everyone believe that everything is still operating as it should be."

"That does little to explain what they want with us," I said.

"I can only speculate; perhaps they want your genetic material to add to their stock, which makes sense. From what we have tested, they have very little variance from one person to the next. Their gene pool is significantly smaller than it should be, which is not necessarily a bad thing when you are simply making clones, but I'm thinking that at some point they are hoping to return to a more traditional existence; there could even be problematic evolutionary occurrences that they cannot ignore. Of course, another likely scenario is they want to offer you up to the Stryvers as a peace offering."

"*What!?*" Cedar asked.

"We...took a human a few years back. He was injured from a battle, would not have survived anyway." He gave this as a justification for their actions; I don't know who he thought we were to judge them. "Humans are changing fundamentally, whether they want to or not. Eight percent of that man's DNA could be traced to Stryver origin. Last month, we obtained samples from another human, a female, and the percentage was close to ten. This represents a significant increase, enough that the race is starting to exhibit not only mental shifts, but their physiology is changing as well. Her entire body was covered in thick, wiry hairs that closely resembled those found on Stryvers. At the pace they are changing, it may only be a matter of two decades before they are indistinguishable from the enemy they have been attempting to purge. Or they could be dying out; it is difficult to know."

"Why now?" Lendor asked.

"They have struck a turning point, one which we believe they will not be able to recover from. At least not without an infusion of new DNA."

"If that's the case, no one on Earth will be safe," Cedar said.

"They can collect DNA without killing the host," Porter added.

"But at what cost? Death is preferable to captivity. We will not be their experiments," Cedar said.

"Speaking as a species that suffered a similar fate, I understand completely."

"We have to get home."

"And you will, but first we need to get to Bristol."

"Then what, Porter?" Lendor started. "If you haven't noticed, we will be no match for them when they return. Are the Genogerians going to help us?"

"They cannot, not yet. There are treaties in place…"

"I know you're not forgetting what they did to the *Ogunquit*." Cedar was seething.

"My father was aboard that ship. I do not believe I will ever forget. We are simply not in a position to challenge their dominance." And with that statement, he left the discussion and went to the front of the ship.

"I don't like this at all," Serrot stated. "We are missing great swaths of information. Each side seems to be giving us small pieces of what they want us to know, whether to protect us from the truth or keep us in the dark, or, in this case for our own safety. I do not know. The only ones I trust are right here and those we left back at earth. We need to get back to them at all costs."

As one, we looked to the front. If this ship had the capability, we would have had a mutiny right there and then. Getting back to Earth in decades was not going to help anyone. We would have to wait until we were in a position to make a difference, and I told the others just that.

"That doesn't make any of this any easier to swallow," Serrot said.

"This is what we'll do. Winter and I will continue to learn how to fly this ship, and even the bigger ones. If they don't take us home right away, we'll find a way to make it happen. In the meantime, there is a vast database that discusses all of the Genogerian weapons. I think we should all become very familiar with how they work and what their effect is. We are not going to win this war with swords, bows, and spears. Sorry, Lendor," Cedar said.

"We are seven against armies, Ceed. How are we going to do this?" Tallow asked.

"I'm sure Michael had those same thoughts once upon a time, and for a while they won," she told him. Cedar got the others to a small console before sitting down next to me. "I know what you're thinking, sis."

"I can't help but think this is all our fault." I was close to breaking down.

"We're supposed to be here, right this very minute. Michael knew it or else we wouldn't be. He could have destroyed the shuttle building at any point. If I don't learn to fly, we never get discovered. It's as simple as that. The Stryvers wipe us out and we're just so much chattel in the annals of human history. We have a greater purpose; we have a chance here to make us who we once were." She paused to think. "And I don't think Earth was forgotten. I think maybe they did not believe it to be inhabited, at least not by people. We were found because of that ship."

"You say that, but what about those men I encountered on the other side of the river? They were talking about other worlds; they must have had a ship."

"Not sure, Winter. They might be people we want to talk to. They could have the ability to hide from those very sensors."

"More people against people?" It hurt my head just thinking about it. I wasn't as convinced as she was, but I knew one thing for sure: chance favors the prepared, and we were going to be just that. Porter had to know what we were up to, but he never said a word. Who knows, maybe he was on the side of not going through diplomatic channels but couldn't say as much out loud. The answers to the hundreds of questions I had took a back seat to learning as much as we could. My home was in trouble from all sides and getting back and leading her defense was all that mattered. The rest would have to wait.

It was five days later when we made contact.

"*Deep Onyx*, this is the *Bristol.* You will respond with the appropriate codes or you will be fired on. You have one minute to reply."

"Good thing we didn't suffer damage to the communications array. Porter, you're going to want to come up here quickly!" Cedar yelled. He must have heard it because he was moving fast.

"You don't know the codes?" Tallow asked Cedar.

"Nope." She seemed a little irked about that. Whether because she didn't know them or because she never even knew there was such a thing, I don't know.

"*Bristol*, this is the *Deep Onyx*, one zero two three five dash one zero three."

There was a delay on the other side. "If you deviate from the coordinates you've been assigned, we will open fire without any prior warning."

"These guys sound like oodles of fun," Cedar said. "Um, Porter, you remember that time not so long ago where you were walking around in space?"

"I will have nightmares about it for the rest of my days."

"Yeah, so sad," Cedar said though she didn't mean the words. "So, if I hadn't worked my tail off finding a way to get you back in the ship, how would we have just convinced your friends out there to not blow us up into tiny bits?"

"It is regrettable that I did not factor that into my decision making."

"Oh well, that's alright…just an oversight on your part. An oversight that could have got us all killed, but, you know, it's alright because you find it regrettable." It was unusual to see so much anger from Cedar. He attempted to apologize a half dozen times; she rebuked every one of them.

We landed on what was called a tarmac—basically a huge, flat, hard-packed ground area. Three ships hovered above us and more than two dozen heavily armed ground troops and seven armored vehicles awaited our debarking. Porter was greeted cautiously as we exited; that turned quickly to suspicion and was rapidly heading to open hostility. We were a movement away from being wet splotches on the surface of this strange planet. Three moons, in varying stages of their cycles, were low on the horizon, and the sun, which was halfway up the sky on the opposite side of the world, was a dark orange, giving us a surreal coloring effect.

"If we weren't about to get shot, I would tell you how good your tan looks," Cedar told Serrot. He didn't seem to care. Can't say I blame him.

"You dare to bring the Others here, Portaliton? Our father would be extremely disappointed."

"Graylon, these are not Others. They are from Earth. In fact, the two women are direct descendants of Michael Talbot."

There wasn't much in the way of oohs and ahhs or gasps, but plenty of the soldiers did look around at their brethren.

"And you have proof of this?" Graylon did not appear to be of a mind to believe his sibling out of hand. When Frost and Ferryn showed themselves, there was a shift, and it was difficult to tell if it was for the better.

"What have you done, Portaliton?" Graylon asked. "These are the beings Commander Breeson is looking for. If we do not turn them over, you will be bringing the might of the Human machine down upon us. We are not prepared for this type of war."

"Prepared or not, Graylon, war is here. Commander Breeson fired upon and destroyed the *Ogunquit* with our father onboard."

"This is not possible!" he roared. "Our ships showed up as the *Iron Sides* was battling a Stryver destroyer and another craft we have yet to identify. We forced them from the area at great cost; that was when we were told that the *Iron Sides* was helping the *Ogunquit*."

"What you were told was a lie. Michael Talbot facilitated the escape of those I have with me. He brought them to the *Ogunquit* in the hopes they would be safe. We barely escaped with our lives."

"When the rest of us were learning the subtleties of war, you were often found with your head in the clouds, Portaliton. It does not bode well that you still drift there. The time for fantasies has passed. Michael Talbot has been dead for centuries."

"Is it so hard to believe that the man who manipulated time to defeat the Progerians and the Stryvers could have found a way to come back one more time? Perhaps I do enjoy speculating about the realms of that which isn't, but have I ever walked in my delusions? Have I ever thrust them forth as truth?"

Graylon was staring at his brother, maybe trying to find some falsehood in his words. "Earth, Rhodeeshians, heirs to the legend, and now the legend himself. I am not sure what to believe."

"Believe me, brother, these are all things I have witnessed myself."

"If what you say is true, what do you propose we do with them? We cannot go to the high council and say Commander Breeson has declared war against us without proof."

"You can check the *Deep Onyx*'s computer; all the proof you will need is housed there."

"Excuse me, er, Graylon. Once you finally realize everything he has said is true, we need to get back to Earth," I said.

Graylon swiveled his massive head my way. "Yes, we will go against our entire alliance to ensure your safe return."

"Good to know," Cedar said sarcastically when she realized that Graylon had not meant his words.

"Earth is no longer a safe haven; Breeson will tear the planet apart looking for you," Porter said.

"All the more reason we need to get back there and defend it," I said.

"Do you possess ships?" Graylon was curious as to what we could bring to the upcoming fight.

"Whatever you give us." Cedar stood defiantly.

Graylon let out a low, growling grumbling sound that soon spread to the rest of the soldiers there. It was laughter. "I would no sooner let you go than I would willingly hand myself over to a Stryver patrol."

"What is going on? Why are we so important? None of this makes sense. The Others have known about Earth, they could have done with it what they would for time untold. Why now? Why us?"

"Portaliton, from which lineage of Michael are they?" Graylon asked, ignoring my entreaty.

"Without tests, it is impossible to know."

"What lineage? What does that mean? How many lineages can one be from?" Lendor asked.

"When Michael and his crew got stuck in time and subsequently found a way out, they inadvertently created another virtually identical series of themselves," Porter stated.

"Wait…what? They made copies of people?" Cedar asked.

"They did not consider themselves copies; they were doubles of the originals."

"Oh, that makes more sense," Tallow replied.

"Any of this making sense to the rest of you?" I asked.

"The descendants of that original crew began to exhibit some special abilities. Most were negligible; some had the ability to lift very small objects, subtle changes to their surroundings, but others were able to manipulate time to a degree. But none more so than the offspring of Michael and Tracy Talbot."

"Because they were both aboard that ship," I said, putting it together. I was thinking on my ability to slow down time when I fought an opponent. I did not know it then, but it was a gift given to me long ago. And it could probably explain how Cedar had learned to fly a ship with the skill she had in such a relatively short time. Was she manipulating time to learn more? "There are others on Earth with ability." I was thinking of Brody and even Haden, who, thankfully, was no longer a problem. And what of the boy that had crossed the country to be with my mother? Certainly, he wasn't alone.

"And what of it? So we have some special abilities. What about that makes us so desired or dangerous?" Cedar asked.

"You admit to powers? Show me," Grayson demanded.

"I'm not a carnival pony. Show him, Winter."

"Gee, thanks. You have hand to hand training weapons?" I asked Graylon.

He grunted something in his native tongue, and within a few moments he had in his hands a ten-foot pole that was thick around as my body. The end was wrapped in some heavy looking material offering some padding. Didn't matter, though; if he hit me with that, there was no chance I could survive the collision.

"A good old-fashioned sparring competition!" Graylon shouted.

"What are you doing, Winter? My brother is a combat teacher; he has never been beaten in training or on the field," Porter said.

"You got something people-sized I could use?" I gulped.

"She wishes a child's truttle!" His soldiers laughed again. Within a few moments, I was handed a five-foot pole that was roughly ten pounds heavier than my sword and difficult to wield. I swung it around a few times to get familiar with it.

"Come!" he yelled. "First, we will have a good meal. I have missed my brother. Afterwards, we will head to the arena."

"Arena?" I asked Porter.

"It is a throwback to the days of the Progerian rule. Warriors of all races were sent into the terraforming arenas where they fought to the death. Now they are mostly used for training. Every once in a while, though, they are used to settle a grievance…even more infrequently as a form of justice."

"Win, this is nuts! These beings are crazy. We need to get out of here," Tallow said as we were being led to a supposed feast, surrounded by a sizable force of Graylon's people, who now seemed downright jovial at the thought of the spectacle that awaited them.

"I'm listening to whatever you might have in mind," I told him.

"Yeah, we'll fight our way out with the giant cotton swab," Cedar said sourly.

The food was surprisingly good, though I could barely identify any of it. Although thinking on it, rat would have been delicious after the two weeks of the protein bars we'd been relegated to eating. Graylon was boisterous as people came up to him and clapped him on the shoulder or wished him luck in the arena. But they were laughing as they said this, like they knew it for the slaughter it was expected to be.

Porter had worked his way over to his brother. It was loud around us, but I could still hear them talking.

"Graylon, I do not presume to ask you how to conduct your battle, but I am imploring that you do not kill the human."

"If she is who she says she is, then she should be all right. If not, we solve a lot of problems by her demise. How can we possibly explain their presence here? It would be better for all involved if they ceased to exist."

"Can you use that thing?" Cedar broke me out of the conversation I was listening in on. "It's pretty heavy," she added, as if I didn't already know.

"Win, this doesn't seem like a good idea." Tallow was looking from me to the much larger Genogerian. I didn't think it was such a good idea either; I couldn't tell him that Graylon wanted to make it look like he had inadvertently killed me.

The Genogerians were having a grand old time as we headed to the arena. Whereas my group was looking a little sullen, which was not doing my psyche any wonders. If I could not prove my worth to Graylon and his troops, it was likely we would find ourselves disposed of in a rather inconvenient manner. And by inconvenient, I mean we'd be dead.

"Bring them to the South entrance," Graylon told Porter. We were escorted by a dozen of Graylon's troops.

Porter appeared to be warring within himself. "Winter, we do not know each other all that well and I have no idea your fighting ability. Challenging Graylon to combat plays into his strengths. There is something I must tell you." He leaned down so I could hear him better. "He does not wish for you to exit this clash; I fear that I have brought you and your friends here to die. That was not my intention; I thought you would be the flashpoint that would ignite the rebellion that has been long overdue. My brother is not willing to see it, yet. And by the time he does, it may be too late for you."

"It is my understanding that Genogerians are very spiritual beings. Has that changed?" Frost asked.

"No, that is very much still a part of our culture."

"Then you must have faith that Winter will have the ability to show your people the correct path," she told him.

"Thank you, Frost. I appreciate your confidence, even if

I'm having a hard time finding it for myself," I told her. "Plus, I didn't challenge him." I felt that I needed to make that clear.

"Graylon already believes he has defeated you; use that against him," Frost said.

"She's right. Much like Haden, his hubris is his undoing," Lendor said. "But if you wish, I will gladly stand in for you."

I was shaking off the doubt. "No, I will not send someone else in to do what I must."

"Come. The rest of you will follow me to the spectator section," one of Graylon's men spoke. I'd like to say he was a host, but he was a guard, making sure we did nothing to disturb what was to happen.

"I love you, Win." Tallow kissed me before he was pushed away and in.

"If he hurts you, just know that every one of us is going to rush him," Cedar said. "You touch me and I'll break your face!" she shouted at the guard getting ready to move her along. Incredibly, he just pointed to where she needed to go instead of ushering her along more forcibly.

I was alone, well, except for Porter and three guards. I should have felt better knowing that they thought it took three of them to watch over me, then I figured that they were probably here to make sure Porter didn't do something stupid.

"I am sorry, Winter," Porter said as a guard opened the door I was supposed to enter. I don't know what I'd been expecting when I walked in, but this wasn't it. I was in a large, round area, a wall more than three times my height circling the entire perimeter. There were filled seats surrounding the arena. The Genogerians were buzzing with excitement for the spectacle they were about to witness. The crowd stood and turned to where Graylon had entered; there was a thunderous applause to greet him. He put his stick-laden arm into the air; this small action stirred them into a frothy frenzy. I found where Tallow, Cedar, and the rest were. They were dwarfed in a sea of the massive bodies and they were the only ones looking in my direction. Cedar was pointing at something; I followed her line of sight. How I'd missed the weapons hung at random intervals on the wall, I'm not sure. Most appeared entirely too heavy to wield, as they were created for much larger beings. But there was a spear and an axe that looked like they might do, if need be.

"Genogerians of the Warring Forty-Seventh! We have a special event for you today!" A voice boomed throughout the entire stadium. "In the challenger, we have a legend in the making! She is a direct descendant of the man and woman who helped to free our kind from the yoke of slavery!" The announcer paused for dramatic effect and the crowd was eating it up. "Winter Talbot!" If the announcer was expecting them to be riled into a raging passion, he'd missed the mark. The place couldn't have been any quieter if it were empty. "Winter Talbot!" he shouted again, maybe thinking they hadn't heard him say it the first time.

He moved on quickly, realizing he wasn't going to get what he was looking for. "In the champion's corner, we have the one and only leader of us all, Graylon!" There was a smattering of claps, but nothing like the rush of sound there had been when he had first entered. I suddenly realized they were stunned by what was going on.

"Roll changes!" Graylon growled, he was not a fan of the sudden change in the atmosphere of the arena.

I stepped back as the blank gray terrain before me began to shimmer and shift. The ground was now a brown, sandstone color and was laced with low, rolling hills throughout, peppered occasionally by stunted plant life. It would have been hard to miss the vicious thorns that protruded from most of it.

"We cannot allow this to happen!" Porter shouted. "Is this how we treat kin to the one that put us on our path to greatness?" The crowd somehow became even quieter, then a small hissing sound began which slowly grew in volume. I didn't know what it was, at first, but when I saw Graylon looking around, I noticed that each time he turned, he looked angrier. The sound was something he didn't like. Like maybe they were booing him.

"You do not understand the danger they bring upon us!" he yelled. "You will thank me for this!" He slammed his stick down and picked up a large spear. Well, any pretense he had of this being an exhibition was over; he was going to drive that thing through me like I might spear a fish. I was terrified like I'd never been before. He was storming toward me and I could do little more than watch him come. I figured I would still be like this as I felt the spear tip break through my sternum.

"Get your ass moving, Winter!" Cedar yelled.

"What she said!" Tallow echoed.

I gave a quick glance over to them, thankful for the figurative slap across the face, because Graylon had spanned half the distance between us while I was mired in my dread. I reached down in my mind, concentrating hard on that part Brody had worked so diligently for me to find. I felt a ripple at the base of my neck travel up and over my skull before exploding outward. I don't know what happened, but Graylon suddenly appeared to be several feet further away than he had been.

"…moving Winter!"

"What she said!" Did they really just say that again? My mind was racing while time itself seemed to be dragging out. Graylon looked like he was traveling through a thick tacky syrup, his face a mask of anger, his spear was dipping down for a better killing strike. All of this I was watching in vivid detail. As if that weren't strange enough, I watched a droplet of sweat fall from my head; it shimmered and pulsed as it fell through the air. I could see a tiny upside-down reflection of the crowd through it. When it hit my hand, the splash happened in what I would consider real time, but the minuscule spray that flew up from the impact were once again much, much slower.

"No way." I was astonished. I knew the time dilation gave me an advantage in that I could see what was happening at a very slow speed, but it had not previously given me any added speed; I wasn't faster than my opponent, I just had the benefit of knowing what they were going to do a fraction of a moment before they did it. That seemed to have changed. I would be like the rabbit running around the mountain. I moved toward him; I was many strides closer; I could see as his eyes grew wide as he attempted to adjust his weapon. I reared back and struck his exposed knee with a resounding thwack. He stumbled from the contact and pain. He was turning to once again face me, but I had already circled around and leveled a crippling blow to the back of the leg I had hit before. My stick broke in half from the force and he fell to that knee.

The noises coming from the crowd were drawn out; they sounded low and menacing. I couldn't tell if they were cheers or jeers, and ultimately, I didn't care. Graylon had made this a life or death struggle, he'd brought this on, and I was going to take that seriously. I went to the wall to rearm. I seriously considered taking a large metallic ball with spikes protruding from it. My first concern was whether I could even lift it; secondly, would I be able to wield it? A distant third was, did I want to kill Graylon? Not only did he threaten my life, but the lives of those I cared for. *Fair is fair*, is what I would have said as I stood over his body, the large ball forever embedded in his skull. In the end, I took the axe. I would imagine for the Genogerians it was used as a hand axe; for me, it was a two-handed weapon, and even then it was exceedingly top heavy. I stayed a considerable distance away from Graylon as I removed myself from whatever phenomenon I had created. The crowd had quieted—except for Cedar. She was jumping up and down and cheering like a mad woman.

"Do you yield?" I asked my opponent. His knee was still resting on the ground. His mouth was open and his eyes half-lidded in pain. He begrudgingly stood. He said not a word.

"I will not ask again," I told him. He motioned to me with his free hand to come closer. "Fine, have it your way." He braced as I moved. I stopped once again, reaching inside my mind for the back of my neck where it seemed this power resided. I felt the small vibration as I initiated the sensation.

When I looked up, I realized how close I had come to losing my life. Graylon had thrown his spear with enough force that, had it connected with me, I would have flown through the air and been pinned into the wall by it. It had come no more than five feet from my midsection before rewinding twenty feet. I stepped to the side; at first, I was going to let the projectile harmlessly pass me by; instead, I swung with my axe, shattering the shaft into pieces. The front end spun into the air and landed tip first into the ground. Graylon's features changed from the satisfaction of knowing he had delivered a killing blow, to the astonishment that he had somehow missed. And soon he would be once again registering a blistering pain.

"That is not possible!" he roared. "What sorcery is this? My spear traveled backward!"

I was confused; hadn't I somehow rewound time? If that was the case, did not his memories go back as well? Not only was he angry he had not struck, but now he might realize he never could. I was shaken; some by how closely I had come to carelessly yielding my life, and some from the fact that he had witnessed it. Then, instead of falling to his knees and begging for mercy, he grimaced and spun, heading to the nearest wall and the fearful metal ball weapon I had forgone. If anyone still harbored any ideas that this was merely an exercise, they had been nullified the moment Graylon had attempted to impale me at the end of his tree-like spear.

It appeared to all involved, meaning me, that the only way I was going to be able to end this was with his death, and no part of me thought that would give us a free ride out of here. I took a step toward him, unsure what I was going to do when I got there. That was before I was hit with a crippling dizzy spell. The arena spun circles around me, though I wasn't moving. I was certain my eyes were swimming spirals inside my skull. My stomach cramped up and I fell over; I was on all fours, attempting to regain some sense of equilibrium. The crowd was quiet as Cedar's voice rang out.

"Get up!" she urged. "No time!"

"Win, I'm coming!" Tallow shouted out.

It took everything I had to concentrate enough to raise one hand up in a stopping motion. He would be killed before he ever landed a foot on this false terrain. I turned my head enough that I could see Graylon's massive legs making their way to me. I took a macabre sense of satisfaction in the fact that he was dragging the injured leg. Not sure where that was going to get me when I was melded to the ground with a metal spike through my head, though. I never once heard him ask if I yielded. Lesson learned. When you have the chance to finish a brutish opponent, do so, because they will not hesitate. All I wanted to do was curl into a ball and die. If I stayed like this, I was going to get half my wish. I swayed like tall grass in a field as I pushed up and onto my knees. It bought me a few seconds as Graylon assessed how much of a threat I was. If he got close enough, I'm sure I could have bitten hard on his ankles.

I could see Cedar, Tallow and the rest leaning up against the wall, a ring of guards around them. Their expressions were panicked. From their perspective, they had no idea why I was down on the ground. It must have looked like I was wounded. And I was; just not by my opponent. I stood up with some effort, somehow still holding on to the axe. I no longer looked like tall grass in a breeze as I got onto my feet. Now I was a tree trying to dig its roots deeper into the ground as savage, gale force winds threatened to rip me free from my moorings. Even thinking of taking a step sent my head into a mind-numbing vertigo. Graylon could sense I was struggling, but he was not so comfortable as to take me head on. He was circling to the side and I was doing all I could to shuffle my feet enough to always keep him in front. Really, if he had just rushed me, this would have been over long ago, and I might have actually welcomed it. Graylon motioned for me to attack him. I laughed. It was absurd.

"Your turn," I told him, unsure why I was goading the giant.

He snorted out a great gust from his nose and muzzle. If

he was looking to intimidate me, he was doing an admirable job. Slowly, I was coming back into my own, and Graylon's opportunity was diminishing, but I couldn't let him see that. My next attack would likely be my last, and that meant the same thing for my enemy.

"Do you yield?" I asked one more time, not because I expected his answer to be any different, but it gave me a few more seconds.

"You look as if I were to blow on you too hard you would fall over," he snorted.

"Yet, you do not attack." That quieted him quickly.

He raised the weapon up and over his head; seems I'd pushed him enough. His left leg staggered and locked as he came closer, but it was not going to be enough to stop him. He began his arc, starting the swing of the enormous weapon. I stumbled backward as it whooshed by me. The momentum moved him a few steps to my right; I could hear him grunting as he had to use his injured left leg to halt the progress and bring it back around. He finally let it fall from his hands when the task became too burdensome. "Arrrh!" he yelled out as he spun-hopped around.

This was my chance; I would not let it go again. I got everything I had left in me and raised that axe above my head. He was just turning back to me when I swung; it was high over my head when it crashed into the left side of his skull. His eyeball exploded outward in a thick, viscous bulb. As he was falling over, I fell with him; his arms had come up to fend me off but did not seem to be working of their own volition. His entire body was twitching with violent spasms; they were his death throes as we collided to the ground. I rolled off to the side and before I could even consciously think upon it, the shiver struck out from me once again, with the rewind. Graylon's heavy weapon had, for a second time, thudded to the ground. I fell over; my entire body an electrical storm of bright pain flaring along the edges of my mind. I could not see. I could not think. Moving wasn't even on the list of possibilities.

I thought I was dead, but how horrible would death be if it was a neverending all-encompassing pain-fueled ordeal? A killing blow repeating endlessly, a fall...pain, repeat. Life, even with all its aches and heartaches, would be a world better, but what chance did I have? I was on the ground, writhing in agony. As far as I knew, Graylon was rearing up to drive me into the dirt now that I'd given him a second chance, again. Between the static-laced micro-bursts floating through my field of vision, I could see Graylon's legs as he straddled my body.

"I yield," he stated as he reached a hand down to help me up. My brain wasn't firing well enough that I even knew what was happening. I remember a ride in his cable-like arms and then sweet blackness as, I believe, I passed out.

CHAPTER TEN

NEW FRIENDS

My eyes opened slowly. I thought something was wrong with my vision, as I could not focus. Seemed about right that I had somehow made my brain explode, because that was sure how it felt. Come to find out it was an over-zealous Tallow hovering less than three inches from my face.

"What happened?" His breath washed over me.

"Give her air, you oaf." Cedar pushed Tallow away and somehow got even closer than he had. "Yeah, what happened? You alright?"

"Where am I?" I gently pushed Cedar away.

"Genogerian meddie facility. Their beds are huge; we can almost all fit on it!" Cedar said, bouncing up and down.

"I want to make it abundantly clear, Winter, I did not lie down on the bed with you," Lendor said in all seriousness. I smiled at his modesty.

"Some strange things happened on that arena floor," Frost said. "I am unsure as to what I witnessed, or if I even did so."

"Yeah, she keeps saying time was running backward, but the rest of us didn't see anything like that." Cedar was once again coming in close, looking at my eyes.

"What are you doing?" I asked.

"Trying to see if you had a stroke," she replied.

I didn't know what that was and so I couldn't say if I had or hadn't. I let her go about her business, though I scooted up so I was in more of a sitting position. I had expected the swimming swirling sensation to return and was thankful when it had not.

"Why did Graylon not kill you?" Serrot asked.

"Are you that big of a dummy?" Cedar smacked his shoulder.

"I mean," he backpedaled, "obviously I'm glad he didn't, but you were on the ground. He didn't have to do much more than step on you."

"Seriously, Serrot? This is my sister you're talking about."

"I'm just saying! We all saw it…one second Graylon is going all beast-mode trying to kill her, the next he's cradling her in his arms declaring her the victor. Does any part of that make sense to you?"

"Does it need to? She's alive and that's all that matters," Cedar said in no uncertain terms, she even folded her arms across her chest as if to reiterate her point.

"What did you see?" I croaked out; Tallow handed me a large container of water.

"Sorry, they don't have anything people-sized," he said as he helped me tilt the large carafe up to my lips.

"It was really weird, Win. There was like this shimmering wave, like you see sometimes off in the distance on a hot day. Then there was the smashed spear, which no way you should have been able to dodge, much less shatter—but I'm thankful for that," he added quickly before Cedar could wind up and deliver a punch to him as well. "Then the part at the end…he dropped the mace and went over to pick you up. The shimmer happened again right before that. Frost kept saying something about time changing, but if it did, no one else saw it and nothing happened to any of us."

"Is that what happened?" Cedar asked.

"I really don't know what happened; it wasn't anything I planned on. I was looking for the time dilation that Brody had worked on with me and it felt like it broke…or I guess broke through."

"What's that mean?" Tallow asked as I furrowed my

eyebrows trying to figure out just that.

"All boys can't be this thick, can they?" Cedar asked of no one. "She's trying to figure it out too, you head bone. Wait, no, that's not it." She looked up as if she were trying to remember something. "Bonehead. Yeah, bonehead."

"Brounds vright," I said as Tallow tried to drown me with the water. I had to push it and him away.

"Sorry." He smiled mischievously as he saw the front of me was soaked and that was maybe what he had been attempting to do all along.

"I did make time go backward. The first time I just thought it was a mistake of perspective on my part. Graylon had been coming across the arena and then just suddenly he was further back than I expected. Then I attacked his legs and it happened again. Then I killed him. I buried that axe in his head; we fell over. Then the pain…it was like my brain was on fire."

"Interesting," Frost said. "The Genogerian remembered his death?"

"I guess," I said.

"No wonder he yielded." Lendor was looking me over.

I was not at all happy with the amount of scrutiny I was receiving.

"None of this makes sense." Serrot was pacing the room.

"I think perhaps it does," Frost interjected. "I think it is safe to say which set of descendants you two are from."

That struck me; the story of my family was confusing, no doubt about it, and it also contained a separate tree which in itself was wholly unique. Knowing which tree we belonged to meant more than I could put into words.

"Whoa…you think I have powers too?" Cedar was looking at her hands as if she more than half expected lightning to issue forth from them. "MaryBeth from *Ten Gables and the Stablehand* was able to heal with her touch. Wouldn't that be something?" She was reaching toward me.

"Get away from me with those! Knowing you, if you touch me I'll suddenly have a love for all things plaid." We were laughing and smiling, having come through another life or death situation.

"What's the matter?" Cedar asked as my face quickly lost its smile and a serious expression took over. She saw what I was looking at; Graylon was standing in the doorway. I felt a pang of regret for what I had done to him, but also a sense of pride at the large bandage on his leg.

"May we have a moment?" he asked those around me.

"No," Cedar told him. "You tried to kill my sister. There is no way I'm leaving you in here alone."

Serrot, Lendor and Tallow stood in a protective line. Without weapons, I was not sure what the three of them could do, even though each was an accomplished fighter. It was that Graylon was orders of magnitude stronger and larger, faster even. If he wanted us dead, odds were highly in his favor he could accomplish that, with or without the brace on his leg.

"My intentions are honorable." I could see him grimace; he was in pain. Good, because so was I.

"Your intentions are honorable? What are you planning on doing, taking her on a date?" Cedar appeared to be getting more and more worked up. She hopped off my bed and was moving toward the Genogerian. She shouldered past an astonished Lendor. She hardly reached Graylon's midsection, yet she was all fury as she looked up at him, her arm outstretched and a finger coming close to the bottom of his jaw.

"The sister," Graylon said. I would swear there was a note of fear in his voice and he turned his head slightly as if he was making sure he had an exit, in the event he needed to make a quick getaway.

"It's all right, Cedar, let him in," I told her. I sat up more, trying to make myself look as imposing as possible.

"You're lucky she's so tender-hearted. I would have left you to bleed out on that arena floor, might have even had a snack while I waited." Cedar did not move but rather made the much larger beast find a way around her and he did and also made sure to not touch her in any way as he passed. Graylon stood over my bed; he finally sat but still, I had to crane my neck to look at him. He turned to look at my honor guard.

"I'll be fine. Can you guys maybe find some food? I'm suddenly starving."

"Remember what I said about the snacks." Cedar was again pointing at Graylon's head before she walked out with the others in tow.

"She is a fierce little creature," Graylon said as he watched her go.

"You have no idea," I said nothing more as I was curious as to why he was here. He sat in silence; he seemed reluctant or hesitant to talk about the nature of his visit.

Finally, after long minutes, he appeared to have gathered the nerve and the words he was looking for. "It is no easy feat to die." Again, he was quiet. I did not interrupt. "For a moment there was an all-encompassing blackness, then I was traveling. I had the sensation it was with great speed. Perhaps I saw a pinpoint of light far off in the distance, I do not know." His head was looking toward me, though his gaze was far off, perhaps as far as another realm. "Then I remember being wrenched back into the world. It was very much like being born again; even had all the pain that goes along with it, and this time, unfortunately, I remembered the process."

Did I want to tell him I was sorry? Because, really, I wasn't; it had been me or him and I'd chosen me.

"I do not know what you know of Michael Talbot's history." He stared off into the distance. "He and Drababan were prisoners aboard a Progerian vessel. Drababan was an arena champion with unrivaled wins and Michael was crowned the Earth champion through a series of contests he was forced to fight."

"Forced to fight?"

"It is a long story and one better suited for another time. They were to the death, these contests. For Michael's next and last fight, he was pitted against Drababan. Our champion was expected to kill Michael handily and would have, had not the Earthlings intervened. Even Drababan himself experienced a change of heart, thus securing Michael's escape."

"Why are you telling me this, Graylon?" I was tired, sore and angry. Angry I was still here.

"I do not believe much in chance, of random, convoluted events without meaning. That you are here is something much bigger. Fate has brought us together."

I chortled, but it was issued with no mirth. "Fate brought us together? Like lovers from Cedar's books? I don't think so."

His head tilted slightly. He wasn't sure what I was talking about. Was I? "Portaliton has told me everything that has transpired. Could chance possibly have brought you from your tiny prison on a forgotten world, light-years away, right to me? How many 'random' events must have occurred for that to happen?"

"Are you going to let us go?" That was all I cared about, all I wanted to know.

"No, I cannot."

I was getting up, ready to show him round two.

"Sit back, please. I do not profess to be the warrior that Drababan was, but the rest of it? The similarities? They cannot be ignored. I do not and cannot expect you to trust me yet, but I will do all in my power to earn that from you, to fight alongside you, much as my ancestor did with yours."

"What are you saying?" I asked cautiously.

"For far too long we have sat upon this rock waiting for the lightning strike that is this revolution to ignite us, to…unite us. And I wholly believe, Winter, that the spark is you, and I vow my allegiance and that of the Warring 47th to you."

"What?"

"Aren't you listening, goofball?" Cedar was peeking around the door. "We're going home and we're going to kick everyone's ass!"

CHAPTER ELEVEN

BRISTOL

Bristol was a beehive of activity as Genogerians gathered supplies, packed ships, and continued to train. The purpose we now shared changed their demeanor. They were excited for what the future entailed. I wasn't of the same enthusiasm. Yes, I was very much looking forward to getting back to Earth, to making sure my friends were all right, to taking revenge upon Breeson and the *Iron Sides* for what they had done. I was prepared to strike fear into the hearts of the Stryvers and into our new, unknown enemy, if they had one.

"Two weeks? How can it take that long?" I was out of bed the very next morning and ready to leave.

"We are moving an entire base, Winter, and Graylon is attempting to gather more allies to the cause," Porter informed me.

Cedar was less impatient than I, but only because she'd been promised all the flight time she could manage in the time allotted. For good or bad, they did not possess flight simulators, so she was required to go off-world. I went with her mostly to learn to fly, as she had, but also because to sit there and wait was driving me crazy. The first week we had an instructor, then without warning, and seemingly without jealousy, came the moment that Sevtral said we had outdistanced her skill and that she would only be a detriment to our continued growth. We were allowed to fly solo, as it were. I stayed with Cedar another three days; she was a ferocious learner and a patient teacher. I did not at any time think I could master it with the ease she had, but I had a firm grasp of how to control the war machine. I still preferred battle on the ground, but that was highly unlikely. However, this war was won, it was going to be in space, and I was going to do all I needed to ensure we came out victorious.

"We need call signs." Cedar was doing spins through space. I was getting nauseous watching her.

"We've been out here for fifteen hours; aren't you ready to go back? I'm hungry, sis," I told her.

"I told you to bring some food up here."

"We are in single-seater fighters; I'm not bringing food and water. What happens when…" I left it at that.

"Hate to get into the grubby details, sis, but this suit takes care of that."

"NO! Absolutely not!"

"Prude." She was laughing. "That's it! I have your call sign. I shall call you Prudence!"

"You do that, and I'll call you the Soiler!"

"You wouldn't dare!"

"What's the matter? Don't you think Serrot would like that?"

"Fine, fine…we'll work on something else."

"Seriously though, when are we going back?"

"Are you whining? Tell you what, we'll have a dog fight. You beat me, we go back. You don't, then you can get more familiar with your suit."

"I hate you," I growled, she laughed. The weapons had been disabled for our exercises, but the firing and the radar systems still worked, so it was essentially the same except for the explosions, the screaming, burning and/or freezing in space. Other than that, just the same. Cedar was off to my right and slightly ahead. "Fine, we'll do it your way," I told her as I gripped my joystick and turned toward her.

"I see how it's going to be. Nice warning, by the way." She dipped her ship down at a severe angle and so quickly she was out of my field of view in the beat of my heart. I started twisting and craning my head to catch sight of her.

"You have to trust the radar systems. Stop 'looking' for me."

"How do you know what I'm doing?" I was still looking through my canopy.

"I can hear your suit rustling around." Two seconds later, my radar warned me that I had been painted with a weapons system. "Boom," she said just as an alarm chirped in my cabin. "I think that's a record. I love you, sis, but there are going to be times when we are out for even more extended periods of time, and the enemy is not going to be firing bolts of light. You can't take any of this lightly."

"Cedar, you're a natural-born pilot. Maybe the best to ever sit in a cockpit, according to Sevtral. How can I possibly beat you? Oh god, I can't even stand the sound of my whining. Sorry. Let's go again."

"That's my sister!" She fired again. "Boom." The alarm let me know once again I had been scattered all over the cosmos. I pushed the joystick down as far as it would go; Cedar gave me a second or two before she followed. "Pull hard left, Win! Don't stay too long in any one direction."

My system had alerted me that I was being lit up again, but it was brief as I moved away from her firing trajectory. "Locking on with missiles."

"What do I do now?" I knew those would follow me no matter what direction I turned.

"Deploy counter measures."

I did as she told me.

"Weapons away," she informed me.

There were a number of ways to foil missiles; now I just had to hope I was doing it right. I shut my engines down as I simultaneously sent bright flares rocketing from my tail section.

"Good one, but these aren't heat seeking; they're intruders."

The moment she'd lit me up, the weapons had locked onto

this vessel and would not stop until they ran out of fuel or hit their preordained destination. I was looking on the panel for my next step when I got the warning that I'd once again been reduced to parts. After another six hours, I could barely keep my head up. Cedar relented and we went back to the base. I considered it a minor victory that for the briefest of moments, I had made her screen light up in warning. Although, in fairness, I think she had fallen asleep.

Every day we would head back up into the sky. Something which I had initially been doing to while away time began to seep into my blood. While I ate, drank, and slept, I thought about going back into the sky. My skill was growing by leaps and bounds; the problem was so was Cedar's. I had mistakenly thought she was at the ceiling of ability and all I needed to do was catch her there; how wrong I had been. Her training missions with me evolved into training missions for all the pilots who would watch it back on base. They would exclaim their praise for all she had done right while picking apart everything I'd done wrong. My ego should have suffered a great bruising, but I'd risen above that. Drive, the ambition to become better, to match my sister—it was all-consuming. And two days before we were to head out, I got her. I shouldn't have been so excited I'd "killed" my sister, but after one hundred and seventy-two defeats, I felt justified.

Took the final day off. I wanted to spend time with Tallow, Serrot, Lendor, Frost and Ferryn. I had a feeling that very soon, a time would come when all of us meeting together would become a rarity, if not an outright impossibility, and I wanted to leave that thought right where I left it. Most of what needed to be done was done, and now the rest of the Genogerians on base were waiting, as were we. An expectant relaxation, if such a thing exists.

It was Graylon that disturbed our peace. He came into the large room and tossed a piece of equipment against the wall hard enough to shatter it. Whatever it was, it was safe to say it was never going to work again.

"Cowards!" he yelled. Porter was right behind him, doing his best to calm his brother down; it wasn't going so well. Every time he laid a hand on the other, it was shrugged off. "Fellow warriors!" Graylon now stood in the center of the room, all eyes upon him as others began to stream in to see what had upset their leader. "We have received word from the Progerian High Council. It should come as no surprise to anyone here that they will not join us in our fight, that there is not enough proof that the humans attacked and destroyed the *Ogunquit*, even after I showed them the footage. It seems that even after all these years, we have yet to achieve equality in their eyes, though they will say otherwise. It was unwise of me to expect more from them. They are a scourge to both our proud species!" He nodded to our table.

There was an abundance of hisses and snarling sounds signifying their displeasure at what they'd heard. There was more to say; Graylon was waiting for the din to die down.

"What I did not expect, what none of us could, was that the Genogerians have forbidden us from this crusade. Have ordered me to stand down. They are sending two battalions here to ensure we do nothing that could jeopardize peace." He was taking great strides across the room as he allowed the troops to intake the new information. "I want you to think about that. The Genogerian High Council has told me that we cannot avenge the unjustified and savage attack upon my father, upon your kin, upon our race!"

The looks of shock were turning to fury.

"It is unlikely that where we go, we will return. The moment you became part of the Fighting 47th, you forfeited your life for the greater good of all Genogerians, no matter what some of them may think!"

"One heart, one mind, one life to give, yet many to take!!" The collective had stood to repeat the mantra they lived by. I was swept up in the moment of it, and by the third go around, I had joined my voice with theirs. I was not alone; the rest of the table had as well, Tallow even getting atop it.

It was long moments before it quieted in the great hall. Graylon had not attempted to silence them; he merely waited patiently as all eyes fixed on him. "I thought perhaps today we would rest and celebrate our lives and the victories we are sure to garner, but that is not to be. Even as I speak, their battalions are racing here. I am disgusted at their gutlessness, but I have no desire to war with our own. We will be leaving in an hour." With that, he turned. The room thundered at his departure.

"These Genogerians are fearsome creatures, but I fear that they are making a tactical mistake." Serrot made sure to say it quietly enough as to not be overheard.

"Even a thorn can take down a lion," Frost said.

I looked to her, there was a glint in her eyes.

"Cedar, Winter, you have the best understanding of the great war vessels these Genos have; how do they compare?" Lendor asked.

I nodded to Cedar. Whereas I was doing my best just to pilot, she had, again, gone several steps ahead and was learning about nearly every flying vessel known. She told me that she wanted to be prepared in any eventuality. I had been giving her a hard time when I asked when she thought we might have the chance to fly a starship, and she had immediately replied with: "When did you think you'd be flying a Genogerian fighter?" My mouth closed faster than it had a right to.

"It won't be easy." She hesitated. "The *Iron Sides* is considered a battleship, useful for battles in space, in planetary air, or in support of ground incursions. The armor, the defense mechanisms, the offensive capabilities can hardly be rivaled. The Genogerians, by comparison, have two newer destroyers and an older generation starship. The starship, in her day, would rival just about anything any enemy could throw against it; that's not quite the case anymore, though her capabilities cannot be ignored by us or by those she finds herself going up against. The destroyers are (now this is compared to the *Iron Sides*) much lighter. They are much nimbler when gravitational pulls are a factor."

Tallow sheepishly began to raise his hand.

"If we find ourselves close to a large planetary boundary or perhaps within an atmosphere, the destroyers will have more maneuverability than the battleship, but Breeson is no fool. He will know this as well, and never allow that advantage to be used against him."

"The fighters though, we have bunches of those." Tallow seemed pleased he had found what he thought was our saving grace.

"You want to tell him?" Cedar asked me.

"There's four hundred and ninety-seven fighters here," I started.

Tallow whistled at the magnitude.

"And the *Iron Sides* alone has over a thousand."

Tallow gulped.

"And it is highly unlikely she will be alone in this war, as we have declared it upon nearly everything else out there," Cedar added helpfully.

"I liked our chances more when Graylon was speaking." Tallow looked dejected.

"Do not fret," Lendor said as he placed a hand upon Tallow's shoulder. "You are mighty Dystancians. You have defeated Klondikes and Hillians, befriended Brutons and Comanchokees; all is not lost…until it is."

"That mostly makes sense," Tallow told him.

Porter was threading his way through the throng that was moving quickly for the exits. The imminent departure had most wanting to finalize their preparations.

"How are your spirits?" he asked. It was easy to see he was truly concerned and not just making conversation.

"We're ready," Cedar spoke for the group, even smacking Tallow's shoulder so he would look up from the floor.

"We will be on the *Traverse*."

I looked over to Cedar as Porter spoke the words; of the three ships, this was the one she said was the most vulnerable.

"That is the safest place," Porter assured us. "The ship will be behind our vanguard."

"We won't be in the thick of it?" Cedar asked, clearly perturbed.

Porter looked baffled for a moment. "Until we know 'what the thick of it' looks like, that is the wisest decision. Once the high council realizes who we have aboard the ship, it is likely they will change their minds about placing ships in the sky. In the meantime, it is imperative that you stay alive to make sure that becomes a reality."

"So now what, we're just props? Something to be displayed? Something to incite a revolution?" Cedar was full-on angry.

"Exactly. I am glad that you comprehend the intention behind this," Porter replied.

"I don't think you're comprehending it, Porter. She's not on board with this," Serrot said. "It might be better for you to retreat before she goes off."

"I do not understand."

"And you don't need to. I'm helping you here." Serrot urged the Geno to leave.

"There's something I don't understand." I was thinking. "Graylon is great at inciting his unit, but he never said where we're going."

"Not Earth?" Tallow asked.

"No." Now I had Cedar thinking. "That wouldn't make sense. There's nobody there yet to fight."

"He's going to strike a target that forces the Genogerians," Lendor said.

"We're listening," Tallow said.

"He destroys something the Others have…a small base or maybe a ship. No matter how much the Genogerian High Council says they had nothing to do with it, the Others won't believe them. They'll be forced to jump in to defend themselves from retaliation.

"Forcing allies? I don't like it," I said.

“There may not be another way,” Cedar said. “And honestly, I don’t care what it takes to put all of our enemies to rest. I’m going to grab my things.” And with that, she headed out; we quickly followed.

CHAPTER TWELVE

THE TRAVERSE

We hadn't been on the *Traverse* for more than an hour when the Imminent Arrival warning sounded; this was immediately followed by the message to prepare for a buckle.

Cedar was pouring through manuals, as she always did while we were in the buckle, but the moment we pulled free from the strange mode of travel, she said she was going to seek Porter and was out the door. I went with her. He ended up being on the bridge; we got a few glances as we walked in, but the crew quickly got back to what they were doing and paid us no more attention. Porter was manning a station off to the side. A Genogerian I'd not seen before sat upon the commander's chair.

"Porter, where are the destroyers?" Cedar asked.

"They are not here," was his terse reply.

"I can see that; where are they?"

"You two are allowed on my bridge, but disturbing my personnel while you are here is not allowed," the commander said.

"Then, I'll ask you." Cedar approached him. I was astonished with my sister; she had absolutely no fear. "Where are the *Lyman* and the *Arundel*?" she asked, referring to the destroyers.

"That is no concern of yours."

"Wrong answer," I mumbled.

"This war is our war, too. What happens to you, happens to us as well. I think we have as much right to know what is going as anyone."

He regarded her for a moment. I thought he was going to motion for some guards to remove her from the bridge and have her detained. Instead, he surprised me.

"I am Commander Kabon, and you are correct. Porter, send the feed to the viewing screen."

It only took a moment until we saw Graylon's ship, the *Arundel*, engaged in battle. They were above a world that did not look familiar. Cedar told me that the ship under fire was the Others' version of a frigate. The *Arundel* must have caught it off-guard as the human ship was ablaze in a half-dozen locations, every opening venting material out into open space. Fighters buzzed all around the larger ship. The view switched to the *Lyman's* feed as the destroyer came in and started sweeping the much smaller ships away like a person will a mosquito. I swallowed loudly with how easily the ship I had just learned how to fly was being defeated.

"Something's wrong," I said. Cedar was watching the screen. Moving closer to it, in fact.

"You are watching the vastly superior Genogerian forces destroy the Others," the commander said triumphantly.

"Yeah, sure, whatever you say," Cedar dismissed him. "Get them out of there." There was no alarm in her voice, just conviction.

"Without finishing the job? Do you Humans not have the stomach for this? Perhaps you should go back to your room."

"Don't *ever* speak to me like that. I have no problem with dispatching an enemy that stands between me and my freedom or threatens my family and friends, but something there isn't right. Get them out now—I'm telling you, it's a trap."

She cut off the commander before he could speak.

"Before you start with the whole propaganda about how great you are, that ship, those fighters, they're ancient, and I don't think they're manned."

"Why would they do that?" Levant asked.

"To set a trap. Get them out of there!" Now there was a

rising sense of dread in her voice as she figured the jaws of the trap were poised to spring.

"Graylon will not do it."

"Do you outrank him?" she asked.

"It is not quite as rigid in the Genogerian forces as in the Human ranks," Porter informed us.

"Lie," I said. "Tell him you have spotted three battleships coming from the other side of the planet. He will surely not stand to fight a battle he cannot win."

Kabon had stood. He looked to the screen, really studied it, then at Cedar and me. "Tell them, Porter, tell them that three Human battle-class ships are even now approaching and that they must leave."

Porter did as he was ordered.

"Commander." Graylon showed on the screen. "My scans show no such approach."

"I have known you for more years than scars I have on my body," Kabon said.

Graylon bowed his head to this saying, "And I you."

"Leave the area immediately, Graylon."

Graylon tensed but again nodded. The next few seconds were chaotic. We were watching the feed from the *Lyman*, the trailing ship. The *Arundel* had moved quickly and in the blink of an eye with its buckle drive spun up, it winked out of the picture just as a green column of light nearly as large as the ship itself flowed up from the planet's surface. Fingers of splintered light shot off the main bolt, destroying what remained of the fighters and the frigate. There were none of us aboard the *Traverse* that didn't believe that beam would have utterly destroyed the *Arundel*; what would have been left would have fit in the bowl I'd used for my last meal. The feed was lost as the *Lyman* wisely joined her sister ship before the weapon could be aimed at her.

It wasn't long before Graylon's stern face showed up on the same view screen. He would have been hard-pressed to miss the looks of astonishment on our faces, yet he pressed with his own anger.

"I was destroying them, Commander! They were no match for my might and still I show no signs of the battleships you used as an excuse to warn me off. Have you suddenly gone soft for our enemy? Do you wish to back away from this challenge? To sit safely with the high council upon their thrones?"

Kabon growled.

Porter quickly interjected. "Graylon, Winter and Cedar just saved your life and those of your crew."

"*Winter and Cedar?* I was removed from attacking Humans by Humans? Does that not seem suspicious?"

Porter rolled the recording of the mysterious green energy beam.

Graylon watched it four more times before looking at us. "My apologies." And then he ended the communication.

"At least he was grateful," Cedar said. She had a book in one hand and lunch in the other. "Hope that's not a new ship weapon." She then proceeded to take a big bite of food. All eyes turned to her as she chewed thoroughly and deliberately. "Sorry," was muffled around the food in her mouth. "I'm hungry," she said when she'd swallowed more. "What? Why is everyone looking at me?"

"Why are you concerned about the weapon being mounted on a ship?" Kabon asked.

"Seriously? Weren't you guys watching the same thing I was?"

"Maybe just explain it," I prompted.

Her widened mouth hovered over her food as she prepared to eat more. "Will you let me eat in peace if I do?" I nodded.

"When whatever that was, it blew up from the surface in a straight column, headed right for the *Arundel*, then, when it seemed to detect that there were other targets in the area, smaller beams fractured from the main part and sought out those new targets. Everything that was out there in the general area of that thing was obliterated. That, more than anything, proves it was a trap." She seemed content with her answer as she once again took a bite bigger than she should have been able to.

She held a hand up, chewed for a few moments. "Srop rooking at me," she managed to say. "Ohmigod. I'm never going to be able to eat in peace! Winter noticed it first…you tell them."

"Umm." I wasn't quite sure how to start. Can't say I was overly thrilled with the attention I was receiving. "It was what the fighters were doing, or not doing, I guess, that made me suspicious. They weren't dodging or evading; they seemed to be flying on autopilot in preprogrammed sequences. Nobody flying would do what they were, and that was my first thought: that they weren't being flown by people. And if that was the case, why weren't they? Why sacrifice so much machinery?"

"To set a trap." Kabon was thinking on her words.

"To set a trap," I echoed.

"A few moments later and this rebellion would have been crippled. We would have lost a ship we can ill-afford to and a leader of Genogerians; that would have set us back considerably."

It had been seven days since Graylon's attack. We weren't doing anything. Okay, that's not right. Lendor, Serrot, Tallow, Cedar and I were constantly doing weapons training. The ship was equipped with a rifle range, and at times we even went through our hand to hand combat skills, though how this might work on a Stryver, I wasn't confident. When we weren't doing that, Cedar and I were out in the fighters, training, or having the Geno technicians retrofit the fighters so they were more our size and we could stop feeling like small children using adult tools. Other than that, nothing. The three ships were floating out in space, not going anywhere, and as far as I knew, not waiting for anybody.

"What are we doing here?" I was staring up at the ceiling, lying on the oversized bed in the room I'd been assigned. Cedar, even though she also had her own room, spent the majority of her free time with me. She was currently sitting on the bed with her back against the wall, her nose buried in a book.

"Shhh. Marigold is spying on her sister Francesca."

"Why is she spying?" I really didn't want to know, but I was bored, and bothering her seemed about the only fun thing to do at the moment.

She let the book drop to look at me. "You really want to know?"

"Sure."

"That's not very definitive."

"I'm on 'pins and needles,' as you say."

"Fine. Marigold is in love with Edward and Francesca knows it. Francesca, being the older sister and more beautiful, according to those around her, has decided she wishes to crush her sister's spirit."

"Why ever would she want to do that?" I had flopped over, so I was on my stomach, propping my head up with my arms. I even batted my eyes for effect.

"See, you sound sincere enough, but when you say it like that, I'm not so sure."

"Tell me. I'll be good."

"Secretly, Francesca knows how much more beautiful Marigold is, both on the inside and the outside, so she wishes to do everything in her power to ruin her."

"That's horrible! How could she be so cruel to her sister?"

"She is childish and insecure and knows no better ways to cope with her world. I believe her to be much like you."

I was taken aback for a moment before I reached to my

side, grabbed a pillow, and smacked her on the side of the head.

"That's what I'm saying!" She wrenched the pillow from my hands and proceeded to beat me into submission. I had my hands outstretched and was begging for mercy when Porter strode in.

"I rang the bell but no one answered. Is this a bad time? Do you wish me to come back later?"

I ran to him and hid behind his back. "Save me, Porter! She's a savage!"

"Oh, that's real grown-up of you. Go and hide behind the first giant being you come across. So like you, Winter."

I stuck my tongue out at her. Cedar tossed the pillow; it caught Porter square in the snout.

"Truly, I can come back at another time."

"It's alright, she was just telling me some lame story."

"I will cut you," Cedar said. "What can we help you with?" she directed to our guest, though, technically, she was my guest as well.

"I thought that the two of you would like to know that the Progerian High Council will be meeting us here in a few hours."

"The Progerians? Not the Genogerians?" I asked.

"We have messages out to the both of them; the Progerians, however, were the first to respond."

"Hmm." Cedar was thinking.

"What's hmm?" I asked. Porter was looking to her as well.

"You have a strained relationship with them?" she asked.

"It is something we have been working to overcome for seemingly ages," he responded. "They believe themselves to be superior to us in every way."

"Why would they come here?" she asked.

"I do not understand the question," Porter said.

"Your relationship is strained. Graylon's attack on the Human base would have only compounded that, yet they are the first to respond to your call. It doesn't make much sense."

"Perhaps they now have seen the error of their ways," Porter said naively.

"Just now, just this very moment in history, after untold years of enmity, they have finally come to their senses? Does that ring true with you?"

"I thought it sounded strange, but why would I doubt them? And their help would be a welcome addition."

"Are you just being paranoid?" I asked Cedar.

"Were you?" she said, referring to Graylon's attack and subsequent trap.

"Good point. Where's Commander Kabon?"

He didn't immediately escort us off the bridge once Cedar and I voiced our concerns; that alone led me to believe he was questioning what was happening as well.

"It is my sincerest hope that you are mistaken, but you are right about one thing; we cannot risk the chance if you are correct. I will talk to Graylon and see what he wants to do."

For some reason, I found the lack of true leadership among the Genogerians disturbing. It made moving ahead with any degree of quickness a difficult and frustrating undertaking.

"Do you wish us to stay?" Cedar asked.

I grabbed her arm. Porter had told us that his brother was angry that he had so willingly fallen into a trap that had nearly destroyed a ship. He was not mad at us for alerting him to that fact; my guess was embarrassment, though I wasn't yet sure if they suffered from that emotion. In either case, I thought it best that this conversation happen between them without interference from me or Cedar.

Apparently, the memory of what had almost happened was very much in the forefront of Graylon's mind. A remote drone was planted where we were supposed to be, and we were assured that we had been moved a significant distance away and should be safe. When Cedar asked for clarification on "should be safe," she was not answered. As the time approached for the Progerians to show, the ship alerted us to the Imminent Arrival. Porter told Kabon that the signature was that of the Progerian vessel *Traitorial.* It was only Cedar and me that were struck by the name. We looked at each other.

"That's a little much, don't you think?" she asked me.

I shrugged my shoulders. "It's probably the name of one of their great leaders; no one here seems upset about it."

Cedar and I weren't overly shocked when Breeson's ship, the *Iron Sides* showed up along with another vessel. We did not get a chance to identify it as the drone was targeted and destroyed. Graylon's face was stern; the muscles on the side of his jaw were clenched as he spoke to Kabon.

"The Progerians are in league with the Others," he said unnecessarily. "How can this be? Yes, we have warred in the past…*but to side with them?*" he spat. "It is an affront to our shared world, our shared heritage." His emotions quickly changed from shock to outrage to a desire to wipe them from the face of the galaxy. It seemed our quest was losing steam; we were piling up enemies, and as of yet, had not found a friend.

We were in a difficult situation now, disavowed by the Genogerians, betrayed by the Progerians, and actively hunted by the Others. There were not many places to turn.

"Might as well head to Earth," I said as I sat at the war

table with Porter, Graylon and Kabon.

"They will surely be waiting for us to make that move," Porter interjected.

"Counting on it," I told them. "Cedar and I were talking last night—" My sister took it from there.

"It seems to me Breeson wants his measure of blood," Cedar began.

"And us," I added, sticking my finger in the air.

"Correct me if I'm wrong; the Genogerians do not want to enter into this war…" Cedar said, but it was left as a hanging statement.

Graylon answered with a growl.

"Fair enough," she continued. "And the Progerians have shown whom they are aligned with, but they were noticeably absent from the ambush, so I don't think they want any part of it. Still good?" She looked around the room. "That leaves Breeson and this other ship we don't know about. According to scans before we were so rudely interrupted, it appeared to be of the Others' origin. Right now, it is Breeson attempting to contain this before it spirals out of control. I don't know the politics of what happened when the Progerians sold us out, but I do know from reading enough politically-charged conspiracy books that it is likely that the high council wants this dealt with quietly, to make this go away before populaces begin to find out."

"So there will not be an armada waiting for us." Porter solved the puzzle quickly.

"We do not know this for sure," Graylon spoke. "But either way, Breeson must be dealt with. If we neutralize the Others' greatest commander, they will be forced to escalate."

"Then," Cedar began, "with the vast mobilization, news will spread of what happened."

Kabon stood. "The Genogerians will have to declare at that point. They will not become traitors to their own kind! Even the back-stabbing Progerians will receive pressure to align with us!"

"That's the conclusion we came to as well," I said.

Porter spoke. "An all-out war benefits no one, but this one is a long time coming. To not do so now only delays the inevitable. The Others will be more Stryver than Human soon enough, and they will know no other way."

"I have read up on the ships that all the races have, quantities, capabilities. The Genos and the Progs combined will not be a match for the war machine the Others have assembled. We will not be able to fight like you wish to, Graylon," Cedar said. "We cannot stand against them and trade weapons fire." She explained what needed to be done.

"You wish us to come out of hiding? Throw a punch and then retreat again? That is not the noble way to go about it. I would rather die attempting to destroy them all than in running off into the recesses of space!" he roared.

"Your greatest hero and ancestor, Drababan, accepted this tactic when presented by Michael Talbot. Are you doubting the wisdom of those that went before you, and for a while, at least, gave peace to the cosmos?" she asked, shutting him down almost immediately. He wasn't happy about it and appeared to want to say something in retort, but did not.

Lendor was shaking his head as Cedar spoke, easy enough to know why. He was from a Death Squad; their main tactic involved running headlong into the teeth of the enemy, and if that didn't work, they mobilized to do it again. He did not understand space battles, openly disliked shooting from hundreds, even thousands of miles away. The measure of a warrior was in witnessing firsthand death being dealt or received. If you could not see the eyes of your opponent, you were cheating the process, not giving Death the proper respect it so richly deserved.

Cedar would pull him aside later and explained that, more than likely, he would get his wish, as she had read multiple times that hostile boarding parties had breached ships and needed to be repelled. I found the gleam in his eye strange. Killing was necessary on our world; on all worlds, really, but actively looking forward to it? We did not share the same viewpoint.

"She is right." Porter was talking directly to Graylon. "If we die now, what we are attempting to achieve dies with us."

Graylon did not specifically reply to his brother, but I could tell he sensed a rightness to the words. "And you two believe Breeson will go to Earth for you?" he asked.

"We do. His ego compels him to do it, with or without blessing from his high command."

"Then that is what we will do," Graylon said. "Kabon?"

"How is it that once again everything centers around that tiny little planet so far removed from the rest of the known universe? Yes, killing Breeson and destroying the *Iron Sides* will send a powerful message, one that must be issued, but we must remember that this single act will lead us into a much larger war. Once the Stryvers realize the greatest threat to their existence has been taken out of the equation, they will bring everything they have to bear. There are many unknowns and the variables we are aware of could play out in any manner."

"These Gendruns we have heard of, is there any chance we could talk to them? Might they side with us?" Tallow asked.

Now it was Porter who was shaking his head. "We do not even know why they fight. They do not attempt to conquer territory, they do not take resources, and as far as we can tell, there is no area they are defending. They fight, kill and die, seemingly to do just that. We have sent envoys to attempt parlay; none have ever returned. We have captured some, but if they realize they cannot immediately escape, they possess an enzyme within themselves that they release; it kills them, and from watching, I can assure everyone here it is a painful process. Why they would rather do that than talk eludes me."

"I hope we don't run into them," Tallow said.

"That would be for the best," Graylon echoed the words.

"Can't forget about the giant floating germ we encountered either," Cedar said. "Where the Stryvers dug them up and how they got them to fight alongside them, I don't know."

I hadn't been thinking on it much until she spoke and then thoughts began to flood into my head. "Commander Kabon, could we get a meddie up here?"

"Are you all right?" Cedar came to my side immediately, feeling my head. "You don't have a fever. Are you planning on having a fainting episode? Swooning was big during the Victorian age; I knew I should have brought my fainting couch with me…or at least a cushion."

"What are you talking about?" I asked, shrugging her arm off my shoulders as she directed me to a bench in the back. "I have a question a meddie might be best equipped to answer."

Cedar gave me a strange look. "You're going to talk to a Genogerian meddie about that?" She looked down. It took me a moment to register what she was suggesting.

"Ew, no! What is wrong with you!?"

Commander Kabon, as of yet had not moved. "Should I call for medical personnel or not?"

"I need one well versed in germs," I said.

He didn't ask why. Five minutes later, a Genogerian on the smallish side, who still towered over all the Humans came inside. He was pushing a table full of medical supplies.

"Under-Lieutenant Hebern, sir." He nodded to the commander. "Is there an injury that needs tending to?" He was looking around but saw no one in distress.

"Thank you for coming, Under-Lieutenant. I have some questions, but first you need to see something," I said. "Commander Kabon, would it be possible to show him the attack on the stealth ship?"

Commander Kabon did as I requested. We watched the ensuing battle, the destruction of the *Ogunquit,* which still stung. Porter and Graylon were stoic; we continued to watch as the Stryver ally sent tendrils and gelatinous spheres to attack all the other ships in the area, including ours. Hebern took a great interest in what was happening. When I motioned for it to be shut off, I turned to the meddie.

"Have you identified what that was?" he asked, looking around the room.

"My sister thinks it looks like a germ," Cedar replied.

"Turn it on again, and pause on the subject," he asked. He studied the picture for long minutes before he spoke. "Virus," was the first thing out of his mouth. I do not believe he was speaking to any of us directly.

"Again?" Kabon asked.

"Virus, Commander. It behaves more like a virus. Viruses need a viable host to survive, and that is what this appears to be doing; looking for one. Where most lie in wait to come into contact with one, this is actively searching for something to latch onto. Once it gets into a host cell, in this case metal, it uses the machinery to replicate. It will then consume the host until there is nothing left. It appears that once the host is dead, the virus itself dies with it."

"Biological warfare," Porter said. "This is not another enemy; it is a great and horrible weapon created by the Stryvers."

"That's good and bad, isn't it?" I asked.

"What good can come from this?" Porter looked alarmed.

"I cannot even pretend to understand how this works," Hebern said. "It would appear that the Stryvers have found a way to inoculate themselves against it. If they can, there is no reason to believe we couldn't do the same."

"A vaccination?" Cedar asked.

"How does one give a ship a shot?" Tallow asked.

"Perhaps something sprayed onto the surface," Hebern suggested.

"Or a signal." It was the first thing out of Serrot's mouth since this morning. "The viable part…I'm hung up on that."

"You're a genius!" Cedar went over, grabbed either side of his head and kissed him. "A substance that can somehow tell the virus the target is an inhospitable host."

"Of course!" Porter was excited. "We need to have specialists go over these recordings; it is very likely they will find the signal Serrot has alluded to. Once we know what it is and can duplicate it...." He left it at that; the significance was already known throughout the room.

"We have a real chance." Cedar had a gleam in her eye. I didn't quite share in her outlook, but her good cheer was infectious.

"I'm just happy we're going home," Lendor said.

Serrot and Lendor did something I had never seen before. Cedar's boyfriend raised a fist up to Lendor, who immediately bumped his own fist against it.

"What was that?" I asked.

"The Genogerians call it a broken fist, something that was done in olden times. Michael used to do it with Drababan and BT."

Cedar put her fist up for me. "Don't leave me like this!" she said. "This is going to be the symbol of our revolution!"

I broke my fist with her; seemed silly, but everyone cheered.

When Cedar and I were once again alone and it was nearing time to sleep, doubt began to creep into my soul. When everyone was with me and the tone was spirited, I didn't think there was anything we couldn't achieve, but alone....

"Do you think we can win?" I was staring up at the ceiling.

"Do you want a book?" she asked.

"What's that going to do?"

"It's going to take your mind off the hole you're headed down. Do I think we can win? Sure I do. Don't know for sure, though, and honestly, I don't want to think about it, because if the worst happens, that means good people start dying."

"How can you not help but think of that?"

"Because right now I'm on the streets of 19th century France with Kassandra, the English spy, and the French diplomat, Mathieu, that she has fallen in love with."

"It's that easy for you?"

"It has to be. I don't want to be neurotic, like you."

"I still have a pillow."

"I dare you. We're going to win, Winter. Yeah, Breeson might be a brilliant tactician, but he is egotistical as well. He will underestimate Kabon and Graylon and most of all *us*. He will never expect the piloting we can do and the damage we will deliver."

I was thankful for her optimism even if sleep was going to elude me for the remainder of the night.

It wasn't long afterward when the bleeting of an alarm simultaneously told us to get to our battle stations and also of our impending arrival at Earth. Cedar and I were racing for the hangar. I knew we'd be fighting, just hadn't figured it would be the moment we arrived. Fighters launched by the score when we were in proximity to our home. I was dazzled for a second by the blue brilliance of Earth. That quickly changed to dread as I saw the ten or more ships waiting for us. They had their fighters out as well—not as many as we did, thankfully, but they were vastly different from anything we had thus far seen. There was a towering dorsal fin and two sleek, massive wings halfway down the body, forming an inverted V.

"Cedar?" I called over the radio.

"Don't know."

As of yet, no shots had been fired. Clearly, it was not Breeson, because he would not have waited this long and given up the element of surprise.

"War ships *Arundel*, *Lyman*, and *Traverse*, I am General Hamilton, or as you may know me, Brigend of the Renaissance. Stand down and prepare to be boarded!"

I wondered what was going on; if these were the Others, we had vastly miscalculated how they would handle the situation. Our fighters were in a large formation called "the tip of the arrow." We had not moved. The fighters on the other side were in a hodgepodge array that gave no indication of unified command or structure.

"Hold for orders," Under-Commander Germund, the leader of the fighter squadrons said.

Cedar and I were close enough together that we could see the looks of confusion we mirrored.

"Pirates," one of the Geno pilots hissed under his breath. "I hate pirates."

"Steady," Germund ordered, as one of the pilots, most likely the one that hated pirates, was moving forward, independent of our line. If he started firing—no matter the pirate general's intentions—we would be in the midst of a dogfight.

"Earth by right is our home. You being here is in direct violation to that fact. We will defend what is ours." Brigend broadcast.

"To the death," Graylon added.

"Wait, wait!" Cedar shouted as she moved forward.

"Cedar, what are you doing?"

"You dare to bring them here?" Brigend shouted. "Prepare to fire!" he ordered his fleet.

"Wait, wait!" Cedar shouted again. "Earth is our home, too; we are defending it as well!"

"Pah!" Brigend said. "You tainted ones think you own everything. That stops now!"

"We're not tainted!" I moved to be next to my sister. "We are from the planet's surface!"

"Lies, all of it lies. You will do anything to save yourselves. It is the Genogerians that I am most disappointed in; we are aware that you know what my distant kin are becoming, but still you side with them. Makes no difference to me; we will kill the enemy and the sympathizers."

"Sympathizers? You insolent scum. The Others deserve to die and so do you!" Graylon was itching to get the conflict underway. I was not.

"Brigend, General," I urged. "It's true; Graylon has broken pact with the high-council. We are attempting to start a revolution that will overthrow the Others."

"The people on this planet are like newborn babes; they know not what happens in the heavens above them, and they certainly do not have pilots among the Genogerians," Brigend said.

"Not so long ago that was the truth," Cedar replied. "We found an old shuttle hidden away. I learned how to fly it, and before we knew it, the Others had come for us."

"You set off their sensors. Very foolhardy of you…if any of this is true."

"We were prisoners aboard the *Iron Sides*, saved by…" Cedar paused, not sure how she should broach how exactly we were freed, "Lodilin. And for that, he was blown from the sky. We barely escaped with our lives."

"Hell of a tale, huh boys?" Brigend said, his men laughing.

"Are you daft?" Cedar asked. I sucked in my breath at the provocation. "When have the Others ever tried to explain themselves or lie so extravagantly?"

"Whenever they attempt to save their skins." There was a loud cheer from his men.

"There are Rhodeeshians with us," I said. Brigend said nothing. "Graylon, who is speaking, is a direct descendant of Drababan. I am Winter, and I am here with my sister, Cedar. We are direct descendants of Michael Talbot. Ever heard of him?" Again, nothing.

"Stand down. All ships: stand down," Brigend ordered.

"Graylon?" I asked. I could hear his heavy sigh through my headset.

"Perhaps we should only destroy one of their vessels," he said.

"He's a kidder, that one." Cedar laughed.

"We require proof," Brigend said calmly.

"The proof is that we haven't wiped the skies clean of your

filth!" Graylon started.

"This is ridiculous! Will you both put your very large swords down? Winter and I will come to your ship; my understanding is a simple blood test can prove what we say."

I switched to a private channel. "I realize by some of the stories we heard that Michael may have been insane; have you decided you would like to retrace his footsteps?"

"Relax, pirates are all swashbuckley."

"I don't even know what that means."

"I wonder if Brigend has a parrot? Come on, Winter! Let's go give blood in support of the war effort."

"Are you sure you're my sister?"

She laughed. "Commander Kabon, we'll be right back," she said, switching back to the broad band.

No one ordered her back, which I found unnerving.

"Follow the lights," Brigend said just as one of the ships turned to its side, affording us a view of its hangar. "You deviate in the slightest and we will not hesitate to fire."

We landed the fighters, waited for the airlock to do its job, and then stepped out just as a bevy of armed men jogged toward us. They were not uniformed, like Breeson's; in fact, they appeared disheveled and had grabbed whatever suited them at the time.

"Weapons?" the one closest to us asked.

"Are you looking at this flight suit? Where would I hide one?" Cedar asked as she turned completely around, a little more slowly than I thought necessary.

"What about you?" He motioned with his gun.

"Same, and no, I'm not turning around like my sister just did. I saw the way you looked at her."

"Buzzer, check her," Brigend said.

Buzzer walked around me. "She's clean, boss."

The leader nodded to a camera on the wall. A few moments later, Brigend strode in. He was tall, had on a leather jacket that swept past his knees, and a tricorne hat perched atop long, black hair that flowed past his shoulders.

"Oh, he has a patch!" Cedar restrained from clapping, but I could tell she really wanted to. A black patch obscured his left eye, but his right burned a brilliant blue as it settled on us.

He looked at us; there was almost reverence in his eye. "Blinder, put the guns away."

"General…" Blinder started.

Brigend put his hand up.

"Sir, they could be a suicide squad. The taints have been trying to kill you for years."

"Blinder, I know history was not your strong point and that's not why you're my second in command. But I want you to think back to the early days of Earth's resistance."

"What about it?"

"Buzzer, pull up a display on that fancy watch you lifted," Brigend said.

A swirl of light in the form of a cone shone brightly from a small device upon the man's wrist.

"Now search out a picture of Tracy Talbot."

There were whispers among the crowd, sounded suspiciously like worship. The light swirled quicker, blends of color began to mix in, and then in a flash, the cone became a floating head of light and shadow. It was Tracy; the woman we had just seen, maybe a few years previous to that, but her all the same.

"What am I look…" Blinder stopped as he looked from the picture to us. "Well, shiver me tambourine."

Cedar giggled. "That's not quite how the saying goes," she told her.

"It's her. It's her twice." Blinder's eyes had grown wide as she looked from the now shaking wrist of the man holding the display then to us; back and forth she did this, multiple times. "It can't be. This is some sorcery on the part of the tainted."

"I am afraid that what Blinder says cannot be completely discounted. While the tainted don't actively seek us out, they still do all in their power to destroy us when they find us." Brigend motioned to a man holding a small box, roughly the size of a loaf of bread. It almost contained as many lights and buttons as the dash of my fighter. He walked closer to Cedar, the box outstretched in his hand. He started at the top of her head and stooped to get down to her boots. He then did the same to me.

He spent a minute looking at a small display screen before turning to Brigend.

"Clean, both of them."

If I hadn't thought the whole thing strange before, it got weirder; many got down on one knee with their heads bowed. Cedar began walking around and touching each on the crown of their skull.

"Arise," she would tell them regally. We were born in the same place, from the same parents, but most of the things she did confounded me to no end.

The men were hesitant as they glanced over to Brigend, who looked bemused.

"You scurvy lot! Tracy Talbot wasn't a queen, and neither are these two. Get up."

"I'll allow it," Cedar said.

"Come to my bridge. We have much to discuss." Brigend turned and we followed. As we walked, I began to notice things. In the hallways and some of the areas I could see into, men and women were dressed in the blue uniforms I had seen, seemingly a lifetime ago, when I had tested the Pickets. There was more here than Brigend was letting on. The men in the hangar, the variety of clothes and weapons, they wanted to give the appearance of Earth pirates, but from the little I could tell, I was having my doubts about it. If we had engaged those fighters, would we have been surprised at how they flew?

"You seeing what I am?" I leaned into Cedar.

"Oh yeah." Her gaze fixed on the back of Brigend's jacket as it moved when he walked.

"Cedar!" I said, louder than I should.

"You mean the structure on a seemingly disorderly ship? Or are you referring to the people in uniforms? Last thing I read, pirates were pretty much anti-uniform. I bet the patch he so casually wears isn't even to protect his eye."

"You are right," Brigend had turned and flipped up the swath of fabric, his left eye just as brilliant as the right and full of mirth.

"And just so you know, it's *brigand*, not Brigend," Cedar said.

As we got to the bridge, he took off his hat and jacket and placed a cap on, much like Breeson's, though this was emblazoned with an Eagle in flight, holding lightning in its claws.

"My real name is Brigend Hamilton; you are looking at the proud remnants of the United Earth Marine Corps."

"What?" was all I could manage to say.

"First, let your ship know all is well, then sit. This might take a minute to explain."

"Graylon, Kabon, this is Cedar and Winter. We're fine, and it looks like we have the potential for some decent allies. So don't screw this up and shoot anything you're not supposed to. Cedar out."

"Does your sister speak her mind like that all the time?"

"You have no idea."

"Once it became apparent that Earth was about to have a civil war, your greatest of great grandfathers, Michael Talbot, began to do some completely radical things. He wanted to bring the war off planet as quickly as possible. The earth had seen so much destruction and he knew they couldn't win."

"What?" Cedar and I both interrupted him.

"Some of the brightest minds ever known to man belonged to the tainted."

"The Others," Cedar said.

"The Others," Brigend said, thinking on the moniker she gave them. "As good an explanation as any. The Others, as you call them, had not only been preparing ways to completely eradicate their enemies but also people. There was a growing segment of their population that felt they were the next step in the evolutionary process and that regular Man would only try to keep them from achieving their perceived greatness. They might have succeeded, if not for the one called Mad Jack."

"The one that started it all," Cedar said angrily.

"He is an easy enough scapegoat, but if not for him, humanity would have been wiped from the annals of history long ago. Much like J. Robert Oppenheimer."

For once there was a look of confusion on my sister's face; she did not recognize the name, nor did I.

"He was the father of the most destructive weapon mankind had known at the time: the atomic bomb. The technology was used to end the worst conflict that had ever been waged upon the planet, but in doing so, he unleashed this terrible technology, which would hold the planet hostage to the threat of its use for decades. It was created with the goal of doing good, but was eventually warped into great evil."

"What about Earth? What about the people left behind?" I asked. "You left us to rot in the Pickets."

"You might not want to hear this, Winter, but you, the rest of you, were better off there, undisturbed. The lives we inhabit are full of hardship, strife, war and death."

"That sounds just like home," Cedar said. "Maybe not on the same scale as what is going on here, but lives lost are all the same in the end."

Brigend nodded solemnly. "I cannot argue that point."

"I saw some of your men on the surface; you knew we were there, yet you did nothing."

"It is only recently we have returned. We have spies that

tell us the Others are once again interested in Earth, though we do not know why. We began watching them and watching out for those still there. It was impossible, at first, to figure out the reasons for their interest. They placed sensors and tracking systems all along the surface. Even took some people."

"You let them?" Cedar shook with rage.

"I don't know what you think we can do about it. In terms of populations, we are nearly equal, except that they have more ships, more weapons, more technology and more resources. Everything we have has to be acquired or built in absolute secrecy."

"They just think you're pirates," I said, the thought coming to me. "Do they know you're human?"

"That they do, but they think us small, not unified, not worthy of the might they could bring down on us. Not yet, anyway. If we showed our hand, that the United Earth Marine Corps still exists, we would be in an open, active war we would have no chance of winning."

"So you skulk about on the peripheries, not really doing anything?" Her words shot forth like daggers. I wasn't sure she meant the caustic things she said, but it did not appear she could control herself; so many wrongs had happened and they had stood idly by, I could not blame her for the anger.

"This might come as a shock, but we've been fighting, killing and dying for a good long while. I don't need a whelp to question what we may or may not have done or are doing for a small population surviving on their own."

"We could have helped, those of us left behind," I said, wanting to diffuse a situation that was becoming volatile.

"How, Winter? Your people are using bows and arrows. How effective do you think that will be up here?"

"No thanks to you." Cedar kept looking for buttons to push on the man. I wasn't sure what would happen when she found the one that set him off.

I put my hand up to my sister, hoping she would take the hint and ease up on her brewing tirade. Like placing my hand in front of a wild dog, hoping it wouldn't bite.

"Most of us, especially in the Pickets…we are without hope. In a short time, Cedar has learned how to become a pilot, and I bet one of the best there is." I was glad when Brigend didn't roll his eyes or say something derogatory. He was smart enough to be diplomatic, if nothing else. "She taught me, and if I can learn, what could others do? We know how to fight, Brigend, we've been doing it all our lives. Replace the arrows with something that will work in space; a weapon is a weapon. Give us hope for a better future—or let us die trying."

Brigend regarded me, both of us, really, and was on the verge of speaking when the ship warned of an imminent arrival.

"More friends of yours?" he asked.

"We know who it is, but they are unlikely to be friends," Cedar said. "We have to go." She stood.

"Who might this mystery guest be?" he asked.

"I would imagine Commander Breeson and the *Iron Sides;* don't worry. Winter and I will debark quickly so you can take your caravan here and go hide in some dark and dusty corner of the universe. Let those who know how to fight take care of this battle."

Brigend shook his head. There was a small smile hidden under a stern set to his jaw.

"Wow, sister," I said as we moved quickly through the ship to get to the hangar. "Why didn't you just shoot him? That would have hurt less."

"How can one be an arrogant coward?" she asked just as she was climbing into her fighter. I could only shake my head.

"We can't possibly know what they've been through."

"True enough. All I care about is what happens going forward." And with that, she shut her canopy. In less than a minute, we were racing back toward our ship.

"You live," Graylon said flatly through the radio.

"You had doubts?" Cedar asked.

"Pirates are not widely regarded as being courteous to their guests," he said.

"You let us go into a place you did not believe we would have survived?" Cedar asked.

"We would have avenged your deaths with honor," he replied.

"Is he kidding?" my sister asked me.

"Doubtful," I told her.

"Now I don't know who infuriates me more: Brigend or Graylon."

Brigend's ships had not yet moved, though we were told that their buckle systems were online and ready to go. They were going to wait to see what showed up and then make a run for it. We, on the other hand, were staying. The fighters were ordered to stay on patrol. I loved being in the fighter…and I didn't. To be in control of one's own fate was all I'd ever asked for; going to war willingly and being forced to fight for unknown and unknowable reasons had nearly driven me mad. But being alone, isolated in space like this…I don't even know if I have the words. The loneliness was as vast as space itself. Soon we were going to fight a war that could very much determine the fate of the world I had grown up on. I could very well die up here and my friends wouldn't know, or even worse, my friends on the planet would die without having any idea of why.

"How you doing, Cedar?" I asked, wanting—no, needing—to hear a friendly voice.

"Not so good." I could hear a hitch in her voice.

"Are you crying?"

"No! You're crying," she shot back.

"It'll be all right, sis," I said. "We'll make it through this."

"Huh? I know that, silly. It's Frederick; he got into a duel with the scoundrel Domingo to preserve the honor of Josefine. He was shot through the stomach; he's in a hospital, but very rarely do people recover from that. Josefine is proclaiming her everlasting love for the man and he told her he would wait.

How romantic is that, Winter? Frederick is going to walk the world a ghost as he waits for Josefine to pass so that they cross the bridge together!"

"A *book*, Cedar? You're reading a book right now?"

"What should I be doing?"

"I don't know? Thinking about what could happen, maybe?"

"Why would I want to do that? What's worrying going to accomplish? I can think of a thousand different scenarios that don't end up good and I can think of a thousand different scenarios that do end well. But that's the thing, Winter; none of that thinking changes anything. Only doing can accomplish anything. So instead of listening to my insides roil, which is much the same sound as a milkmaid churning butter, I prefer to get lost in a story. To fully immerse myself in the written word, to retreat into my mind, instead of laying it bare."

"I hate when you're right."

"So basically all the time. Is that what you're saying?"

"Shut up. Does Domingo get what's coming to him?"

"Now, you're talking. This is where it gets good. Frederick, like I said, plans on waiting for Josefine. So while he walks the world a ghost, he uses his free time to haunt Domingo. Finally drives him insane, and the man has to be institutionalized. He is force-fed drugs that make him drool and babble incoherently and are supposed to remove the demons from his head, but they don't. See what happens…."

She was cut off as Graylon warned that the ship approaching was less than five minutes away. "Fighters, get into position. Scum," he added at the end. I thought he was referring to Breeson. "Pirate buckle drives are winding up," he added.

I was watching Brigend's ships when the mystery ship that had been with Breeson showed up. It was wholly unremarkable in its appearance. It shared a vast majority of its architectural design with a brick.

"Fire!" Graylon ordered. Streaks of brilliant blue and red

flew from the great ships. There was no return fire, nor did a bevy of fighters release from her bowels. Brigend's ships had still not moved, nor fired. I think I was even angrier that they were merely spectators, as if this were some sort of sporting event for them.

"What have you done?" This from Brigend.

I was too busy watching for the enemy to wonder what he could be going on about.

"We cannot leave!" he shouted. I had hoped he meant it as a way to prove his loyalty, but there was too much anger in his voice for that to be the case. He couldn't leave for a reason I did not know yet. By the looks of the derelict ship, it was most likely a maintenance issue.

"If you can't leave, perhaps you should fight," Cedar said. "If you can't already tell, our weapons are having little effect on that ship!"

I was so intent on watching for threats that had yet to materialize, I'd not taken notice that Cedar was right; the weapon beams, which were concentrated plasma and lasers, dissipated into tiny sparks of light and fire as they traveled toward the ship. Instead of massive beams of energy pounding into and through the hull, it looked more like a dazzling show of lights dancing atop the metallic surface. Cedar banked hard to the right and was moving quickly toward the strange ship.

"What are you doing?" I asked.

"Fighter sixty-six return to formation," our squadron commander, Germund, told Cedar.

"Wondering what a missile will do," was all Cedar gave way as explanation.

"That was an order!" Germund reiterated.

Good luck with that. I thought. Couldn't remember the last time anyone ordered Cedar to do anything she didn't want to. If my sister was getting closer to the ship, then so was I.

"You sure about this?" I asked her.

"It'll be fun."

I had my doubts about that last statement, but I was not

going to leave her alone. The ship must have had something to fear from us because as we approached, it was easy enough to see the large gun emplacements rise up from their storage compartments.

"Are those for us?" The barrels on the weapons were twice as long as the machines we were flying.

"Remember your training, Winter, and I love you," Cedar said. I watched the blue from her afterburners as she pushed forward and at speed. A beam as thick around as a tree blew out from the cannon; Cedar turned hard away from it, but the bolt turned as well, not as quickly and not as severely an angle, but it was adjusting, coming back around in a wide arc.

"You seeing that?" I asked her.

"Well, that's *different.*" She corrected her flight path and was heading toward the ship. "Missile away." A bright red glow was all I could see from the missile as it streaked toward its target. The *Arundel* and the other ships were still firing; unfortunately, it was with the same result. I had a hard time believing the small StormBringer missiles would have any effect if the cataclysmic weaponry wasn't doing anything. Had to think Cedar was of the same mind because when the missile did strike and there was an explosion, she couldn't help but yelp excitedly.

"Graylon, missile strike confirmed. Repeat, missiles effective. Coming back around to fire everything."

The large cannon was swinging around, following her every move.

"That's not going to do." I had my targeting guidance system up and locked on to the large array. "Missile away." A short burst managed to come out just as my missile hit the base. The explosion was enormous; the entire array listed and was forced into the side of the ship, causing an even larger hull breach.

"Nice one!" Cedar told me as she streaked by. What happened next was in the span of one heartbeat to the next. The Genogerian ships had stopped with the ineffectual weapons and had fired missiles of their own. Brigend's ships were moving further away, although not by means of buckling. Where it really got interesting was when the *Iron Sides* showed, releasing everything in its large arsenal, including its fighters. Cedar and I were caught in no man's land—The *Iron Sides* to our rear with the Genogerians even further still and the strange ship to our front. The *Iron Sides* could not get an effective shot off for fear of striking its sister ship, but that wasn't the same problem for the ten fighters heading our way.

"Go toward Brigend's ships," Cedar told me as she pulled her fighter up and was going to fly over the top of the ship we'd been shooting. There were three gaping holes that were venting a thick black smoke into space; one was large enough that, had I been of a mind, I could have flown straight into it. If not for the pursuit, I would have, at the very minimum, sent them an explosive present.

"Genogerian ships, do not approach!" Instead of Brigend's communication officer, this came straight from him.

"Too late for that," Cedar told him. "But feel free to tell that to the *Iron Sides* fighters. I'm sure they'll listen."

"Son of a bitch," I heard him say before he cut off comm.

Cedar had us heading straight for the *Renaissance*. If they wouldn't actively help us, she was going to force them to defend themselves.

"Brilliant," I said aloud.

"I know, right?!"

Brigend was attempting to move his ship even farther away, but the fighters were quicker and more nimble; he would not so easily escape. We were being fired upon but the fighters, as of yet, had not locked on. Pulse cannons from the *Renaissance* started firing. I had a moment of doubt where I thought perhaps they might try to shoot us down so as to give no reason for the *Iron Sides* to fire upon them. I was relieved when the shots went far to our right.

"Splash two," Cedar said. "Follow me, sis." We were diving down. "Stay close to the *Renaissance's* hull."

"How close?"

"Close enough you could trade finishes."

"I don't like being that close," I told her.

"Yeah, but it will mess up the fighters' firing systems. It will most likely lock on to Brigend's ship as opposed to us—unless they switch to manual."

"And then?"

"Ever heard of a sticky widget?"

"No."

"Then don't worry about it. Just stay close to me."

"Sounds like something I should very much worry about," I said softly. I was sub-consciously ducking my head we were so close to its underbelly. The weapon fire from the ones pursuing us was scorching the hull where it struck. We continually passed gun emplacements that were firing on the fighters. My display registered that they were losing fighters at an alarming rate.

"They're pulling back," Cedar said just as we came out from the shadow of Brigend's ship and to the other side.

"What the hell kind of stunt was that?" Brigend shouted at us, and before we could even answer, he again wanted to know what we had done to his ship.

"Don't know what you're talking about," Cedar told him. She pulled next to me and motioned to turn around and go back. I nodded at her.

"What did you do to my buckle drive?!" he asked.

"We haven't done anything," I answered. I was confused; we were in fighters. We hadn't shot at him, and as far as I knew, nothing the others had done would have been capable of doing that either.

"We cannot buckle."

"And here I thought maybe you'd grown a conscience," Cedar said as we rocketed away. We were taking a wide arc, to stay away from the long arm of the *Iron Sides*. The *Traverse* was taking the brunt of the attack from the *Iron Sides*. We could see fighters weaving in and around each other, killing blows signified by miniature explosions, in comparison to the massive wounds the ships were inflicting on each other. We could hear the chatter as we raced to get back into it and do what we could.

It was Porter talking from the *Traverse*. "We are taking damage; seven decks have collapsed. We do not yet know casualties. We are in danger of total destruction."

"Buckle, Porter. Get out of here. We will deal with them as they need to be," Graylon said. It was difficult to discern through the speakers and the normal gruff way Genogerians spoke, but he definitely sounded concerned.

There was a moment, then Porter came back through. "Buckle drive is offline. All systems show normal, but it will not start."

"It's the brick ship," I said, the realization hit me. I was as sure of it as I was Cedar was my sister.

"Makes sense. Got to be why Brigend's ships are down. You hear that?" She was asking the pirate captain.

"Just because I know what the problem is doesn't mean I have a solution."

"If you won't fight for us, maybe you should do it for you," I said.

"Full bank of blister arrows," Brigend said.

"Blister arrows armed," his weapons officer replied.

"Fire." There was no inflection in the word; he could have been asking for someone to hand him a cup of coffee. I was alright with his lack of enthusiasm as long as he was in the fight.

"Winter! Hit your afterburners!" Cedar said with alarm. I did as she said before looking around at the threat. It was Brigend's blister arrows; they were each easily over a hundred feet in length and forty feet across. They were enormous. The only part that had any resemblance to an arrow was the tip, which came to a sharp point that looked capable of piercing even the toughest of hides. The Others knew the threat for what they were. The *Iron Sides* was swinging around to get better firing trajectories and her fighters had all disengaged and were heading to do what they could to keep the massive missiles from making contact.

"We need to let those hit," Cedar said as she banked back around.

"You just said we need to get out of here," I told her as I followed her lead.

"They will not be paying us any attention. It will be like shooting fish in a barrel."

"Why would anyone shoot fish in a barrel? Seems to me you've already caught them."

"You're funny, sis."

I wasn't meaning to be, but I'd let her think that. We were streaking toward the fighters that were streaking toward the missiles, that, yeah, were streaking toward the brick ship. I didn't even bother with the gauges that determined velocity and acceleration; the numbers were far too staggering to comprehend. Right now, everything I did was going to come down to instinct and training, and I'd had the best teacher anyone possibly could. Cedar had brought us higher than the *Iron Sides'* fighters and now we were flying down toward them with our deadly armature, primed and ready. Cedar began to fire first. She took two down; a third was damaged and spiraled away as it was hit by debris.

"Bogies above! Bogies above!" a panicked Others pilot shouted as I fired. His transmission ended in a ball of fire. We strafed their entire formation, inflicting as much damage as we could, though we were two against hundreds. Our noses were vertical to them as we dove down.

"Switch to the private channel," Cedar said. "Let's get in behind them. Keep your public channels on monitor. I want to know if they plan any surprises." We were leveling off and coming into position as the first of the blister arrows hit. Our canopies instantly and automatically darkened and still, the light was so intense I had to turn away, my hands reflexively coming up to my face to shield from the blast.

"Pull up! Pull up!" Cedar yelled.

My hands flew to the controls and I did as she warned. *Iron Sides'* fighters were being blown back toward us. Many on fire, others attempting to escape the effects of the blast. Ships were being tossed around and into each other, the forward lines of the fighters were vaporized. Nothing remained. As the ring of destruction radiated out from the initial blast zone, it wrought absolute carnage. We were flying upside down in relation to the others as we scrambled away. Below us, the fighters were doing the same. Right now, we shared similar destinies; not enemies, but rather fellow combatants attempting to survive.

The wave of slaughter was gaining and at the leading edge were the tumbled and twisted wreckage of the ships it was carrying with it.

"Into it, Winter. We need to fly into it."

I thought her insane, but what does that make me if I followed? We had turned just as the front of the ripple flowed over our nose cones. Alarms blared wildly. I could not see any of my instruments as they shook into an indeterminable jumble. The fear was so great in me, I'd not even noticed when my mind expanded and collapsed back in on itself. Everything had slowed to nearly normal levels. My ship warning of collision threats; the alarm now a long, drawn-out warble. The objects hurtling at us ranged in size from that of a lonely bolt to complete inoperative ships. I could see the pilots screaming as they tumbled around. Anything hit our ships at these speeds and it would be disastrous. Even with the advantage my condition afforded, avoiding everything coming my way seemed a daunting task; possibly undoable.

Where my moves were hesitant as I tried to look two or three hazards down the path, Cedar was, in contrast, moving fluidly and with a grace bordering on precision. There was a loud screech off to my right as a headless helmet scraped down the length of my wing. At least I hoped it was headless; either way, it spelled disaster for the owner that had worn it. We were halfway through the debris field when another arrow struck the side of the brick ship. My canopy again darkened, and though the desire to was intense, I did not shield my eyes. The ship listed heavily to the side from the impact. Fires bloomed from dozens of spots along the hull as panels the size of small mountains were forcibly ripped from their moorings.

Dodging flotsam was one thing, but avoiding flying walls was an impossibility. There were more explosions as the large slab of steel obliterated everything in its path. A broom could not have been any more effective. I knew what Cedar was doing the moment she spoke and her fighter turned. We were going to attempt to get in behind the road cleaner. That was going to bring its own set of challenges as the two concentric circles created by the explosions warred with each other for domination. We had roughly ten seconds before a third was added. The merge point of the large energy fields was so intense it shook apart fighters that had been previously damaged. I hoped the Genogerian constructed fighter could hold up to the assault. Even with everything slowed down, it was nearly impossible to see. The shaking was so violent, sparks began to issue forth from my console. I had to place both my hands upon the flight control joystick to keep a grip on it. The ship's engines were in a full-throated whine as they tried to move us in the direction I desired to go.

My arms throbbed in pain as my muscles struggled to hold the ship steady. I kept my mouth closed tightly, fearful I would shatter my teeth or bite my tongue off if I opened it. If not for the safety harness holding me tight to my seat, I would have been tossed about, repeatedly slamming against the interior sides. As it was, it felt like my brain was very much doing that anyway. I had stopped trying to fly and was now merely holding on for dear life; whatever the fates had determined for me, I was in her hands. I hoped she was a loving master. Just when I thought my brains might start to push through my skull and out my ears, everything quieted. I had a moment where I thought I might have died; the immutable silence after such a roaring din was discordant.

"Winter, you all right?"

"I'm alive?" was all I could think to ask.

"Well, if you're not, we're now traveling to the afterlife together, and I'm okay with that." I could hear the mirth in her voice. "One more round, sis. You ready?"

"God, no," I told her truthfully. This time the explosion came to the rear; didn't need to see it to know this was the death of the brick ship. It had already been in its violent death throes; this next missile would merely put it out of its misery.

"Don't get too close to this hull section. Its most likely going to start to spin when the concussive wave strikes it."

"Can't tell you how wonderful I think that is."

"Do you have a concussion?" she asked.

"The better question is, how do you not?"

"My brain is bigger; it presses up tight to the side of my head, so there's no room for it to go sloshing around like yours."

We were riding the wave of the previous blast. The gigantic panel in front of us was plowing an obstruction free path; it would take time before the last wave caught us and by then most of its force should have dissipated. We were moving further from the battle. Now that it was relatively calm and there wasn't anything we could do, I turned up the volume to listen in on the distant ships. It was not a surprise to me when Brigend had his ships buckle after the annihilation of the strange ship that had somehow blocked their efforts to escape.

"Not sure if I'm angry or appreciative," Cedar said as she witnessed what I had.

"He didn't do it for us," I told her and that I knew for the truth. Perhaps at one time, Brigend's Marine Corps had been a full-fledged fighting force, but now, after so many years of small raids and ambushes, they appeared to know no other way than to strike and run. On the far extreme was Breeson, who did not look like he knew the meaning of the word retreat. Immense portions of the *Iron Sides* were consumed in fire and still, he battled. His fighters had nearly been wiped clean from the playing board and even that did not deter him. His anger and need for revenge and retribution rivaled anything I had thus far seen.

The *Traverse*, our current home, was nearly unidentifiable. So many parts of it had yielded to the battle, it was not recognizable as the ship we had left seemingly years ago. How that was even remotely possible, I wasn't sure. They were ordered to abandon ship. Shuttles were leaving in droves. Breeson, proving he was who he was, targeted more than a few of them. The *Arundel* was taking savage swipes at the Others warship to the point where the *Iron Sides* could not continue to sustain the damage it had. Before it buckled away, it turned everything it had on the brick ship. There were cries for help, even as the ship was completely and utterly destroyed. My mouth hung agape at the act of cruelty Breeson had performed on his own.

"He doesn't want us to get ahold of the technology," Cedar said as we flew back toward the *Arundel*. The area was littered with debris; heavy rumbling percussions came forth from the *Traverse* as she died a violent death. The *Arundel* and *Lyman* were sending their own shuttles with nearly suicidal pilots to off-load who they could from the doomed ship.

"Raven Wing 1, this is Raven Wing 8. We have fighters making a retreat," Cedar announced.

"Pursue, do not destroy. We will catch up shortly."

"Don't destroy them my ass."

"Cedar?" I interrupted her.

"Why don't they want us to destroy them after everything they've done? Everything they've destroyed and taken?"

"Prisoners, I would think," I answered, though I wasn't entirely sure. "That's not really why I'm asking a question though."

"What's going on, Winter?"

"We're a long way ahead of our support, and there are fifteen fighters out there. What are we going to do if they decide to turn around and fire on us?"

"They can hope God will have mercy upon their souls."

"I had a feeling you'd say something along those lines."

"Come on, sis."

The Others' fighters were faster, but we were gaining.

"They're conserving fuel," Cedar said.

"Breeson must be coming back for them."

"Let's make sure there's nothing to come back to," Cedar replied.

They were running and we were chasing; yes, we had beaten them, but they still had long teeth and claws and could turn and fight at a moment's notice.

I didn't need to see Cedar to know the anger she had coursing through her. It oozed through every word she spoke.

We were gaining and had just reached range when five of the fighters slowed down.

"They're turning to fight," Cedar said as she let loose with her twin cannons. One of the fighters dissolved under the assault, the other four were turning. I shot, blowing a wing off of the nearest to me. The fighter flew away in tight circles. I was focused on the one furthest to the right as another took a wide arc in an attempt to get behind us. Cedar peeled away to cut him off. I appreciated the gesture, but now I had two coming straight for me.

"You've got this, Winter. Stay focused," Cedar said. I was thankful she was keeping tabs on me; I'd be happier when she was by my side again.

An alarm went off that I was being targeted. I dove down and released a dozen flares. Once they were away, I pulled back up. I was looking straight at the bottom of the fighter that previously had me in his sights. I blew four holes straight up and through; his end came swiftly. The other was diving down to meet me. We were both locked on when he received impacts from the side. Cedar, after having killed the fighter she was engaged with, had come and broadsided the last of the five sent to slow us down or take us out.

"Let's get the rest of them," she said without losing a beat.

My radar showed that our reinforcements had gained

during our dog fight but were still not close enough to assist us, should the rest of the Others turn. We were once again gaining on the remaining ten. I was good; Cedar was otherworldly with her skills. Still, two on ten might be odds we could not overcome.

"*Iron Sides'* fighters. You will shut down your thrusters and your weapons systems. We will escort you back to the *Arundel,*" Cedar announced on the universal channel.

"Like hell we will!"

"Fire when ready," Cedar said to me. "She was bluffing or she wouldn't have said it over the broadcast.

They kept running. None had yet turned to fight. Cedar flipped back to private.

"Looks like they're going to need convincing."

"You sure, Cedar? It's one thing when we're fighting, but they're running away."

"Breeson was firing on evacuating shuttles; pretty sure anything goes with them."

She fired—her shots went wide to the left. She never misses; she'd given them a warning…one that they did not heed. Again she let loose a wave of projectiles. These were the less lethal 30mm cannon rounds, hellacious to ground forces, fighters could generally take a few before suffering irrevocable damage. The engine compartment of the one she had shot at blew out in a large blue burst before thick black smoke poured forth.

"I can do this all day," she told them. "Or you can surrender." We flew past the stalled fighter. Nothing. Crickets rubbing their legs together two miles away would have made more noise. If they were talking, it wasn't to us.

The fighter we'd left in our wake took an ill-advised and badly-aimed shot; he or she paid for it with their life as our vanguard cleaned up the stain upon the inky blackness of space.

"And then there were nine." Cedar almost sang the words.

I was having a moral dilemma. On one hand, they were

trying to get away, but it wouldn't be forever; whoever we let go here, we would very likely meet again, and it was impossible to know what damage they could inflict next time. I fired. I'd chosen which side of the line I wanted to be on. I was assured this would keep me up at night, but I could also rest assured that no one would die from these fighters because I didn't do what needed to be done. Unlike Cedar, I hit it with my front plasma cannons; there wasn't much left as its parts blew outwards.

"Needed to be done," Cedar said, somehow knowing what was going through my mind; it was going through hers as well.

"You need to stop," I told the eight left.

"It sounds like two girls, Wombat. I can take them," one of the pilots said.

"That was very similar to what the five I sent to stop them said." It was a female voice and I assumed, Wombat. "*Arundel* fighters, we are powering down."

"Are you insane?"

"Beaker, what's left of this platoon is now under my command. You will stand down!" Wombat yelled. It was easy enough to hear in her voice she was losing her grip.

"I'll be damned if I'm going to become Geno food." Beaker banked hard to come up on us.

"I've got him," I told Cedar. "You keep watch on them.

She said nothing. It's difficult to cheer someone on when they're going to kill another. Even when they were the enemy, it just isn't a celebratory event. Not sure what was going through Beaker's mind, but as he was pulling out of his turn, he was firing wildly and yelling a loud "*ARRRR!*" as if he already knew the outcome and was preparing for the finality of it.

"Wombat, this is insane! Are you just going to let him die?" another of the squadron asked.

"Deuce, I outrank you. I was pinned with my wings before you. He's flying against a direct order. You want to join him, go ahead," Wombat replied.

"Deuce, you so much as turn that engine on and I will splash you," Cedar said icily.

Something in Beaker had snapped; seemed he wanted to die much more than he wanted to be captured. He turned his ship so that I was looking at the top of his canopy and wings. I strafed him as he flew past. There was a cry of release and then nothing more as his ship kept flying, its sole occupant long past caring where it was headed. By the time I got back to Cedar, we had a squad of back-up fighters with us.

"You have done well here," Under-Aviator Denathin said as we were escorting the fighters back to the *Arundel's* hangar.

I had not been prepared for what awaited us there. We had to wait to board as the hangar floor had become a triage for those injured in the battle. Many Genogerians were burned beyond recognition, though somehow they were still alive. Bones protruded from various arms and legs, blood ran in rivers from the number of injuries. Meddies were running back and forth doing what they could to stem the tide of death that had swept across our ranks. I was so engaged with my battle it had never occurred to me the sheer number of casualties that had been suffered. I nearly doubled over when I remembered that Tallow, Serrot, and Lendor had been on the *Traverse*.

"I don't see them." Cedar had grabbed my hand.

"What will happen to us?" Wombat asked. She was kneeling on the deck, her hands clasped above her head just like the six with her. Two Genogerian guards were preparing to handcuff them and get them to a cell. I didn't even look her way at the entreaty. Absolutely didn't care if they were released or eaten. If something bad were to happen to them, they would have deserved it.

"I asked what are you savages going to do with us!" she screamed hysterically.

I couldn't contain myself. Even through my fear and angst, I spun on her. "Savages? Who attacked who first? Who shot at defenseless shuttles trying to bring survivors to safety? That can all be laid at your feet. Whatever happens to you now is fine with me!"

She sagged down at first, as one of the guards put cuffs on her hands and then roughly pulled her to her feet.

"Where are they?" Cedar was looking through the scattered carnage of broken bodies, searching for those we cared about.

Breathing was becoming difficult as panic surged inside of me. Came across Porter; he had a bandage wrapped around his head and his arm was in a cast. He was sitting up, a dazed expression upon his face.

"Porter!" I yelled much too loudly. I was concerned for him, but I needed to know. "Are you all right" and "Where are they?" came out in one long sentence.

"I will be fine. And I am sorry, Winter. We were together for a while, but in the confusion and explosions, I lost consciousness. I do not know what became of them."

I saw the lithe form of Frost bounding in our direction. "It is good to see you well. Gather your sister and come with me." If possible, my heart sank further.

"Cedar! Let's go!"

"I haven't found them."

"Frost has."

We were racing down the massive hallways, doing our best to keep up with Frost. That we were running gave me hope. Because the dead will wait. But it also could be that they were so badly injured it was imperative that we get there as soon as possible. How bad were they that they had jumped to the head of the line and were now in the hospital? As we got closer, I saw a huddled form with his back against the wall, his head in hands.

Cedar was slowing down. "It's…it's Tallow. Where is Serrot?"

"Tallow?" I asked, coming to a stop right in front of him.

He looked up. He had a shiner that did little to hide the fact that he'd been crying. "Winter?" It took him a moment to recognize me, maybe because of the haze of tears or the crack he had taken to the head. He stood with a slight wobble. "It's good to see you," he sobbed into my shoulder.

"Where's…where's Serrot?" Cedar begged.

Tallow let out an involuntary cry before looking to her. He released me and moved toward her. He said nothing but the action implied the meaning.

"NO! You will not hug me! I will not accept this!" she screamed. She was going to push her way through the doors that led to the surgical section.

"Cedar please." Tallow had his arms outstretched; I think to comfort her as much as himself. Frost's tail was swishing back and forth in an agitated manner.

"Who's in there!" she demanded.

"It's Lendor. We were all together, heading for the shuttle when an explosion ripped through the side of the ship. Serrot, he saved us…he tossed me out of the way and covered up Lendor with himself."

"You're wrong! He's alive! I'd know if he had died. I want to see him!"

"He did not make it over," Frost told her.

"You left him there? How could you leave him there? I need to go back and get him. He'll be so alone and scared."

She turned and was heading back to the hangar, I would imagine to go and grab a shuttle.

"Stay with her," Tallow said.

"What about Lendor?"

"Internal bleeding…but they think they got to him soon enough. Go."

Cedar had a head start and she was running on pure adrenaline. I could not keep up with her. She was weaving through those on the hangar and was heading right for where I thought she might be. I caught up to her just as she began arguing with a guard to get out of her way.

"I have to get over to the *Traverse*! You will move."

He was as understanding as he could be, given the circumstances. "There is nothing to go over to."

"I will determine that for myself!"

"Look through the ports, little one." He was pointing to the far wall. Cedar seemed reluctant to leave the shuttle area, as if this were some trick on his part and he would hide the ships from her before she could get back. She moved slowly, not wanting to see the truth. The longer it took for her to get there, the longer she could hold on to the belief that everything was going to be all right. I didn't attempt to stop her, to hug her in solace or even give her the worst words that one could in this situation: that it would be all right. Because it wouldn't. Not now and not for a good long while.

I stayed a few feet behind her as she made her way over; didn't even need to look to see how bad it was. The glow of the burning ship was flooding through the windows, bathing her face in a ghostly light. Deep shadows formed under her eyes. Still, she moved closer until she could place her hand against the indifferent glass.

"Why didn't I know?" she asked me. "I should have felt his passing, right? Shouldn't I?" She had not turned to me. "He must…he could still be alive."

I took this opportunity to look at the *Traverse;* what was left of the giant ship was a raging inferno. I tenderly touched her shoulder and pulled her away. She did so without fighting me. We sat in her room for an hour, never once did she cry.

"I'm so tired, Winter. I'm going to get some sleep. Please go and check on Lendor and Tallow." Her deep racking sobs chased me out the door. I cried for her, I cried for Serrot, I cried for all that were lost and all who remained to suffer the loss of someone dear to them. Just because Genogerians displayed their emotions differently did not belie how strongly they had been affected today. More than a few times I saw them walking around with what I can only describe as a hollow expression. So profound were their depths of misery, they could not interact with those around them.

When Graylon spoke over the ship's communications announcing that we would be buckling soon, I knew that was where I wanted to go: the bridge. The Geno meddie had cleared Tallow; he had a mild concussion and needed a few days' rest. And Lendor, he would "make it or he wouldn't." Those were the doctor's exact words, and though my friend was out of surgery and in recovery, I could not yet see him. I got Tallow to bed and went to see Graylon.

He saw me as I entered. "You fought courageously."

"You as well," I replied.

"Yes, but not well enough to save our ship. The lives lost will not be forgotten nor replaced. We have suffered a great victory here at great cost. We will not be able to bask in the glory of it."

I'd yet to encounter a Genogerian well versed in sarcasm, though I was certain that Graylon's last sentence was steeped in it.

"Why are we leaving? We haven't even gone to the surface. We fought for this; isn't Earth our spoil?"

"Commander Breeson will be back, and if he shows up with another of those buckle drive inhibitor ships, we will be forced to fight a battle I do not believe we will survive."

"So we are running, like the pirates?"

"This ship is damaged, as is the *Lyman;* we are not in a position to force our might onto anyone. As it is, finding safe harbor for repairs may be difficult."

"So that's it? It's over?"

"Far from it. It does not make sense to stand one's ground merely for the principal of the matter. I wish to win this war, Winter, not make a statement."

"Did you know that the pirates are really part of the Earth Corps?"

"I did, though they are merely a shadow of their former greatness."

"Are you so sure about that? Those missiles they fired destroyed that Buckle Stopper."

"They did indeed. If you are thinking they would make a good alliance, I should tell you that they have never aligned with anyone. What they did, they did so they could escape. With that being said, they did send a burst message directed to you before they left."

"A burst message?"

"A highly compressed data stream that is directed precisely, and if not picked up by the intended receiver, dissolves into nothingness. I've had my communications officer isolate it and place it on a computing device not attached to the ship's system."

Pretty sure my eyebrows kept furrowing.

"A virus can be sent this way," he offered as explanation.

"To make people sick?" I was still lost.

"A virus that can infect machines."

"There's such a thing?"

"Mm. Incredibly dangerous events on a ship."

"Where's the computing device?"

He pointed to an empty workstation. The display was attached to the console, like all the others. "This one?"

"Yes. It is not wired into the mainframe."

"Winter, Cedar," was written in large letters. I touched the screen and the message revealed itself. "We need to talk, one ship." And then there were a bunch of numbers.

"Coordinates." Graylon was next to me.

"What are we going to do?" I asked him.

"It is most likely a trap; they are pirates, after all."

"I think it's worth it."

"How worth it will you believe it to be when they capture all of us and you are enslaved by the Others?"

"Not so much, but I still think it's a chance we need to take."

"Why?"

"You said it yourself, Graylon, not in so many words, but we need help. Maybe they're offering it. If they wanted to push the issue, they could have stepped in and helped Breeson or waited until he was gone. We weren't in much shape to take him on. No, he had a chance to take us and he didn't."

“There is logic in what you say, but that does not make me like the words any better.”

“When do we leave?”

Graylon eyed me while he thought. “We will buckle to a safe zone nearby to this rendezvous point and then we will bring the *Arundel* to him.”

We left just as the warnings came that enemy ships were less than ten minutes from breaking space with us. For five hours, I was on the bridge repeatedly; I would check the infuriatingly small message for any signs of deceit. It wasn’t just me that was walking into a trap. I was bringing half the rebellion. It would be a loss we could not recover from. What kind of bounty would the Others pay for something of that magnitude?

“I would like to give the crew a few hours to rest and the medical teams to catch up on the injured. We will buckle shortly. Do you harbor doubts?”

“Would you believe me if I told you I didn’t?”

“No,” he responded.

I went and checked on Cedar; she was having bouts of fitful sleep. Her legs kicked out and she would scream occasionally. I sat down next to her head and talked soothingly to her while I wiped her sweating brow.

Her eyes opened quickly. “Serrot?”

“It’s me, sis.” I gently hugged her.

“I thought for a moment that he had come back to me. I was dreaming that.” She started crying again. “I never thought I could feel pain like this,” she said.

“I’m so sorry,” I told her. I could not fathom the depths of despair she was going through, though when I thought Tallow had died, I thought it would be the end of me. She cried until she had nothing left to give. Her body gave out and she was once again asleep; I truly hoped her dreams offered some comfort. I kissed her forehead and headed over to Tallow’s room. He still slept and soundly; I would not bother him as I went to the Medical Bay.

I had my first bit of good news as I heard something metallic clanging in the next room over and then a groggy-but-alive Lendor shouting to let him out of the damn tube he was in. When I went in, there were two Genogerians going about their business, clearly ignoring him. He looked like he'd got into a fight with a Stryver and lost, but still, I smiled as I walked over. There was a large port through which I could see him, and he could see me.

"Winter!" he shouted, then coughed. "Broken ribs, sorry." Didn't stop him from trying to sit up where he proceeded to bonk his head on the top of the vessel he found himself in.

"You should tell him to be calm. The hyperbolic chamber will speed the healing process." The Geno to my left said. "We have tried but he will not listen."

"How long has he been like this?"

"Long enough. I am trying to get the doctor to authorize the use of sedatives."

"Lendor, did you hear them?"

"I heard, Winter, but I'm in a tube. I don't like enclosed spaces."

"The less you rustle about, the sooner you get out."

"How is everyone?" he asked but I was fairly certain he had an idea.

"Serrot didn't make it."

He looked straight ahead toward the ceiling. "He died for me."

"It would appear so."

"There is a debt there that I must repay."

"He's gone, Lendor, what could you possibly owe him?"

"What he left behind in life; it is now my duty to care for. It is the way of the Brutons. It is called Gunnowism."

"All he left behind was Cedar." As soon as the words left my mouth, I knew what he now meant. "She's not a possession, Lendor, you can't just take her, and don't even think about telling her you're going to 'take care of her.'"

"It is not meant that way, only that I must do all that I can to ensure she is cared for," he said without offering any clarification.

"Tread lightly, Lendor. She's going to need a lot of time to heal."

"I will only be there when she needs me; of this, you have my promise."

"I am glad to see you mostly well."

"Mostly?"

"You look terrible."

"I feel decent, Winter. I was assuredly going to die. I had said my final traveling prayers and was ready. The meddies somehow brought me back; it was a strange sensation to have traveled so far into the realm of spirits, to wake finding myself in a tube. You can see how I could be upset."

"I do. Rest; I will visit later."

There was a small hiss, a bluish release of gas entered into the chamber and in a moment Lendor was asleep.

"Got the sedative," the Geno meddie said. "Now perhaps I can get some work done in peace."

I wanted to go back to the bridge, but I was running out of energy. My legs were getting stiff and my head heavy. I detoured to my room, letting Graylon know to get me up before the buckle. I thought I might need some of that blue gas Lendor had received when my head hit the pillow, as my brain, unlike my body, was spinning on its axis. I was going to get up, when inexplicably, my thoughts began to calm, and I found myself sleeping. I was whisked away to a field; Tallow, Cedar, Serrot and myself were gathering blueberries and eating them by the score. I knew I was dreaming because I was enjoying the fruit. Didn't matter; it was good to see Serrot. He smiled and waved goodbye to me as a voice came into my room telling me I was needed on the bridge. I don't know much about the other side, but I know that was Serrot and he was letting me know that he was all right. I thanked him for the message as I arose.

When I walked onto the bridge, Graylon was there. I didn't

feel overly rested after my small nap but worlds better than he looked. He had not left his station, and he looked exhausted.

"Has sleep clarified your thoughts or are you still of a mind to go through with this?" he asked.

"I am. Are you?"

"I do not like it, but I fear you may be correct. We are not in a position to turn away help, wherever it may come from. That, above all, has me concerned. It is not too difficult to believe that Brigend knows this as well."

He was right, but still, Brigend had passed up an opportunity to finish us—or hurt us more, anyway. Graylon gave the order to buckle.

"We will be there in an hour."

In terms of a buckle, that was fast, but the number of miles traveled was still staggering. We'd no sooner stopped when my heart lurched, not due to the strange mode of travel but rather at what awaited us. Brigend had a ring of ships around us. We were one to their twelve. I had wrongly assumed when he told us to come alone that he would do the same. It was an oversight I would learn from, if given the chance. Graylon was a heartbeat from giving the order to buckle again.

"I did not think you would come." Brigend's face was displayed on the comm screen. "Although, it is good you did."

"Is this a trap?" I asked point blank.

"It would be the ideal set-up, but no, Winter, this is not a trap. I have someone here that may be able to put you at ease."

"Johnjon?" I was thankful Graylon was so close; there was a chance I would fall over and I could use him to prop me up. "Are you prisoners?"

"Hey, Winter! It sure is good to see you. We're all here; your Bruton squad, the Dystancians, Comanchokees…all who would come."

"What do you mean 'all that would come?'" I didn't know what was going on.

Brigend spoke up. "We've been watching Earth for a while now. Use it as a place to get away when we need to. Caught wind the Others, as you call them, were now very interested in the place and it goes without saying they did not have good intentions. We have been off-loading people from the planet's surface for a couple of months now. We have everyone who wanted to go. Some stayed; can't blame them. Earth is all they've ever known. In fact, they never even knew other worlds existed. Difficult to convince people to get on a ship that flies the stars when most have never even been on a horse."

He was talking but I couldn't process the information quick enough. "Why? Why did you do that?"

"We're human, Winter. It's what we do."

"I thought you were a pirate, only out for yourself?"

"Have you not listened to anything I've said?"

"No. The first impression you made has stuck with me."

He laughed. "Graylon, get your other ship here. We will be traveling far to our home. We can get the repairs you need, and we will talk further about what needs to be done to win our world back."

"That's it? We're going to leave those that are left to their own devices?"

"There is nothing more we can do; time has run out. They have chosen their fate, though I argued loudly for them to change their minds. Some would not."

"We have to go back."

"Breeson has an armada parked around the planet now. Going would do nothing except spell our doom."

"Graylon?"

He was still looking at the screen; I had no idea what was going through his head.

"We are no match for Breeson's fleet; not like this." He finally turned away and to me.

"I tried, Winter. As an officer and a gentleman in the United Earth Marine Corps, I tried. We saved who we could, and when we can, we will save the rest."

"Johnjon?"

"We were among the first picked up, Winter; he tells the

truth. I went down on more than one excursion trying to convince people. Many times we were even attacked, and still, he pressed."

"Sometimes, the imprisoned know no other way. We have seen it before; a regimented life is a difficult thing to break free from. There are those that are content being told what to do, their lives defined by the structure, even if it is of a harsh nature. Fear of the unknown can be a hindrance many cannot overcome."

I was stuck, but he was right. How could we help those that didn't want to be helped? We couldn't force them, and even if we tried, all we would be doing was exposing ourselves to even greater danger. We'd already suffered so much. I instinctively knew if I pressured Graylon, he would begrudgingly go back. But what would that prove? And the blood of those lost would be my fault. I could not, I would not do that.

"I'm ready when the rest of you are." I resigned myself to what was happening.

The Genogerian sister-ship showed up in a few hours; we explained what was going on. When Brigend sent the coordinates over to Graylon, I noticed surprise in the Commander's features.

"Truly?" he asked, looking up to the screen.

"How do you think we've survived for so long?" Brigend wore a wry smile. "We should probably get going; even with the buckle, the journey is not a short one."

"What's it mean?" I asked, looking at the chart.

"It's a black hole."

"A hole in space? Aren't all holes black?" I had no reference to what he'd said.

"It is created when a star dies and collapses in on itself; the gravitational pull is so strong that nothing can escape, not even light."

"So that's where the name comes in," I deduced. "Doesn't seem like a place conducive to life."

"It isn't." Graylon was again looking at Brigend.

"We live on the edge of the pull, just out of its reach."

"There is no world there."

"You'd be surprised what you can find out in space."

The journey took nearly a month. I thought I would go crazy with worry of all those still behind; it was Cedar, of all people, that prevented that. She had her own demons that she needed to escape from, and with a single-minded determination, she threw herself into training. She was a woman possessed, and I was along for the ride. She did not talk of Serrot at all; I felt like she thought if she never brought it up, then it never really happened. I wasn't sure if she was in denial, until one day, after a grueling fifteen hours of training I had walked with her back to her room. She'd no sooner closed her door when I heard her sobs. She was still very much suffering; she just chose to do it alone. My heart grieved with her and for her.

CHAPTER THIRTEEN

THREE YEARS LATER

The Horizon wasn't a planet—not a naturally occurring one, anyway. Of that, Graylon was right. What we stopped at, some three years previously, was, in a word, astounding. It was a human-built structure; I was told it was nearly the size of the moon. It shared some similarity in shape in that it was partly round, though the middle stretched out to make it look more like the rings of Saturn. It was the color of an angry storm cloud and was woven together by nanotechnology, machines that were apparently too small to see with the human eye. The beauty was that they could also detect damage and repair it before it ever became a problem for the inhabitants. I tried not to think of them much; I couldn't get the image of electronic spiders out of my mind when I did.

For three years, we trained, we gathered resources, sought out allies, and I watched as Cedar slowly healed. She had more of an edge to her than before; she wasn't quite as happy all the time as she had been, and that change was difficult to witness. Sometimes, when she didn't think anyone was looking, I could see the smile she had, be quickly replaced by a sadness that ran deep within her. When we would mock-fight during our training exercises, she would go all out with a deep determination to destroy the enemy. Losing was not an option, and on those rare occasions when she would, she was nearly insufferable. Sort of like today.

"Watch it!" she told Tallow as she sat down and hit his side and arm, causing him to drop a forkful of food.

"You realize I was here first, right?" he asked as he moved slightly over.

"Yeah, well now I'm here." She dug into her meal like it had somehow offended her. She did not eat with any signs of enjoyment, but rather something that needed to be done to keep her running at optimum performance. It was not overly difficult to foreshadow what was going to happen next as we had often heard this diatribe.

"When are we actually going to do something? These exercises against each other aren't doing anything to defeat the real enemy. All we're doing here is wasting time."

The first few hundred times, we had attempted to explain what was going on or how beneficial all the training was, only tended to add fuel to the fire. And once Cedar got going, well it wasn't too good of an idea to stick around. We'd since learned to say nothing or change the topic of conversation until she moved on. It sounds worse as I write this down. Cedar hadn't changed fundamentally, but she'd been affected, as had we all. Dinner was done and I knew where she was headed as she got up.

"She heading to the simulator again?" Tallow asked, shaking his head.

"You know that's what she does when someone bests her."

"It was seven-on-one, and she took out five of them, something no one else on this weird planet could do. I don't think she should beat herself up about it."

I knew what was consuming my sister, powering the relentless drive. She would tell others differently, but she wanted revenge, and if possible, to single-handedly end the regime that had taken Serrot from her. It wasn't so far-fetched to believe she could deliver on that vow.

Tallow and I had gone to the observatory; I found myself here whenever time permitted. The spin of the station kept us in constant view of the black hole. There was a destructive beauty there that I could not help but gaze upon.

Tallow couldn't understand my fascination, for the life of

him.

"You know it's just a giant hole, right? Hey, you think maybe there's a library in there?" he asked, joking.

"You see that bright light there?" I was pointing. "Brigend told me that's a planet, been circling this black hole for over a hundred years. He said the scientists here believe that it most likely had life on it. Can you imagine?"

"Can I imagine that what you consider a normal life is completely and abruptly different from things that happen in space? Yeah, surprisingly, I can wrap my head around that, Win."

I nudged him in the shoulder. "It's just hard to fathom the power of that. To be so powerful as to rip matter apart into individual atoms and maybe those don't even survive. What do you think happens to everything that goes down there?"

"If those brainiacs walking around in the lab coats don't know, how could I?" he shrugged.

"I think whole new universes are created. All that matter is torn apart and rebuilt; it's a fresh start."

"Most people's idea of a fresh start is to move to another city," Cedar said as she walked through the door. "Not violently rip themselves apart into sub-atomic molecules."

"Cedar! Did you stop obsessing?" Tallow asked.

I smacked him in the arm.

"What? It's not like she doesn't know what she's doing."

"Is it difficult being a dolt?" I asked him.

"Not so much." He was smiling.

"Can I talk to my sister?" Cedar asked Tallow.

"Of course you can," he said, not moving.

"She means alone," I told him.

"I knew that," he said sheepishly and headed for the door.

When she was sure he was gone and the door was shut, she took a deep breath before she began to speak. "Major Rettings is putting together a team to test out our new fighters and the weaponry."

"What do you mean? We've been testing them for

months."

She was looking at me, an intensity in her eyes. "In real-life situations."

"I don't understand."

"Our long-range surveillance systems have picked up communications about the location of one of the Others' patrol ships."

"And?"

"And we're going to attack it."

"Just going to fly out and attack a ship?"

"Exactly. What do you think we've been training for all this time?"

"And you're going?"

She nodded.

"Why am I hearing about this now?"

"I cut my training short because I just heard about it. I told the major I would find you and ask you."

I turned back, so I was watching the black hole and the millions of twinkling lights that circled the rim.

"When are we leaving?"

"An hour."

My heart leapt as fear and anxiety warred within it.

"Did you tell Lendor?" I asked.

"No need. Fighter pilots can request their own mechers, and he's mine."

"He's still an apprentice."

"There will be other mechers there if he gets in trouble, and this is a quick in-and-out mission. What could go wrong?"

"Did you really just say that?" I asked.

"You'd think I'd know better," she responded with a devilish grin.

"What do I tell Tallow?"

"That's easy," she said. "Tell him you'll be back in a week."

I turned, a look of surprise on my face. "They're that close? Have we been discovered?"

"Doubtful, nobody has left since the pick-up on Earth."

"Maybe found one of our probes?"

"Unlikely, and even if they did, there's no way to trace them back. Best guess is that it's an outpost just keeping an eye on things."

"We also testing out the new cloaking system?"

"Not really a cloak, it just masks the ripples in space that a buckle creates. I'm told we can't get past the quantum physics of how a buckle works, but there is a way to make it undetectable. Something about wave cancelling technology."

"A trial by fire."

"Best kind. I've been waiting for this."

"You promise you're not going to do something rash?"

"Me, rash? I mean, personally, I would never do anything like charge down a slope at a line of Stryvers. If you're talking something like that, no, definitely not."

I grimaced at her. "I mean more like flying a ship into hordes of the enemy or I guess more correctly, crashing into them."

"When'd you get so funny? Come on, we've got to go, and you've got to tell Tallow."

Tallow looked like I'd stuffed his shirt with hornets as he blustered about the room throwing his hands up in the air. His face was red and when he spoke, his cheeks were puffed out.

"It's only a week." I tried to placate him. Might as well have been driving the stingers in myself.

"A week, Win, where I have to wonder and worry what's going on. How am I supposed to deal with that? Try to think if the roles were reversed!"

"Oh, that's easy enough…I wouldn't let you go," I told him.

"Okay, then that's what's going to happen. I forbid you from going!"

I laughed just as Cedar walked in. "I can see this is going well."

"Oh, thank you for that," I told him as I placed my hand

against his cheek. "If it gets difficult at any time, I will always have this moment to smile about."

"Not fair, Win. This isn't how people treat each other."

"Make no mistake, Tallow," I told him, "I have no desire to leave you, or to fight. It's just something that needs to be done. The sooner we're rid of the Others, the sooner we can live our lives like they were meant to be."

"Come back to me," he said.

"That's just what Gwendolyn said to Grendal as he went off to war with England; that's so romantic. It is a little weird that the roles are reversed though," Cedar said.

Tallow was desperate. "How did it end?"

"Well, Grendal died in Scotland, dragged behind a horse, I think, but Grendal's brother Kellan ended up comforting Gwendolyn and then marrying her."

"Cedar, if I die, I don't especially want you to be with Tallow," I told her.

"What? Eww! He's like my brother, Winter!"

"Don't, because if he's your brother, he's mine too."

"This is getting weird. I don't want to be anyone's brother."

"Smart, leaving the door open." Cedar smiled, tapping the side of her head with her finger.

Tallow rolled his eyes at her. "Just come back," he said to me. "Both of you," he added.

"Sometimes the denseness between you astounds me. Is that right?" Cedar looked up and off into the distance. "Never mind." She shook her head. "Tell her."

"Tell me what?" I asked.

"Tell her what?" Tallow echoed.

"O.M.G." Cedar palmed her hand to her forehead. "Not only do I need to be the beauty of the outfit but the brains as well? Fine, fine, I can take on the added burden. I want you both to listen carefully."

"Is she serious right now?" Tallow asked.

"Shush!" Cedar snapped her forefinger and thumb

together. "I've been told that every time we go out on exercises that you, my dear, pining, Tallow, manage to find your way into the control room."

He blushed.

"Even on our extended training missions, he never leaves," she continued.

"Is that true?" I asked him. "You've never said anything."

"I find comfort in it."

"I talked to the duty sergeant. He says you have a basic understanding about the displays and a natural knack for reading the three-dimensional read outs."

"Yeah? So?" he asked.

"The denseness is thick in this one," she said. "Can you take it from here, Winter? I'm starting to get a headache."

Took me a second to see where she was going, I finally got there. "Oh!" I clapped once, much like Cedar, then caught myself. "Um, you could ask to apprentice in the tower."

"Why would I do that? I'm a soldier."

"You're right, Cedar, if not for that face…" I smiled. "If Lendor can be a mecher apprentice there's no reason you couldn't get assigned to the tower as an apprentice."

"I'm a sold…oh…I get it now. I can do that!" He was beaming.

CHAPTER FOURTEEN

THE SURPRISE

Brigend was leading the raid. The new buckle drive system was less stable than the more traditionally used one and he didn't trust anyone else to monitor any fluctuations as closely as he did. Off-duty, the Commander could be very affable; when he was on, he was all business. The ship was much smaller than what we'd been used to. They called it a *carrier.* Large enough to carry five squadrons of fighters, it also had a heavy weapons punch, reducing the living space that much more. The pilots were given five areas, including sleeping quarters, where they were expected to stay and not be in the way of the crew running the ship.

"How does it feel less claustrophobic in a fighter?" I asked Cedar as I ducked down before banging my head on a bulkhead doorframe. We were headed to the cafeteria where we pretended to eat, or at least I pretended. Cedar seemed wholly unaffected as to what was coming up and had no problem fueling up on her food and most of mine.

"You going to eat that?" Her mouth was full as she asked.

"Well, now that you sprayed over it all, I think I'll pass."

"Sorry," she said sheepishly, belatedly pressing a hand to her mouth.

"Tell me again what we're facing."

"You realize you're not quite a blonde, right?"

"What's that mean?"

"It means I've told you three times already."

"You got somewhere else to be?"

"You're lucky you're my sister," she said swallowing her food. "It's a Destroyer-class ship. Bigger than us, more firepower, fewer fighters. Really, our only hope of success rides solely on surprising them and getting two or three heavy punches in before they can strike back or buckle away."

"Do you think we'll surprise them?"

"The tests look good. If we don't, probably not going to have to worry about it too much."

"Why?"

"Really? I'm eating. When you figure it out, let me know."

"Oh." It dawned on me. "Why aren't you worried about that?"

"Nothing I can do about it. We either go and punch them straight in the face or we don't. Me losing sleep over it changes nothing. I'd rather use the energy for other more productive things."

"Like eating, apparently."

"Good one," she said as she thrust her full spoon out at me.

The closer we got to our destination, the quieter the pilots around me got, except for Cedar, who was abundantly jubilant. Partly I figured it was to keep up the spirits of those around us, but an even greater portion I think was because she was finally going to be able to exact some measure of revenge.

Brigend told us when we were twelve hours from our buckle point, then advised we should get some sleep. I don't know how Cedar did it; she could shut herself off better than a machine. I looked over jealously at her sleeping form.

"Stop staring at me," she whispered without opening her eyes.

"I thought you were asleep."

"I am, and so should you be."

"I'm trying."

"Can't dream about being back on Earth with Tallow eating blueberries if you don't."

As sage advice as I had ever been given. I nodded off in under five minutes. The lights slowly came on in the pilots' quarters before a voice announced we were three hours from our approach.

"Want to go and get something to eat?" Cedar was sitting on the edge of her bed in full pilot gear.

"How long have you been up?" I stretched; most of the other pilots were already gone.

"Hour, maybe? Been reading; now I'm starving."

It was useless to argue against it and the more I thought of it, the more I decided I was hungry, even if I was concerned that this could be my last meal, or worse, my sister's.

Got my first surprise of the day; I would have been content to not have any more ever. Frost and Ferryn padded up.

"It is good to see you both," Frost said.

"How did you get here?" I asked.

"Who would stop us?" she replied; there was mirth in her voice.

"I'm glad you're here." I scratched under her jaw, she purred affectionately. I gave Ferryn a head nod; he wasn't much into contact, and I respected his space.

With an hour to go, we were in the hangar doing our pre-flight run-throughs and getting final instructions from Brigend.

"What we do out there today is the first step in a very large campaign that will determine the fate of Humans and Genogerians. We must show them that we are capable and willing to fight. That we can beat them. Our victory today will send reverberations throughout the entire realm. The Others' alliance with the Progerians will be weakened, and once it is on shaky ground, we will press the attack until they are forced to declare a side."

We'd heard this before, but then it had seemed in the abstract, something that would eventually happen. But now that we stood on this great precipice, it was difficult to not look down the sheer cliff. If we won, it would be but the first volley in a war that was far from over. If we lost, it would be with great difficulty we'd be able to change the public's opinion on the necessity of this conflict. Most might be happy to hide in the remotest corner of the universe, to live out their lives on the artificial planet. There was an appeal there, not dying violently being at the top of it. But me, personally, I wanted to be back on the ground, to feel the grass and dirt on my feet and the sun shining on my face.

Not only was the buckling technology new, but so was the way we were going to launch. We were going to use the momentum of the of the buckle to shoot our fighters through tubes like torpedoes of old, so I was told. The idea behind it was the full two minutes we arrived ahead of the carrier would put us in a better position to attack, as we would be more difficult to detect. There were some that didn't agree with us being exposed for all that time without the back up of a war ship. Cedar wasn't one of them. Two minutes, if they knew we were coming and under a heavy assault, could seem like hours.

"Launch in twenty," the computer announced. Didn't have to do much during this part except hold on for the ride.

"Remember, Winter, when we come through the buckle onto the other side, we're going to be traveling much faster than we're used to."

"I was next to you when we were doing the simulations."

"Yeah, that was more for me than you."

I swallowed hard; that meant my sister was nervous, and that didn't seem to be part of Cedar's DNA. If she was concerned, then we all should be.

"Let's keep the chatter down," Captain Banks said. He was in command of the Dagger squadron, which included us. There were twelve bays and we would be sent out first, followed immediately by Saber squadron, then Lightning squad. Thirty-six fighters in total.

"Launch in five…four…three…two…"

I kept my hands off my controls as I was taught to do, sat back and got ready for the ride of my life. I attempted to stay as relaxed as possible as I was forced back into my seat. The lights of the launch tube streamed past and then we were traveling through space faster than any fighter was ever designed to. There were long moments we were enshrouded in complete blackness and the effect of the buckle before we were thrust into normal space.

"Pull up, pull up!" Cedar screamed.

I had barely managed to unseat my head from the backrest as I looked upon the entirety of the Others' hull. My entire field of vision was the gray-blue material. Without even pausing to think on my sister's warning, I did as she instructed. My entire panel was flashing red; somewhere in the cacophony, I heard an alarm trilling. I would have shut it off if I wasn't using my entire body weight to pull back and up.

"Ahhh!" someone cried out as he was too slow and plowed into the side, exploding in a fiery ball. Two forced their ships downward; it was the wrong direction. I didn't see either of their collisions. My ship was bucking wildly as I fought the inertia and was willing my fighter upward. I had my teeth clenched waiting for the impact that would snuff out my life. My imagination, or possibly reality, had me convinced I was scraping against the destroyer as my ship shook violently.

"This is Captain Banks! Delay launch, delay launch! Critical collision!"

I hoped the message got through, but at this very moment, I was doing all I could to not be one of the first to die as the revolution began.

"Almost there, Winter," Cedar said through heavy breaths. "Captain Banks—they've launched fighters."

It made sense; they wouldn't fire their own weapons as we were too close. I banked around when I was finally clear; I could see wildfires pouring out of four gaping holes in the hull of the destroyer. The fighters had acted as high-speed projectiles and punched straight through—no telling the damage they had wrought. Fighters were scrambling forth from the hangar to the front of the ship where Cedar was waiting for them like a fox might a juicy vole, picking them off as they came forth from their hole. She would only be able to do this for so long before she was overwhelmed by sheer numbers. I was moving vertical to her position, cutting through fighters just as they cleared their ship.

The ones behind had seen their compatriots being sliced from the sky and began to come out at varying angles, making it much more difficult to zero in on them. By now we had a half dozen ships in place, but they had more than double that out in the fray. We would not be able to hold our position any longer.

"Dagger squadron, regroup, far side," Captain Banks said.

Cedar had worked with a technician aboard the Space station; in my right ear would be Banks and the rest of the squadron, in my left was Cedar only. There was a small button next to my trigger that I would depress if I wanted to say something only she could hear; she had the same array.

"It's not that I don't trust Banks," she had said when she was going through all the secrecy to get our special gear rigged. "I just trust myself more. If I think he's about to do something that's going to get us killed, I'll let you know."

"What if he finds out about this?"

"Don't know, don't care. You're more important to me than anything he can do."

"The tech won't tell?"

"I told him if he said anything, I would sick Frost on him. Nobody wants to anger a Rhodeeshian."

"Frost know about that?"

"She was with me; figured it would lend more credence to my threat."

"You're a scary person, sis."

"I know." She smiled.

I was confident in my abilities to fly, but knowing I had my sister in my ear was comforting.

"You good?" she asked as we came around the far side.

"Heart is still threatening to pound out of my ribcage, but yeah," I told her as we came out to the far side of the destroyer. I had thought the damage to the near side had been severe until we came around; the fighters had been traveling with such velocity they had punched right through the far side. The exit wounds triple or more the size of the original strike. Space was littered with debris and bodies; we rose above it to avoid micro-collisions. There was a part of me that felt for all those that lost their lives. The interior of the ship was an inferno. I could not understand how they even had the ability to launch fighters, which we were now attempting to evade as they regrouped, this time with the numbers on their side. The destroyer listed heavily as two more fighters blew through and onto our side. Captain Banks' message must have been received too late.

"What's going to happen when the carrier comes out of the buckle?" I asked.

"Dagger squadron, full thrust away!" Captain Banks ordered. We were pulling what remained of the destroyer's fighters with us, and now we had Saber squadron behind them. Shots from both sets of fighters were streaking past.

"Oh, I don't think so," Cedar said as she pulled straight up.

"Dagger three, what are you doing!?" Captain Banks asked her.

"I'm no one's bait" was all she said. I followed her suit. We were looping back around; two of the enemy fighters attempted to follow us and were cut down by Saber squad. We were just pulling out of our loop when the carrier showed, the hapless and helpless destroyer directly in front of it. Those who had still been clinging to life previously aboard the ship no longer were, as the *Talbot* severed what remained into two halves. The carrier was doing its best to bank away from the destruction.

"Destroyer *Integrity*, this is Commander Brigend. Surrender. You have nowhere left to run."

The reply we got could barely be considered human. It was a guttural response that devolved into a rising and falling pitch, underlaid with a hissing. I thought perhaps the one trying to talk had been injured. By now, Lightning squadron was in position and it devolved quickly into a shooting gallery where nothing from the *Integrity* was going to escape. There was more hissing, but they never did stop trying to fire. In less than a half hour, we were sweeping past the front of the *Talbot*, looking for damage. The carrier had been traveling so fast and the structural integrity of the destroyer had been degraded so much that the damage to the *Talbot* was hardly more than superficial; the nano-technology was already at work.

Dagger squad had been ordered back to the hangar when we received the warning that an imminent arrival was incoming. We landed and Cedar and I headed straight for the bridge. Brigend had given up on us following protocol.

"Good job out there," he said as we came aboard.

"One of ours?" Cedar asked, though we already knew the answer. We succeeded or we failed this mission on our own. There was no help coming, had we needed it.

"They could have got a call out for help," I offered.

"They could have and probably did," Brigend said. "But there is no way it could have arrived so quickly."

"They're meeting someone," Cedar deduced.

"That's what we're figuring," Brigend told her. "The question is who. Why did they have to come out to what they figured was the loneliest place in space to do this?"

"I think I know," Cedar replied.

"Inform us." Brigend was not humoring my sister; he'd come to respect her opinion, and unless I was completely misreading their interactions, he was totally infatuated with her, something she either consciously or unconsciously chose to miss. For someone who was so focused on what she did, I had a hard time believing she could not see it.

"We know the Others are rapidly evolving or devolving into Stryvers; however, you want to look at it. I think they hit critical mass. When you asked them to surrender, they were hissing—or what we thought was hissing; I'm betting it's a lot like Stryver language."

"Captain Felder, compare the fighters' transmissions to

Stryver language," Brigend ordered as he turned to his comm officer. "Give me a translation, if there is one."

It was ten tense minutes later when the captain responded. "Sir, it's not a direct translation, but there are more similarities than disparities. It's a mix of Human and Stryver. To use an old phrase, almost a pidgin language of the two. Makes sense, given the Others' vocal cord restrictions. They wouldn't be able to use the same dialect as the Stryvers."

"What's it say?"

"I'm not completely sure, but something along the lines of 'death to all those that oppose us.'"

Brigend turned quickly. "Cedar, I'd like you to take me and a small group out in a shuttle."

"Of course," she told him.

"Major Retters, how much time until our guests arrive?"

"One hour, twenty-two minutes," he replied.

"What are we doing?" Cedar asked him.

"We're going to need a body. Need to see what has happened to them, why their physiology has changed so dramatically over the last three years."

We were aboard the shuttle and doing the pre-flight check when Cedar nudged my shoulder. Tallow was up in the tower. He waved and I waved back. I knew this was driving him crazy, the waiting and watching, but there was nothing I could do about it. I told him that he should perhaps learn some skill in the control tower so that at least he could watch firsthand. He'd taken to that idea immediately. He was still in training but was getting better by the day. It was also nice to know he was only a radio call away.

We were navigating through the debris field left over from the battle. We were going much slower than anyone would have liked. Knowing there was a timer running made every minute we spent looking seem interminable. We'd come across a few bodies, but they had been so mangled or burnt as to be beyond recognition. Brigend was hoping to find someone who had the misfortune to have been sucked out into the vacuum of space relatively unscathed.

"How much time do we have?" Brigend was behind Cedar, looking through the front shield.

"Fifty-eight minutes," was my response.

"We're going to have to turn around soon." I could hear the strain in his voice.

"There." Cedar was pointing off to the left as she turned the ship.

I gulped; it was the upper half of a man. He'd somehow been cut neatly in half. We were staring at the wound, which had frozen completely. Twinkles of light radiated off his midsection from the frozen blood.

"It'll have to do. Get ready," Brigend informed the capture crew.

"He doesn't look right." I was straining to see his features.

"Other than missing his bottom half?" Cedar asked.

"No, she's right. Magnify," Brigend said, stepping closer.

It was difficult to make out as we moved closer, but there appeared to be thick, wiry hairs protruding from odd angles on his forehead, cheeks and chin.

"Damage from the battle?" I asked, more than hoping that was the case.

"I…I don't think so," Cedar gulped.

We got close to the body. The three-man team quickly retrieved it and placed it in a sealed bag. With less than twenty minutes to spare, we were back aboard the *Talbot*. The body was sent down to the lab.

"I want to know the moment you have anything," Brigend told the tech taking the body.

Technically, Cedar and I were off duty, and I also wanted to hear about it the moment they had anything. "I'm going with them," I told her.

"I don't eat cahol chips, but right now, I'm going to see if anyone has any," she replied. There was a disturbed look in her eyes.

I don't know why I was so determined to find out what was

wrong with the man. Maybe it was because I wanted them to be less human; it somehow more justified our fight against them. If any lingering doubt was left, it quickly vacated as the two technicians undid the seal on the body. They were wearing biological suits and were in a negatively pressurized room; I watched from the safety of a glass partition, yet we all still backed up a step when the man's arm flopped out of the bag. It was a blue-gray color that could be attributed to the severe temperatures he had been exposed to, but that could not explain that pencil-thick hairs that protruded. Also, his pointer finger and middle finger were fused together; it could have been a birth defect, but I didn't think so. As they pulled him free from his bag and clothes, the differences became more evident. The strange hair was haphazardly placed all along his torso and his jaw. It didn't look right.

"Beginning of a mandible?" one of the techs asked as he hesitantly reached out to touch it.

"Get a blood sample," the other one said as he lifted one side of the man to look at the back.

Within five minutes, I had all the information I needed to know. The man was now more Stryver than Human, by two percent. Whatever was happening to them was moving at an accelerated pace. This new information was explosive; whatever alliance remained with the Progerians would be blown away like a fallen leaf in a gale. *If* we could get them the information, that is. We still didn't know who was coming or why. I made it to the bridge with three minutes before arrival, but far after news of the Stryver-Man hybrid in the meddie center. Brigend looked grim, and most of the crew appeared as if dinner had not sat well.

The Others weren't originally some hostile alien race bent on the destruction of all others; they had originated from the same place we all had. It was just that their ancestors had made some questionable decisions and now they were faced with the consequences. Brigend wanted to know why the change was happening so rapidly over the last few years when previously it had moved at a glacial pace. I heard phrases like, "tipping point" and "evolutionary markers," or that the Human side was no longer able to keep the invasive aspects of the Stryver contamination at bay. That their immune systems had finally succumbed to the onslaught. Whatever the answer, it didn't matter. They were Stryvers now.

"Wind up the buckle drive," Brigend ordered with less than two minutes before the other ship showed.

"Coordinates, sir?"

"Get us close to the Bootes constellation."

"Sir?" Major Rettings turned to look at his commander.

"I've got a feeling I know who's coming, and I'm not bringing them back to our home."

"Stryvers? He thinks it's Stryvers?" I asked my sister.

"Makes sense, and since we know they can somehow track a buckle, it's the right thing to not go home."

That didn't make me feel any better. If it was indeed Stryvers, they could follow us forever.

"Thirty seconds to arrival."

"Release the drone. Have it send microburst transmissions. Set the self-destruct for thirty-five seconds," Brigend ordered. "And get us out of here."

"What's he doing?" I asked as I felt the familiar pull as the ship was now traveling faster than the speed of light.

"Every second head start we get on those who would pursue us, the harder it will be for them to pick up our trail. Anything more than a minute, it should be theoretically impossible to find us. Now you're going to ask: Why we didn't leave, then?"

I nodded, wondering how she knew all this.

"The drone and the microburst message will only travel so far…"

"And if we left at a minute out, we'd never get it," I completed her sentence.

"Look at you, getting all smart."

"Funny," I told her.

"Incoming transmission."

"Put it on the screen," Brigend said.

The ship that appeared was as menacing looking as it was huge. There was no definitive shape; it looked as if it had been lumped together by a variety of individuals with not a care for what the being next to them was doing. It was clearly not something meant for an atmosphere, as there was nothing even remotely aerodynamic about it. Somehow I didn't think that would matter, as some of the larger arrays appeared to be weapons of some sort.

"A new Stryver ship?" I asked Cedar. She prided herself on being familiar with all the known ships. She said when decisions had to be made in an instant, it could be the difference between life and death.

"It's not like anything I've ever seen, though it does share traits with a few," she replied.

"If the Others' outward appearance has changed, does it not make sense that they have changed inside as well?" I asked. The entire deck crew looked at me.

"You're saying it is of Others origin?" Brigend asked.

"Makes sense, right?" I answered.

"Why meet out here? What's the big secret?" Cedar asked.

"The big secret is what they're turning out to be; maybe it hasn't spread to the populace. If they unveiled this ship at their home, news of it and those that are changing would spread like wildfire." Brigend replied.

"How could they possibly be hiding this?" I asked.

"Is it possible this is a faction?" Cedar asked. "That maybe they're not all like this?"

It was boggling to think of what their nearest brethren might think of them. As if Brigend knew what I was thinking, he continued.

"This could be something we could exploit. Maybe there are those that don't know."

"How could they not? The resources alone to build that ship…" Cedar replied.

"Look what we've done undetected," he answered, referring to our new home.

"Who do we tell?" I asked.

"Everyone," Cedar and Brigend said in unison.

"Sir, we're being followed," Major Rettings said.

"Looks like someone isn't quite ready to reveal their secrets," Brigend said.

"Or they're angry about what we left behind," I said.

"There's that. Either way, I don't want to be around to see what that thing is capable of. Major, let's move to the Berringer scenario; ultimate destination still the Bootes constellation."

The major looked out of sorts with the entirety of what was happening.

"Cedar, can you tell me what's going on in normal terms?" I asked her, trying to stay out of the way of all the activity.

"You want me to start with Berringer or Bootes?"

I looked at her like I had no clue, because really, I didn't.

"Fine, fine, Berringer it is. Early on during the war, there was a famous general—umm, maybe infamous. Jury's still out on that one."

"Cedar." I was trying to keep her on course. Sometimes she had so much knowledge in her head it leaked out in random bursts.

"Sorry. So Berringer was out on an unsanctioned raid, stumbled across three Stryver ships. He fought for a while, but only long enough to make an escape. Of course, the three ships followed him into the buckle; it was only a matter of time before they caught up, and…want to know why they were so angry?"

"Not really."

"He was rounding up Stryver young for experiments, to find better ways to kill them, maybe to keep them from ever maturing or being able to reproduce. It wasn't a popular position, especially with those ruling, who feared retribution."

"Cedar."

"Just giving context."

"Less context, more facts."

"Those are facts."

"The relative ones."

"They're all relative because relatives are pains in the butt," she mumbled. I gave her another look and raised my arm to punch her. "He knew he couldn't outrun them, and because he was where he wasn't supposed to be, there was no help—no help that could get to him in time. So he did something that had, up to that time, never been done. They rigged a shuttle to be able to ride the buckle. I won't bore you with the incredible technical aspects they had to overcome; let's just say it was a pioneering effort. As soon as they were ready, they launched the shuttle out at the same time they removed themselves from the buckle."

"That's not possible; wouldn't the buckle have stopped without the ship driving it?"

"Like I said: groundbreaking."

"What happened?"

"They got away. The Stryvers followed the shuttle. I figured that was evident; I mean, otherwise, how would he ever have had a maneuver named after him? Still, almost got court-martialed for risking the crew and the resources."

"So that's what we're going to do? Launch a shuttle in the hopes the Stryvers follow?"

"No, that'd be a waste of a perfectly good shuttle and anyway, the Stryvers wouldn't fall for it, not again. No, now it's a machine that mimics the effects of the buckle so that their sensors won't be able to tell when we drop out."

"Won't they know?"

"Most likely not. This is all new stuff. As far as I know, it's never been done in a live situation."

"Is it going to work?"

She shrugged.

"Okay, and the Bootes Constellation?"

"Really, Winter, you need to pick up a book."

"I already live in space, sis. We ever get back to Earth, I don't even think I'm ever going to look up again."

"The Bootes Constellation is one of the strangest, remotest, and completely unexplored parts of the galaxy. It is a void that has never been traveled before."

"A void like a black hole?"

"No, it's somewhat different; there's absolutely nothing in it, no visible light. It is so enormous, that if you were in the middle of it and only had your unaided eye, you would not be able to see any stars."

I realized that the universe was vastly larger than I could even comprehend, but an area so large as to not be able to see anything past it was a staggering thought.

"And we're going there why?"

"Because no one goes there."

"I'm thinking with good reason."

"Major, send out the word for everyone to get strapped in," Brigend said before turning to us. "Both of you as well," he said as he pulled a harness across his lap and chest. "The launch of the decoy, along with the abrupt exit from the buckling stream, is…" he paused, "jarring."

We watched the countdown displayed on the screen. With thirty seconds left, there was a high-pitched whine, and I could feel the tightening of the harness. With twenty seconds to go, the force was so great I could no longer pick my head up to watch as the time ticked off. I tried counting in my head; if this went any longer, I was positive my eyeballs were going to be sucked to the back of my skull or I was going to press through the straps, pieces of me sliding to the far bulk. There was an intense shudder before the pressure subsided immediately. I gasped for air I hadn't realized I needed until just then.

"Didn't enjoy that at all," Cedar said beside me.

I nodded in agreement; not sure if she saw me.

"Start the buckle again," Brigend ordered.

"Sir, that's not advisable."

"Neither is getting destroyed by an alien ship."

There was a loud thumping as if the machinery was protesting to the stresses it was being put under, and once again, we were underway. Brigend undid his restraints and stood. “Let’s hope that did the trick.”

“Um, sir,” Major Rettings started.

“You have got to be kidding me?”

“I wish I was. It gets worse. They got much closer with our stoppage.”

“How much time do we have?”

“Five days.”

“I don’t understand,” Cedar said. “New buckling technology is so much faster than it used to be; how can they possibly capitalize on that and move closer?”

“If we ever had any doubts that the Others were more Stryver than Human, this puts that to rest. It is not all necessarily about the speed. The Stryvers have advanced technology that we have never been able to get a hold of that allows them to use the stream and inertia of the ship they chase as a means to increase their own speed. Some of our greatest minds have attempted to puzzle this out; when they could not, they assumed wrongly that adding more speed would somehow shake our pursuers loose.”

“How far to Bootes?” Brigend asked.

“Eight days,” the major said.

At some point, it became evident we were going to have to turn and fight.

“Get my fighter squad leaders to the war room,” Brigend said before leaving the bridge.

Like all the other pilots, we had to wait until that meeting was over. The cafeteria was a hotbed of talk; everyone had theories about who was chasing us and what would happen when we were caught. Not much of it was good, though many pretended to relish the idea of standing and fighting. Even in the crowd, it would have been difficult to miss Lendor; he was somehow sitting at a table by himself, in fact, with an even larger cushion of emptiness around him. He’d created his own starless void.

"He looks surly," Cedar said as she smacked my arm and we headed over. "How's it going?" she asked, wrapping an arm around his shoulder. At first, it appeared as if he might bite her, then there was something more…anguish, perhaps? Was Lendor longing for Cedar? It was something to keep an eye on.

"I am angry," he said, swiftly moving past the brief, questioning look I caught.

"Can't imagine how we would be able to tell," Cedar said. "Could be the way your eyebrows are drawn tight or the scowl on your lips. Possibly the way you sit; I mean, it speaks violence. This room is shoulder-to-shoulder and you have all this space to yourself." She made sure to sidle right up next to him, extinguishing any hope he had of retaining that buffer between himself and…everyone else. I think that irked him further; Cedar couldn't be this clueless. Could she?

I sat across from him.

"I'm your second in command, Winter. It is impossible for me to protect you while you are in that confounded contraption." He was downright sullen.

"That's all right! I'll watch out for her." Cedar was now tracing his eyebrows, which were nearly touching.

"It is not the same. And stop that." He went as if to move her hand away but did not. "I am sworn to protect her, yet whether I had stayed back at the base or sit at this table makes no difference. There is nothing I can do."

I reached across and grabbed his hand. "Knowing you're here Lendor, gives me peace. It makes me stronger when I'm out there."

"Truly?" he asked, looking to me.

"Look, sis, you made him so happy!"

"I sometimes feel as if I have rubbed up against devil's root when you are around," he said to her.

I stifled a laugh.

"I make you itchy and break out into a rash?"

"Something like that," he answered her. I had to once again stifle a smile as he blushed ever so slightly.

"Cedar, give him his space."

"I kind of like that I irritate him. He always seems so unflappable; this is a different look for him."

"Hey!" Tallow waved from halfway across the room. Frost and Ferryn were with him. "Thank you," he said to the female Rhodeeshian. "Wouldn't have been able to find you without their help." He sat.

Ferryn sat on the floor, his head level with the tabletop. Frost climbed up and sat on the bench.

"I'm glad I'm here," Tallow had said. "I've been on enough ships to know how this works. Never know where you're going to end up, and no way I'm staying back wondering what's going on." His words reverberated with all of those sitting with us.

"Do you know what is happening?" Lendor asked me.

I had an attentive audience, but I wasn't sure what I was or was not supposed to say. "We're still being followed." Didn't think I'd given away anything everybody didn't already know; beyond that, I didn't know much.

"Brigend's in the war room now," Cedar said, grabbing some of Lendor's food off his tray. "What? He's not eating it."

"Another space battle which I will take no part in? I cannot wait," Lendor somehow looked even more morose.

"Yeah, the view from where I sit isn't so great either," Tallow said, referring to the control tower.

I watched as a look passed between Frost and Ferryn; the large male quickly trotted off and was gone. I wondered what that was about, but if they'd wanted me to know they would have told me. We talked for a while longer after the crowd had thinned; Lendor settled into his perpetual scowl, seemed more himself. Ferryn came back at this point. It was easy enough to tell he and Frost were having a tense and in-depth conversation. Whatever they were speaking about, they kept secret.

"We will need to talk later," Frost said as they departed, the words only spoken to Cedar and myself. I was unclear how she was able to do that. Cedar looked over to me as I shrugged.

"Looks like my lunch is over. I'd better head back. My sergeant is notoriously hard-nosed." Tallow leaned over and gave me a kiss before he left. Again it was just Lendor, Cedar and me; the rest of the room was completely empty.

"My fortune is tied with yours, Winter, and I would not change that. I just wish I could do something to hold up my end of the agreement."

"You're a good man." Those words felt strange on my tongue. Yes, he was a man, in deeds and actions, if barely in age, as he was only slightly older than me and there were times I didn't yet consider myself old enough to be a woman. Maybe it was because I wanted to once again be that kid that ran in the Dystance fields, hunting for berries—a difficult life, to be sure—but so much simpler-seeming. "This war has just started, Lendor. I think you will have plenty of time to fulfill a debt I do not believe you to owe."

He smiled at that.

"Now, as your commander, I am ordering you to go and get some sleep."

He rose and bid us goodbye. Before leaving, he spent a few extra seconds looking at Cedar. I thought he was going to say something; instead, he turned abruptly and left.

"Was he acting weird?" Cedar asked as she played with her hair.

"How can you be so smart and so dense?"

"Huh?" was all I got. "What do you think Frost wants?" She moved on.

"Don't know, but when Ferryn came back, it seemed urgent."

"Ferryn left?"

"How could you not know?"

"Did you not see me flirting with Lendor? Do you think he likes me?"

"You cannot be that thick. Come on, let's go find Frost."

"What? Thick? Why?" She was hurriedly following me.

Finding Frost was not a problem, as she'd sent Ferryn to gather us and bring us back to a maintenance room. Wasn't much bigger than a closet. In the cramped quarters, I was face to face with everyone present.

"Couldn't find somewhere a little bigger? No one's in the mess hall; we could have had this meeting there."

"I would rather we were in close proximity so you can feel the full weight of my words," Frost said. "And also, there are no monitoring devices in here. I do not wish for anyone to suspect us; there is little going on aboard this ship that we do not know about."

"Spill it," Cedar fairly demanded.

"The fighter commanders and Brigend are planning a diversionary battle to the enemy that follows."

"Okay, that's to be expected," I said, wondering what had them so concerned.

"The fighters assigned will all be voluntary," Frost finished.

Cedar's features got hard; there was a set to her jaw. "A one-way mission."

Now I was the lost one. "Huh?" I asked.

"We pull out of the buckle, launch fighters, and as we're about to engage, the *Talbot* buckles again. The fighters will be left behind with the mission of keeping the enemy busy long enough that the trail goes cold."

"Then they'll come back to pick us up?"

Cedar looked at me with concern. "I wonder if our mother dropped you on your head as a child. I mean, maybe not onto a hard floor, something soft, like thawing ground in March, but dropped nonetheless."

"I get it, I get it. They're not coming back. What happens to us?"

"Nothing good. We get destroyed out there, or the enemy leaves us to chase after them. Eventually, we run out of food, fuel, water…in terms of ways to go, can't imagine it's too good of one."

"Neither of you can go," Frost hissed. "Do not let your pride be your undoing."

"Frost, if we don't, that's two other people taking our spot. I would feel directly responsible for their deaths," I said.

"What she said. There's hardly a choice in the matter."

"There is always a choice!" Frost spun on her quickly. "There are more important things that need to be done and none of them involve your deaths. Promise me neither of you will volunteer for this."

Cedar and I were silent.

"I will have Ferryn keep you company in here until this foolishness is done."

"Prisoners? You're going to make us prisoners?" Now I knew why she'd picked a closet.

"If that is what it takes to be reformed from your errant thoughts, yes. That is exactly what I will do. And if that is not enough incentive, I will go and get Lendor and Tallow and tell them of your plans."

I took note that Frost was between us and the door. How long could she really keep us captive? And if push came to shove, what would she do?

"I promise we will not be doing anything rash." That was all I could give her.

I'm not sure if she was appeased by my words. She turned to look at Cedar.

"Rash, nothing rash," my sister said with her hands in the air.

"All pilots please report to the control room." This came through the ship's comm system. Frost's tail was swishing back and forth in an agitated manner.

"We have to go," I told her.

She chuffed, her lips blowing what sounded like a raspberry. She was not happy about it, but she was going to let us go. I sidled past Frost to open the door and we all exited.

"What do you think she would have done?" Cedar asked

as we hurried away and down the hallway.

"Not sure I want to find out," I replied honestly.

"That's the truth." She turned. "They're still watching."

"Move faster."

CHAPTER FIFTEEN

WAR COUNCIL

"I know it's crowded in here; I won't make this long," Brigend said. He was at the front of the room, looking over at all the pilots. "As I'm sure all of you know, we are being followed by an enemy and we're not entirely sure of their capabilities, though they have origins rooted in an ancient opponent of ours. Not only are they following, but they have the technology to gain on us. We have five days." That caused quite a bit of murmuring among the crowd. Brigend held his hands up. "We cannot allow them that opportunity, I have been discussing strategy with my senior officers and we have come up with a plan that we believe will give us an opportunity to break away from them."

Cedar and I looked at each other; we already knew where this was going. She grabbed my hand, which I willingly took. He began to speak of the specifics of the diversion and attack; my heart was pounding in my chest when he finally got to the part that mattered.

"Make no mistake; this is a one-way journey for those that will be out there. We cannot come back for any that may survive. We cannot jeopardize the main mission. It is imperative that this ship, that this ultimate outcome, is achieved. That is why it can only be by volunteer that this mission is undertaken. I will not order any of you."

I felt myself being gently guided to the front. We ducked under or pushed people out of the way.

Cedar raised her hand. "I volunteer."

"As do I," I said.

Brigend's lips pursed. I got the distinct impression he was not happy with that turn of events. Within ten seconds, nearly all had raised their hands.

"I have never been more proud to call you women and men part of my Earth Corps. I will get back to the fifteen I need by tomorrow with more details. Dismissed. You two, stay here," he said as the rest filed out of the room. "You two are among my finest fighter pilots; are you sure about this?"

"We're fighting for Earth," Cedar said. "I'm not sure you have two other people with more at stake than us."

I tapped Cedar on the shoulder; she turned, and we were both looking at Frost, who was peering through the door.

"Uh oh," she said.

"Listen, I appreciate your willingness to do this. I do. But you both are the face of this rebellion, the symbol of everything we stand for."

"You yourself just said this ship is the most important thing, not any individuals," I said.

"This could go wrong in a hundred different ways. It's possible they don't even take the bait, that as soon as we buckle again, they follow and leave you stranded."

"Then it would probably behoove you to make sure they cannot," Cedar said. "You hold up that part, and we'll make sure they're stuck for the time you need."

The weight of command appeared heavy to him at the moment, as his head dropped a bit. "I'll get back to you. Dismissed."

"Behooved?" I asked Cedar as we headed to the door. "Did you make that word up?"

"It's a good word. What do we tell Frost?"

"Maybe worry more about Tallow." Cedar pointed to where Tallow and Ferryn were running toward us.

"That's not cool," I told Frost.

"Tell me it isn't true!" Tallow demanded, nearly running past us when he couldn't quite stop himself.

"Nothing's finalized," Cedar told him.

The look he gave her was pure anger wrapped in a healthy dose of hurt.

"You volunteered? Both of you?" His gaze swept back and forth between the two of us. "How could you? How could you be so selfish?" he demanded.

"Selfish? It's self-*less*," Cedar defended.

"What about me, Lendor, Johnjon…all of us you plan on leaving?"

"Tallow, we're not the only ones with friends and families. It's not right to expect others to sacrifice if we're not willing," I said.

"It is that Talbot blood that makes you speak so," Frost said.

"The same blood that has kept us linked for time untold?" Cedar asked.

"I wish I could argue against your words," Frost replied.

"We don't know anything yet. Everybody there volunteered; no sense in worrying about it before it happens." I said the words, but my stomach and brain thought otherwise. I was nervous and telling myself it would probably be fine wasn't having a calming effect.

"If you go, I'm going," Tallow said.

"There's no room in the fighters," I said.

He tucked his tongue in his cheek as he thought. "Maybe you're right. Sir." He motioned to Brigend, who had not left the room yet. He walked past us and shut the door.

"Well, that was rude," Cedar said.

"No worse than telling him we're leaving and not coming back."

"This is about me right now, Winter."

"It's always about you, Cedar."

"As it should be. I'm going to go read. That way I won't have to think about what we just did."

"Got a book for me?" I asked.

CHAPTER SIXTEEN

DECISION DAY

It was two days later, and we were back in the war room. It was a lot less crowded. There were twenty of us.

"What is Ludlow doing here? She's a shuttle pilot," Cedar said.

"So's Grennin." I nodded over.

"Before we get started, I want to ask those I have brought here if you still wish to volunteer. No one will think any less of you, especially me, if you decide to withdraw your offer." There were glances all around, but no one reneged. At that point, I figured it would have been more difficult to step back than stay the course.

"Well then, let's proceed," Brigend said. "As I'm sure most of you have noticed, it is not all fighter pilots in here; some changes were made after conferring with my senior staff…and some others." He looked over to Cedar and me. "Some insisted if you were going, so were they, if only to bring you back. You will be accompanied by shuttles."

"Tallow," I fairly hissed. "What has he done." Dread settled over me like a wet blanket.

When the meeting was over, I didn't know if I wanted to punch Tallow or hug him.

"Who knew he was brilliant?" Cedar said. "I just figured he was a pretty face."

"I'm going to kill him." I was huffing and puffing as I did all in my power not to break out into a run. I was heading for the hangar area, where the assault teams were training. I'd no sooner walked in when Lendor sped by.

"Oh, hey, Winter." He was smiling and firing his rifle. They were specially designed for training purposes and shot a much lower-powered ray. Still, when you got hit, there was no doubt, as it caused a fair amount of pain and would put the unlucky victim out of commission for a few moments. Cedar yanked me out of the way as a yellow bolt traveled past my shoulder.

"Sorry!" Tallow yelled from behind a stack of boxes.

"Can I kill them all?" I asked.

"Do you blame them?" Cedar asked. "Yes, I know you want them all to be safe and that is why we're doing what we are, but don't think for a minute that those aren't the same thoughts going through their heads."

"Don't you have a book to read?"

She smiled.

We stayed and watched for over four hours as they trained hard, getting yelled at or shot when they made a mistake.

"They are in their element," Cedar observed.

"Unfortunately," I responded.

Cedar looked up from the book she was pretending to read. "True."

A whistle signified the end of the exercise for the day. "For those of you that got shot, I want you to burn that feeling into your memory, to make sure it never happens again. Get some chow and I want you back here at 1430; we're going to go through the breaching exercise again," Sergeant Balline said. There were groans, not for having to do more training, but rather for the sore and aching muscles that they were enduring.

"This was my idea!" Tallow was beaming as he came over to us, putting the rifle away in a nearby rack.

"Finally, I can make use of my many talents." Lendor had stripped off his soaked shirt; I would have had to be blind not to see Cedar ogle his abs.

"Maybe you should just touch them," I whispered.

"Think he'd mind?" Cedar reached out a few inches before thinking better of that.

"It would seem, Ghost, we will finally fight together again!" Lendor wiped his brow.

"Does he realize what he's doing to me?" Cedar asked.

"No, he's a man, which basically makes him clueless." She laughed outright at that, maybe slightly too loudly, and with a nervous titter. "Okay, don't do that again," I told her.

"What do you hope to accomplish?" I asked Tallow.

"Same thing as you. To stop the enemy from following this ship. And don't give me a hard time about not having any right to do this. I have more right than most, and just as much as you. We're from Earth; if there should be anyone fighting for it, it should be us."

He was basically echoing the same words we had given Brigend.

"He's right," Cedar said as she attempted to keep the fury that was building within me bridled.

"All will be well," Frost said as she and Ferryn entered.

"You two, as well?" I asked, although the answer was self-evident.

Like Tallow and Lendor, Frost and Ferryn seemed thrilled with the prospect to finally be able to do something. That night after their training was done, Brigend had a feast for all of us who would be on this mission. I could not get the idea of this being our last meal out of my mind.

"Lighten up, sis. What did I tell you about worrying?"

"Someone has to," I said, looking over a fair amount of the people laughing and singing as they drank something called beer. I found the beverage to be entirely too bitter, but that didn't stop Cedar from downing more than a few.

"I rink if I knew bout this struff earlier maybe I wouldna been so eager to fright." She hiccuped and giggled at her slurred words, as she sloshed a fair portion of the liquid onto my shirt.

"I rove roo, sis."

"I rove roo, too," I told her as I swept her hair from her face.

"I'm going to ask Lendor to dance with me." She grew serious, then busted out laughing.

And she did. It was strange to see the scowl he generally wore fade into a smile as she made her way to him.

"Good for you," I said as she grabbed his hand. I thought perhaps he would be reluctant, but he went out and made moves that looked like dancing, to my untrained eye.

"Ah, young love," Tallow said as he plopped down in the seat next to mine.

I grabbed his hand and we went and found some private quarters. I wanted to think on something different, and we succeeded. For a while, at least.

CHAPTER SEVENTEEN

TURNING POINT

The next morning, I had never remembered seeing so many people look less likely even to be awake, much less fight. I mean, of course, except for Cedar; she looked like she'd just slumbered peacefully for the last twelve hours.

"What's wrong with everyone?" she asked.

"I think it was the brew."

"Hmm, maybe I didn't drink enough of them."

"I think you had plenty."

"Where's Lendor?" I asked.

"How would I know?" she said much too quickly.

I left it at that.

Brigend was walking around clapping shoulders, talking animatedly with everyone that was going. He was all smiles in appearance, but his movements were stiff; he was doing his best to hide the burden he was carrying, of basically sending us all to our deaths. Maybe that was why he gave everyone the brew, so that they would be too distracted to be able to see through his façade. Unlike last night, lunch was a somber affair. There was little talking and even less eating. Again, except for Cedar; she was eating leftover meals from everyone next to her.

"How can you eat?" I asked as I pushed my tray over to her.

"How can you not?" She gladly took it away from me.

"I mean, with what's about to happen?"

She studied me, her eyebrows furrowing. "We're going to

kick ass today. And I'll let you in on a little secret: we're not dying."

She said it with such absolute ferocity she had me half convinced. I was doing fine—right up until I watched Tallow and Lendor walk into the shuttle and the doors shut behind them. It was about that point that my legs got weak. I looked to the ladder that led to my fighter and wondered how I was going to make it up with dead legs. Cedar was standing at the top of the platform for her fighter, whistling while she checked something in her helmet. She swept her hair back and forth before donning it. There was not any part of her that was not a warrior; I did my best to mirror her. Did surprisingly well until I stumbled on the second step.

"One foot in front of the other, sis!" she yelled over.

I gave her the gesture she told me was for swearing; she laughed.

"Wrong finger!" Then she hopped in, the canopy closing and locking.

I stuck each finger up in turn; one of them had to be right. Coordinating the launch made it necessary to not only sit in our fighter for an extended amount of time but also within the confines of the launch tube. Claustrophobia, which I didn't suffer from, was worming its way into my head.

"This is Raven Two." It was Cedar; she was second-in-command for this mission. Should have been first, but it was difficult to tell a Colonel he now had to listen to a Captain, even if she could fly circles around him backward, as she would tell me. "Each of you on this mission are among some of the bravest souls I have ever had the honor to know. Today we are going to accomplish something that our forefathers could only dream of. We are going to pierce the heart of the beast. A lesson will be learned here that will be talked about for generations. And you want to know how that is going to happen?"

There were more than a few smatterings of: "How?"

"I am going to personally make sure that this story lives on, because all of you here will be telling it to your kids and grandkids. Nothing? Tough crowd. Listen, people, this isn't the end; this is just the beginning. If you think I joined this thing because I thought I wasn't coming back, you're just crazy. Though I walk through the valley of death, I will fear no others…."

"Launch in fifteen," interrupted her.

"This day is ours, Raven squad! And don't you ever forget that!" she yelled.

"Ten."

"Victory is ours!"

"Five."

Now she got the triumphant yells she was looking for, as we screamed through the launch tubes. I felt like I could finally breathe, though the space I was allotted had not grown. We got into a loose and very spread out V formation; Colonel Rafferton was front and center. The three shuttles of troops were behind us and hopefully, adequately protected. And with the *Talbot* to our back, for the time being, anyway, it felt like maybe Cedar was right; we could make it through the day. Then the alien ship showed, and if everyone there didn't feel the dread wallop them in the chest like I did, then they were stronger than I. It caused discordant feelings just to look at it. It did not look like any vessel we had thus far encountered. I might have stayed there with my mouth hanging open for another few moments if not for Cedar spurring us on.

Brigend fired two of those ship-busting missiles seconds before they had even appeared. Evading them was all but an impossibility, though the enemy fired as well, but by then Brigend had buckled away and the *Ordnance* flew harmlessly off into space. With the departure of the ship went the illusion of safety.

We were close enough to the Others' ship that we had to avoid the debris that flew free from the missile strikes. I was happy they had hit, but I had misgivings; if they did destroy the ship and now we were out here for virtually nothing, what would the point have been? I'd expected more, for them to keep firing, for a buzzing of fighters to exit and attack. Something. In the meantime, we were performing strafing runs along the hull in preparation for the shuttles to breach through the opening the missiles had made.

"Any idea what is going on?" I asked to whomever wanted to answer. "They give up?"

"Something's going on," Colonel Rafferton said. "There's a yellow glow rising along the surface."

"Pull back! Everyone pull back!" Cedar announced.

"I did not give that order!" Rafferton replied.

"If you want to live, move now!" she shouted. We were peeling away from the ship as fast as we could. The ship started to glow so brightly it was difficult to look at. The slower shuttles were having a difficult time keeping pace. I was matching pace with Tallow's shuttle when the percussion wave radiated out from the Others' ship. Those, including the colonel, who had not heeded Cedar's advice, were instantly blown apart. We could see as the spherical energy ball radiating out further and further, quickly catching up to those that had reacted too slowly.

Two more ships, including a shuttle, were caught and exploded into fragments—and still, the ball came.

"Get that shuttle moving," I hissed.

Cedar pulled up alongside me.

"This is Raven 7." Lieutenant Cooper was speaking, a man I'd not talked to more than a handful of times. "I've been hit…still here, but my engines have shut down." I located him on my radar; he was bearing our same direction and at speed, though apparently, he had no control.

"Who else is without power?" Cedar asked.

Two more ships reported in. The question was, what did we do now? If they had been stopped, we could have potentially pulled a shuttle up to them and made a transfer. It wasn't without risks, but it beat the alternative. As it was, the fighters were traveling too fast; the shuttles would not be able to keep up.

"Winter, Captain Faulkner, we're going to stop those runaway fighters. Shuttles, stand by for orders," Cedar ordered. "I've got Raven 7; Winter, you're on Tunney, and Captain Faulkner, you get Brentner."

I was about to ask her how we were going to get them when she continued.

"This is the plan." I shook my head back and forth the entire time she talked. "Now get to it."

Facing a Stryver with a small knife would have been less harrowing. At least, if the Stryver killed you, it was only one person; this crazy maneuver endangered both pilots. What was worse was we had lost comm with the fighters; whatever had taken out the engine had also now shut down the electrical system, so we couldn't even tell them what we were about to do.

"Gotta move fast people; their life support systems are most likely offline. The clock is ticking."

"Thanks, Cedar, I was hoping we could have a little more pressure."

"You've got this. Shuttles, stay close."

I pulled alongside Tunney; she was a small brunette which she more than made up for with her loud and boisterous attitude. She was one of the most well-liked and well-respected pilots out here. She had a small flashlight in her mouth, her head down; she was attempting to get the ship back up and running. I pulled slightly ahead of her until she finally noticed. I put my left hand up; she was looking at the back of it, then I brought my right up in the same manner, moved it slightly past the left and placed it in front of my right hand and then pulled back.

She put her thumb and forefinger together in an OK gesture. I was glad she was alright with this; my guts were churning. Although really, what choice did she have? Her life was void in a few minutes, once the freeze of deep space got to her. I sped up before turning my thrusters off. Pulling in front,

I hesitated before I slowed. If I did this wrong and the nose of her fighter didn't strike the center of my rear end, there was a chance she could damage my engines, or worse, she would begin rolling, and once that happened, there would be no chance of this working.

I had to silence my collision alarm; the maneuver had to be done completely by the radar system, as I could not see her once I pulled ahead. My hands were sweating within the gloves. I would have felt so much better if Tunney could have at least verbally guided me. Then the heavens finally felt the need to bless me.

"Just a bit to the left, Win." It was Tallow. "We're watching you on the screen…almost perfect. Right there, that's it."

The harness kept me tight to the seat; didn't prevent the jarring impact that jerked my entire body as I slowed enough for contact to be made between us. If we lived through the day, I was going to pay for it in soreness. I eased the backward thrusters on; my ship began to shake as Tunney's ship wanted to keep moving forward.

"Ease off," I said softly. If I applied too much pressure on her, chances were Tunney's ship would skitter off to the side. There was another bump, not quite as bad as the first. I again applied some backward force. This time my ship was not shaking nearly as much. I kept slowing down, careful to ease off if I began to shake again. The grinding, grating noise as we scraped together echoed loudly through my cabin; I would imagine it was just as bad for Tunney. Alarms warned of structural damage to my ship; it was all I could do to block out the extraneous noise and concentrate on getting her as close to a standstill as possible. It must have been working, as the shuttle was catching up.

"Good job, Winter! I'm going to help Faulkner," Cedar said.

"Show off," I said through gritted teeth. The other shuttle was already in the process of bringing the pilot over.

"When you've got it, there's no sense in hiding it." She sped off.

Tunney was basically crawling now; I felt as if I could finally breathe.

"Good job, Win. We've got it from here," Tallow said. I watched the shuttle door open. Tallow was suited up and tethered to the ship. His thrusters moved him closer to the dead fighter as Tunney popped her hatch and free floated out, making sure to keep one hand on the canopy—I would imagine as a sort of safety blanket.

"Push off, Lieutenant," Tallow told Tunney. He wanted her to be free of the ship. If either of them hit the still-moving ship, they could be forced away and possibly slam into the shuttle with bone-breaking results. Her movements were hesitant, but she knew she only had the few moments of safety that the suit and helmet afforded her. She pulled herself close to the ship and pushed away. Tallow deftly maneuvered and caught her gracefully. I wasn't sure when he had become so proficient with the controls, but he made it look effortless.

"Pull your arms in. Got you," he said as he wrapped his arms and legs around her. "All right, Lendor, bring me in. And not as fast as in training when you thought it was hilarious."

"But it was," Lendor responded. "Arms flailing about like a rag doll."

I gave the shuttle the thumbs up sign as I sped off to see if there was anything I could do to help Cedar and Faulkner.

"Ease up, Captain!" Cedar exclaimed just as they were coming into view.

"I've got this." The tremble in his voice was a sign that he didn't.

"I can do it," Cedar told him.

"I've got this," he said again. A metallic crunching sound came over my headset. "Dammit," he muttered. "Looks like I destroyed my starboard engine."

Brentner's ship had skipped off the back plate. There was a bright blue flame out as the engine was wrecked. Faulkner was doing his best to keep his fighter stable, Brentner was very much in danger of spinning.

"Move!" Cedar ordered. "Winter, going to need you to tap Brentner's wing. Wait until I get into position."

I raced around to come up and behind, waiting for her order.

"Few more seconds. Winter, the very moment you tap that ship, dive down and away. You got it?"

I knew the dangers here. If I did not move out of the way, we would very likely be involved in a deadly three-way collision as Brentner's ship smacked into Cedar and I plowed into and through both of them. The sense of accomplishment and peace I had been feeling moments before was wiped away in a sea of anxiousness.

"Ready, Winter."

I was easing closer, my heart concussing in my chest so violently it was sending tremors into my extremities.

"Now!" she demanded.

I tapped the wing and dipped down using after burners to get away. I more than expected to hear my tail wing being torn off and was pleasantly surprised when it wasn't.

Cedar was still struggling to get Brentner under control as I came back around; a steady stream of sparks was shooting off to the side from the contact.

"There's fire," I told her. From my angle, I didn't know if it was the back end of Cedar's ship, the front end of Brentner's, or both.

"How bad?"

I got as close as I dared. Brentner was frantic; his cabin was filling up with toxic fumes. I could see a dancing of shadows inside his canopy as the flames had traveled up the nose, and his cockpit was on fire.

"Better hurry," was all I told her. The shuttle was too far back and still losing ground. Even if she stopped the ship in the next minute or so, Brentner would be cooked alive before his ride could get him. His hatch blew away as he must have hit the emergency release. Luckily, he had not ejected yet. If he had, he would forever be tumbling into space, strapped to his seat. The lack of oxygen did what he intended and snuffed out the fire, but that only meant his life support clock was ticking loudly. The suits weren't designed for much more than five minutes exposed to the extremes of this climate—or lack of.

"Cedar, he blew his hatch and the shuttle is too far out."

"You have got to be kidding me."

"Not much choice in the matter."

"How far back are they?"

"Ten minutes at most."

"Win, we're eight out," Tallow said. "Coming now."

That was many minutes too long.

It took a few more minutes to get Brentner's ship stopped. His movements were getting sluggish, as if he was trying to move rapidly freezing blood through his system, which could very much be the case. I was less than thirty feet from him; I was going to watch him freeze to death.

"Tallow, hurry," I told him but there wasn't any more that they could do.

Cedar and I were side by side; I was doing my best to keep him in sight and active. He weakly waved one hand, then it dropped down into his lap. I got above and turned my ship slightly, so I was looking down on him; his legs had been burned, and now where the suit had melted away was crystallizing. He wasn't going to make it. Even if by some miracle he lasted until the shuttle got here, there was nothing medically that could be done for his extensive injuries.

"Captain Ludlow, I am ordering you to hurry your ass up!" Cedar shouted to the man piloting the shuttle.

"Cedar." I got her attention. When she looked over, I shook my head.

I could see her smack her dashboard.

Brentner's head fell forward.

"Almost there," Tallow replied.

"Head back," Cedar said with little inflection in her voice.

"Didn't you hear me?"

"Captain Ludlow, head back and please try and keep your crew under control and off the airwaves," she said.

"Understood." I watched as the shuttle turned back around. I went to join them; Cedar lingered a few moments longer, giving a short, solemn prayer to the deceased before she also turned and joined us.

It felt like we'd been away from the battle for days; in truth, it hadn't been more than fifteen minutes and yet nothing more had happened. The ship hadn't buckled, nor fired any more weapons. Our fighters were keeping a respectable distance, considering what had happened the last time.

"Raven squad, get into attack formation. Captain Ludlow, once we have the ship covered I want you to breach the hull," Cedar said.

I switched to our private frequency, not wanting to question her orders in front of everyone.

"What are you doing? The plan was to take the hangar if we could. They breach the hull, you know as well as I do about the DNA detectors in the halls."

"That ship is as offline as the fighters were."

"Are you sure enough to send them in there? To send Tallow in there?"

"Is this what this is about? Are you worried about Tallow?"

"What kind of question is that? Of course, I am. I know what he's out here for and I know he's quite capable of performing his task admirably, but you're placing him directly in harm's way on what, a hunch?"

"I'm not sure if you're aware, Winter, but we're all in harm's way. I've yet to detect anything on that vessel that even slightly resembles a hangar area. In fact, I'm not even sure they have one. We are running out of time and that thing might be our only chance. The pulse that came off that ship…I am mostly certain that it was due to damage from the strike. It had the same effect on them as it did us. And yes, I am willing—no, I am *ordering* them into harm's way because there is no other way. Do you want to freeze in your fighter like Brentner did? I don't. I'm much too angry, and I want to take it out on somebody, and they're right there. We done here?"

I said nothing. Yeah, I was angry too, but I had a different idea of who I wanted to punch just now. Cedar moved us in closer to the ship, but not so close we couldn't escape if the strange pulse started up again. We waited there for indeterminable moments before we moved in closer. I didn't like this; I felt as if we were being led into a snare and it would spring the moment we were close enough.

"The rest of you stay here. I'm going to get a closer look," Cedar said.

I wanted to be mad at her, but what she'd said was true, and there was never anything she'd make anyone else do that she wouldn't do on her own, again proving those very words. She took her time, thoroughly going over the entirety of the ship. I never let my guard down, fearful that the moment that I did, something catastrophic would happen, some strange new alien device would lash out and destroy my sister's ship. When she began to fly to the far side and out of our sight, I decided there and then that I would disobey a direct order. Figured the chances of a military tribunal convening were slim.

"Pretty sure I told you to stay put," she said to me just as I came over the top of the ship. She was much farther down, once again crawling along close to the hull.

"My headset must have got damaged."

"I don't see any hatches or openings of any sort, except for the ones we put there. No windows, portholes…I can't even tell where the sensors or gun emplacements are." She turned her ship so she was perpendicular to that section of the hull. Her front mounted lights came on and illuminated the area. "I'm looking into the exit hole; no activity, no lights, no signs of life. I know what you're thinking because I'm thinking it too, Winter, but if it's a trap, it's a really elaborate one. We're going to have to risk it."

"I know," I told her.

"The hole here is big enough that the shuttle will easily be able to fly in and land. It must have been a storage room of some sort; it's massive. It's empty now; everything is scattered across the universe at this point. Captain Ludlow, I'll need you down here. Raven squad, I want you spread out evenly across the hull. Anything so much as stirs on this ship—shoot it. Lieutenant Grennin and Delfines, I want you both to stay where you are."

"Understood," they replied.

"Winter, I want you down here with me. We can cover the assault team when they get inside."

The closer I got to the ship, the less I thought they were feigning dead. It felt truly dead. Now I had to wonder: what good would it be for us? We had people here with engineering experience, but to what point? If the technology was as alien as the rest of the vehicle, it would be a small miracle if they could even work on it. The shuttle off-loaded its team without any incident. Cedar and I had our lights trained in the room along with our cannons. Flashlights bobbed around from the dozen soldiers inside.

"Nothing, no movement," Tallow reported. "We're going farther in."

"Roger that," Cedar said.

As their lights faded away into the darkness, the panic within me began to well again. I wanted to blast holes through the hull, so I could watch their progress.

"Got something here." Tallow was on. "It appears to be a pressure-tight door. Definitely put in place after the strike. Must still have some live ones inside."

There was silence as Cedar mulled over what to do. There really weren't many options.

"Use the explosives. You need to get inside."

"If they're alive in there, twelve people might not be enough," I replied to her.

"Sis, we need to find out. We're in floating caskets otherwise."

I wasn't sure if trading out the one I was in for a much larger box was worth it.

"I'm going in," I told her. "I'm better with boots on the ground."

"Winter, you don't have the right suit on if the atmosphere in there is compromised."

"They have spares in the shuttle."

"Thought this out, have you?"

"Cedar, there're no fighters to engage; the ship isn't firing on us. All I'm doing out here is waiting. I'd rather be doing something."

"Permission granted," she sighed.

I was happy she acquiesced, but I was going regardless. I switched over to regular communications. "Tallow, I'm coming in."

I expected him to protest; he knew better. Maybe he was finally learning.

I flew into the large ship and landed close to the shuttle. In a couple of minutes, I was suited up like the rest of the team. Have to admit, it felt good to hold that rifle in my hands. There was something very different about fighting an enemy you could see up close. From the cockpit, something that was a very intimate matter became an abstract one. Killing another being should be personal; I guarantee the one dying feels that way.

"Good to have you here, Ghost," Lendor said. "We've placed charges upon the door; at your order, we're ready to go in." There was an eagerness to his voice.

"Let's get in there." We moved back to the relative safety of where the ships were parked.

Tiegs, the demolition expert of the group, was ready to go.

"Fire in the hold," he shouted.

"It's hole." This from Cedar.

"But it's not a hole, not yet," Tiegs responded. "Three…two…one…" There was a slight rumble under our feet and then a much larger one, enough that we had to grab onto what we could so as to not be tossed about.

A blast of fire and debris blew past our location and into space. This was immediately followed by four bodies, Others that were standing too close to the door. Didn't get much of a chance to look at them, but it would have been impossible not to notice there was something wrong about them, and not just that their bodies were broken and burnt.

Lendor looked over to me. "Shall we?" he asked.

"Yes, and stop smiling."

"This is my war face."

"It very much looks like you're smiling."

"A warrior is much more comfortable in his skin when he is warring."

I poked my head around the corner; the fire had been extinguished, though the borders of the hole were still glowing a dull red.

"Jerdig, I want an explosive round through the door," I ordered. He came up alongside of me with his special rifle. It launched a shell that, upon impact, would blow apart and a concentrated blue plasma charge would radiate away, sheering through anything in its path.

"Firing," he announced.

We watched as the ordnance slammed into the wall next to the hole; I grabbed Jerdig and pulled him back. The round had bounced and was heading back as its shell exploded. I landed on top of him as the blue rays snaked out. When it was over, Lendor ripped the weapon away from his grasp. For a moment, I was concerned that he might beat the other man with it.

He turned the corner and fired another round, this one neatly deposited within the confines of the enemy-held portion of the ship. I was just getting up as the glow dissipated. Lendor roughly shoved the rifle back into Jerdig's hands.

"I think not," Lendor said as I was attempting to move to the front.

"I know how to fight, Lendor."

"That is without doubt. Until you can learn how not to die,

I will lead. Let's go you lot."

As we were cautiously moving forward, Lendor held up his fingers for me to switch to another channel.

"These men have trained well, but I do not know how they will hold up in a combat situation. I long for our squad."

I knew what he meant; there were soldiers that could do all the right things while they were in the regulated safety of a training exercise, but when your life was in mortal danger, some just froze, their minds no longer working correctly.

"You two going to chat all day or are we going to go get this done?" Tallow asked, after having intruded into our private line.

I switched back. "One at a time through the breach, then fan out, hold a perimeter until we are all through," I said.

Lendor was first through; he motioned for the rest to follow.

"All clear." This from Tallow. Between the missile strike and the plasma grenade, the immediate area was a twisted, jagged display of metal bent at varying angles. To our immediate front was another breach sealing door. From the small area we were in, a corridor led off in each direction.

"Can we seal the damage we did?" I asked. I would rather fight with my helmet off; I felt more in tune with my surroundings relying on my own senses than those of the equipment I was wearing, even if it did have thermal imaging and life-spotting radar. There was nothing within the range of the helmet, which meant we had at least a hundred-foot circle around us free from the enemy.

"Got a torch in the shuttle, should be able to weld something back in place. That creates another problem though," Kolder said.

I knew what he was referring to; if we needed to make a quick getaway, we could be in some trouble. But I had to think in the long-term. If we were going to make this ship our home, we needed to be protected from the violence of space.

"Kolder, get it done. Jerdig, you go with him, watch his

back," I said.

We stayed alert as I gave Cedar an update about what was happening inside. She did not share in my outlook, said it was too much like sealing a tomb. Kolder had started welding the door when we got our first warnings on our displays. It was an occasional blip as something would run by, right on the periphery of the helmet range. With Jerdig helping Kolder and Tallow and Lendor with me, I divided the rest. Each team was responsible for anything coming down their assigned corridor. It was not a large fighting force, and a ship this size could potentially have thousands of personnel.

On more than one occasion, I got the urge to tell Kolder to stop what he was doing and open it back up. We would just wait outside and go quietly into the night…then the realization would hit me: die a slow, miserable life out in the vacuum of space, or die a quick, painful one inside. What was the difference? I only had one life to give; I wanted it to count.

"Just finishing up, Lieutenant," Kolder told me. Took more than a moment to realize he was talking to me.

Detter was my Staff Sergeant and had been in charge of combat training. She was one of the most capable people I had ever met, male or female, in hand-to-hand and small arms fire fighting.

"Staff Sergeant, send someone down each hall see if they get hits on their cams."

"On it. Leadtoes!" That was Corporal Leddings; he got the nickname Leadtoes because at two hundred and fifty pounds, he sounded like he had heavy metal in his feet when he walked.

He started down the hallway to our right.

"Blanks." That was Private Blanks, four months ago she had been working the galley when she decided she wanted to do more. What she lacked for in real-world experience she made up for in enthusiasm.

"Yes, sir!" she yelled much too loudly; my headset squelched, as did all of ours.

"Ease up off the throttle, private," Detter told her. "Go

down the hallway. As soon as you get a hit on your helmet, let us know.

Leddings had made it all the way to a hatch; he shook his head when he got there. "Nothing."

Blanks hadn't made it more than twenty feet when she stopped. In direct contrast to her previous boisterous reply, this one was much more subdued. "So many targets have shown up they are registering as one massive blob on my gear."

"Come on back," Detter told her. "Lieutenant, we need to find a more defendable position."

There was only one option. I motioned for the hallway Leddings had checked out. The Staff Sergeant twirled her finger around for Leddings to do an about-face. We had three watching our back as we moved down the hallway in a column formation. Leddings was out in front. He stopped three-quarters down.

"Got movement. Four, no, five bogeys. Looks like they're running."

"We can't let them get into position. Go!" I ordered. We ran for the door.

Lendor turned the heavy handle, pulling the door inward; Leddings was the first through.

"Another hallway," he announced.

We could see a small group running perpendicular to our location. Three-dimensional imaging showed them to be ten feet below us.

"They're on the deck below. They will attempt to surround us," Lendor said.

Unlike the dark hallway we had just vacated, this one was partially illuminated, though the lights were flickering, causing a strobe effect that was unsettling.

"One good thing about the bad lighting," Tallow said as he pointed to a small pinhole in the wall above. It was a camera port. "Most likely they can't see us."

That was a plus for our side, now we just had to hope they didn't have some other sort of sensors. But for now, it was one small victory at a time.

"They're coming up," Leddings said, though we were now all in range to see what he had. I turned just as a hatch slid to the side. I fired into the surprised face of a monster that would have forced me from a nightmare. I kept firing as another one came up the stairs; I neatly removed its head before it fell back from where it had come with wet, heavy percussions that echoed in the small chamber. A third scurried away before I could get it.

"What in the name of fried chicken am I looking at?" Leddings had shouldered past me and was looking straight ahead. "Next time, Lieutenant, maybe don't shoot it in the face; could have got a better idea of what we're dealing with."

"I'll keep that in mind," I told him.

Tallow was beside me now. "Its body doesn't look right." Besides the thick hairs that had poked through most of its clothing, the chest was abnormally large and irregularly shaped; it could not be attributed to my shots.

"Excuse me," Lendor said as he leaned down to the body, a knife in hand. He cut away its shirt, revealing two, small, misshapen arms that were tucked close to the body. They were wet and covered in a thick slime and pinned close like a newly hatched bird's might be. There was more than one gasp as most of the squad saw the deformation.

"What is going on here?" Tallow asked.

"They're turning into them," Lendor replied.

"No time to gawk." My headset was displaying multiple incoming.

"He doesn't look so good," Tallow said, staring closely.

"Would you?" I asked.

He shook his head.

"They're going to surround us." Lendor was looking at the same convergence as I was.

It wasn't going to be that difficult; our squad wasn't big enough to truly challenge them for supremacy on this ship. We would have been better off staying out in space and blasting them apart piece by piece, but that avenue was now blocked.

"Cedar, we're in a bit of a bind. Give them something else to think about," I said.

"You get yourself killed in there, sis, I am going to track you down and knock some sense into you. Hunker down."

"You heard the woman." We fanned out to keep an eye on the doors leading into the room we were in. The hull rang like a bell as the fighters and the shuttle gave an all-out barrage. There was a momentary pause to the Others, but they did not stay frozen for long, nor did they retreat. There was a distant explosion; a few seconds later the deck under our feet rippled with the concussion.

The first of the warped Others ran through the door. His speed seemed otherworldly, and if he hadn't been coming straight for me, I'm not sure if I would have been able to track him fast enough. I put two in his chest, sending him sliding back to the door he had just exited, his body impeding the next one out. It was Lendor's shot that took off its head. There was a moment where the body had not realized it had been decapitated and stood like a sentinel—a monument to all those who had been beheaded. Then, as he was falling, he was pushed over by the next soldier trying to come in. This one was shot by a multitude of rifles.

I thought their strategy was going to be throwing enough bodies at us that we would be overrun. The door was nearly blocked with the dead of those trying. I felt like we could hold out forever; that all changed when a canister no larger than a tin of food was tossed in over the dead. I ducked my head and covered up just as a deafening explosion rang out. Even though my face and eyes were hidden, a brilliant light still managed to shine through…and then there was nothingness. I could not hear, or more importantly, I could not move. I could not help thinking that I was dead; the only thing that made me question that was the incessant ringing in my ears and the savage pain that stabbed at the back of my head. I felt hands wrap around the lower part of my legs. I could not even manage to turn my head as I was dragged along, my face scraping against the cold, metallic surface.

As the noises in my head began to subside, I could hear a sort of guttural speech, mixed with words I could understand. I was still reeling inside from whatever the weapon had done to me, but I knew enough to realize I had been captured. Blood coated my entire face as I was dragged through the remnants of someone or something; I was not sure as I could not see anything else besides the floor in front of me. I'd now wished I'd left the protective device upon my head, luckily the comm units were built into the suits and not my long gone helmet.

"Winter!" Cedar screamed. "Answer me!" She sounded panicked and right now she had every reason to be. I wanted to answer, but just getting my chest to take in air seemed about the best I could muster.

"Answer me, dammit!" she screamed, and I felt the ship shudder as she let her frustration out on it.

"Winter…" A voice no louder than a whisper heard from across a fogged meadow.

It could have been Tallow.

"Do not speak!" boomed out and was followed by the solid strike of a boot on a body. There was a sucking in of air and wheezing and still, I didn't know who it was. Though I couldn't move, my heart seemed to be making up for it as it fluttered wildly, struggling against the invisible bonds that had been placed upon me. Iron chains would have been preferable.

"Do you think Lokken would mind if we ate a couple of them before we brought them to her?" one of the voices asked.

I was disgusted almost to the point past revulsion. They looked Human enough to realize that this was wrong.

"We are not them yet!"

For a second, I thought I had a champion that would maybe not fight for us but might at least fight for his humanity. That didn't last long.

"First to Lokken, then we feast."

As I was pulled from the room, I heard the distinctive

sounds of teeth gnashing and the loud slurping of liquids. A single tear was able to escape my eye as I mourned for whoever had fallen victim to the cannibals.

"You're going to wear her face away if you keep dragging her like that."

"I care not. They have damaged our ship and killed countless of our crew."

"You may not care, but Lokken wants them in reasonably good shape so she can interrogate them."

I was dragged a few more feet before the other muttered some swears. He bent down and turned me over. We were staring face to face.

"Well, aren't you a pretty one? And all that blood; it looks like you're basting in it. I am going to drain you dry." He smiled as he licked his lips. Then he opened his mouth wide; there was a squelching noise within. I watched as his throat began to move like a gulping fish out of water. That was when the true horror started; a gray, pointed protrusion pushed past his lips. What looked like venom dripped from the tip of the single fang. I desperately tried to turn as he dragged it lightly across my face.

"Sogell, what are you doing?" someone asked from behind. The appendage quickly reeled back into his mouth; he was still sneering.

"We'll continue this later," he said as he hefted me onto his shoulder. I caught a quick glimpse of the room; there were at least two of my squad dead. Other than that, I don't know who lived. My vision was once again obscured as my face was buried into Sogell's back; black spiny hairs abraded against me, scraping more than one wound open. The ship still rattled as it was attacked and Cedar continued to try and hail me, though I had the feeling she had an idea of what was going on, as she would be able to hear the Others speaking.

"Winter, I don't know what's wrong, why you can't speak, but your vitals still show as good. Elevated heart rate, but other than that, fine. I will keep monitoring you and I will get you out of there."

I silently thanked her. I may have managed a grunt in reply.

"Where does Lokken want the meat bags?" Sogell asked. "The dining hall?" He laughed at his quip.

"Prisoner containment," was the reply.

"Looks like you're in for some tenderizing before we eat." Sogell laughed. He walked for a little while longer before he lifted me off his shoulder and tossed me unceremoniously onto the floor. I had a flash of panic as the air was forced from my lungs and I could not get enough in to sate my desire. With some difficulty, I was able to roll from my side onto my back. I was staring up at an illuminated ceiling. I shut my eyes as I willed my slumbering limbs to work. I could feel my fingers curl and uncurl, though I could not lift my arms or my neck to actually see it happen.

"It's awfully quiet, Winter. What's going on?"

"Trying," rasped out of my throat. If I hadn't known I'd said it, I would not have believed that to be my voice.

Once she heard me speak, she rapid-fired more than a dozen questions. I had to tune her out as I was desperately attempting to not be so helpless. When I was finally able to lift my head and look around, I was alone in a small cell. It was another five minutes until I was finally able to sit up.

"Cedar." My throat was so dry it came out more as a croak.

"It's so good to hear you. Are you all right?"

"I'm alive," I managed as I put a hand against the wall, doing my best to get my legs under me. "They attacked with some sort of paralysis bomb. Lost at least two people; I don't know who." That came out more as a sob. "I'm alone in a cell. Someone named Lokken, I think it's their commander, is coming down to talk…to interrogate me. I need to get out of here. I need to find Tallow and Lendor and the rest." I couldn't bring myself to add the last part: *if they're alive*.

"I know you can hear me in there." Cedar must have

opened up the channel. "I will tear this ship apart if you do not let all of the prisoners go."

She repeated that message two more times before someone responded; it was a distinctly female voice, though it had a strange resonance to it.

"Have you not already done enough? Unprovoked you have shot missiles at us, doing irreparable damage. And now that our ship is crippled you still fire upon us and send landing teams—to do what? Perhaps finish what you have started?"

"You will let the prisoners go or…"

"Or you will what? You have already proved you will destroy us whether we have the prisoners or not. I think you will be less likely to do so if we still have what you want. I will meet with you, and you alone, but only if you cease fire immediately. If not, be careful where you shoot, as the holding cells are on the outer perimeter and the most likely to suffer damage."

Cedar growled out a "Fine, open up your hangar and I'll be there within fifteen minutes, but I'm going to let you know now, I have my fighter packed with enough explosives to break that part of the ship apart and if this is some sort of trick I'll do just that, taking as many of you with me as I can. And if you hurt anyone, well, let's just say none of us will have to worry about how this negotiation goes."

I knew that first part was not true; I could only hope Lokken thought it was. The second part, was as certain as the sun rising.

"That will be completely unnecessary. I would just like to talk with the person in charge of so callously attacking us."

"All the same, I don't think I'll be off-loading my package anytime soon."

"I don't think this is a good idea," I told her.

"Don't you worry about a thing. I'm going to get you all out of there," she said back on our private channel.

The front of my cell was clear. I placed my hand up against the see-through barrier; I could feel a slight tingle from the power that passed through it. I gave it a slight punch; it had absolutely no give to it. I thought about kicking it but refrained. "Hello, is anyone else around?" I yelled, hoping to hear a response. "Tallow? Lendor? Leddings?" I was angry at myself; I'd led my team into a trap and now had no idea how to help them…or whether they were beyond help.

"That's a useless way to think. How about getting yourself out of this jam instead," I said, trying to use anger to disrupt the anxiety welling within.

I could hear voices approaching, though I could not, as of yet, see who they belonged to.

"Who is the leader of this rabble?" the woman that had been speaking to Cedar asked. That meant at least one other person was alive, as she was not speaking to me. "Get up!" She was yelling now. I was waiting desperately to hear a voice, any voice, but selfishly, I wanted to hear the one of the man I loved. All I got in response was a grunt.

"Pull them from their cells. Beat an answer out if you need to!"

"Me," I said hoarsely. Then with more force, "I am the leader."

The woman was in front of my cell in a moment.

"You? You're the leader? I don't believe you."

"Honestly, I don't care what you believe." I was still fighting through the effects of the charge I had received.

"Get her out."

Two guards came to my force field. I noted that they did not press anything that I could see to deactivate it; either someone else had done it out of my view or they wore something that allowed them access. Or perhaps they had some sort of biometrics coded to their uniqueness. That was possible; maybe not likely. Chances were on occasion they had to use these cells on their own kind, then what good would it do if they could walk out at any time.

The men ushered me out but did not touch me. Not sure what they were worried about; that I could walk under my own power was still iffy.

"Tell her to stop," Lokken said.

"Let me see the rest of the prisoners."

"You're in no position to make demands."

"And yet I have."

Lokken nodded her chin to one of the guards, who punched something into a large device that wrapped around his left forearm. I turned just as the doorway turned from a smoked brown color to opaque and finally clear. I walked past one, got a thumbs up from Staff Sergeant Detter, the next held Leddings, who was on the floor but breathing. Kolder was sitting on a cot holding his head in his hands. He looked up to see me but said nothing. My heart leapt as I got to the next one. Lendor was pacing the room like a caged animal.

"You are all right!" he said, coming to the barrier.

"I am. We'll be getting out of here soon."

"Good to hear. Does she know it yet?" he asked, pointing to Lokken behind me.

"She will soon."

"Enough." Lokken roughly shoved me.

"Are there any more?" I tried to keep the tremor out of my voice.

"This is all that survived your malicious attack."

I turned slowly just as a guard was whispering in her ear.

"Oh yes, there is one who is in surgery now. You see? Because we are not barbarians, we will even treat those that would attack us."

"You will take me to him, and please feel free to stop with the self-righteousness. Our kind have been fighting for seemingly ever. You can pretend with the indignation, but the truth is more obvious. If you had been given the chance, you would have attacked first. The nature of war does not dictate that an enemy must announce his intentions; it should always be assumed that bloodshed will follow confrontation."

"What is to prevent me from spilling your blood right now then?" she sneered.

"I would imagine it's the threat of your ship being slowly torn apart by the barrage it's receiving. There's that, and what makes you think you could kill me?"

"I was beginning to like you; I may have to change my perspective. Those with delusions of grandeur rarely survive."

"They're only delusions if they're not true."

"Perhaps it would be for the best if you remained silent as we travel to the infirmary; we can hope that the attack being waged on us does not interfere with the sensitive electronic equipment as our prisoner is being operated on. I could not help but notice your expression as you looked upon the captured; you're looking for someone, someone special, I would wager. I do hope he's the one we're going to see. For your sake, I mean."

I was angry I had tipped her off; it would do no good to attempt to dissuade her to the importance of who I was looking for now. I decided to keep silent.

"Ah, the first intelligent thing you've said today," she said in response to my quietude.

I did my utmost to quell my feelings as we arrived at a window that overlooked the infirmary. Down below, housed in a clear tube and being administered to by no fewer than three machines, was Tallow. The desire to run down there to comfort him, to make sure he was all right, to sweep him up in my arms and make a run for it, was nearly unbearable. All of that warred within me, yet I shrugged as though disappointed. I turned to Lokken.

"I would like to know when he is out."

"So he is not the one. I would like to say I'm sorry, but that would be a lie. He will be fine. He had a concussion, a broken rib, and a laceration on his liver. Should only be another hour before he goes into recovery. Again, that is if your cohort doesn't destroy something vital. Come. We are running out of time." She spoke something too silently for me to hear as we traveled down toward the hangar.

We watched from behind a viewing port as Cedar's ship

landed; the area was repressurized and Lokken, myself, and a dozen guards entered.

"So much for alone," Cedar said. "Lieutenant, it is good to see you."

"Same, Captain." We kept our speech as formal as possible as to not give Lokken anything to work with.

"And the rest?" Cedar asked with concern.

"There have been some casualties," I told her.

Cedar wanted to ask me a dozen questions but wisely said nothing.

"Come, come. It would appear we have a family reunion taking place; I do not think it would be uncalled for if you two hugged."

"Commander Lokken, I was under the impression we would be meeting alone," Cedar said, ignoring the other's jibe.

"This is my ship; I will do as I please. And under no circumstances will I make deals with a terrorist. Take her prisoner as well." She motioned for her guards.

"Hold up there, spidey," Cedar said. "I realize that you didn't heed any of my words, but remember the part where I said I would be bringing a package aboard?"

"We all know that blowing yourself up is not a terrific bargaining chip," Lokken said.

"Blow myself up? Oh, certainly not, but do you wish to see what I have?"

"I have no time for these games. Grab her!"

"Yes, Frost, grab her," Cedar said.

Lokken gasped as Frost's fangs brushed against the commander's neck.

"Captain, feel free to grab a weapon," Cedar said.

"You cannot work them," the guard said as I walked over and grabbed his rifle.

"Give me the wrist tablet as well."

He looked over to Lokken, who was as still as a sculpture. She nodded her head ever so slightly; if there was ever something that terrified her, this was it. The fear of

Rhodeeshians must be ingrained deeply within the psyches of Stryvers.

I no sooner attached the arm device than the rifle lit up and indicated it was ready for use.

"The rest of you might as well put those down," I said, motioning with my gun. "That wasn't a request." Again, they looked to Lokken; this time she did nothing.

"I am told that the venom from a bite is one of the most excruciating ways one can vacate the living," I said.

Lokken's eyes were closed but still, there was a nod of ascension.

"That's the most intelligent thing you've said today," I told her.

When the guards were on the ground and unarmed, Frost finally released her grip on Lokken's neck, though she stayed close.

"How dare you bring one of those filthy animals aboard my ship." Lokken was fairly quaking with rage.

"There was a time when at least half of what you are fought alongside their kind," I said.

Lokken shuddered.

"Well, maybe less than half now," Cedar added.

"What are you planning on doing?" Lokken asked.

"We're going to need this ship for starters," Cedar said, very matter of factly. "What are the chances you'd just give it to us?"

"That is not going to happen."

"Here's the deal. We're stranded out here."

I looked to Cedar, wondering why she was freely giving information away.

"With nothing else to do, I plan on using this ship as target practice until such time as I run out of fuel, air, or munitions, or more likely, until there is nothing left of this bucket worth wasting a round on. Our scans show your buckle system offline and your life support hanging by a thread. We've not been able to get a read on your weapons, but since you're not fighting back, I don't think I have to travel too far down a limb to say they are either damaged or offline as well. Maybe you get your systems up and running in time, maybe you don't. But what are the odds I don't have another Rhodeeshian, even now, roaming through the tightest crevices of this ship, placing charges in some of the most vulnerable locations?"

Lokken kept her cool, though her eyes narrowed.

"So with all I've said, how do you feel now?"

"I would rather we all die out here than I ever turn this ship over to you," she replied.

"I figured this wasn't going to be easy. I mean, sure, I hoped, but one can never tell. So this is what we're going to do. You're going to allow us to get the captured, wounded, and deceased. When that's over, I will begin the process for your capitulation."

"Do you believe that I am just going to allow you to remove the only bargaining chip afforded to me at the moment? What kind of option is that?"

"Well, as far as I see it, there are no options other than you all die. I'll leave that decision to you. Now go send some of these guards to round up my people."

Lokken did not look as if she was going to comply; that ended the moment Ferryn came into view.

"It is done," he said as he paced around the men on the ground.

"Crager, get the prisoners." The man closest to her got up; he made sure to skirt around Ferryn as much as was allowed.

"We have one of yours in the infirmary. To move him now would only speed up the outcome you seem to most desire," Lokken said.

Cedar looked over at me. "I'll stay with him," I told her.

"Are you sure?"

"I don't trust her."

"I'll give you a remote for the explosives. Don't worry, Commander; if you somehow got it from her, which you won't, it can't be deactivated from there."

Within fifteen minutes the four from the raid were led out. Cedar called in one of the other shuttles to pick them up. She again looked over at me when she saw them. I gave her a terse nod.

She gave me a hug and leaned in close. "Are you sure about this?"

"I have to stay with him."

"Completely understand. Be safe."

I wanted to laugh out loud at the lunacy of that statement. How I could possibly "be safe" on a ship full of the enemy was ludicrous. "I'll do my best," I smiled.

Anxiety increased within me as I saw them all leave.

"Come. We will wait at the infirmary." Lokken appeared to have got herself back under command with the removal of Frost and Ferryn.

We were no sooner in the room when three guards came in.

"You will surrender your weapon."

"Not really a fan of that idea." I had my rifle raised, as did the Others. "I'll just hold on to it. Maybe all of you should just leave, then there won't be any unneeded tension."

"Very well. Although you do realize there will be guards posted outside," Lokken replied.

"Not a doubt in my mind."

She was heading out the door when a thought crossed my mind.

"Why are you really saving his life?" I asked.

"Is it not enough that we are?"

"No…I appreciate it, just doesn't make much sense. Your ship is crippled and…and you…" I wanted to state something about the mutations they were undergoing, but left the thought unsaid.

Lokken waited until the guards were out of the room, she closed the door and directed me to a seat.

"I'm going to stand."

"As you wish." Lokken strode across the room and sat

down. "We are changing from what we were. At first, we were nearly gods among men; our minds vastly superior to those we had deviated from. It wasn't until much longer that the side effects began to manifest themselves." Lokken stroked some of the fibrous hairs on her arm. "What we fought so hard to separate from, Humankind and their foibles, we now desire to recover. We've been falsely convincing ourselves we are still Human, even as more of the disadvantages of our 'upgrade' reveal themselves. It was when we first discovered that we could begin to talk to each other telepathically that we knew our end was in sight."

I gasped at the notion that they could now listen in on each other's private thoughts.

"Oh yes, it was as disconcerting, as you might imagine. Human minds can be a cesspool of errant, deviant, sometimes evil thoughts. Fighting amongst our own became the norm as no secret was safe. This calmed down as we became more like Stryvers, and we began to understand the fact that we were all moving toward the same goal. There are a great many among us that are welcoming the change, no matter how far it brings us away from who we originally were, and still others, like myself, are doing everything in their power to halt or even repeal the changes. I very much remember what it is, or was, like to be Human; I do not want to be a Stryver. That, and the process…" She hesitated.

"It's painful," I answered. I could see the anguish in her eyes. We may be enemies, but that didn't mean I couldn't have compassion.

"It's that." She looked up at me, "and more. It's frightening to the depths of my very soul. To lose one's self so completely."

Then it all came rushing back, all I'd heard, all I knew. "This is why you want Earth. Why you're saving him." I pointed to the window. "What can you hope to accomplish?"

"There are some among humanity that are naturally immune to the Stryver DNA. Their bodies completely reject the foreign cells, destroy them, in fact, and pass them through with no more difficulty than food."

I grew suspicious; my eyes narrowed as I looked upon her. "And how do you know who's immune?"

"There are two processes. A very unobtrusive test that merely requires a small vial of blood, and another more…*invasive* measure that involves injecting the DNA into a host."

"And?" Alarms set off in me, much like my fighter when it's under attack.

"The unobtrusive method requires time: a luxury we can ill-afford."

"So what? That's your plan? Inject as many people on Earth as you can and see who rejects it? You selfish bastards! You made your choice and now you want to take that away from others?"

"What would you have us do? The need to survive, to flourish, is hard-wired into all of us."

"But at the expense of everyone else?"

"You are not that naïve. Isn't war all about surviving and flourishing? Haven't you killed to ensure just that?"

"This is different. And don't you try and justify it with some superior-sounding moral compass. Those people, they're not your enemies. They're not fighting you!"

"What rose-colored glasses you wear. They have—no, they *are* a resource, and all wars revolve around resources. Whether territory, precious metals, food…what does it matter what the resource is? They have it and we need it."

"You've known for ages your kind are changing; why didn't you go to Earth and do the testing when you still could?"

"As I said, there are those that don't wish to alter the course. They feel it is our evolutionary right, and unfortunately, these people are high ranking members of society; senior military officers. We have not had authorization to travel to Earth until recently, when your sister's ship was detected. Oh, look at that face; it's priceless. In saving you, she ultimately doomed you. How ironic."

"And Tallow?"

"Your precious boyfriend? Don't look so surprised. It's my job to know everything."

"*What about him!?*" I raged.

"We'll know in the next twenty-four hours if he can fight off the injection. I have to admit, the odds are not in his favor. I'm told only one one-thousandth of the populace can."

"I am ashamed to know that we share any DNA. Reverse it. Get it out of him!"

"I can no more do that than I can rid my own body of the poison."

"Want to bet something you didn't know?" My reflection in the glass was a mask of hatred; a part of me shrank away from it, another reveled in it. I leveled the rifle on her. Her head disappeared in a misted shroud of bone, blood, brain, and hair. The detritus had no sooner settled when a guard burst through the door. I sent him back into the hallway with a fist-sized hole in his midsection; blood poured from his mouth as he fell over. Another guard ran past the door but not in. I heard a loud yell as my shot hit his trailing leg. I heard him fall over but knew enough not to stick my head out the door and see if I needed to finish the job. I looked down to Lokken; her chest still rose and fell; her body didn't know quite yet, she no longer lived. I would have not taken note of it had it not lit up at that exact moment; she was wearing an arm device much like the guard, though hers was bigger. It was warning her that her vitals were slipping…if it only knew how far they would sink. I suspected she would have access to things a guard might not; I ripped it free from her arm and tucked it into my pocket. Then I ran across the room and secured the door by shooting at the electronics panel. I had no idea if that would work or not, but as of yet, no one was trying to gain entry. My only exit was through the glass and to the infirmary floor, one story down.

"If that glass is plasma-proof I'm in trouble." I was angry

at myself for not properly thinking this through. My anger had clouded my judgment and I had put Tallow in even more jeopardy than he already was. The glass dissolved under the assault of the rifle charge. The two technicians working on him looked up. One was reaching for something; I shot him before he had the chance to get to it.

"Move!" I ordered the other one to the far side of the room. Ten feet wasn't extremely high, but certainly high enough I could break a leg or roll an ankle. My best bet was to climb out and hang down the sill, making the drop as short as possible.

"Hurry!" I could hear hammering on the door behind me and an alarm trilling.

"Winter, what's going on?" Cedar asked.

"Change of plans. Hold one," I told her as I dropped down, bending my knees to take less punishment. "Get him out of there!"

"He's still being worked on." The tech raised his head, his arms held high.

"Will he live? Will he live if he gets out of there early?"

"I…I need to check where in the process he is."

"Get up then, hurry. You do anything I don't like, you'll end up just like him." I pointed to the other tech with the barrel of my rifle.

He stood and went over to a panel, punched in some information and was reading it. "You know we're justified in what we are doing," he said. "You're nothing but savages bent on destroying everything you encounter."

"I'm glad I gave you everything you need to alter your perception of us, enough to justify your horrific actions, I suppose. Will he live!"

"You realize he's now one of us, right?"

"And yet, I'm the savage. I'm losing the reason I need you any longer."

"He'll live; he'll be in pain, but he'll live."

"Get him out of there."

"He'll be too weak for you to make good on your doomed escape attempt."

"You let me worry about that."

"He's already sacrificed enough; why not leave him here? See if his life will be worth anything."

"I'm done. Can't reason with the unreasonable." I neatly removed his left hand from the rest of his body. He cried out as he held up the stump, the wound neatly cauterized by the heat generated. "What would you prefer to lose next? And you might want to hurry, before shock sets in."

He moved to the cocoon device Tallow was in and pressed a series of buttons; there was a hiss as gas escaped. Tallow's eyes fluttered; at first, they were dim as he fought upwards from the depths of the sleeping agent, then they flew open and he sat up quickly.

"Oh no." He wavered, gripping the edge of the machine.

"Winter?" Tallow and Cedar asked at the same time.

"Come on, we need to get out of here."

"Where am I?" He was doing his best to crawl out.

"The Others' medibay." I slung my rifle over my shoulder to help him. The technician had retreated to the far corner of the room and slid down the wall, his right hand had gripped his forearm and he was staring at the void where his hand had been. He was rapidly going into shock.

"Where's everyone else?" Tallow was now partially standing on his own.

"We're it. Can you walk, preferably run?"

"Win, I can barely talk right now."

"Cedar, I'm going to have to shoot my way out. Did you hear what Lokken said?"

"Every word. I regret that we're not going to be around longer so I can send them where they all belong."

"Not quite dead yet," I told her.

"We'll keep them busy out here. You going to be able to make it to your ship?"

"Doubtful. Tallow doesn't have a suit."

"He can make it for a minute, maybe more."

"Not the way he is now."

"Head that way. There's still a shuttle."

I didn't like that idea, though I didn't tell her. The Others were detestable beings, but they weren't dumb; they would know that was where I was heading. I wondered if the wristband I was wearing would give me authorization for one of their ships. The hangar was really my only shot. I would have headed to the bridge if I'd known where it was.

"I need a weapon."

"Maybe once you can hold your head up we'll get you one. I'm afraid you'll blow your toes off." He was shuffling along as I went over to the door; it opened, and I was relieved to not see anyone in the hallway. The alarm was still bleating, and I was worried that it would cover up the sound of people running toward us. I motioned for Tallow to follow.

"She's in infirmary room eight," came from behind me.

"This is what happens when you show mercy." I came back into the room and finished what I had started, only a few moments too late.

Tallow managed to look back. "We're in it pretty bad then?"

"What gave it away?"

"Gotta cut me some slack; I'm still out of it, and this shrill noise in my skull isn't making it any better."

I looked over at him with a questioning stare. "The alarm, you mean?"

"Oh, thank goodness." He did not explain any further.

"We have to move." It became an elaborate dance of propping him up, moving and keeping my rifle at the ready. In a ship full of hostiles, it wasn't optimal.

"I'd ask you to leave me behind, but I feel like that would be a waste of energy."

"And yet you said it," I grunted as I hefted more of him. "Cedar was right; it's a good thing you're pretty." I mostly dragged him to a point hopefully far enough away from the medical bay. "You're right though, we're not going to make it like this. We need to hide until you get some strength back. Here, hold up this wall."

"How am I going to do that?" he asked as I let him go.

I flipped my wrist electronic at the nearest door. The way things were going, I was fairly sure it was going to be crew quarters and I was going to be staring at a couple of hundred surprised soldiers. Instead, I got a darkened room; there was someone on a bed surrounded by all manner of machinery. This was a meddie room; seemed as good a place as any for Tallow to rest. I prodded the strapped man on the bed; he did not stir. I quickly went back and helped Tallow in. He had slid down to the floor, his head nearly in his lap.

"Just need a minute," he said as I wrapped my hands under his arms, and instead of waiting for him to stand, just pulled him along on his backside. It was then I heard the pounding of many booted feet heading toward us.

Tallow was using his hands to force himself backward as fast as possible.

"Now you help," I teased him. I let him fall to the floor as I quickly shut the door. I could hear people yelling.

"Shoot on sight. She killed Lokken. She's armed and dangerous."

Seemed safe to say negotiations were over.

"We need to get you on the other side of the bed."

"Was kind of hoping I could stay here," he whispered.

Again I dragged him.

"Stay down and stay quiet."

"I can do that," he replied when I got him on the far side of the room and away from the slightest of prying eyes, anyone took longer than five seconds to look would find us.

"Winter, need an update."

"I've got Tallow. We're laying low; he's in no shape to fight."

"Are you safe for now?" my sister asked.

"For now."

"That'll have to do. Let me know if anything changes or when you're on the move again."

"I will. I love you."

"I love you, too," she said. I heard her radio cut off.

"She's not here!" This was followed by a loud sound of things crashing against a wall and floor. "Check the rooms!"

"Uh-oh." I had been close to the door; I went and checked on Tallow, who had the good fortune of being asleep. The only place I could even remotely hide behind was the large machine that was monitoring the patient. It would be just big enough if I pulled my legs up against my chest and kept my head low. It would put me in a vulnerable position, but there weren't many alternatives.

I could hear them coming back down the hallway. Furniture within the other rooms was being tossed around, absolutely unnecessary, as there was no place to hide. There was zero chance I would go undetected. It would be a short firefight, but I wasn't going out with my back to the enemy.

"Cedar, if you've got any tricks, now might be the time to use them."

"I've got just what the doctor ordered," she said.

I'd stopped long ago trying to decipher everything she said. Maybe someday she'd write a book detailing Cedar-to-English translation, but for now, I got the feeling she meant to help. It had better be soon because they were in the room next to mine and were sounding angrier by the second. The floor underneath me rippled; had to be Cedar. The machinery began to wobble; through it all, Tallow slept. Not sure if it was going to be enough. I could see the light from the hallway under the door. I raised my rifle up, attempting to keep it steady, though my heart was threatening to push it to the side from its heavy percussive beats. My finger on the trigger, sweat rolling down the sides of my face, my irises narrowed as light began to filter in. The man coming in was violently tossed to the side, as was I. I had to twist to keep from landing on top of Tallow. It would do no good if he sat up and yelped in pain or surprise.

The lights in the hallway were flickering. As I sat back up, my rifle rested on the legs of the patient, whom I noted was strapped down, his blanket having shaken free. I recoiled from the thing that was there. It was a blend of Stryver and Human, though it looked nothing like either one. It was made more grotesque by its familiarity. Dealing with the natural repulsion of a Stryver was one thing, but this? I had no words. It was a fundamentally wrong creature that had no right to exist.

"Is this what's going to happen to you?" I asked Tallow. He let out a small snort; more likely he was dreaming of the sweet cakes he liked to eat so much, rather than in reply to me.

"Come on. We need to pull back!" This from the man that had been ordering the troops.

I didn't know why until I smelled the smoke. Cedar had saved me momentarily, but we were far from safe.

"Winter?"

I didn't say anything because the door was stuck partially open, and the men were leaving but were not completely gone.

"Don't know what you did, but it got them out of my area. Thank you." I said, after the last of the Others left.

"Don't thank me yet; we damaged their life-support systems. You've got ten to twelve hours at the most to find a way off that ship. It's going to get cold in there in a matter of hours."

"Not sure I'll have to worry about that," I said as I got up to look out the door. Fire was sweeping down the hallway with outpouring jets of an unknown propellant being added from the rooms.

"The Others there?"

"No, fire."

"Are you trapped?"

"Not yet. I've got to get Tallow and get moving. Stay on the line with me; I like hearing your voice."

"Anything," she said. Even over the electronics, I could hear the concern.

I went over and stroked Tallow's cheek; when that didn't work, I pinched his side.

"Ow, Winter! I liked your hand on my face better."

"Maybe next time wake up. How you doing?"

"Do I smell smoke?"

I nodded.

"Well, I was feeling better."

"We have to get moving."

He reached up, grabbed the bed and moved his legs so he could prop himself up.

"I know you feel like crap and I wish I could let you sleep for two days straight, but that's not going to happen. I need you to be able to walk under your own power."

"I've got this," he said, looking directly at me. I could see the strain in his neck just from him holding the gaze. "What the hell is that?" He stumbled backward when he saw the thing on the bed.

"Not sure; nothing we need to worry about now." My heart folded in on itself thinking that right this very moment that same DNA was coursing through his veins. I then had a flutter of hope it would all work out, that maybe his system would fight it on its own. "Cedar, I need to talk to Kolder."

"You planning on making repairs?" she quipped, though a moment later she had him patched through.

"Kolder, this is Winter."

"Hey Winter, you all right?"

"No time for niceties. I have in my possession a wrist device that gives me access to weapons and opens doorways. Is there any chance you can gain access to their computer? There's some information I very much need."

"Where'd you get it?" he asked.

"Lokken."

"The commander? Holy pokes. What happens when you touch the screen?" He asked.

I pulled it free from my pocket and touched it. A red warning screen came up to alert me that the biometrics did not match. I told him as much.

"Any chance you can make her unlock it?" he asked.

"Does she have to be alive?"

"I can see that's going to be a problem. I can hack into it, but I'm going to physically need it in my hand to do that."

"Understood." Now I was feeling the weight of Tallow's immediate and long-term well-being pressing firmly down on my shoulders.

"You coming?" Tallow asked me, although he had only made it ten feet away.

"Yeah, not sure how I'm possibly going to be able to keep up with you. Let's go find you a weapon."

"That would be helpful."

CHAPTER EIGHTEEN

RECLAMATION

"Staff Sergeant Detter, can we put a team together to perform a hull breach?" Cedar asked. She was monitoring Winter, but switched to a private channel so her sister couldn't hear.

"It's possible, Captain, but putting together a large enough team to be able to locate them is going to be a trick. If we knew where they were, perhaps we could do a surgical strike. That ship is enormous; we'd be putting more lives at risk with very little reward."

Cedar wanted to rail at the man. Just looking for her sister was reward enough, but she knew better, no matter what her heart told her. To risk over a dozen lives for a near futile rescue attempt made no sense…and then it did. The clock was already ticking for all of them.

"What about thermal imaging?"

"We can pick up a little from those close to the outer hull, but we don't have a way to differentiate them from the enemy," he replied.

She'd not heard from Winter for a few minutes. Occasionally she would fire on the ship out of sheer frustration. She knew she was being slightly childish and didn't care.

"Where are you, sis?" She was now flying around. "Wait—she said there was a fire."

"Excuse me?" Staff sergeant Detter asked.

"A fire. Winter said there was a fire. Wouldn't thermal imaging pick that up?"

"Kolder, you heard the captain! Get on it!" Detter yelled.

It was tense moments before she heard anything back.

"Good news and bad news, Major," Kolder said. "Good news is, yeah, we can pick up the heat from a fire; bad news is there are seven raging right now. That leads to more bad news."

"Can't wait," Cedar replied sardonically.

"Those fires are going to eat through their oxygen supply."

"Faster than the cold seeping in?" Cedar asked.

"It cuts the amount of time they have to get out of there in half."

"Detter, how much time to break into a hull?"

Detter knew what she was asking. "We're going to need a bit of luck; we can conceivably check out three, maybe four of the fires before we run out of time."

"You have your orders."

CHAPTER NINETEEN

THE HUNT

"Winter."

"Little busy," I whispered. I had poked my head around a junction point. There were a half dozen people scrambling to move farther away from this damaged section.

"Need you to stay near a fire. We're going to try and find you, pull you through a hull breach."

"You know where I am?" I asked. Hope, which had been in short supply, loved the idea of this.

"Well, down to seven places."

"How long?"

"If everything is on our side, I'd like to say half an hour."

"And if not?"

A response was not forthcoming.

"So, I'm found quickly or I'm not?" I knew the implication she wasn't voicing.

"We're going to find you."

"Cedar, I can't really stay where I'm at. The fire is producing a thick smoke. We'll die from inhalation long before the flames do us in." I was thinking on the logistics of what Cedar was suggesting; the odds it was going to work were not in our favor. Even if they found the right blaze, they could punch through above or below or even on the other side of the fire. My best chance still lay with getting a shuttle.

"I'm okay," Tallow said for no reason. I didn't find that comforting.

"Get to the hangar Cedar; that's where I'm going."

Cedar may have growled or sighed in frustration; either way, it sounded the same. I tapped Tallow and had him follow me just as the smoke billowed down toward us and forced us into action. It was clear as far as I could see, but I could hear activity and it was close.

"Stay close to the wall."

"I can do that," he answered; he was already leaning against it, so that wasn't going to be a problem.

I stopped as a door opened immediately to my left. The man took a quick look at me then shut it. Already spotted and we had barely begun our journey. The door opened again and a rifle blast blew through a display not a foot from my face. He was adjusting his aim when my shot struck his weapon; the molten metal flowed onto his hand and merged with his body before he could let it go. He was howling in pain as he backed away; even with the door shut, I could hear his anguish.

"Think he told anyone?" Tallow asked.

"Don't think he had enough time." I was happy to notice that Tallow had more color in him; that pale gray had not been flattering.

"Think that gun still works?"

"You going to pry it from his hands?"

"Probably not."

We were moving as fast as we dared. I constantly kept looking behind us waiting for any stragglers or even a squad lying in wait to come out and find us.

"Someone's coming," Tallow said. He was ten feet behind; he'd stopped when he heard something. We were not in an advantageous position—no rooms to hide in and absolutely no cover.

"I'd take a sword right now," Tallow said as he moved closer to the noise.

I wanted to kill him before he got killed. Two men and a woman rounded the corner, Tallow threw a punch that buckled the knees of the first man and sent him sprawling to the ground; he was unconscious before his head snapped off the deck. The woman was reaching for a small firearm at her hip—Tallow reached for it before she could, pulled it free while at the same time sending a kick to her knee. The loud crack of bone as her knee locked was followed immediately by her cry of pain.

"I surrender," the other man said, his hands in the air as Tallow pointed the pistol at him.

"Sorry, no prisoners," Tallow said as he whacked the man in the side of the head with the firearm.

"Whoa," I said.

"Been practicing with Lendor and the Earth Corps; they call it hand-to-hand combat. All things considered, I'd still rather have a weapon," he said, holding the pistol up.

"Whoa," I repeated. "You're going to want to take her wrist device or that thing won't work." The woman was on the ground, cradling her damaged leg.

"Leave me alone," she screamed.

"Just need the thingy on your wrist," he told her.

"I'll brick it!" She had a wild look in her eyes.

"Not sure what that means, but if you break it, I'll be forced to do something I won't be proud of." Tallow moved closer.

She watched him, gauging if he would make good on his threat. Finally, she extended her arm so that he could take the wrist device. "You're both going to die on this ship. And I'm going to laugh over your broken bodies when it happens!"

"Not like you're getting out of this floating coffin," I told her. "Come on, Tallow, let's go."

"You want to leave her conscious?"

"I just want to leave her."

We'd no sooner rounded a corner than she began to scream for help. Tallow paused.

"No time; come on. Feeling better?"

"Crazy, right? Could hardly move and now I feel better than ever. Not sure what they did, but I feel like I could have taken five of them on. Wish I had a rifle, though."

"Having a little barrel envy?" I asked.

"What's that even mean? Forget it, I'm sure it's something Cedar told you."

We'd gone down two more halls and had seen—and more importantly, heard—nothing; that was when our luck ran out. Five soldiers were waiting for us at the next intersection. They were behind a blaster shield that prevented us from getting any clean shots off. We did not suffer that same luxury. We were far enough away that it was a difficult shot for them, but our escape route was effectively blocked.

"Door!" Tallow yelled, pulling, more like dragging, me back as shots were fired. We fell into the room in a heap, quickly scrambling to get back up. "Empty."

Empty of people, that is. The room itself was full of steel slab tables and either medical equipment or stuff used for experiments, or both, though I didn't want to think of that. Glass bottles full of various colored liquids lined the walls; more than a few had an unidentifiable mass floating within. Some were not unidentifiable; those I did not stare at long. To our left was a series of glass panels that looked into the next room.

"Come on! We have to get to the next one before they surround us." I grabbed Tallow, who was watching the door we had just entered. I took a chair and hurled it through the glass, the noise alerting anyone nearby to exactly what we were doing.

I had just turned to Tallow and was looking past him as the door opened. A canister was tossed in. My mind flowed out and snapped back; again, the last of the glass was crashing down to the floor. I reached and grabbed Tallow's shoulder, adrenaline giving me the strength to pull him toward me, I pushed off with my legs; we were halfway through the new opening I had made when the concussive force of the canister exploding rattled my skull. We landed awkwardly, me on my shoulder, Tallow taking the brunt on his head.

He was shouting at me. I couldn't hear much; there was a warble in my skull, followed by a voluminous echo. He was asking if I was all right, though I figured this out only by the movement of his lips. The taste of blood was in my mouth. He was dragging me away from the broken windows, colorful rays were blasting past. Glass was exploding all around us as the Others' assault team moved closer. I still could not hear, and my head felt like it was stuffed full of cotton, and apparently, I was bleeding. None of that kept me from moving as Tallow and I struggled to get behind a table.

When Tallow realized I could not hear, he began using hand signals he had learned. They were basic enough, but right now, I wished I had attended a few more of his training sessions. He held up two fingers and pointed back the way we had come. Then three fingers to the door we were now facing. He wanted me to cover the entrance as he shot at the two behind us.

"Be careful." I could not tell if I actually said the words aloud. He rose his head just high enough to take a look. Placing his rifle on the steel table, he fired and ducked down just as the door I was looking at opened. I fired before anything or anyone had the chance of coming in. Tallow spun just as another canister came through. I thought for a moment perhaps I had dilated time again because of the speed with which he moved. He caught the small explosive before it had a chance to hit the floor and flung it; it clipped the doorframe before flipping back out into the hallway. His forward momentum brought him crashing into the wall in front of me. He grunted as he collided. The explosion tore the door from its frame and sent it hurtling not inches from his head.

CHAPTER TWENTY

CEDAR'S DEEDS

"That's new," Cedar said as she looked upon a section of the ship that was changing. It was morphing from its box-like structure into something she could not identify, and it left her with serious feelings of foreboding. She moved in closer to get a better look.

"We're going to need help, Cedar!" Winter sounded out of breath. "Surrounded…somewhere close to the medical bay."

That information didn't help her as she still didn't know much about the layout of the ship.

"Captain, this is Lendor. Request permission to board."

She was going to tell him no, that he would have no idea where to go.

"Frost says she should be able to easily pick up their scent."

"Get it done." The words no sooner out of her mouth when a lightning bolt of energy blew past the front of her fighter and slammed into the nearest one behind her. The pilot didn't even have a chance to scream in the face of death. "Pull back! All ships pull back." Another fighter was taken down. Cedar began firing on the strange weapon. She had one missile left and hoped it would be enough. She fired just as the metal surface began to shift in her direction; she took that as in invitation to leave the area.

"Lendor, belay last," she said as the bolt streaked past her aft. "You won't be able to dock."

"No worries," he told her. "We've been practicing for this."

"That shuttle will not be able to evade their weapon." She was diving, rising, and moving side to side, doing her best to keep whoever was manning the gun from locking on.

"What the…?" Cedar said once she felt that she had got far enough away from the ship that it would not be a threat. She watched as eight soldiers hopped free of the shuttle. They hit the thrusters on their suits and were going headfirst toward the Others' ship.

"It is a halo dive, generally done in atmosphere, but we are adapting," Lendor said.

Cedar didn't like it one bit.

"We're coming, Ghost," he said as he streaked through the sky, the edges of his suit illuminating silver.

"Hurry," she replied.

"Godspeed," Cedar told them. She wondered how they were going to get into the structure. She watched in great detail as she magnified the image. "Maybe should have done this when I was looking at that stupid gun," she said. Lendor's group moved with a choreographed gracefulness, the routine practiced until it felt natural to them. They turned and slowed as they came close to the ship, landing softly upon the hull. There was a flare-up; then they began to disappear.

"We're inside," Lendor said. "Live feed on." Cedar watched her display shift from the radar array to a shaky camera image as, presumably, Lendor pulled his way through a tangle of cables and optic wires.

Cedar winced as she saw him pull on more than one apparatus emblazoned with a red skull.

"You realize those mean danger, right?"

"Everything we're doing right now is dangerous," he responded.

She nodded. Couldn't argue with that.

"Inner hull. Access panel. Hold on, might be some blowback if it's pressurized." He spun around and Cedar watched as he kicked out two times, striking the panel hard before it fell away. He then pulled himself through and landed with a solid thud. "Not pressurized, but we have gravity. No lifeforms within proximity. Everyone in."

"Are you kidding me?" Cedar asked, making sure she wasn't broadcasting. She watched the lithe form of Frost bound on by; she was wearing a specially designed suit. "How long had they been planning this?" she wondered. "How can she possibly smell anything with that on?" That, she voiced.

Lendor stopped to reattach the panel as best he could, then he moved to his place in front again.

"Be careful, Lendor; they're finding ways to get their systems back online," Cedar said.

She watched as they came to the end of the hallway, a large, sealed door directly in front of them.

"Weapons ready," Lendor said as he moved to the controls. He was looking through a small port at another door not ten feet away. It was a pressure lock. When it opened, they would be extremely vulnerable in the small room while they awaited normalization.

The small room illuminated red when he pulled open the door. Cedar held her breath while she waited to see the green that would allow them entry to the rest of the ship.

"Bogeys," Tiegs said. "Straight ahead, dozen."

"Pull back, Lendor. Try a different point."

"This was a one-way flight," Lendor said. She thought she detected a bittersweet humor in his voice. She knew what he meant; the suits only had so much fuel, and they must have used a good portion on their impromptu flight. "Plus, we wouldn't be Great Saviors if we turned back now."

"This isn't about heroics; this is about staying alive," she replied.

The light finally turned green. Lendor rushed through and was ready to lay covering fire as the rest of the extraction team got into position. She watched a round object pitched forth. Lendor looked down on a display he had; it showed the controls for the rolling bomb. He moved the gyroscopic device closer to where the Others' breach-repelling team had mustered. There was loud grunt behind Lendor as one of his team ducked from a bevy of rounds coming down the hallway. Cedar, as of yet, could not see the enemy; she imagined it was the same for the team down there.

"Captain, this is Kolder. I think I found them."

"Can you be sure?" Cedar asked.

"With a high degree of certainty, yes. Thermal imaging is showing massive forces moving to one location."

"That has to be them. Send me the feed." Cedar watched as hundreds of individual dots were coalescing on one spot. If she could get past that new gun, there was a good chance of getting help to her sister; they were fairly close to the hangar. She was studying the best route when an alarm flared on her console. She looked up quickly and pulled her yoke to the right, believing she was being fired upon, only to realize she was being warned of an Imminent Arrival. "Dingo's kidneys! My dance card is just plain full right now!" she yelled.

"Captain?" Kolder asked.

"Someone's coming. Okay, we need that gun emplacement taken out. Who has munitions?" she asked.

"I've got two missiles," Tiegs responded.

"Squadron, form around Tiegs. We need to protect him." She wasn't sure what to expect from the men and women she was commanding; she was sending them on what was very likely a suicide mission, armed with nothing more than small weaponry. Within a few moments, they were shaped into a flying V with Tiegs off to the left of her lead position. The mounted weapon swiveled to meet the new threat.

"Disperse! Tiegs, you stay to my left and follow me in," Cedar ordered. Fierce bolts flew from the weapon; it seemed the gunner was attempting well-aimed shots, but when those weren't having the desired effect, they hoped to make up for the lack of targeting with sheer volume. It looked like a high-pressure water hose shooting a constant spray of death. It was somehow easier to avoid, as you could see the beam moving in your direction, but still, it sliced through two of her fighters, incinerating them immediately. Cedar growled in anger as she and Tiegs flew closer.

"We're in missile range, Tiegs, let them loose."

"Just a little closer," he responded. She stayed glued to his side.

The beam was sweeping their way.

"Tiegs, we have to break off. Let them fly! That's an order!"

"Almost there..." he said calmly.

"Yeah, we're almost there...almost too close! Let's go!"

"One heart, one mind, one life to give, yet many to take!" he screamed as he hit his thrusters.

"Tiegs!" Cedar screamed. She saw what he was going to do and thought about nudging him away, but the speed needed and as close as they were to the ship, they would both collide.

The bright beam was sweeping closer to Tiegs, who was diving straight down toward it. Cedar could not stand to watch but she could not turn away; she owed him that at least. It was anyone's guess what had made contact first. The resultant explosion flared on her equipment, her face shield darkened in response to the intense brightness and still, she was left with sunspots completely obscuring her field of vision.

Frost was waiting at the next bend for Lendor and the rest to catch up; she had removed her suit and was perched on the body of one of the crewmen, his neck ripped out, blood gurgling from the wound.

"I have their scent and I have found a way to them. The next corridor contains a squad of armed personnel; you would be wise to avoid it," Frost told them.

"Avoid? To engage is my destiny, little one," Lendor told her.

"If this is indeed your fate, I can only wish you good luck," Frost told him as she bounded away, Ferryn hot on her trail.

"Come," he told those with him. "We do not have many chances in this life to prove our worth, and I will not miss the opportunity." He and the rest ran with determination into the fray.

When Cedar's eyes finally cleared, she was looking at a great maw in the side of the warship. She'd not even had a chance for a plan to form in her mind as she made her ship dive forward. Fire still burned within the opening, and the metal around the edges glowed a bright red from the intense heat that had not yet dissipated.

"Like threading a needle," she said, though she'd never done that particular task. She illuminated her front lights; they cut deep into the darkness before her. Tangled piles of equipment were intermingled with bodies and great swirls of dust. The tips of her wings had less than a foot of clearance on either side as she flew inside. She fired rounds, obliterating whatever got in her way. She could see damage more than three decks in. Somewhere deep in her memory, she heard Serrot saying she would someday fly inside a cave; he'd not said whether it would be natural or manmade…a bittersweet smile pulled at the corners of her lips. "I'm coming, Winter," she whispered as she landed the fighter and exited, pulling her pistol from its holster on her thigh.

"Captain?" Kolder said, "We have company."

"I'll deal with them when I'm finished here," she said as she was picking her way through the debris.

"Don't think that's going to be a problem, Captain," he responded.

"It is good to know I have not missed all the festivities!" Graylon's voice boomed through Cedar's headset.

CHAPTER TWENTY-ONE

WINTER'S SALVATION

The corridor beyond the missing door was a twisted ruin of metal. I raced over to help Tallow up. When I was certain he was all right, I quickly ducked my head out the opening. The Others had effectively sealed off that approach but had also effectively removed our only avenue of escape. Tallow and I got back behind the table to wait for the next barrage.

"What are they doing?" Tallow asked.

"I'm sitting right next to you."

"That mean you don't know?"

"It means whatever happens, at least we face it together." We could hear movement, but as of yet there were no shots, and thankfully, no more exploding bombs. Luck was only going to get us so far. Although, tough to call the situation we found ourselves in "lucky." I had to remind myself that we were alive; that counted for something. A shot hit the ceiling above us—happily, not that close. I peeked up and over to take a look; the half dozen soldiers I could see were all looking up, rifles in the same direction. Something held more of their interest than we did. I saw an opportunity and took it, firing rapidly into the surprised group. Three fell instantly in the hail of fire; the other three ducked down and away.

"Hello, Winter," Frost said with a hint of gleefulness; mostly, it was ferocity.

"Is that…." Tallow began.

I put my finger to my lips.

"Frost…what are you doing here?" I asked.

"Where should I be?" she answered cryptically.

"There are at least three in the next room and I have no idea how many beyond," I told her. "Be careful."

"It is me you wish to be careful? You do realize, Winter, there are over a hundred of the Others surrounding this area, do you not?"

"I hadn't, no." Even with Frost's help, the possibility of escape vanished. "Wait—is there a way for us to follow you out?"

"That is not an option; this passage is much too narrow," she replied.

I could hear cries from the rooms we were near, some of surprise and pain, others of men and women urgently shouting orders. They were under attack.

"It would appear Lendor and his team have arrived," Frost said.

"How?" was all I could ask.

"The time has come to do my part," the Rhodeeshian said.

There were more shots fired into the ceiling. I would give her the cover she needed to do whatever she'd planned. I stood; there were still more than seven others in the next room. I felt acutely exposed as I began firing and moving closer so I could keep angles on them. Two fell with blistering wounds before they even realized their folly of looking away. Tallow was moving to catch up, firing his pistol as fast as he could. Just as their attention was being pulled to us, Frost broke through a panel, leapt to the far wall, and seemed to defy gravity as she ran across it for a few steps then launched into the midsection of the nearest soldier. She ripped a chunk out of his neck larger than my fist, then bounded off of him before he could even raise his hands in a futile bid to stem the flow of blood.

She was moving quickly, taking out soldier after soldier, but there were too many of them. She went from trying to kill Others to trying to save her own life. That was when Ferryn joined the fray, and the tides of the small battle turned. He cared not at all for himself as he launched down and into the head and face of a soldier ready to shoot his mate. The screams of terror and pain were otherworldly as Ferryn stripped skin and meat. The soldier was running around the room, blood pouring forth, the pain so intense he could not even touch the wound. In less than a minute the four of us had secured the area. A large explosion rocked the ship; Tallow wrapped his arm around me to keep me from falling over. Intense fighting could be heard down the hallway, though it was not close. Frost tentatively walked to the door, looked both ways before coming back in.

"Whatever is going on, they are not focused on this area," she said.

There was a heavy vibration throughout the hull of the ship and the much louder racket of weapons fire and explosions. It sounded as if the ship were being ruptured in two.

"What now?" Tallow asked as he took a quick glance out. "Do we try to escape while they're not looking?"

"Escape to where?" I asked. "I think I'd rather stay and take their ship like they are trying to take our lives." Tallow did not attempt to talk me out of the insanity of my idea. Clearly, to escape now only meant a drawn-out death in space. Our only chance stood here. I was out first, going across the hallway and into a small recess where an access panel was located. I waited until Tallow was in position. The soldiers at the back of the battle up ahead were not looking our way; that changed the moment we opened fire. A dozen or more had been shot before the confusion was overcome and they assembled to return fire. By that time, it was too late as Frost and Ferryn had run teeth-first into their midst. Tallow and I rushed to aid them. We needn't have worried; in the close combat, the wily animals had all the advantage. Our peril was being shot from panicked trigger pulls. The Others were firing wildly, many times injuring or killing their own in a bid to stop the attack.

The Others, in a desperate bid to get away from us, were

running into the backs of those ahead of them, creating even more congestion and panic. The carnage was horrific. I had to keep reminding myself that they would not have thought twice over our demise and that of every Human. We once again sought an alcove to shield ourselves as we could no longer advance; the Others had nowhere to go as well. The corridor they found themselves in was blocked by structural damage. It would not be long before they once again rallied.

"WIN!" Cedar screamed.

"Cedar!! Are you all right?" I was alarmed at her volume through my headset.

"Oh, sorry." I could almost see her blushing. "Been blowing things up, I think I've lost some of my hearing."

"Where are you?" I asked.

"Coming toward you."

"You're in the hangar?"

"Umm…not really. Found an alternate entrance."

I didn't know what that meant, and right now, I could not begin to speculate. I was right; the Others had finally thought to defend their flanks. Sheets of volleyed shots blasted down the corridor. We were once again pinned down; this time, though, it did not appear they were in much of a hurry to rush our position.

"Where are they?" Tallow was referring to Frost and Ferryn.

"My guess? Back up top." We were pressed tightly against the wall; the shots had slowed, though not stopped.

"If we get out of this, Winter, do you want to marry me?" Tallow asked.

I paused to look over at him; I couldn't help smiling. "This is the romantic scenario you've waited for to ask that question?"

He shrugged.

CHAPTER TWENTY-TWO

THE ARUNDEL

"What have we missed?" Graylon asked as the *Arundel* appeared. He was staring at his screen.

"Commander, this is Lieutenant Kolder." He spent the next couple of minutes bringing the Genogerian leader up to speed.

"Launch fighters and every breech-worthy vessel we have," Graylon ordered. "Also, see if you can get that intergalactic scum on the communications." He sat back down at his command chair before speaking softly, "I am coming, little ones. Do not go and die on me now."

CHAPTER TWENTY-THREE

A SELF CONTAINED FORCE

Cedar was moving quickly through the hallways, surprised at the lack of personnel she was encountering. "I guess that could have something to do with that giant hole I smashed into the side of the ship." She was saddened for the loss of Tiegs, but proud of his sacrifice. She would not let the opportunity he created go to waste. She was being cautious, but not overly so. In her haste to get to her sister and Tallow, she'd barely had time to react when the shot came from an open doorway. It blasted through the side of her suit and into the large pocket on her thigh; she looked down to see a sheaf of burning pages. Her gloved hand pounded repeatedly at the yellow flame.

"You bastard!" she screamed. She shot with vengeance as she advanced. "That was my favorite book!" Her pistol out in front, multiple blasts struck the shocked soldier in the chest. "Where am I going to get another copy of *Highlander in Time*!" she yelled over his prone body. Cedar was still fuming as she rounded the next corner and stood in a corridor, witness to a battle raging at the end of it.

"Someone is going to pay for this," she said, looking down at the smoldering hole in her uniform. With her rifle up, she focused her anger and took carefully aimed shots as she moved ever closer. The Others fell away from her withering fire; again, confusion strangled their ranks as they were caught in a crossfire. Cedar pressed the attack; she thought she caught a glimpse of Lendor moving across from her. She had a sudden urge to wave but thought better of it. From time to time, she glimpsed the swish of a white tail. Now she knew the real reason why the Others could not marshal their strength; they had the numbers but were in complete disarray.

On occasion, a shot was fired in her direction, but it was hastily made and without any true aim. She'd not given much thought to her personal safety; that was right up until she heard the heavy footfalls of dozens, if not hundreds of boots coming toward her from the way she had come.

"Winter," she said, when she realized her folly. "I die today, knowing I did everything in my power to help you. I love you, sister, and look forward to seeing you on the other side." She turned to face the new threat, determined to make them pay dearly for every step they took.

"I'm coming! Hold on!" Winter yelled into the headset.

Cedar knew any help would take far too long. She had her finger on the trigger and her shoulders squared to the approach. "So many books unread," she lamented as the first of them came around the corner. Her laughter rang out.

CHAPTER TWENTY-FOUR

REUNITED

"NO!" I cried out, running headlong into the enemy. I had to get to Cedar—nothing else mattered, certainly not my own life. Tallow and I were bringing down the Others in bunches, and then something strange began to happen. The soldiers first put their weapons down, then got on their knees with their hands clasped upon their heads. I had no time to accept surrenders; I shoved them over and aside as I rushed to get to my sister.

"What's going on?" Tallow asked as we navigated pushed and sidestepped among the kneeling or dead Others.

"They've surrendered…or this is the worst trap ever created. Cedar?" I asked, terrified of not getting a response.

"You're not going to believe this," she replied. We met up in a juncture point of four hallways. A bloodied and battered Lendor, along with Frost, Ferryn, a hundred or more heavily armed Genogerians, and thankfully, my sister.

"We did it," she smiled.

I let my rifle clatter to the floor as I hugged her tightly. We'd taken the ship. It was going to need months of work to be battle ready again, but even more invaluable was the data contained upon her onboard computers: the locations, the defenses; armaments of the entire Stryver and Others' fleets. It was everything we needed to ensure our victory.

EPILOGUE

Where does one begin as you approach the end? So much had happened after Brigend had buckled away. I never did get a clear answer on how Graylon had come to our rescue. It seemed to be some great secret between the two that they were reluctant to share. Brigend, when cornered, would smile and look up. "One cannot question the motives of the heavens." This was his standard reply.

Graylon was even less satisfying with his response. "Is it not enough that we were there?" After thinking on it for a good long while and conferring with Cedar, we came to the conclusion that somehow Michael had passed a message on. Both Brigend and Graylon would have gladly taken the credit for it if they could have; that they didn't spoke volumes.

It was comforting and it wasn't, knowing that somehow we had a distant ancestor that had the ability to look out for us. There was no telling what other secrets he had planned or had planted, waiting for us. I pained for the desire to spend more time with Michael and Tracy. Having been deprived of it for most of my life, I could think of nothing more important than family. I was thankful for my sister and the new family of warriors around me.

After hearing so much about it from Cedar, Tallow and I had a commitment ceremony, something very similar to what were called marriages. It didn't make much sense to me. We'd been committed to each other from the beginning; whether we had a ceremony or not made no difference. But it meant a lot to Cedar and Tallow. I told them fine, if they were so into it, then perhaps they should be the ones that had the ceremony. Ended up being a beautiful occasion; all of our friends were there, and the good cheer poured that day helped to fondly think on those that had passed instead of the constant sorrow that afflicted us all. Tests for the Stryver virus had begun on all the uninfected, Tallow was indeed infected. He wasn't one of the lucky ones who possessed the rare, natural immunity. Still, it was my hope we could find a cure; either way, I planned on living every day with him as if it were our last. For truly who could tell if it wasn't? That day would surely come for us all; today, tomorrow, no one could say when.

Cedar had two suitors for her affection. I found it funny that she had pushed me to a commitment that she herself was having the most difficult time making. It wasn't that Brigend and Lendor weren't ideal suitors; I think it was that she was unwilling to open her heart back up after having it shattered by Serrot's death. I understood that. I don't think I'd ever be capable of love again if Tallow died. How does one pick up all those tiny pieces and put them back together? There would always be holes and jagged parts where it was rebuilt improperly.

The Progerians had needed no further impetus to join our cause than when we were able to bring a half changed Other to a council meeting. It had caused quite a disruption but there had been no dissenting votes.

The unending war had a new beginning, one which we could win, one which we could end. It was the dawn of a new era. We could fulfill the hopes of our ancestors, put the mistakes of their past behind us, and create our own destiny. Together, we would move forward, and I, for one, for the first time, anticipated with hope what our future held.

AUTHOR'S NOTES

I truly hope you enjoyed this book and this series. I know it took an abnormally long time to get it completed. This was a difficult one for me, as it was a labor of love and sometimes a constant source of frustration. I painted myself into corners more times than I care to remember! I think perhaps my foray into the Young Adult Dystopian world has come to a conclusion. It is high time to let Winter, Cedar, Tallow and the rest find their own ways among the ink-filled pages they inhabit. I will miss them as I miss any character that I leave behind. I came to love Winter's stoicism and Cedar's quirkiness. Who knows, maybe I'll find a way to bring them along to another world!

About The Author

Visit Mark at www.marktufo.com

Zombie Fallout trailer

https://youtu.be/FUQEUWy-v5o

For the most current updates join Mark Tufo's newsletter

http://www.marktufo.com/contact.html

Also By Mark Tufo

Zombie Fallout Series book 1 currently free

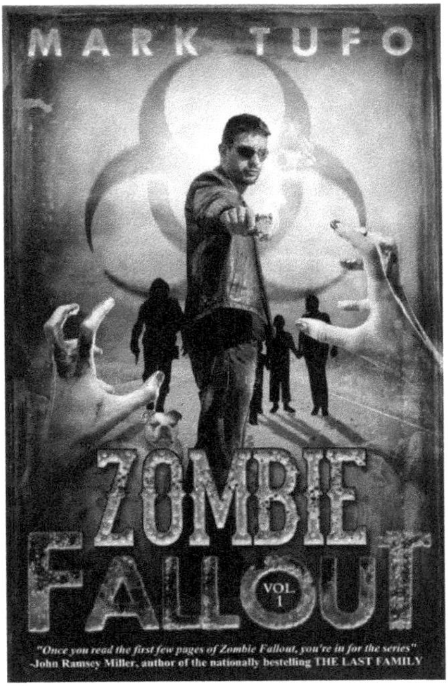

Lycan Fallout Series

Indian Hill Series

The Book Of Riley Series

Also By Devil Dog Press

www.devildogpress.com

Caldera By Heath Stallcup

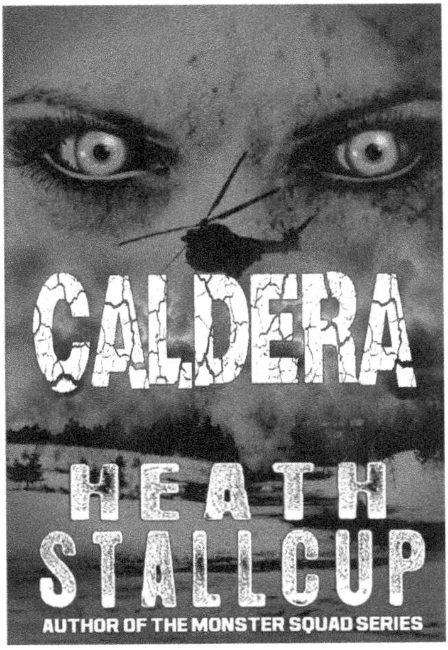

All That Remain By Travis Tufo

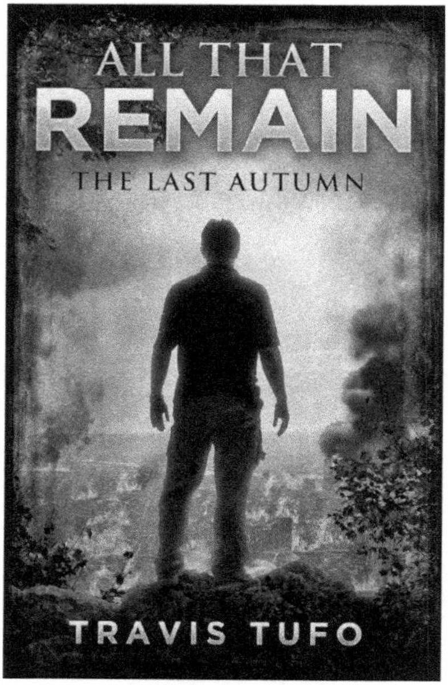

Heart Of Jet By Sheila Shedd

Prey By Tim Majka

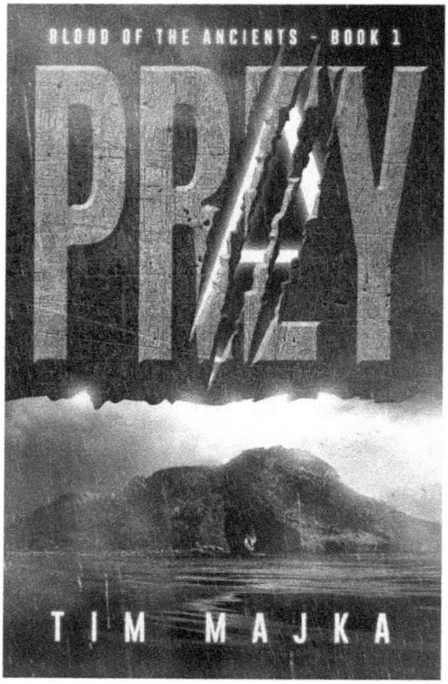

Thank you for reading Dystance 3: Edge of Deceit.. Gaining exposure as an independent author relies mostly on word-of-mouth; please consider leaving a review wherever you purchased this story.

CUSTOMERS ALSO PURCHASED:

SHAWN CHESSER
SURVIVING THE
ZOMBIE APOCALYPSE

WILLIAM MASSA
OCCULT ASSASSIN
SERIES

JOHN O'BRIEN
A NEW WORLD
SERIES

ERIC A. SHELMAN
DEAD HUNGER
SERIES

HEATH STALLCUP
MONSTER SQUAD
SERIES

MARK TUFO
ZOMBIE FALLOUT
SERIES

CPSIA information can be obtained
at www.ICGtesting.com
Printed in the USA
LVHW041456141019
634126LV00001B/262/P

9 781694 163905